living words

UNWRITTEN TRUTHS DUET BOOK ONE

JENN BULLARD

Edited by Amber Nicole

Cover Art by Veronica Lancet

Formatting from The GravesYard

Published by Jenn Bullard, 2022

To all of the Toris of the world, who need a Tesa as a bestie.

foreword

Living Words is the first book in the Unwritten Words Duet. This is a why choose duet, which means the heroine will not make a choice in this book or any other between the guys in her life. Tori has an unfortunate relationship before meeting her guys that is toxic. There will be moments where you're upset at my characters, and that's quite alright. They have a lot of growing to do. I promise his unaliving when it happens will be satisfying. Please understand that there will be a happy ending at the end, but Tori has quite the journey to get there. This book does have some content that may be considered triggering. If you have would like the full list, please email me at <u>jennbullardwrites@gmail.com</u>.

content warning

Living Words is book one of the Unwritten Truths duet, a dark contemporary RH romance. Living words deals with darker themes including but not limited to mental and emotional abuse, non-con, stalking, bullying, self harm, and book ends on a cliffhanger. If these topics, or any other dark themes bother you, then this book may not be for you. For a complete list of potential triggers, please email the author at jennbullardwrites@gmail.com.

prologue

TORI

I stand in a sea of caps and gowns with a smile. We did it! We graduated and the rest of our lives are ahead of us. Four long and amazing years of college, where I took my classes, made incredible friends and connections, and met my boyfriend, Anthony. The only people missing today are my parents, and they physically can't be here since they passed away in a car accident my junior year. Instead, I'm wearing my locket with their photo in it to remind me how proud they would be if they were here. Everything's coming together perfectly.

Well almost perfectly. My smile slowly disappears as I think about the comments my boyfriend has been making recently. Anthony doesn't want me to go out in the cute outfit that I put together tonight for postgraduation drinks. He said something about not wanting everyone to see me 'like that' and that it reminded him I had gained ten pounds since I met him. Did I? I glance down, but I can't really see my body through the graduation gown.

Today is important, and I don't really want to have another fight. I don't want what should be one of the most important memories in my life this far ruined. So I won't let him. I'll wear something else. I'll be good, I'll smile just the right amount, and I won't drink or eat too much either. And then it'll be fine. We'll come home and have sex, and tomorrow will be a new day. That's all I want. To have one amazing memory.

When we first started dating, Anthony took me to the beach; it was about an hour north of Georgetown, South Carolina and the drive was gorgeous. We spent the day in the water, he packed a picnic, and was so sweet. His hands ran all over my body, like he couldn't get enough. This is what I cling to when my boyfriend isn't nice, or acts possessive.

We started out great, but now I don't know. Maybe it'll be better now that we're out of school. I'm starting a new job next week at a publishing company. Entry level but, whatever, it's my dream job. Anthony's starting a position with his dad's accounting firm, and he'll be less stressed. Hopefully, crossing my fingers.

I squeal in surprise as my friends jump on me yelling, "We fucking did it, Tori!"

Yes, yes we fucking did!

one

TORI

ONE YEAR LATER

I stare unseeingly at my computer monitor and blink, shaking myself out of my daze. I didn't sleep well, but that's par for the course these days. I sigh, and make myself concentrate on the manuscript that I'm editing. It's a paranormal romance with wolves and a girl who doesn't know that she's fated for them. *Hmm. Fated. Must be nice.* I shake my head again and tell myself to get it together. This book is being launched next month. I need to finish editing it and talk to the author about the tweaks that I need to make. They're minor thankfully, but it just cleans up the story a little. *Okay, put aside all of the crap you've been dealing with the last few days, Tori, and help this author publish an amazing book.*

K...*good talk self.* I edit for a few more hours until my stomach starts to grumble. I save my work, and grab my lunch from the staff room. I need to change gears, so I'll eat in my office while I read a book on my kindle app on my phone. Then I'll be ready to button up the book I'm editing and make the call that I need to make.

I let myself get pulled away into a duet about a college student who wants to get into a sorority as her mom's dying wish. It's an Amber Nicole book that I've been wanting to read, but was told that it would likely make me cry. I'm feeling really emotional lately, and probably need a good cry under the excuse that it's a book.

I need to figure out what to do about Anthony and the things that have been happening, but work is my safe place. I won't let him ruin my passion for reading, editing, and the satisfaction I get from helping an author's hard work and dreams come true.

Cara from Amber's *Forever Changed* duet fills my thoughts, and takes me away from my own problems. Instead I'm pulled into someone else's struggles, and yummy man sandwiches. Yes, this is exactly what I needed.

A knock interrupts me. I jerk my head up, and I'm aware my body is flushed. Damn my Irish roots and red hair. I call out for them to come in, and close out my kindle app.

It's my coworker, Tesa, and I smile happily.

"Are we still on for this weekend? I wanted to be sure that nothing last minute happened."

She looks at me with a raised eyebrow at my flushed skin, knowing my guilty pleasure of reading smutty romances during lunch.

She chuckles and asks, "Girl what are you reading? You look guilty or horny, I'm not sure which right now."

"Fucking hell Tesa, way to call a girl out," I laugh.

I tell her about the book, she grins and opens her phone, making a note to download it later.

"I'm so glad it's you though, and not someone else. I needed a distraction from my day, and here you are." I wink at her and she mock curtseys.

"How are things going? You're editing the Taylor book, right?"

We talk about the book, and the small challenges that I need to talk to the author about before it launches. Things are nice, normal, until she asks the question that I hate having to lie about. I shouldn't have to lie about this, but still I do.

"How are you and Anthony doing? Y'all went out last weekend, right?"

I smile tightly. That night was a shit show. He took me out for dinner and drinks with his friends. Ordered a salad for me, and a vodka soda, before smiling condescendingly at me, and telling his friends that I was on a new diet because my job required me to sit more than I was used to. He also told me not to drink too much since I was joining him on a run in the morning. And that was just the beginning of a really excruciating night.

But I don't tell her that, instead I say, "We did! We went out with some of his work friends and had a good time. Then we went for a run in the morning. We've decided to make sure that we're exercising since we're both working desk jobs now."

Tesa's not an idiot, and her eyebrow raises at my blatant lie.

"That's...nice." She murmurs. "He does know that you're five-foot-two, and your ass didn't get like that by sitting, right?"

I roll my eyes and snort. "Yeah, yeah."

I grin and lean to the side, deprecatingly smacking my ass.

"It's here to stay, it's well known. So...what are our plans for this girls night anyway?"

Tesa thankfully lets it go, smiles and says: "Dancing, drinks, and shots, of course!"

That's going to go over real well with Anthony, but oh

fucking well. I'll spend the night at her house. What he doesn't know won't hurt either of us.

————

I THROW my keys into the dish as I walk into the apartment, pull off my shoes, and put them in the closet. I move into the hallway and put my bag on the kitchen table. Was Anthony home yet?

"Hey baby, are you here?"

Part of me misses him when I'm at work, but then there's other parts that have broken edges and flinch from the thought of him.

"Yeah babes, I'm in the kitchen."

I pause and take a small breath. He sounds like he's in a good mood. I follow his voice down the hall where he's putting a baking sheet filled with asparagus, carrots, and chicken thighs into the oven. It's all healthy, but at least it's food. I breathe an internal sigh of relief that I don't dare let loose.

"Can I help with anything?" I ask, in an effort to keep his good mood going.

He smiles at me and shakes his head. "No, I have this covered for now. Why don't you put something more comfortable on?"

I smile gratefully, I can't wait to throw on a tank top and sweatpants. I give him a quick kiss and then turn, hurrying to change, suddenly happy to be home.

When I return, we talk about our days, eat dinner when it's ready, clean up, and then snuggle on the couch. I crave nights like this. Our life together isn't all bad, but the bad has started to outweigh the good.

I yawn and glance at the clock. It's closing in on midnight and we both have early mornings.

"Hey babe, I'm going to head to bed, are you coming with me?" I ask.

He's scrolling through his phone, quickly making the screen go black when he notices me looking, then turns, giving me a smirk.

"Yeah, I'll be right behind you."

I walk to our room, and start getting ready. I throw on some sleep shorts, because I'm too hot to sleep in pants tonight, brush my teeth, wash my face and go through my facial routine. Anthony steps behind me, sliding his hands up my hips, over my stomach, pulling my shirt up to expose my breasts as he squeezes them. I feel a tingle that I haven't felt with him in a while, and I relax against his chest.

His mouth slides over to my ear and he growls, "These are mine, aren't they, baby?"

He's kneading with both hands, sliding his thumbs over my nipples, and lightly pulling.

I sigh and push into his hands.

"Y-yes," I gasp. He kisses down my neck and I can feel myself getting wet.

"Such a good girl. You like that?"

"Yes," I moan arching into his hands.

All too quickly, his fingers twist hard and pinch my nipples. I wordlessly scream, squirming in his arms to try to get away. His hands went from teasing to punishing in a blink of an eye, and the room spins from how fast this changes.

He slips his left hand into my hair and pulls hard, before dragging his right hand down my front and into my shorts.

He grabs me hard and murmurs, "Is this pretty, wet pussy mine?"

I don't know what has gotten into him, but I don't know whether to be turned on or upset. Can I be both?

I cry out that it is, as he slides a finger into me, then adds a second starting to fuck me. He licks up my neck as he continues to slowly finger me. I'm right there, but something tells me that this isn't going to be an easy orgasm. There's an edge of danger as he grinds his cock into my ass. He's so hard up against me, and I wonder where this is going.

"You looked so pretty today when you walked in. Who did you see? Hmm, was it that boss of yours? The one that watches you like you could be his? Did you let him bend you over the desk? Did you let him fuck you like the whore you are?"

Wait, what? I shake my head, crying out at all of the sensations that are going through my body. I'm feeling overwhelmed. He pulls down my sleep shorts, dropping them to the ground, and makes me watch ourselves in the mirror. Before doing the unthinkable. He slaps my pussy, causing me to writhe and cry out.

"That's for letting anyone see what's mine. *This* is mine."

He slaps me again and I gasp. It shouldn't feel or hurt this good. *What the fuck?* He drags his finger through my wetness, and circles my nub.

"Whores don't deserve to come. You're going to take everything I give you, aren't you baby?"

He pulls my hair, and my back arches. He turns my head to kiss me forcefully and my body writhes. I whine as he grinds his hand against my clit, shoving three fingers into my pussy.

"You take my fingers so good, just like you take my cock. So tight, stretched, so good."

I don't know what to do, how to feel, and I can feel my toes start to tingle, aching to come. Clenching on his fingers, he yanks them out and shoves me forward. I catch myself on the counter with a cry. He pushes me down until I'm flat against the cold marble. Pulling out his cock, he spreads my ass cheeks to stare at my center. He grabs his cock and slaps it on my pussy. It's heavy, hard, but feels different from when he slapped it with his hand. I cry out again at the attack. He rubs his cock against my clit and I shudder.

"You're such a pretty little fuck toy," he growls, grabbing my neck and gripping me firmly.

"A cock tease in your little dresses and swinging your hips."

He thrusts against me again, coating himself in my arousal. I don't know where he's going with this, but I can tell this is not going to be for my enjoyment. He shoves his dick from my pussy to my ass, using me to fuck himself. He continues to push against me calculatingly, squeezing the base of his cock, and then thumping against my pussy. He squeezes the hand around my throat tighter and tighter, cutting off my air, until I'm on the verge of either blacking out or combusting. I'm surrounded by sensations.

He continues to take his cock, and pushes just the thick tip inside of me.

"Dirty little whore. You'll take what I give you and you'll like it."

He continues to thrust shallowly into me, taking the base of his shaft and jacking himself off with me as his favorite lubricant. Pulling my head up by my neck, he bows my body even more as he squeezes tighter and I keen.

I have no words, no air to breathe, and everything feels like too much yet not enough. I just want to come. I need to come, but I know now he won't let me. He's going to use my body, taking everything I am and giving nothing back.

On and on it goes. My eyes are rolling back into my head, and I wonder if I'll pass out. After a few more thrusts I hear him grunt, as he comes inside of me.

He lets me go and it's like someone cut my strings. I collapse, gasping and crying in frustration. I don't know what the hell got into him. He storms out and the front door slams moments after.

Good, I'm glad he's gone. What the hell was that?

I undress the rest of the way and take a cold shower. I don't even bother touching myself. Who knows what he'd do if he found out. I snort out loud. *If?*

He always has a way of finding out when I do something against his wishes.

two

I open my eyes to Anthony leering at me. He grabs the blanket and yanks it off.

"Get up lazy bones, time to get our run in. Let's go!"

Every single morning, he does this. He insists that we run together, because it's good for me, and it's 'good for our relationship'.

I snort to myself, then quickly change into a pair of running shorts, jog bra, and a loose tank top. I grab my arm band for my phone to play music, a bottle, and prepare for torture.

You'd think that after the fiasco of people 'seeing what's his', that he wouldn't want me to wear these tiny shorts, but since it's five-forty-five in the morning, no one is up to care.

So, every morning, we rush down the stairs, out the door, and on a two mile run before work. I wouldn't mind so much, if he didn't set such a grueling pace with punishments if I slack off. If I don't keep up, he yells and hits my ass and thighs with harsh smacks. One time I couldn't sit for hours afterwards, and I had to edit standing up, because I had welts from his huge hands from moving too slow.

So now I try to run like the wind, or as fast as my short legs can carry me.

I can admit these crazy workouts are paying off. I'm the fittest that I've ever been, a little malnourished honestly with all of the salads that he makes me eat when we go out, but my body is looking good.

Ugh, salads. I am so over them. Thank god they're becoming more rare as I work later hours and he has been schmoozing with clients and colleagues. I'd honestly rather our paths cross less and less lately, the way his moods have been. What does that say? That I feel safer when we aren't together lately.

We finish up our run, and I hobble up the steps to our apartment. I'm going to be feeling sore today. I walk into the bedroom and march right to the shower. I know the drill. It's the same almost every day now. We shower together. We dress together, and I pray that we can leave without some rude remark or biting comment.

Today isn't one of those days.

I finish dressing when he grabs me by the base of my bun and pulls back my hair.

"Are you gonna behave today, Victoria?"

Ugh, he and my parents are the only ones that call me that. Freaking cringe. I hate my full name, and he calls me it because he knows how much I dislike it.

Taking his thumb he smears my lipstick across my mouth, then brings his lips to my ear and growls, "And now you look exactly like the whore that you are. Don't wear red lipstick out today. Or I'll find you at lunch and smear it again."

I fight not to tremble and internally groan. He's been making it a habit of finding me when I go out to eat with my coworkers lately. He texts me, criticizing what I'm eating, who I'm eating with, and describes how he'll punish me for my transgressions. Those are the days that I dread going home. I fight not to drag out my work day as long as possible. But I know that would only incite him more.

"I won't. I'll be good, I promise."

My voice shakes a little as I say this and I hate it.

Lifting his left hand up quickly, I flinch. He laughs, grabbing my face and pinching it tightly, before raising an eyebrow.

"Oh darlin'. You're so lucky that I don't hit you. Your life is practically perfect in this apartment, with me taking care of you and helping you become your best self. Don't twist how special we are to one another," he says cruelly, getting in my face.

He kisses me roughly, then lets go, striding away before walking out the door. I sigh, and walk into the bathroom to fix the mess that he made of my lipstick. I grab a makeup remover wipe, then fix my makeup, choosing a dark brown instead this time. I survey the change as if someone else was in my body. I turn my face from side to side, already preferring the red over this color.

"Nothing can be done about it now, Tori. Time to suck it up and get to work before you're late, baby girl." I say with a sigh.

I stare at myself a moment longer, noticing the pallor that my skin has. I add a little blush, blending it, before giving myself a glare. I'm really starting to dislike the person that I see. I'm becoming someone that lies to cover up the actions of others and I think I've started lying a little to myself. I think it's time I finally come clean to Tesa. A little heart to heart when we're out and I spend the night. Maybe it will help. We'll see if I can muster up the courage to do it.

Feeling a little lighter now with that decision, I grab my things and head out to work.

———

IT'S HALFWAY through the day, and I'm really happy with all the progress I've achieved. I was super productive today. I met with a new author on a Zoom call, talked about her book, and she asked me to edit it. I'm excited for this new project.

My boss is all about adding a personal touch, and wants to be sure that everyone meshes. It's important for him and the publishing company that the author has a personal connection with the person reading their words and editing. I've learned a lot from him and his ways are effective. I serve as a developmental editor as well as line editor, before it goes on to be read one last time by my boss. And if all the boxes get checked, it goes off to be published.

I love my job, and I excel at this. I love being a part of someone achieving their dreams and getting their words out there among the world. My boss, Peter, took a chance on me as a new graduate, and I appreciate him so much. I may have the job, but now my goal is to show him that I deserve the promotion that he's been teasing me with. There are eight editors that are all vying for this. I just have to keep showing him that I'm the girl for the job.

I sigh and check the clock. It's lunch time, and I'm going out with my coworkers for a quick bite. We try to do this two times a week at least. Get out of the office and have some girl chat time. I usually love it, but I keep thinking back to what Anthony said this morning.

"I'll find you at lunch and smear it again."

If this was anyone else, I'd roll my eyes. But I swear he has a tracker on me somehow. He has a knack for finding me even when my outing is impromptu. He knows that I'm going out with coworkers today. I told him, but I didn't tell him where. Not that that would stop him. I can't knock my gut feeling that he'll just *know* today too.

Determined to have a good time after such a good morning at work, I grab my bag and head out to meet my coworkers: Tesa, Taylor, and Austin. They grin and wave at me as I arrive.

"I'm so hungry," Taylor groans with a laugh.

"I swear my stomach was talking during our staff meeting today," Tesa sighs with a shake of her head.

We head out to a small eatery in Georgetown that's by our work, *The Daily Grinder*. They serve the best soups and sandwiches, and their outdoor area reminds me of a secret garden. It's not too cold yet since it's only October, but there's a great breeze that plays with my hair as I sit down.

We order and laugh and talk. Everything is going swimmingly until I feel my phone buzz. I force myself not to stiffen, and keep my smile on my face as I pull my phone out and glance down.

***Anthony*: I see that my pet can follow directions**

I know that he means my color lipstick, and I force myself not to respond. I go back to my lunch: a pastrami on rye with French fries, knowing that I'll be running extra miles for this meal. I get another text, and I think *'called that one'* deprecatingly, thinking how sad his routine is to torture me.

***Anthony*: I hope you enjoy my cock stuffed in your mouth later as much as you're stuffing it with that sandwich, little whore**

My eyes widen. I didn't expect him to go there. I don't know what to say, and I feel a little dirty as I push my plate away.

I've suddenly lost my appetite and can't enjoy it anymore. I know that text wasn't just an idle threat. He will gag me with his cock when I get home, and if he wasn't such an ass about oral, I'd be excited to take care of him. Instead, I know that he will find a new way to punish me tonight.

"Aren't you hungry?" Tesa asks, glancing at me as she eats.

"I lost my appetite," I murmur. "I think my eyes were bigger than my stomach." I say with a small laugh, trying to salvage things when she looks concerned.

I don't want her to think that I'm coming down with something when we're supposed to go out this weekend. Two days left until our girl's night. I can make it.

"I'm really looking forward to going out this weekend," I tell her with a smile.

She fist pumps and says," Yes!! I want to take you to that bar that is off First Street. They have two dollar shots and the best DJs."

I laugh in surprise because that sounds like trouble, honestly, but why the hell not. What's the worst that can happen?

I get another buzz on my phone, and I decide to ignore it. I am trying to have a nice time with my friends and his attitude right now will just bring me down.

I'm finishing up lunch, then stand to walk out, when I feel a hand on my elbow. I'm spun around, and Anthony pulls me to him with a cruel smile. *Oh god, please don't let him embarrass me in front of my coworkers.*

"Fancy seeing you here, darlin. I caught sight of you as you were walking out, but you were so caught up in what you were doing, that you must not have seen me."

I take a deep breath and smile tightly, "I'm sorry, Ant, I was in a rush to get back to the office. I have deadlines, and this was a quick lunch to enjoy being outside before getting back to it." I try to pull my arm away, but he pinches the inside of my elbow, drawing me in and causing me to hiss in pain.

"Just a kiss then, before you rush off to do all the superhero things that you do as an editor..." Anthony says with a smirk.

I know he's taunting me now, he's never really taken my job seriously.

He leans down as if to kiss me, grazing his mouth to my ear and says, "I won't smear your lipstick like the whore you are, because you were such a good girl and didn't wear the stripper red that you were wearing earlier. Just know that you'll be painting my cock with your lips tonight."

My heart starts to pound at his words and my lips pull into a grimace. I don't have it in me to smile right now. He gives me a peck on the lips as my coworkers realize I'm not behind them.

"Hey, Tori, you coming?" Tesa asks.

I slowly pull my arm back from Anthony

"Sure thing! Ran into my boyfriend, and wanted to be sure I said hi before going back to work." I tell her, forcing my breath to stay even.

There, I think as I turn, mildly worried to be turning my back on a predator.

Taking a step forward, starting to breathe easier, I look over my shoulder to say to Anthony, "See you at home."

He drags his thumb over his lip, the left side twitching in amusement.

"I can't wait to see you. Have a great rest of your day."

His response was so mild, and yet I can't help the shiver as I nod, and walk away. Maybe he'll forget? Maybe he'll have to stay at work late. Gah, a girl can dream, right?

three

TORI

L ater, I get a call on my way home. It's Anthony, telling me that he had to go out of town for a meeting, and that I should be 'good' while he's gone. I hate that this gives the impression that everything else I do that he doesn't agree with is considered 'bad'.

I'll have to be extra careful while he's gone. This means that I still need to get up at five-forty-five in the morning to run and keep my regular routines. He has cameras in the apartment that he turns on when he's out of town to watch me, so that also means no junk food either, and I've been craving chocolate, something fierce. I can only blame the stress of this week since I recently had my period.

You know, I never thought anything of it when the cameras were installed, because he said that they were for my protection, or in case we ever had a break in. Now, I am starting to understand it for what it actually is: control. Control of what I eat, what I wear, who I see. I have even less freedom, in some ways, when he's gone. How will he know if I run or not? Even when he's gone, he still controls me. He makes me take a before and after photo and then judges how hard I ran based on the selfie.

If he thinks that I haven't run hard enough, the threats to redden my ass and thighs start, and I know that when he comes back he'll fulfill every word. I know that spanking to some is considered a turn on, but it isn't for me. To me, it feels degrading as he holds me down and takes a belt or hand to my ass and thighs. I always have to call in sick the next day, because everything hurts. I don't want to put myself through this if I can help it.

So I run even harder when Anthony isn't behind me, telling me that my ass has expanded and my thighs jiggle as I run. He's five-foot-nine, but his body feels more imposing with all of his muscles and long arms that find me, no matter how hard I run. His slaps that find my ass and thighs when he is here keep me in the moment, meant to punish, pushing me to run harder.

As scary as the smacks are because they come in irregular patterns, along with the slurs that I'm a lazy whore, the unknown of how much worse his punishments and corrections can be, keep me running longer and harder.

I'm feeling extra on edge, as his threat about choking me with his cock from lunch still lingers in my mind. I hope that he'll forget now that he'll have a few days to cool off and is distracted. I always feel like oral should be different than it is with Anthony. I didn't have a lot of experience before I started dating him, so I don't know any different.

I can't enjoy oral with him, knowing that he's punishing me with his cock. Anthony uses blow jobs to shut me up, take his own pleasure, and punish me. All the while, he taunts me about how good my mouth feels, that I'm such a good whore, and asks how many cocks before his I've sucked. For the record, it's only his and he knows it.

Sighing, I walk slowly into the apartment, knowing the cameras are probably on. This place hasn't felt like a home in a long time, now it's been feeling more and more like a cage. As I look around the space, I realize that very few of the things in the apartment are mine. My things are in storage, because Anthony wanted us to wait to have more room.

I shiver, but know that it's not because I'm cold. All the same, I change into a pair of sweatpants and an off the shoulder sweatshirt, snuggling into the fabric. I need things that bring me comfort right now. I make myself some spaghetti squash with veggies and meat sauce. This is as close as I get to pasta these days, but the bonus is that I enjoy eating it.

It also helps that no one is hovering over me as I eat this meal, shaming me for every bite. I know he can see me with the cameras, but he won't be able to find fault in what I'm eating either. It's a miracle that I haven't developed an eating disorder, with the anxiety that I sometimes have surrounding food. I shiver, knowing that's not entirely true, because I do carry a lot of anxiety around food. Thanks, Anthony.

After dinner, I grab my phone, open my kindle app, and settle in for a night of reading. It's so quiet, I melt into the couch and just let go of the stress of the day.

I used to handle stress differently, but it's been ages since I've danced for fun. My muscles lock in panic just thinking about the jealousy in Anthony's eyes. I worry about going out with Tesa this weekend, because he's conditioned me so well to respond to the growl and bark of his voice. Will I be able to just let go and let the music lead me? I just want to forget that this is my life now. I sigh. How did I get here?

Before bed, I take a bath. I can't take one when he's here because I can't relax. He'll lean on the bathroom counter and talk to me the entire time. It should have been nice to wind down and talk to my boyfriend, and I should feel grateful that he wants to hang out with me. He even brings me a glass of wine after a long day in the office. These are all the actions of a good boyfriend right?

Everything about Anthony is so deceiving. As the bubbles pop, I know he's assessing me. My body, possible flaws (we all have them), and how much harder I'll have to run the next day. I personally love my body.

I have curly red hair down my back, I'm a solid D cup, and I have curvy hips. I'm five-foot-two, so I'm literally all curves. I love my warm blue eyes, my lips that are always slightly curved in a smile, and even the way the corner of my eyes crinkle too. You'd think that the man that I loved and spent so much of my time with would too. All of the running has given me a relatively flat stomach, so I can't fathom what else he has to pick at. However, he always finds something.

My phone buzzes in my hand where I've been reading on my kindle app. Anthony is calling. I sigh and ask myself if I need to answer it. If I was in my bedroom or the common areas of the apartment, I wouldn't hesitate to, because I know he can see me. However, I put my foot down on cameras in the bathroom. I deserve to be able to go to the bathroom without worrying about cameras.

Why would he even want cameras here?! Still, he tried to hide that he put one in here early last year, but I found it and spray painted the lense. I refused to see any reason for there to be one in here. He finally relented and removed it.

Tori: one, Anthony, everything else. I still can't believe that he let it go so easily.

I let it ring to voicemail, and see a few minutes later that he's left a message. I refuse to glance at it. I add a little more hot water to my bath, and go back to being wrapped up in my book.

THE REST of the week flies by, and it's Friday. Tonight is the night I'm going out with Tesa and I cannot wait. I pack my bag in my closet, knowing that there aren't any cameras in here either. I looked it over thoroughly after I found the one in the bathroom. I'm in a pair of comfortable sweatpants, a tank top and sneakers. I feel a little like I'm sneaking around, but if I want to go out and enjoy myself, then I don't have much of a choice.

I have a couple of girls' night out outfits in my bag, and I'm planning to change and do my makeup at her house. I have my hair in a messy bun at the top of my head that has actually already been blow dried and just needs a little time with my curling iron to be bouncy again.

I slip out of the closet, forcing myself to not bounce as I walk in my excitement. I need to act like this is any other day. Grabbing my phone, I walk to the door, shooting out a quick text:

Me: **Hey Ant, I didn't want to spend the weekend alone, so I'm spending it at my friend, Tesa's house from work. We are going to watch movies and hang out. I didn't want you to worry, so I'm letting you know. Miss you, and I hope that work is going well. Xox.**

I had been worried about getting out of the house if he was home. But, because he's gone it's a little harder for him to say no to me without acting like a complete jerk. He likes to be in my face when he acts like that, because he leaves a lasting impression that way.

His threats are still ringing in my ears anyway, and he knows that usually that's enough to keep me in line. Usually it would, but I'm not going to think about that this weekend. It'll be my first carefree weekend in ages. I just want to have fun. I'll deal with the fall out later.

I walk out the door, lock up, and practically bounce down the stairs to the parking lot. My phone vibrates as I get in and I grab it.

Anthony: Send me a photo before you head out, gorgeous. I want to see what's waiting for me when I get home.

My face is bare and freshly washed. I had a feeling that he would do this, and I also know he had to have watched me get ready today in our room. This is why I was so careful about being as fresh faced as possible. I take a selfie of me blowing him a kiss.

It's silly and innocent, and I know that he only asked to verify what I was wearing and maybe show his colleagues a photo of his 'pretty' girlfriend.

Anthony: Such a good girl.

He responds almost immediately.

Anthony: Behave and I'll see you Monday.

I take a deep breath, gather all of the pieces of myself, and then let it all go. He can't hurt me tonight. He can't degrade me. Tonight I'm just going to go have fun.

Tesa lives near work, so I head over that way, and pull up to a super cute cottage like home. I bounce up to the steps, as she flings open the door and screams.

"Bitch, finally! Girl, I was about to send out an SOS and Tori signals."

My mouth drops and I gasp in laughter, knowing she means like a Bat signal. This girl is crazy, and exactly what I needed. She's already dressed, I notice. Her makeup consists of a smoky eye in golds and browns, with fake lashes that look like they're her own. Her blue eyes look extra big with the lashes on right now too. She's added dark purple lipstick that should look out of place, but somehow doesn't.

Looking at her from head to toe of her five-foot-eight frame, she's glowing. Her naturally wavy chestnut hair is arranged in a beachy style, with lots of volume and texture. It looks like it's effortless, but probably took a while to perfect. Her tan skin perfectly complements the shimmery gold dress that stops at mid-thigh and I know that her legs will look sky high in the strappy heels that she has dangling from her fingers. My friend is a knockout. I giggle because she's also super impatient.

"Babes, I was running five minutes behind. I didn't want to forget anything. I'm going to change here and do my makeup. I may need help with deciding what to wear though. Is that okay?"

Tesa grins, knowing how over the top she's being.

"Yeah, we will have no problems making you even more gorgeous! Your messy hair bun gives me all the jelly vibes."

I giggle, knowing that I'll be able to relax and just have fun here. I can be myself, without worrying that I'll be too loud or excited. I have to say it's a really nice change from my normal.

I step inside. The house is cozy and matches Tesa's style. Tesa grabs my hand, and closes the door behind her. She tosses her shoes to the side and starts pulling me through the foyer.

"I am so excited. I can't believe you're here. I've been wanting to hang outside of work forever, but you're always busy. I'm so happy you said yes. I'll give you the full tour later, but I thought we could drink and hang out for a bit first while we decide what you'll wear."

I fake a smile, hiding my guilt. I feel guilty. She's been inviting me out forever now, but I could never get away. I take a small breath and remind myself: *This isn't my fault, and I'm here now.* I'm going to enjoy every second of this. Who knows when I'll be able to do this again, if ever.

As we move through the house, I see light gray walls, blue throw pillows on the living room couch, and a tiny chandelier over a desk in the office. I am only catching glimpses of the amazing decor as Hurricane Tesa pulls me through. She's just as excited as I am. Work has had us pulling long hours, so this is exactly what we both need.

She grabs a bottle of champagne, with two glasses from her kitchen, and we head up the stairs to her room. She puts the bottle down, throwing herself on her bed.

"All right, girl. Show me the goods."

I laugh, then grab my bag, and pull out what I packed. Tesa dives in with a squeal, and I giggle at her. She pulls out a pair of leather shorts, a green crop top that'll show off my toned stomach, and then squeals again so loud my ears hurt.

"Heeled combat boots? Girl, where have you been hiding all of this badassness?!"

"You've only seen me at work, and I dress more conservatively than biker shorts and combat boots," I deflect while chuckling.

"Mmhmm, well I know it's in there now, and that's what matters."

She opens the bottle of champagne and grabs one of the glasses that she had waiting on her dresser.

"Drink up, let's get ready, and have the first of what I hope are many fun nights."

I grin and go with it, knowing all the stars that had to line up perfectly so that this could happen.

I get dressed, put on my makeup; spending a little extra time on my eyes. I have a fun dark smoky eye, lashes on, and I decide fuck it and wear the lipstick that caused such an issue earlier this week. This outfit *is* badass, so I'm going to make sure the rest of me matches it. I roll some big beachy curls into my hair with my curling iron and call it done.

I turn to Tesa with a smile, only to find that her jaw has dropped and she's staring.

"What?" I ask in a slight panic, turning back to the mirror. "Is my makeup smudged? Is it too much?"

"No," she squeals.

I turn and she's shaking her head violently.

"Absolutely not. I'm just once again in awe of how fucking gorgeous you are. And I was thinking that if I was into girls, I'd give that boyfriend of yours a run for his money."

I laugh, now shocked and flattered and shake my head. "Oh my god, you're too much and I love you so much for it."

She grins and raises her glass, "Bottoms up, you sexy bitch."

I giggle and shake my head again, turning to check out my outfit one last time and that my eye liner hasn't smudged. I meet Tesa's gaze in the mirror as she sips, and her eyes sober.

"So I've been wanting to ask, ever since I saw your guy come up after lunch. I got a really weird vibe from him. I kind of felt like he isn't the nicest to you all of the time. Since we're friends, you don't owe me anything that you don't want to tell me, but I need to know you're safe with him." She says it like a statement, even though I see the piercing question in her big blue eyes that seem to see too much all of a sudden.

I'm not sure I like where this conversation is gonna lead, but I say, "He treats me well enough. He's an attentive boyfriend, and always makes sure I'm doing alright."

"Mmhmm. Is that what he was doing at the restaurant?"

"Oh, that." I try to wave it away like it wasn't a big deal. "He was there for lunch with his coworkers, and wanted to be sure that I saw him before I went back to work."

I smile and shrug, letting my eyes drop from hers and slide

to the side. Deciding that I look well enough, I turn and fake smile.

"Every relationship has its ups and downs, and lately we are working through some downs. That's all it is." I tell her.

"And you promise that's all y'all are doing?" Tesa asks.

I notice that her southern drawl gets more pronounced when she's worried. I hesitate and don't want to lie. I deflect and lie enough, I decide. I don't want to lie to her, but I also don't want to ruin our night. Anxiety, you win. Brave Tori will have to win another day.

I huff and look at her and say, "I promise to tell you when it's something that I can't handle. That's all I'm comfortable doing right now."

She scrunches her face in the most adorable way and then nods.

"So when it's something that you can't, promise I'm your first call. Unless it's life threatening." Tesa demands.

My lips part and something tells me that she sees more than I thought anyone did. Usually, people only see what you let them, and fail to ask the important questions. They believe the fake smiles and excuses that I put on. I think I found a ride or die in Tesa. I nod and feel my eyes start to water.

"Yeah. Yeah I promise." I tell her.

Tesa smiles and says, "Nope, none of that. I got my mother-fucking promise, and now we are going to finish our champagne and go have some fun!"

As I turn for my glass I think I hear her mutter, "Something tells me that you don't get much of that right now."

I'm not sure though, so I brush it off and finish my drink.

Quick lipstick checks commence, and we are grabbing our wristlets, then heading out to meet the Uber. Off to have some fun!

four

TORI

The club is hopping when we arrive. I'm a little worried we are going to spend most of the night outside waiting in line. However Tesa surprised me when she smiles, steps out of the Uber, and walks up to the bouncer manning the door. I follow her, deciding to just go with the flow. *What's the worst that can happen, right?*

"Hey, Bear! Can you let my girl and I in? Be a doll and don't tell my brother we're here either, yeah?"

Bear is an intimidating, six-foot-three ebony skinned man, with brown eyes so dark they almost look black. He fits his role perfectly as bouncer because he's huge. It doesn't look like anyone would be able to get past him. He's currently half scowling, half smiling as he looks down at my new best friend.

"Look, Tesa, you know that I have to tell him when you come in. He'll want to check in, make sure you're playing safely." He glances at me, and I look worriedly at how he worded that.

What does that even mean?

"No, no. Baby girl, if you were coming to drink, dance and party anywhere, this is the safest place for you to do that. The bartenders all watch drinks, and we have bouncers inside just in case anything goes sideways. We pride ourselves in being a place where people can come, dance and let loose and just have fun safely. It's just, Tesa's brother likes to know when she comes in."

I smile and nod, knowing that I'll find out why at some point, and not needing to push. I don't need to know everything, and maybe that's silly with my history, but I believe in organic relationships. I find out information as I need to.

"Okay, brat," he says to Tesa. "Have fun, if you see your brother, tell him that I wasn't at the door when you came in. I enjoy my balls right where they're at now. Be safe, and please, for the sake of said balls, don't fuck anyone in the bathroom."

"Bear," Tesa says horrified. "That was one time, and forever ago. Also, you're at the door so I can't fuck you." She pushes past him, and walks in as he rolls his eyes, laughing. I shake my head at her and die giggling.

We walk through the club, skirting around people as it's super busy. The club is huge, and I can see its two levels. The dance floor that's filled with people is to the right and a long sweeping bar made of dark wood sits on the left side. The bar is lit up in purple and blue lights and is gorgeous. We walk up, and Tesa is already swaying a little to the music as she waits for a bartender to notice her.

"Hey cutie! What can I get you and your friend?"

"Can I start with two Red Headed Sluts in honor of my gorgeous bestie, and then two Sex on the Beaches please." I'm so surprised, I snort at her, then cover my mouth in embarrassment.

Tesa laughs and turns to me to say, "That was about the cutest thing I've ever heard. Drink up, babes, because we are dancing after this!"

Fuck yes we are!

We take our shots, and survey the club as we drink our sex on the beaches. Then head up to the second floor, which Tesa swears has the best DJ working tonight. Excited to dance, I followed along. Once our glasses are drained, we head out to the dance floor to swing our hips and let loose.

We spend the next couple of hours dancing, losing ourselves to the music. Tesa was right, this DJ is amazing. He moves easily from popular hit music to Latin music that makes Tesa and I cheer and dance with each other. I laugh and turn my bestie in tight turns as we salsa together to the beat.

I'm a decent dancer, and I took some dance classes in college as an elective. It was fun and I loved it. Then, later, Anthony and I took ballroom dancing and that was fun too, until he started to get really possessive and jealous of people looking at me.

The instructors wanted me to start teaching the beginner level classes, offering me free continued lessons in return, but Anthony blew a gasket and forbade it. I haven't thought about that in a long time. It's funny, but I didn't realize how much I missed it.

A guy comes up next to Tesa and starts dancing, and I wink at her and dance alone, totally fine to let the music wash over me. My hips swirl around, and my head drops back easily. The music has transitioned effortlessly to *Bad Habits* by Ed Sheeran, and I let the notes flow over me. Music is easy and uncomplicated right now.

I feel hands on my hips, slowly moving up and I freeze. "Oh no, please don't stop," growls the person behind me. "I've really been enjoying watching you dance, and I couldn't handle just watching anymore."

I relax as I peek over my shoulder and see chestnut curls over a man's forehead and a mischievous smile. I decide to go with it, and glance around for Tesa. She's happily dancing and she grins at me from across the dance floor. The man behind me moves my hips back to dancing, and I slide back into the music. He gets close to me, without grinding on me, but I can feel the heat of his body against mine.

Song after song, we dance, bodies in tune with each beat, and he seems to get closer and closer. His face is up against mine, and I can tell his body is curved into my body to make himself not as tall. However, most guys have to bend their knees to easily dance with me. He leads me into a bachata dance as it comes on.

I whoop as I dance, enjoying a partner who has great rhythm. He turns me around to face him and I almost stumble. My eyes widen as I take in the most beautiful man. He has sun kissed skin, dark brown eyes, and that amazing chestnut, curly hair that I first noticed when he came up behind me. Even though I'm already pixie sized, he'd make any normal person feel tiny next to him as I take in his muscular arms and chest. He's wearing a crisp white shirt with the sleeves rolled up and dark jeans. I find myself thinking that I just want to rub myself on him.

Wait, down girl.

He grins with full lips and white teeth, "Show me what ya got, *gringa linda.*"

I laugh and say, "Oh, please threaten me with a good time."

His eyes widen a little and he throws his head back, laughing a deep belly laugh that I feel doesn't happen often. He's so tall that I have to look up since I'm standing so close to him. It seems that I have managed to surprise this gorgeous man in front of me, and I enjoy the tingles that I feel as his laughter washes over me. It also makes me want to do it again. I expect to feel guilty about dancing with another man, but those feelings never appear.

He pulls me into him and we dance. Our heads are very

close together, and he turns me into tight turns in our little bubble that we've created for ourselves. His hands have the perfect pressure to move me around as we dance, and it makes me wonder what other pressure he can give me. My body flushes, I wonder if he can tell in this lighting.

What is going on with me?

He pulls me to him and rests his lips against my ear. "Let's get some water and cool you down a little. You look a little hot."

I smile. *Oh god, why can't my body hide anything?*

Taking his hand as he leads me to the bar, I step up on the bottom rung of the stool to sit since I have to climb up into it. He grabs me by the waist and sits me on the chair easily. Leaving his hands on my waist, he nods at the bartender, lifting up two fingers. The bartender nods and grabs two bottles of water and sets them down in front of us. I smile happily because I have been dancing for ages, and I'm super thirsty. He eases back from me and sits on the chair next to me, watching as I break the seal on the bottle.

I'm happy that I'm the one to break the seal because safety first, and I raise the bottle to my mouth and drink most of the cool water in a couple of huge sips. I hear a small chuckle as I come up for air and look over. I see the man raise his hand up for another bottle and put his unopened bottle in front of me.

"I've lost track of how long I've been dancing and I was dying of thirst. The DJ tonight is amazing," I say with a shrug.

He grins proudly and says, "I'll tell him you think so. When I first heard him, he was playing in another club, so I offered him a job here with better pay and more opportunity, and he jumped at the chance. Now, people flock to hear him and dance to his mixes."

My jaw drops.

"I didn't realize that you were so intimately involved in the running of this club."

I sound snooty as hell, but it's my fall back when I'm confused or feeling like I'm missing something important. He smiles.

"I'm Miguel. I own this club. I thought you knew, since you were dancing with my sister."

All of a sudden the chips fall into place. *'I'm so gonna kill Tesa later!'*

I give a weak smile and shake my head, saying, "Tesa and I work together, but we haven't really talked much about you yet."

His right side of his mouth lifts as if he's suppressing a smile."You're totally gonna yell at her later, aren't you?" he asks.

I shrug and straighten, not liking that he can read me so well.

"I trust her, and there's no reason that she needs to tell me her whole life story in one sitting. We're new friends, and I'm willing to find things out as we go."

I realize then that I do trust her, especially after our conversation at her house, though I'm not ready to tell her everything about Anthony and I yet. My eyes must have clouded because he reaches over and rubs my cheek.

"Hey, *gringa linda*, what put that sadness in your eyes? That's not allowed here. Tell me how I can fix it or beat it up, because I'm feeling really shitty, since I think I'm responsible for putting it there."

I blink rapidly at how kind he is, and I don't have the heart to tell him that I speak Spanish and know what he's saying. I even did a summer semester abroad my freshman year of college. I take a deep breath, put an extra push into my smile and pull away to grab my water. I break the seal on the new bottle and take a small swallow to have something to do.

"You didn't do anything wrong at all, I just thought of something that I shouldn't have. Should I go look for Tesa? I don't even know what time it is," I say, looking at the room behind me.

His eyebrows draw down, clearly hearing the lie.

"It's about one am, and Tesa has a way of knowing where the people she cares about are. She'll find you," he tells me.

As if he had conjured her, Tesa bounces up to the bar.

"Tori! You found my brother. Hey big bro, you'll be happy to know that I have been keeping out of trouble and having a fabulous time."

He grins and shakes his head, clearly used to her antics and energy.

"Did it slip your mind to tell her that I owned this club?" he asks her.

She shakes her head vehemently, her brown wavy hair whipping back and forth.

"Nope. I just didn't mention it. I figured you'd find us at some point during the night, and I'd mention it then when I introduced you two. However you found my hot as fuck bestie instead."

He shakes his head and says, "Don't 'besties' tell each other these things?"

She smiles brightly at him.

"I know this girl is gonna be one of the best things that's ever happened to me, and is an amazing person. And that's enough right now. Not all of us can know our best friends from practically birth, Miguel."

A whisper of a Latino accent slips in, and I realize right then and there how silly it is that I didn't realize that they were siblings. They have the same bouncy chestnut hair and wide smiles. However, she has bright blue eyes to his dark brown ones.

We chat and tease for a little longer, and Tesa darts off to speak to someone before we go. Miguel steps forward, tall enough to still be sitting on the stool, while caging me in with his arms on either side of the bar. Usually this would make my body lock up and I'd feel claustrophobic, but instead I feel my body flushing.

"I wonder how far that gorgeous flush goes," he murmurs softly.

It's so loud in here that I could almost ignore it. But he lifts his hand up to my face, and it's cool from the bottle of water he was holding. I inhale quickly, eyes widening. He leans in and runs his nose up my neck.

I moan softly, and he growls into my ear. "Fuck me, if that's not a sound I want to hear again. I'm an impatient man, but I will be patient for you. And you will be seeing me more now that you're friends with Tesa."

"Why is that, Miguel?" I drawl out, raising my eyebrow and feeling a little sassy.

He chuckles with his lips still to my ear, and I shiver.

His hand moves along my back as if to help me get warm and he says, "I'm her neighbor."

With that fun confession, Tesa comes to collect me, wiggling her eyebrows, because her brother's arms are still caged around me. Life is definitely going to get a little more interesting now that Tesa and I are friends.

five

T esa and I had the best weekend together. We watched movies, made food together, and kept conversation on the lighter side. She did confirm though that her brother does live next door to her with his best friends. They've been friends most of their lives, and are pretty tied at the hip.

"They see me as their little sister, so dating can be a nightmare," Tesa tells me. "The boys also come over regularly to bug me to cook for them. I swear if I didn't need my own space, they'd move me in," she finishes, rolling her eyes goodnaturedly.

"I think that's amazing that y'all are so tight. That's really special. My parents died my junior year of college, and I miss them every day," I tell her.

I want to tell her about myself, even if I'm not brave enough to tell her all of my secrets. I miss them even more when I see how close others are with their families. I feel a twinge of sadness because I'll never get another hug from my parents or a middle of the day phone call because they missed me.

"That's really shitty, babes, I'm really sorry to hear that."

Tesa squeezes my hand as she says this with sympathy in her voice.

I smile and squeeze her back. I'm not brave enough to tell her that most of my friends from college have also drifted out of touch, but that could also be because Anthony didn't like it when I talked on the phone when he was home. Outside of Anthony, I haven't had anyone that I can really count on. I wonder if this was what he was hoping for as he'd bitch at me whenever I was on the phone our first few months out of college.

I love that there's no pressure to be something that I'm not with Tesa, or worry that I'm saying something I shouldn't. Even when I slip and say something about Anthony in passing, it's like she catalogs that in her head with other things I've said, and lets it paint a picture for her. However, she doesn't gasp or make a big deal. I haven't let anything truly terrible slip, so that's probably the reason why.

Before I know it, the weekend is gone, and work starts up on Monday. I stayed with her the entire weekend; I had brought work clothes with me in case. I put on a pair of teal slacks, black flats, with a white top and am ready for the day. Nude lips, natural makeup, and I know Anthony won't be able to find fault in my attire if he's back. He kind of went ghost this weekend, saying that he was super busy and that he'd see me at home.

I walk into work with a smile, realizing that usually I'm dragging by this time of the day. However, I slept well, probably because I didn't have any early morning runs or altercations. I'm not willing to look too closely at this yet, so I push it to the side.

My boss calls me into his office, and I give him a bright smile. "Good morning, Peter. What's on the agenda today?"

He blinks at me in surprise.

"Hopefully something that keeps a smile on your face! I can't tell you the last time I saw this lightness in your step," he says.

My smile slightly dims as I realize again that I've let Anthony change me. I used to be really perky and happy, much like Tesa, all of the time. I guess lately I've been a shadow of myself and it's starting to show. Peter, realizing he said something that's shifted my mood, clears his throat.

"Yes, well, so we have a new client coming in a couple of weeks that'll be sitting down with you for an interview. He's looking for a publisher and editor for his book, and he chose our firm. Now I just need to fit him with someone that he'll work well with. I chose you because you have a really gentle approach, but you aren't afraid to push for a change if you think it'll help the overall book."

I nod because that's my working style. Manuscripts are their babies, I'm just here to help polish them up and look for any major plot holes or developmental issues. I don't usually meet beforehand with an author unless there's a special reason for it though.

"...which means that if..."

Shit, I got into my head and missed something important!

"...you do well in this interview and y'all work together well, then I'll be promoting you to an opening that we have. It'll mean more benefits, better pay, and you'll be able to choose who you'll work with."

My eyes light up and I smile at Peter. "Seriously?! Oh my god yes. Thank you for considering me for this. I'm super excited and would love to help with his baby...erm book baby."

I try to save myself but the hand in front of Peter's face hiding his smile tells me I failed to do that.

"Yea, well let's focus on the *book baby* shall we, Tori?"

And...I officially am waiting for the ground to swallow me up. Ugh.

Deciding that I can't contribute anything more to this conversation, I thank Peter again, and practically run out the door. Shit, and there goes his laughter. At least he didn't laugh *in* my face. Still, I'm excited to meet this new author and hope that it goes well.

The rest of the day went smoothly, and since I didn't bring lunch, we went out to eat. The weather is starting to cloud up, so we went to a sandwich shop around the corner that I usually avoid. It's delicious, don't get me wrong, but they're huge deli style sandwiches. Deciding that I'll eat half and save the other half to snack on, I order a pastrami sandwich that I'm now drooling over.

Pastrami is my favorite, but typically something that Anthony complains about when I eat it, like he did last week. My stomach has shrunk now that I've been surviving on a diet of salads and protein rich foods, so I couldn't eat more than a half if I wanted to.

Sitting down, I say to Tesa and another coworker, Taylor, who came out with us, "Oh my god I'm so hungry. I'm so excited for food!"

About halfway through lunch, my phone buzzes. I open up the text and see it's from Anthony.

Anthony: I'm disappointed in your choices, Tori. Did you eat junk food all weekend? Or is that pastrami sandwich the first of your bad decisions? I was busy this weekend, so I forgot to ask you if you did your usual run without me to take care of you. Did you turn into even more of a slob, eating whatever, and packing the pounds onto your ass? I thought that I could trust you, but I can't. Did you cheat on me while I was gone too?

Blinking rapidly, I don't even know what to say. I didn't see him come in, but I learned long ago that he has eyes everywhere. I turn around and search the cafe, spotting one of his coworkers. Tracy awkwardly waves at me, then flips her hair and proceeds to send a text, ignoring me. Oh my god, is she texting him?! Ugh, bitch...what happened to girl power?

My phone buzzes again. I look down, my breath starting to get uneven.

Anthony: **Blaming others for your bad behavior solves nothing. You look so perfect on the outside, but the inside of you is rotten. It's the result of outside influences of friends who turn you against me and bad habits.**

Anthony: **Don't you know by now that I'm the only one that you need? Just admit that you were bad and take your punishment. By my estimation, you also owe me from last week too.**

Anthony: **I'm going to turn that ass red, choke you with my cock, and then lock you away. You won't see anyone outside of work anymore. No more Tesa. I'll find a way to get her fired from her little job too. I'm revoking any small freedoms that you may have had. And then you'll be back to being mine, molded into the image of my perfect little whore.**

The texts keep coming and I tremble, forgetting that anyone is near me and start to cry. I finally remembered what it was like to have some freedom, and I don't want to go back to being under his thumb. I don't want to do this anymore.

A hand lands on my shoulder and I startle.

"Hey, hey babes it's me."

I look up, and see Tesa looking intently at me and then my phone.

She takes a deep breath and says, "Remember what you promised me this weekend?"

I nod my head helplessly.

"I think it's time to reevaluate what you can handle, darlin'," she says, frowning.

I wipe my eyes, sighing as I see that three more texts have come in, all more threatening than the last. I pray that I'm not making a mistake, and slide my phone over to her.

"Help me. I can't do this anymore. I'm losing myself. I'm losing what makes me...me. I don't want to stay, but I don't know what to do," I tell her as my hands shake.

Suddenly I remember that my other coworker had been with us and I feel super embarrassed that I'm making a scene right now. My eyes dart around the table and I relax when I realize that I don't see him.

"Yeah, I told him to head back to the office. Bestie rights. He was cool with it. He's also allergic to tears, so the second he saw one, I swore he was gonna burst into hives."

I giggle inappropriately at that, and realize I'm getting a little hysterical. Tesa squeezes my hand and starts to read the most recent texts tensely.

"That fucking rat bastard. *¿Quién piensa que es? El Rey de Roma?!*"

I snort because that's exactly who he thinks he is. Anthony has a very inflated sense of self. I used to think that was self confidence, but I confused it for entitlement.

"Tori, what do you want from life? 'Cause *that* ain't it. It can't be."

I sigh. "I used to want Anthony before he became a monster. Before he started telling me that I was fat, ugly, and a slut. Things haven't been good in so long, that I told myself that I did this to us. I needed to be prettier, run harder, speak sweeter, so that he would be nice to me again. Now he sends me texts like that pretty regularly, and I have eyes on me at all times."

I stop from blurting out everything, suddenly too embarrassed to, and feeling really dumb that I put up with this for so long. I look down, unable to meet her eyes.

Sensing that I'm hitting an emotional wall, Tesa squeezes my hand and says, "Do you want this all to end? Do you want to stop whatever relationship y'all have right now?"

My tears fall faster down my face and I really think about it. I know that I miss regular interactions. I miss dancing. I miss touches that aren't manipulative, and words spoken in love or at least...*affection*. I think back to the club and dancing with Miguel, and I realize that I miss the heat in a man's eyes when he looks at me, knowing that it doesn't mean he's angry with me, or wants to punish me, and I have my answer. I meet Tesa's eyes.

"Yes. I'm done. I... I had a taste of freedom with you last weekend that I haven't had in a really long time. I need more of that, and less pain. Less hateful words, and being worried about every bite that I consume, and that it'll turn into a fight. I'm so tired of walking on eggshells in my own house."

I stop, ashamed again that my life is this messed up and bow my head. She puts her hand under my chin and lifts.

"You, Tori, are a mother trucking badass and you will survive this. One day you'll feel comfortable enough to tell me everything, and it's okay if today isn't that day. Today is about getting you out from under this *bastardo* safely." I smile weakly, knowing now that her Latina side comes out when she's angry and she's angry for me.

"I could break up with him in person tonight, but I'm honestly worried..." I bite my lip worriedly.

"Yeah, absolutely not." She counters. "There's no way I'm letting you go home tonight to him. Who knows what he'll do if he thinks he'll lose you. I'm not trying to tell you what to do, babe, but I don't think that's safe from the little bit that you've told me."

I shake my head and say, "No, I think it's borrowing trouble. I've honestly been lucky with his temper. I don't want to go home when he's there."

"Well then, there's nothing for it. It's not the best form of communication, but you're gonna have to break up with him over text, and then we'll leave work early so that you can get your stuff."

My mind is racing, trying to plan as I say, "I have savings, I can move into a hotel for the time being..."

"Oh fuck no." Tesa laughs, shaking her head. "Absolutely not, you misunderstood babe. You're coming home with me. Meet your new roomie, bestie. I promise that I don't bring random men home, and I'm relatively neat."

She shoots me a wink. "If you feel like you need to pay rent to feel better about this, whatever, I'll put it into an account and give it back to you whenever you move out. However, you *are* coming home with me. If he's this angry now, and can find you around town, it will get worse. At least my brother lives next door, and his best friend works in private security. You'll be way safer with me."

Swallowing hard, I nod. I'm seriously so lucky and I feel so grateful that she's helping me by leading this conversation because my thoughts are seriously scattered. I pick up my phone and see that there are already a few phone calls along with more texts. I don't bother reading any of them or checking the three voicemails.

Me: Anthony, it's clear to me that we are no longer compatible. We want different things from life, and I no longer want to be treated like shit. I'm ending things here before they get worse. Please stop texting and calling me because I'm blocking your number and all your social media platforms. I just want you to leave me alone. I don't want to be controlled anymore, told what to do, or called

a whore. I won't be there when you get home. We are done.

I send the text without thinking it through and say, "Oh shit. I sent it." I look at her with panicked eyes. She snorts.

"Good, because whatever you sent would have been better than what's been running through my head. Block him and let's go tell Peter we need to leave work early. I don't want him waiting for you when we get there."

I nod, and go to block his number, seeing that he's already left a fourth voicemail. I block him everywhere, seeing that he's also already left me a couple of Facebook messages calling me a 'worthless whore' before backtracking and telling me that 'I'm the love of his life and he'll die without me'.

I ignore them, focusing on blocking and moving on. Tesa and I grab our things, and walk quickly back to work, ready to grab my essentials.

Thankfully, Peter doesn't ask any questions, and tells us to take the rest of the day off. Whether my tear stained face clued him into something having happened, or Tesa in warrior bestie mode beside me does, but he decides to just go with it. Thank god for the best boss ever.

———

TESA DRIVES me to the apartment, and I'm a ball of nerves. I don't have access to the cameras, but I'm wishing that I did, because it would be so much easier to know what I'm about to walk into. I look around the apartment lot, and don't see his car. However, I know that he'll often park where I can't see him. My hand is grabbed and I scream.

"Hey! Shit, Tori, it's okay. It's just me. Do you see his car?" I take a deep breath because if I don't, I'll hyperventilate.

"Nooo...but he likes to hide that he's home when he's mad

at me. So he could have parked around the corner and I won't know until I'm in the apartment. I don't think that he'll hurt me if I have someone with me, but honestly he was messaging me some really scary stuff before I blocked him."

Her lips part in surprise and I know that I just word vomited all that to her without meaning to. I huff out a breath and go to explain and she shakes her head.

"No, you don't get to backpedal on this one, Tori McAllister! I had a feeling that things weren't right between y'all, but he's obviously worse than I thought. Fuck," she mutters. "Okay," she says, huffing out a breath, "I've got a bat in the trunk, so let's grab that, check out the apartment, pack you up and then go. If he is there, I have a mean swing, courtesy of my brother and his friends when they used to coach me through my high school softball games."

Loving her even more, and thinking about all of the things that I don't know about her yet, I nod and get out of the car. My eyes glance around the parking lot, looking for anything out of place, and I take a deep breath. He should be at work, but God only knows where his head is at after I broke up with him.

I'm walking when I stumble. *Holy fuck, I broke up with him. This is how I die, isn't it?* I didn't realize how bad things actually were until I had a little sliver of freedom. Tesa pulls me to her and hugs me, while still walking forward.

"Don't worry, baby girl, this will all be a dream before you know it. A really fucked up dream, but still. Y'all are over and done with. *El pedaso de mierda ya no te puede golpear.* He's done hurting you if I can help it."

Focusing on her words and breathing, we walk up the stairs and to my apartment. I grab my keys, trying to listen for the sounds of things breaking. He would be fucking my shit up if he was here, its his MO to hurt me while putting as few physical marks on me as possible. I don't hear anything so I decide to go for it.

I unlock the door and push it open, then take a step and shiver. All of a sudden the air feels really oppressive. I look over my shoulder and Tesa nods in encouragement.

"Let's go clear the apartment, make sure he's not here," Tesa says.

I raise my eyebrow in surprise, and she grins.

"Greg, my brother's friend with a security company, would have my head if he knew I was doing this without him. May as well do it right."

I huff out a laugh and make sure to close and lock the door behind us.

We check out the apartment, all corners and closets and bathrooms, and I start to feel a little silly when I realize that it's just us.

"Okay, I don't need very much." I say as I walk to Anthony and my room to start to pack.

Tesa follows me and shakes her head, saying, "Tori, get whatever you don't want to be without. You're not coming back. I have a really weird feeling and I'm learning to pay attention to them when it comes to you."

I know that she's feeling the same weird vibe that I am, and then it hits me. The motherfucker is watching us.

"So, there's cameras in the apartment. He's probably watching us." I confess and sit on the bed to face her.

"Excuse me?! He watches you when you're here and he's not?!"

I stare at her and say, "My life hasn't been normal for longer than I care to admit. He's really manipulative, and told me that they were in case of emergencies. However, I know that he turns them on when he's out of town, because he always knows what I'm doing when I'm in the apartment. So I wouldn't be surprised if he's watching now. I just want to pack and get out before he decides that he needs to come home to stop me."

Tori strides to the closet, and pulls down suitcases.

"Are any of these his? I don't want him to say that you took something that you shouldn't have."

I shake my head and start packing my clothes. I grab things that I can't live without: signed books, photos, momentos of my family. After my parents passed away, I may have clung too hard to Anthony, thinking I was making a new family. I ignored way too many red flags for too long.

It takes forty-five minutes to pack everything up. I do a final walk through, and grab all of my stuff from my bathroom too. I don't want to have to buy new things while it's all sitting right here.

I turn to Tesa wide eyed and say, "Why is this so hard? I feel like I'm forgetting things, but I just want to get out too."

She gives me a hug and looks around with a discerning eye.

"You're emotional, and I'm not going to lie, you have every right to be. We are going to unpack all the shit that just happened with wine and ice cream later. For now, the bathroom is done. Your clothes are packed. Memories that you want to take with you are packed. Do you need anything from the kitchen? Anything that someone gave you that means something to you?"

Staring into her eyes, I see that she sees more than I've told her about me and there's sympathy and understanding in her gaze. I shake my head.

"Anything that my parents left me, I put into storage. I was going to pull it out when we moved into a house and had more room. Most of what you see is Anthony's because he always wanted things a certain way. I never completely felt comfortable here."

I know that Anthony liked that I felt off balance here all of the time, because it made me easier to control.

"Okay, then that really is everything. We can take it all down at once, and get the hell out of here."

We grab everything, walk out and lock up. I push the key back under the door, saying good riddance. Then we hustle down the stairs and pack up the car.

"Tori, get in the car, right now! Let's go!"

Hearing the panic in Tesa's voice, I run for the door, and see her doing the same. We jump in and lock the doors when there's banging on the window. Raising my eyes in shock, Anthony is there. I push back into the chair gasping, as if that'll get me farther away from my living nightmare.

"You will always be mine," he snarls, grabbing the door handle, but unable to get in because it's locked.

"Open the fucking door, Victoria! Don't make this worse for yourself and your whore friend. She put these stupid thoughts into your head, and made you think that you could leave me. Ha. Like you're smart enough to think this shit up for yourself. Where will you live? Who will take care of you?"

Feeling like I can't get enough air, I wheeze, "Where I am is no longer your concern. We are done. The apartment is yours, I'll call tomorrow to get off the lease. I can take care of myself and I don't need your special brand of care."

"You're gonna regret this, Vict-"

"Fuck this," Tesa says, having already turned on the car with with a push start.

She puts the car in drive, and hits the gas. Anthony is ripped away from the car, and she flips him off.

"Bye asshole! Go fuck your creepy ass self!"

Tires squeal on the pavement and I'm thrown back into the seat as she leaves the apartment complex.

"Buckle up buttercup, you survived Anthony, we need to make sure you survive my driving too."

Laughing while feeling lighter than I have any right to feel, I buckle my seatbelt.

"Thank you, Tesa." I say, shaking my head. She grins my way.

"Love you too. Don't mention it. You'd do it for me."

Relaxing in the seat, I know then and there that I absolutely would have.

"Wanna pick up pizza on the way home?" Tori asks.

My eyes light up, thinking *'fuck yeah I can eat pizza again!'* "Oh my god. Have I mentioned today that you're my favorite?!"

Tesa laughs wildly, and takes a hairpin turn into the pizza parking lot.

"Not today, but I'm not against it since you're my ride or die, bitch. And I say, it's pizza, beer, and ice cream night, roomie."

Relaxing into the seat, I think about how amazing that sounds and how lucky I truly am to have her on my side.

six

TORI

For how fucked up today was, the end was almost anticlimactic in the best of ways. Anthony couldn't text me since he's blocked, so my phone was completely quiet. I should be more worried about this because there are ways he could get around it, but for now, not a peep. Which I'll take as a win. I'm emotionally exhausted from it all. I need to protect my peace, regroup, and rebuild myself.

Tesa helped me move into her house and she promptly told me to stop calling it 'her house'.

"Look, bitch, I'm making it official and drawing up a room-mate contract. I literally can't handle the idea of you thanking me again," she says, as she throws herself onto the couch and pressed her hand to her forehead.

"So dramatic! I can't even right now. Okay, I'll accept a roommate contract. You really saved my ass today, and I'll never be able to repay you." I sniff as I say this, blinking away tears.

We spent the night eating pizza, ice cream, and just enjoying each other's company. We watched old *Sex and the*

City episodes and had a blast. I haven't been able to just be myself in so long, since I was always on edge with Anthony.

I went to bed that night really happy that I had made this change, and excited for the future. I try to ignore the curl of unease in my stomach because fuck that. I'll deal with the consequences of breaking up with him as they come. For now, it's nice to be able to go to sleep without worrying about an early morning wake up to go running.

————

I WAKE up to banging on the front door and gasp, jumping awake. What's going on? I grab my phone and see its four-forty-five in the morning. Ugh, so much for not having to wake up early. I'm having trouble remembering where I am, and then hear Tesa yell.

"Ay! Who's banging this early? What couldn't wait 'til normal people are awake?!"

Her Spanish accent is out in force.

I relax immediately, remembering that I'm safe now. I tense again, my heart beating wildly, wondering if Anthony may have found me and come to get me. I jump out of bed because I'm awake now, and head to the front door. Tesa is there with the door wide open, arms crossed in irritation. This girl enjoys her sleep, and whoever is here is in serious trouble. I see that she's sassy and angry, and not yelling at me to run, so it must not be Anthony. Coming up behind her, I peek over her shoulder to see Miguel and another man beside him. Why are they here?

"The perimeter alarm went off, so we came to check it out. We thought you may have an intruder... For fucks sake, it's a Tuesday, Tesa, why do you have guests?! Don't you have to work today? Couldn't you have warned us so we wouldn't panic?"

I find myself asking why they would care if someone is here, but then I remember that Tesa said he was super over-protective.

Tesa rolls her eyes at the barrage of questions like it's normal for her sexy brother to be banging on her front door, and tosses her hair sassily.

"Miguel, it's my house. It doesn't matter if I have guests, who's in my bed, or not! My house, my rules, and its too fucking early for y'all to be interrogating me right now!" Tesa yells in anger.

Miguel's eyes widen and then he scowls, his eyes taking me in from head to toe suspiciously. *Oh shit, that's not what she meant!* Realizing what he thinks she's implying, I shake my head.

"Dude, that's not what she meant. For fuck's sake. I'm not sleeping with your sister! We are not friends with benefits." I roll my eyes as I say this.

Tesa looks between us and barks out a laugh.

"Oh that's rich, *idiota*. Not that it's any of your business, but no we are not sleeping together, but we were sleeping and you woke us up. I just want to know why, and then I want to go back to bed with my roommate...in separate rooms you perv!"

Miguel looks like he's been hit by a Mack truck and doesn't know where to go next in this conversation. Seriously, it's his own fault for coming over so early and starting all of this bull-shit. I know that Tesa's brain is a scary place, and that this conversation is all downhill from here. It would be really adorable if he hadn't just implied that I was fucking his sister.

I huff and shake my head. Tesa moves out of the doorway so I can stand beside her, and I see the man next to him hide his mouth with his hand, but I can tell he's amused. I am feeling a little overwhelmed by this early morning visit, but I do notice that he's tall, has light brown hair that is buzz cut, and piercing green eyes.

The mystery man pulls his hand away and says, "Er, well that was a lot to unpack there, babes. It's always such a pleasure being around you, but we were worried. As Miguel mentioned, something triggered the silent alarm in the yard, and it woke us. We wanted to make sure you were okay, and we were surprised that you were with someone. You live alone for a reason. You hate people, so I'm confused as to why she's here. If you *are* sleeping with her, that's a damn shame, because she's gorgeous."

His eyes trace over my body and I feel my nipples tighten. I glance down and realize that my shirt is slightly see through in the cooler air. I had had a sweatshirt on earlier, but I took it off to go to bed. I cross my arms over my chest and the man gives a deep chuckle.

"Roommates, you said? Interesting."

"Ugh, Greg it's too early for this and yesterday was...it was just busy and a little weird. I don't know what could have triggered the perimeter alarm, because we have been here since the afternoon."

She spins to me and points. "Tori, this is Greg; who needs to learn to use the phone and some tact, he works in private security. He and my brother live next door and are a bit overprotective. They like to know that I'm safe in my house. Greg is used to being surrounded by crazy people in his line of work, or people that are trying to kill him. He wired my yard as part of his security for the house, and has it monitored through his company. There are motion sensor cameras outside too."

I stiffen, remembering Anthony and how he used to control

me with his 'security measures', and turn towards her, mouth opening to ask questions. I'm starting to feel panicky, wondering if I made the right choice to move in with her.

"No!" She shakes her head, reading my mind. "Nope, totally different, babes. There's no cameras inside, and the outside security and cameras are activated by motion. It really is just in case of vandals or intruders. They're overprotective, but they wouldn't ever take their need for my safety that far and violate my privacy. You're also completely safe here. If anything, these louts being in front of you right now should show you how safe you are in my house. *Our* house. Understood?"

I shakily nod, feeling like my world just went into a tail-spin. I must be more tired than I thought. I'm having a little trouble breathing, and the very intense looks the guys are giving me are starting to get to me.

"Okay. I'm gonna..."

The room spins as I take a step away to get some air and I feel myself start to fall.

"Tesa, what the fuck is going on?" I hear someone say gruffly before they catch me in their arms.

"Remember I said it was a really weird day yesterday?"

"Tesa," Miguel grunts in warning as he lifts me up into his arms and adjusts me properly.

All of a sudden I'm drowning in his brown eyes as he assesses me and looks back at his sister to say, "You have a lot that you're not telling us, obviously. A weird day is getting a flat tire and having to call me for help, or a guy refusing to give you his number. Not picking up a stray to live with you that you barely know!"

His voice raises with each word and I flinch and gasp, twisting in his arms to get away, because I'm just super overwhelmed. I suddenly feel like my skin is too tight, and I can't get enough air. I can't deal with the harsh words, and the yelling for some reason.

I try to calm down, reminded by his words that it would seem odd that I'm living with Tesa, when we admitted at the club that we were new besties that didn't know everything about each other yet. He just wants to make sure his sister is safe too, even if he goes about it in an overbearing way. It doesn't mean that he has to steamroll over me to do it, though.

Tesa moves forward and gets in her brother's face. "Put my best friend down on the couch and then move away. You're scaring the shit out of her and making me a liar."

He glances down at me as I'm unsuccessfully wiggling to get out and he clamps his arms around me tighter.

"Stop moving before I drop you," he growls.

I still can't get enough air, and this isn't helping. I have felt like this before, and recognize that I'm hyperventilating. *Is this what a panic attack feels like?* The room is spinning. My eyesight is alternating between going dark and then too bright around the edges, and my chest feels too tight. Is this a heart attack maybe?

Miguel sighs, seeing my struggle to breathe. He puts me down on the couch, and then pushes my head between my legs roughly.

"Why is your friend having a panic attack? And what the fuck do you mean that she's living with you now?"

I'm trying to claw my way out of a panic attack, taking deep breaths when I hear a slap ring out in the room.

"Oh fuck, Tesa. What is going on? I don't think I've seen you hit your brother in years."

"Yeah," I hear my best friend say, "It's been a really long time since he's been this much of a controlling dick! Now, Tori has been through a traumatizing experience, and you may have just scarred her for life. She broke up with her asshole boyfriend yesterday, and she's moved in with me. We will be living together for the foreseeable future. When you see my bestie, you will turn around and run the other way. You will not look at her, you will not talk to her. You have lost that right. I know that you and her had a moment in your club, but you've fucked up. Until you can make it up to her, you will leave her the fuck alone. Now get out of my motherfucking house!"

"Tesa..." I hear Miguel's voice, as I continue to try and breathe.

I lift my head, even though I can't get enough air, and he glances down at me. There's an angry handprint on his face and he looks pained at whatever he sees on my face.

He sighs, gets on his knees and puts both hands on my cheeks.

"Okay. It's clear that I misread whatever was happening here. Now, I need to fix this before my sister cuts off my balls. So, *gringa linda*, pay attention to my voice, okay. You're safe. Whatever happened before is in the past. There isn't anything in this house that will hurt you. A few years ago, there was a guy in the neighborhood that was breaking into houses and we were overzealous. We want to protect Tesa. Now you're here, so we want to protect you too. Okay? Nod for me."

He speaks in a soft, calming tone and I start to come back. I nod, but with the calm, comes the tears. It happens when I come down from stress.

"Tesa, please don't hit me again," Miguel groans and looks up at his sister.

Tesa shakes her head and sits next to me, hugging me. "Shh. This isn't your fault, Miguel. This is the release of stress and weirdness. She's fine, aren't you, baby girl?"

I nod again and hug her back.

"To-totally fine," I choke out except the end turns into a wail, and I'm once again embarrassed, so I hide my face.

Greg chuckles. "That sounds nothing like weirdness, but I have a feeling this is girl code and you're not gonna tell us shit, huh?"

"Nope, see yourselves out. You've fucked up our morning enough. Thanks for everything. I'm sure it was just a squirrel earlier that messed with the sensors," Tesa says, shaking her head.

I snort and giggle at the mental image, and the boys stare at me in shock.

"*Esta loca...* Tesa, you are harboring a crazy person, aren't you? Why is it that all the super gorgeous, sexy women are crazy?"

Miguel is shaking his head, completely confused and I don't have the heart to explain all the things that are going on in my head right now. My mercurial emotions are giving me whiplash. I'm too tired, too emotionally wrung out to deal with someone else's confusion right now. Tesa stands up, and pushes the men to the door.

"She's not crazy. She's just been dealing with a lot, for longer than she should have. It's not my story to tell, and it's none of your business. *Vayanse*! Goodbye! Don't let the door hit you on the way out."

She slams the door and locks it, then grabs my hand.

"Let's go back to bed. I want to keep an eye on you, so sleep with me, okay? We'll set an alarm and then decide if we're going to work or taking a mental health day."

I don't have the energy to argue, and I don't really think I'll be able to sleep alone right now. I still feel shaky from earlier. Tesa forces me to drink some water, and then we go back to sleep in her room. I fall asleep surprisingly quickly, and I attest that to the panic attack from earlier.

————

I THOUGHT that my sleep would be restful due to exhaustion, but I find myself being chased into dark alleys, with cruel hands grabbing for me. I dodge and weave to get away from them, but they pull my clothes, tear at my hair, and hit me. Finally, I lose myself in the alleyways, thinking that I've gotten away, that I'm free, until I come to a dead end. I whirl around to find a way out, go back the way I came, but there are now men all around me, boxing me in to-

I wake up with a start to the smell of coffee, and my eyes pop open. Tesa giggles.

"I'm figuring you out slowly, babes. You are definitely a coffee person."

I smile slowly and get upright.

"Oh my god, yes. I'm mean and words are hard without it. You see me after at least a cup and a half in my body by nine am."

"Yep, I figured. Drink, then shower and get dressed. Are you up for work today? Or would you rather call out sick and hang in onesie pajamas, eating ice cream and watching movies?"

I take the cup, and then glance at the clock. I have at least an hour to get my life together. Do I want to stay home and overthink everything or go to work and toss it all into a corner of my brain for later? Hmm. Avoidance wins this one today.

I look back at her and grunt. "Work," while sipping my coffee.

Tesa barks out a laugh and says "I could have called that one. Compartmentalize today, but wine and confessions are coming very soon!"

I nod, knowing that I owe her some hard truths about my past. I'll definitely need wine to get through it all. I don't know exactly what triggered my panic attack this morning, except it felt like I was falling down a dark hole and I was trapped. I shiver and take another sip.

Never again. I will never be trapped again. I will never have my choices taken from me.

seven

TORI

Tesa and I walk into the building, and stride with purpose across the lobby. Neither of us are completely awake yet, but we are making an effort today. I decided to wear my favorite comfortable work outfit that I rarely wore. Gray pants, purple off the shoulder shirt and purple flats.

Anthony disliked when my shoulders showed in my outfits at work. I don't know why, it's just a shoulder. He preferred, threatened, that he wanted my body completely covered. He always accused me of not working, but instead fucking anything on legs. I think we can all agree that he's delusional.

It's kind of a warm day for long sleeves, and I should have worn something else, but I don't plan to be outside much. Tesa and I also brought our lunches. I have to catch up on work from yesterday and get ready for my meeting with the new author that's coming up. I'm prepared for today to be a catch up day, filled with returned phone calls and edits.

Suddenly, my eyes cut over to the guard stationed in the building. It's almost like my brain is warning me to say something. I stop and hesitantly take a step over to him. I should tell him to put Anthony on the banned list for the building that the guard station keeps. But how do I explain why?

Tesa realizes that I'm not behind her, and turns. She follows my line of sight and nods.

"Great idea, let's go see a guard about a psycho, babes."

She links her arm in mine and we walk over. The guard glances up from where he's sitting with a faint smile.

"Hi, Um," I glance at his name badge as I start to speak, they all go by their last names. "Shaw. I need to add a name to the guard list for people not allowed on property. I don't feel comfortable with him being able to walk in, knowing where I work. I don't know if he would, but I just want to be proactive."

My voice is strong and doesn't shake at all, and I take strength in knowing that I can do this. I can do this one small thing to make sure I'm safe when I'm working during the day.

Shaw nods and says, "Y'all's safety is our priority, and usually I would ask a bunch of questions, but you two look like you would have my balls if I did. I have a sister and I know that sometimes guys are just 'd bags' that don't deserve you, and they need to stop having access to you."

He blushes a little, and I find it adorable that this burly man just told me all of this.

"I'm sorry," he coughs, "if I overstepped. I just see a lot of my sister in you. You look like you've had a long week, and it's only Tuesday, so I don't want this to be any harder than it needs to be. What is his name and description, miss?"

I take a deep breath and smile at him in relief. He relaxes into a wide smile and grabs a piece of paper and pen.

"His name is Anthony St. James, and he is five-foot-nine, has dirty blond hair, gray eyes, and a tattoo of a cross on his left forearm."

Shaw nods in thought and asks if I have a picture.

I forward the photo to his phone, and he prints it out, then clips it to a clipboard.

"We stop everyone without a badge or who looks new when they come into the building. He'll have to show his driver license to sign in, and we memorize the list of names of people not allowed to come in. This list is also updated regularly. He'll be escorted from the property and asked not to return," Shaw says.

I bounce on my feet in nerves and nod. "Perfect, I really appreciate it. This way I know that I won't run into him when I'm working, or on my way out after work."

Shaw must have heard something in my voice and his eyebrows draw lower.

"Has he been bothering you? Is there anything else that I need to know?"

I glance at Tesa and she shrugs at me as if to say that the ball is in my court. I bite my lip, not wanting my situation to get around work.

"He and I broke up yesterday, and it was...messy. He's upset I moved out and I just want to do what I can to make sure that I don't run into him."

Shaw grunts and leans back assessing me.

"I'll make sure to tell the next person that comes on shift and I'll update the guard staff at our meeting today. If it ever gets more serious, please let me know. You may need to go to the police about this if it's as bad as it seems."

I gulp because what can the police do? My life is wild enough as it is, no one will believe me. It sounds like a movie when I make myself think about it and I try not to. Taking a deep breath, I force a smile that I'm sure is more of a grimace.

"Thank you, Shaw, for all of your help. I really appreciate it," I tell him.

Shaw nods and goes back to work. Effectively dismissed,

Tesa and I step away from the desk and turn back towards the bank of elevators.

"He totally could tell there was more going on," Tesa murmurs to me as we walk.

"Oh I know he could, but I don't want my business to be the topic of conversation around the building. It's embarrassing enough that I had to leave work early and pretty much flee from my apartment."

Tesa grabs my hand and makes me look at her. "Babes, abuse isn't embarrassing. Embarrassing is walking around with tissue on your shoe for hours after going to the bathroom, or a part of your dress getting tucked into your drawers."

I giggle at the very specific incidents she mentions. Tesa snorts and shakes her head, knowing where my mind went.

"It was just one time, okay? And *that* was embarrassing. An ex-boyfriend that's a 'd-bag'" she so eloquently borrows from Shaw, "is something else entirely. Are you sure you don't want to go to the police department?"

I bite my lip again, worrying at the skin.

"No, because he would know. His brother works in one of the precincts in Georgetown. He always was very specific that he never hit me, they were all smacks that anyone else would put down to some kinky foreplay. Being a dick to your girl-friend isn't a criminal offense," I whisper at the end as someone walks by us.

Tesa glares at them as they stare.

"Keep walking, nothing to see here, Karen!"

I chuckle because one of them is named Karen and they are both pretty judgey. They work on the third floor in the marketing department of the publishing company with Tesa.

Tesa sighs, "I always thought the laws on this were skewed towards the abuser. None of this is your fault."

She shakes her head, "We'll figure it out. I'll see you for lunch?"

I nod with a smile, as we head for the elevator and our respective floors.

———

I PUSH BACK from my desk with a sigh. The day flew by, and I can't believe how busy it was. I had two more manuscripts drop into my email to be proofread, edited, and done by next week. I know that Peter is pushing the promotion carrot hard, but damn. I am really going to have to push to get this all done.

Both proofreads are for established authors, so I'll be watching for continuity of plot and any errors. I've edited for them before, so I know their writing styles. Making a note to go through the first one in the morning, I grab my things to head out. The offices are a flurry of activity, and I look around, wondering if I missed something. Was there a staff meeting that I missed yesterday? It's not usually this busy after five pm.

"Hey Taylor," I said as he hurried by. Taylor stops and smiles distractedly. "What's got you in such a hurry?"

"Oh! We all just took on new clients, and it's been crazy. The turnaround that they're asking for manuscripts is tight, so we all decided to stay late and get ahead of it."

I nod, and he walks away. Dammit, should I stay? I pull out my phone and see that I missed a message from Tesa. I've been keeping my phone on silent at work lately.

TESA: *I have to stay late tonight, to work on teasers for the social media projects I'm working on. Do you want me to bring you the keys to go home? I can take an uber home.*

Me: I **don't think that I'm comfortable staying home alone right now. I'm going to stay too. The editing department has a ton of activity right now, and I have things I can work on.**

Tesa: **I don't blame you in the least bit. I know that Greg is home, but you didn't have the best introduction to the guys. Want to order dinner later?**

Me: **Yes! I'm likely to get sucked into what I'm doing otherwise and forget to eat.**

I HEAD BACK into my office to jump into that manuscript waiting for me.

————

THE NEXT FEW days continued with late nights, and I found myself dropping into bed exhausted. Though one of the benefits of this is that I am too tired for nightmares. It's now Friday afternoon, and I've managed to finish one of the manuscripts completely, including the video call that I do at the end to discuss changes that I recommended and why.

This book had one big plot hole that I found.

"I think that we should talk about Terrance and his feelings for Tracy. Is it believable that she caves to his groveling so quickly?"

Katie frowns as we talk on the video call, eyes looking over where I mean.

"I can definitely see what you mean. I'm having trouble figuring out how much groveling is appropriate. He tried to ruin her life and bullied her."

I wince, feeling the parallels in my life right now. I'll never reconcile with Anthony though. Creepy fucker.

"I totally understand. What if he recreates some of the things that he does to her to himself. How do you think that Tracey would feel about that?"

Katie nods in thought. I don't want to push too hard because this is her book, but I feel like it is missing something.

"Ok, I can see that. It'll bring them together, and they'll be able to move forward from things."

I nod with a smile.

"Let me know if you need anything in the meantime, and send me the update when you're done," I say with a smile.

Kate grins. "You're seriously the best. Thank you for coming to me with this. I'll let you know if I hit a wall. I know you work with other bully romance authors. I'll have the update to you by Monday morning."

I do, and it's odd because I've always felt a kinship with the female character. Now I know why.

"It's seriously no problem! I'll talk to you soon," I say as I hang up the video call with a smile, feeling accomplished.

There's nothing else for me to work on for this book before then, so I didn't need to stay late tonight. Tesa had also pulled late nights, and her marketing campaigns were completed for the week. Triumphantly, we stride out of work.

"Peace out bitches!" She exclaims, throwing her arms up in the air when we reach the parking lot. I laugh and shake my head at her.

"Girl, I have never seen work this busy. It's insane!"

I hadn't told her about the possible promotion yet, and opened my mouth to tell her when I'm interrupted by a coworker.

"Hey ladies, we are all going for tacos and margaritas after this crazy ass week, y'all in?"

I look over at the exhausted but happy faces of my coworkers, but I can't muster up any excitement for it. I just want to chill.

"Thanks for the invite but y'all go ahead. I have a date with my bestie tonight," Tesa says.

I grin over at Tesa because she just gets me.

Leaning over to me, she mumbles, "I just spent more time than I care to admit with those people, I'm pretty over them for the week. Even seeing them Monday morning doesn't excite me right now."

Laughing, I pull her with me to the car, we've been carpooling all week, I admit that she's not wrong. I feel exactly the same way.

"What are we feeling tonight?" I ask.

"I wouldn't be against making dinner, drinking wine, and having a chill night. My poor little brain is so tired," I moan.

Tesa climbs into the car with me and drops her bag into the back seat.

"Girl, who are you telling? If I never have to look at another non-fiction teaser, it'll be too soon!" Tesa says, looking tired.

I groan for her. "Ugh. Non fiction is fine, it's just not my favorite genre to read. I'm really happy that Peter has taken pity on my soul. He tends to give me fiction books that have fun twists and turns. It keeps me going so I'm not bored." I commiserate with her.

We head back to *our*, yes I've started saying our, be proud of me, house, and head up to *our* respective rooms to change. I pull off my work dress, heading to the bathroom. Standing in my bra and underwear, I wash off today's makeup, and toss my hair up into a messy bun. The bra disappears too as I walk back into my room. I throw on a hooded T-shirt with my underwear, and head to the kitchen.

I'm not impressing anyone today, and Tesa dresses similarly at home. I pull out ingredients for chicken marsala and she walks into the room.

"Oh my god, you're never allowed to leave," she squeals.

I laugh and shake my head.

"Will you make a salad for us in a little bit?"

I am craving vegetables today after so much takeout this week. Tesa makes the best salads, and it actually makes me excited to eat one. I've become a little biased against them lately and for good reason.

Tesa turns on some fun club music and I grin. I can see this is going to turn into a night of drunken dancing in our under-wear in the living room. Tesa recently warned me that this would be happening today. When she's super stressed out, she has to dance. It helps her release her anxiety, it's a great work out, and occasionally she scares the neighbor kids who peek over the fence in the back yard sometimes. I cackled laughing when she told me that this has happened no less than three times. You'd think they'd have learned their lesson.

My hips start to sway, and Tesa opens the wine. *Tipsy* by J-Kwon is playing and it very much fits our vibe today. We dance around the kitchen, drink and cook, and by the time we sit in the living room, I can say that I have a really nice buzz happen-ing. We have Blackbear playing low in the background now as we enjoy our dinner.

We are unconsciously doing happy wiggles in our chairs as we eat and laugh.

"Not for nothing, because everything leading up to this sucked, but I'm really glad that you're here, Tori. My brother jokes that I hate people, but it's nice to unwind after a crazy work week."

"This is really nice," I agree.

I take a sip of wine and decide to ask what I'm thinking.

"So why does he think you hate people? Honestly, I don't

know what to think of Miguel. We had fun at his club, but then the other day, I swear he wanted to kick me out. Half the time I'm not sure if he wants to eat me or kiss me."

I roll my eyes with a huff, then realize what I just said. I flush and glare at the wine in blame.

Damn wine! That's not what I meant!

I hear silence next to me, then laughter and a thump. I looked up at Tesa in surprise, because I was in my head again, and find my bestie on the floor, losing her mind laughing. I chuckle at her shaking my head. Okay, yes it was that funny. Tesa tries, badly, to get a hold of herself. She sits up, wheezing from laughing, and takes a sip of water, shaking her head.

"First off, ew. I don't want to see my brother eating my bestie in any capacity."

She fake shudders as a giggle escapes. I worry that she's going to lose it again, but she reigns it back in, breathing hard.

"Second, I don't have a lot of friends outside of the guys, and I pretty much claimed you. You were super closed off, and I'd keep inviting you to do things, and you'd politely decline. Now I know why, it's because you *couldn't* go."

She pauses taking another sip before continuing, "I'm a determined bitch though, and I knew you were mine. We were meant to be besties. So I kept inviting you, knowing that one day you'd tell me what was happening. I'd find out why you were so hard on yourself and said things about yourself that weren't true. Then you finally said yes, and the rest is history!"

She raises her glass and toasts me with a grin.

"As for why Miguel blows hot and cold..." she trails off.

We make eye contact and sputter out laughing.

She shakes her head, mirth in her voice as she continues.

"As I was saying, god we are such teenage boys, Miguel doesn't trust anyone with me. Remember Bear? He wasn't kidding when he said my brother would find me to check in.

My brother and his friends still feel like I'm the eight-year-old girl that followed them around, asking them to play with her. I'm not, and I spend a lot of time reminding them of this."

She stops, glancing off at the door as if expecting them to pop in.

"They tend to stop over to the house a lot, invite themselves to dinner at least once a week, just to see how I am. Most of the time I love them for it, until they get all growly like they did Wednesday morning. God, this week has been such a shit show."

Tesa laughs, shaking her head.

"Amen to that! So he's worried I'm going to what? Hurt you? Take advantage of you? Because I want you to know-"

Tesa scowls at me and slashes her hand in front of us.

"*Basta con esa mierda, Tori.* I don't want to hear it. I know you're not trying to hurt me, but my brother especially is very paranoid. He doesn't date much, and I know that he's very much a one and done serial fuckboy. He deserves more, but he doesn't understand how to open up."

My eyes widen at that.

"My jaw dropped when I saw him laughing with you at the club when y'all were dancing. He doesn't open up easily, yet he expects to know everyone's secrets right off the bat, and that's not how life works. No one just tells you all of their secrets to begin with. So, if you're interested, I will say that there's no better person for him, but he's gonna take work."

I nod, grateful to know that it's not personal for him, but also self aware enough to know that I'm not ready to even think about starting anything with Miguel, or anyone else after Anthony right now.

Tesa finishes another bite of her food .

"Girl, I hope the boys don't get wind of how well you cook, because we'll never be able to keep them out! I think they're probably keeping their distance, or caught the memo that we've been working late this week."

She grabs the remote to the stereo and turns it up. *Queen of broken hearts* by Blackbear is on, and Tesa jumps right in, singing about being the queen of broken hearts and her life becoming dark.

I laugh because sure its dark, but it's also catchy as fuck. I get up and dance with her, picking up the words easily. Shortly after that, the dancing has gotten ridiculous and we are singing slightly off key full blast. I twirl and laugh as the sun sets and see a face. I gasp, but relax when it's curly brown hair, and wide brown eyes, not blond and gray.

Oh shit, Miguel is in the backyard. Tesa is still dancing and singing. She grabs my hand as the song transitions into a faster club song, and I shrug.

You get what you get when you act like a Peeping Tom-Miguel!

I laugh and booty dance with my bestie. Tesa glances at the huge back porch windows and winks at me. *She knew he was there the whole time.* She walks over and yanks the sliding glass door open.

"Hey Peeping Tom! This is just getting creepy, Miguel. What do you want?" Tesa asks.

"I-I knocked on the front door, and I heard music. I didn't want a repeat of the other day, so I came around the house to see you. I didn't want to scare you again. I didn't expect y'all to be dancing around in your underwear! What the fuck, Tesa?"

She scoffs, "You know I dance my stress away. And its been a really fucked up, long week. So I'm introducing my roomie to my weekly dance tradition. You may want to call ahead or something, Miguel. Sometimes Tori walks about naked."

I swear Miguel almost swallows his tongue as he looks between us. I grab the wine bottle and snicker. It really is just too easy to yank his chain. I pour some more wine, and take a long sip while maintaining eye contact with him. Tesa's sassiness is clearly rubbing off, and I'm not at all mad about this. I smirk at him from over my glass.

"Aye, *gringa linda*, you will be the death of me. So bratty, so sassy, I may just take you over my lap one day and you'll like it."

My eyes widen and I wait to feel triggered. Only to find that...I'm really not. *This shouldn't be sexy, should it?* God, why am I so messed up? I feel myself start to get wet and I cock my head to the side in surprise.

Tesa scrunches her face, because it's her brother, and then looks over at me, where I know that my face is hiding nothing from her.

"Oh. *Oh!* Well that's surprising." She chuckles at me, smirking.

"Shut it, Tesa!" I yell with a laugh.

"Why do I feel like I'm missing something? And...ohhh you're into that, aren't you? Hmm, interesting. You are constantly surprising me." Miguel smirks at me.

Tesa snorts and says, "Go be surprised somewhere else, Miguel. Leave my bestie to her vibrator. You aren't ready for her."

"Ay, Tesa, *tan grosera!* Why are you like this?! I don't know anyone that could have raised you to behave this way."

Tesa grins. "No? Remember that you and your friends pretty much raised me. All the testosterone, how else was I supposed to survive?"

She winks and he growls. I don't know why but it kind of does it for me. I never thought that growls could be my thing, but I'm learning all kinds of new stuff about myself tonight.

What the hell, Tori? Down, girl!

I shift uncomfortably, realizing that there's a flood in my underwear. God, how is it possible for this man to ruin me so easily? I flush as I realize that it's a lot quieter than it was earlier. I glance up to see the evil sibling duo grinning at me.

"Tesa, does she blush this easily all of the time?" Miguel asks. "I noticed it at the club, and I have a lot of questions about how far down..."

"Miguel!" Tesa barks, laughing wildly. "Out, you perv. You won't be finding that out today."

She pushes him out the door as he yells, "But you didn't say never!"

I shake my head at them in shock, wondering how the hell this is my life right now. I giggle as Tesa shoves her brother out the door, loving every second of it.

She moves the slider back into place, then waves wildly.

"Thanks for stopping by, big bro! Always a pleasure." Tesa twirls around to me and grins.

"Well that was unexpected, weird, and fun. So now, why don't you change those panties and light them on fire because ew my brother, and let's watch a movie. You in?"

Brain trying to process all of that, I flush again.

"Ya, um yes, that sounds good. Fuck, y'all so open all of the time like that?"

She shrugs. "Most of the time it's so normal for us, that I manage to forget the ick factor that he's my brother. It's also fun that you're so easy and blush the way you do. So, do you need a lighter?"

"Huh?" I ask, completely confused.

"To burn your undies." She grins, and cackles as she goes into the kitchen for more wine.

I feel my face burning as I turn to go do exactly what I was ordered to do: change my underwear. Lord, what am I going to do with growly, sexy men!

eight

MIGUEL

Thoughts of Tori dancing and singing invade my head as I sit at my desk at the club. My cock hardens as I think of every blush and that perky little ass. Her blue eyes widening as she realized I was at the windows.

The door swings open violently and it's none other than my broody best friend, Link. I love him, but his mood swings are worse than mine.

"What's new, fucker? Are you working, or are you daydreaming about your baby sister's new roommate?"

"Gah, Link. Did you have to make it weird? I'm already less than pleased that Tesa moved in a stray. She's a hot stray, but emotionally messy. There's something not right about her. She's definitely got a past, and Tesa won't tell me what's up with her. I mean, fuck, I get the feeling that she doesn't know everything either."

Link throws himself into the chair across from me and rolls his eyes.

"People don't just walk up to you and say, 'Here's my entire life story and every shitty thing that's ever happened to me.

This is how I lost my virginity, and oh look there! That's where-"

"*Ya basta, come mierda!* God, you're the worst at making me feel like an idiot. Seriously, Tesa doesn't know anything about this chick. She mentioned her once when I asked if she had friends at work, she replied that she didn't have any close friends, but there was a girl that she was *claiming*, she just didn't know it yet. I told her that was creepy and not how life works. I bet she's laughing at me now. My sister has always been very specific about who she lets into her life and it's weird that she has someone other than us now."

"Aye, Miguel," Link teases, mocking my Spanish accent.

He likes to go all in when he steps into dickhead mode.

"Are you jealous? I mean, yeah we are her 'people', and she's always been the kid sister that follows us everywhere. But, we are also just as bad: making sure the house is secure, that she's safe, checking in, and dropping by for dinner just because. Though your sister can definitely throw down in the kitchen, we do it to make sure she's okay and because we're so used to seeing her every day. Speaking of which, fuck, with the 'stray' moving in, I haven't seen Tesa in awhile. I don't want to have to be nice when I'm over there. I want to be me," Link whines.

I smile, and then chuckle when I realize that he really doesn't know Tori's name. Link's been avoiding the house since Tori moved in, because he's not good with new people. He is also terrified of people who cry or have panic attacks, so the asshole's been pretending that the entire house doesn't exist. Link hasn't talked to Tesa recently either, so she wouldn't have told him. And then, Greg and I keep calling her *the stray*. Fuck it, I decide, this is too much fun to stop now. Stray, it is.

"Ahem. Excuse me but when the fuck are you ever nice?

You're a broody fucker even in the best of circumstances. It totally fits your 'I'm a writer vibe' that you've got going now. Your hair is in your eyes half the time, and you have to toss it out of your face. You seriously need your hair cut."

Link tosses his hair out of his face, I swear just to taunt me. Fucker. I'm gonna cut it while he's sleeping. Yep, it's happening. I give an evil grin.

"Dude, whatever you're plotting, fuck off. Gah, why is that smile so scary. If I take you out to eat all proper like, will it calm your inner monster?"

I huff a laugh, not wanting to give him any more of a reaction. I mean, I do love my food. I've been working all day, and I may also be a little hangry. The only issue is this rock hard cock I'm being plagued with. *Maybe he won't notice. Don't be suspicious, cock. Just calm down a little.* Fuck, didn't work.

"Yeah, food will save you for now. It's a date."

Praying he doesn't notice, I stand up from my desk. Link's eyes widen and I realize my hips are at his eye level.

Well, so much for that, Miguel.

"Miguel, you really shouldn't have! Is all that for me? I'm flattered."

Unable to contain myself, I bark out a laugh, shaking my head.

"I mean, if it feeds your fragile ego, then fine, wanna suck me off too? Fucker won't go down after thinking about a certain red headed stray dancing around the living room in her underwear. Her ass is so biteable. I just wanna eat it!"

Link snorts, "First you want me to suck you off, and now you want to eat a stray's ass?! My head is spinning with all of this material here. It's freaking gold! Let's start with lunch, and then see where we end up, shall we?"

I groan because I literally walked into that. I adjust my cock because there's no hiding it now, and notice Link's smirk as he watches. I always wondered if the teasing could be more, but then he married that she-witch and entered into his own hell.

I swear the day he married Sheila there was one of the worst storms that Georgetown had ever seen. Greg and I were his grooms-men, and he couldn't choose a best man, so he made Tesa stand in. She looked fucking adorable in a suit and tie five years ago.

The ceremony was in a gorgeous church, but I just had a bad feeling. I kept thinking that Sheila was a bruja that put a spell on Link. They got married within six months of meeting each other, and a month before the wedding he moved in with her.

Slowly he stopped hanging out with us, citing that he needed to spend time with his future wife. I'd understand when I got to this 'stage of life', he said. What the fuck does that even mean? We have always been super tight, so for this bruja, this witch, to come between us didn't sit right to me. And I was right.

Slowly, everything unraveled. He was the link that held the three of us together, I just didn't realize how much until then. We saw him even less after they got married. However, he'd call us rambling while drinking, saying that married life was really hard and he needed to figure out how to keep her happy. Life would even out and be easier if he figured out the secret to marriage. He'd tell us that he was falling down on the job, and that he had to try harder. And then the phone would go dead.

He had his first black eye eight months into the marriage, and I didn't know what to say, or how to ask if she had done it. Sheila weighed one-hundred and ten pounds, and was five-foot-seven. She had him wrapped around her finger. She had blue black hair, hazel eyes, and worshiped Link. How could she have done this?

And then it kept getting worse. He made excuses; said he had taken up sparring in his spare time to blow off steam and got caught off guard. And the first, second, and even third time...I believed him. And I feel like a piece of shit for not pushing harder.

I failed him in those three years that they were married. I should have made an effort to see him, instead of trusting the front he put on for our benefit. I didn't want to believe that this vibrant, amazing man, my best friend, was being physically and emotionally abused by his wife. And then I think about how depressed he got during the marriage, how we almost lost him, and I realize this can't happen ever again. I have to protect my family, my best friends.

This is why we don't date. We refuse to let a woman come between us. We'll scratch the itch...but that's it. This is why Tesa calls the three of us 'fuckboys'. We don't fuck women more than once. She doesn't know how bad it got, how we found Link the night after Sheila stabbed him in the thigh. How he lost his will to see another day, decided that life wasn't worth fighting for anymore. I can't believe that I almost lost him. Nothing is worth that hell of something coming between us for a woman.

The weekend sped by after that uncomfortable and hysterical interaction with Miguel in the living room. Tesa didn't breathe a word afterwards about it, but I would catch her looking at me and smirking. Gah, that girl! Her brother is hotter than sin, but I can tell there's a story somewhere about why he's so suspicious about everyone. I wonder why he's like this? Maybe I'll find out one day what put those shadows in his eyes.

Monday morning comes, and I wake up at five. I lay here confused because I am never awake at this time without *him* there threatening me to get my ass up and out the door for a run. Every morning. Rain or shine. Maybe I miss the routine? I sigh, feeling antsy. I have to move, so I may as well get up for the day.

I'm telling myself that I'm doing this for me today. I don't want my past to dictate my present. I know that *he* broke me in a lot of ways. I stare off for a moment, reliving some of my worst moments, letting it wash over me, then shake off those feelings, and dress in a sports bra and shorts. I'm going to take back running for myself, at my own pace one stride at a time. I used to enjoy it before everything got really bad. Ugh, I don't even like to say his name. It just makes me pissed off.

I put a post-it note on Tesa's door to tell her that I went for a run. I don't expect her to wake up before I get back, but I don't want her to worry if she does.

I grab my cell, armband for my phone, AirPods, then lock up the house. I set up my running playlist, starting with *abcdefu by GAYLE,* and walk down the stairs to the sidewalk. I close my eyes, take a deep breath, release it, and open them.

This is for me. I'm taking this one thing back today. He can't have it! One thing at a time, I'll take back. I'm done with my life constantly being upended.

With this affirmation, I push off and start my run. I haven't run in over a week, so I pace myself. I slowly push up my speed, just to see if I can, without the threats of welts on my thighs and ass. I am flying before I know it, and I revel in the speed. I have short legs, so I know that my pace and someone with longer legs will be different. That's okay. I'm not competing with anyone but myself right now. The sounds of my feet hitting the pavement, my breath and my music is what surrounds me right now and it's exhilarating.

I explore the different streets as I go, careful not to get lost, then run and run until I start to get tired. My feet have been in control of this run, I certainly didn't plan it, because I find that I'm back at the house. Stopping, I bend over to catch my breath. I pushed myself this morning, and the endorphins are hitting hard. I feel amazing, like I'm flying.

God, I've missed the feeling of running just to clear my mind and for me. I slowly straighten up, tilt my head back, and guzzle my water. My playlist has ended, and I suddenly spot a shadow standing in front of me.

I startle and gasp, as someone chuckles.

"You always drink water like it's the last you'll ever have, *gringa linda?*"

I recognize the nickname and grin, pulling out my AirPods. I ran for an hour and a half and the sky is starting to brighten. Soon, the sky will be filled with the yellow, orange, and red streaks of color as the sun rises.

Stepping out from underneath the streetlight shows Miguel and Greg. They look intimidating with all of those muscles, Miguel with his dark features and fake scowl; Greg with his shorn hair. Somehow I know that they aren't here to hurt me. Tesa would have their balls for one, but something also tells me that they wouldn't physically hurt me either. Not like *him*.

I notice now that the two are rarely seen without the other. It's like they are connected at the hip. I smirk, wondering where their third roommate is. I don't even know his name yet. I muse to myself that it's odd no one has said it.

"Uh, yeah," I realize he's smirking and waiting for me to respond.

"I usually forget to drink until I'm dying of thirst, and then drain my bottle. It happens more often than not, so you'll often see me sucking it down."

Miguel gives a dark chuckle as if I was talking about draining and sucking other things, and I distract myself from that thought by seeing what they're wearing. They're both in workout clothes too, tank tops with large arm holes and basketball shorts. I struggle not to blush; they look gorgeous even first thing in the morning.

"You were out before the sun today, you always run like this? We've never seen you when we go for our run."

My eyes shutter a little as I think *'I used to run every day'*.

However, I don't want to be reminded of Anthony, so I force a smile and shake my head.

"I haven't run since I moved in. I've been really busy, and the late nights and early mornings have been taking their toll. Work has been insane recently. However, I figured I'd get back into it, ease myself in a mile at a time. I woke up early and couldn't go back to sleep. I needed to work some of this energy off..."

I think about other ways that I could have worked off my energy as I look at them and I lose my battle and flush.

Greg grins. "Oh Miguel, you didn't tell me that she's so easy to rile up. Baby girl, we could have so much fun with you."

My eyes widen, is it possible this is a dream? What's gotten into him? I've only met Greg once before this, and it wasn't a very good introduction. I wonder if they'll notice if I pinch myself to see if I passed out during my run and maybe I'm dreaming now. There's no way that things like this happen in real life.

The guys circle me, and Miguel takes a finger and drags it slowly down my throat, following a drop of sweat as it falls down. He stops at the top of my bra, and I feel the drop slip between my breasts.

"Man, I never thought I'd be jealous of something so tiny. I really want to go after it and then lick it up."

He leans forward as my breath hitches, and Greg is invading my space behind me, pushing his hips into mine, his big hands around my waist. Slowly, I feel his cock start to thicken. Greg presses his lips to one side of my neck and I squirm. He's slowly kissing down the side of my throat, and his hands are massaging my hips. It feels amazing. I'm already a sweaty mess and I'm quickly getting messier...and wetter.

Miguel presses his lips to my ear and says, "One day you'll-"

"Hey! Miguel! Greg! Are we running or not fuckers? Or are you going to play with the stray all day?"

I jerk like I was hit by lightning. I knew this was too good to be true. Men like this can't possibly be attracted to me. I am a sweaty mess, and it's not cute. Gah, I probably smell right now too. I'm quietly freaking out right now. I can't see where the cruel voice came from, but I don't wait to meet the third man who lives in that house. We are hidden by shadows, and now I'm flushed in shame.

I don't think I like this nickname that they have for me. I don't like the game that they're playing either. These men aren't nice, and they may not have hurt me physically, but my self esteem is definitely being put through the wringer right now. Pushing the guys away, I turn, and start to walk up the driveway.

"Ugh, baby girl, he's a mean fucker in the morning and he didn't mean it like that. Come back. We should have breakfast together after our run and have a proper introduction."

I hear Greg and his teasing voice, but I don't want to play anymore. I don't want anything more to do with them right now.

I shake my head and push my little legs that have always given me such trouble into a faster stride. Tears of anger and shame are racing down my face. I go up the stairs too fast, and miss a step falling down in a heap. I quickly scramble to my feet.

"Woah!"

"Baby girl, are you okay?"

"Gringa linda, you're gonna get me killed by my sister if you leave like this!"

I hear the guys and they move closer. No, no, it'll be a cold day in hell before I let them see me like this. I shove the key into the door, and it turns.

"Yes, yes I'm just peachy!" I mutter.

I open the door and shut it in their faces, one that shows

shame and the other confusion. I am no one's stray and no one's whore.

I lean against the door after locking it. They immediately start to knock and yell for me to open it. I'm gulping in air and worrying they'll wake up my bestie, and then I'll have to answer questions that I don't know the answers to. How did that get so out of hand? I don't know them, but my body gets all hot and bothered, and my pussy is just a hussy.

I glance down at it in anger and mutter, "Down girl!"

"Are you talking to yourself? Why are the boys at the front door? Why are you crying? What happened to your leg?"

I look up in a panic and see Tesa at the bottom of the stairs, confused as hell. Me too bestie, me too.

"Umm, can you get rid of them? I can't handle their big dick energy right now, I'm confused and pissed off and-" I end in a wail.

I hear Miguel say, "FUCK, I'm gonna die. *Querida gringa linda*, you me, we need to talk soon, yeah? Hopefully without my sister around to beat the shit out of me."

I hear the thunder of footsteps as the boys pound down the stairs and leave.

"What the fuck is happening?! You know what, we are starting our morning with mimosas and pancakes. You ran today, so I'll make bacon and eggs because you need the protein too. Go shower, fix your leg, and then we'll talk, okay?"

Nodding because I'm a mess of hormones and confusion, I limp up the stairs because the endorphins are fading and I can feel where I scraped my shin. It's definitely going to be a rough day.

I take a hot shower, hissing as I look down at the blood running down my leg. *Motherfucker*. I'm going to have to wear pants. I get out of the shower, put antiseptic on my scrape, and hurry through my face routine. My eyes are puffy from crying, so I put on makeup, and a deep red lip color.

Fake it till you make it, right?

Tesa strides into my room with a tray of food and mimosas as I'm pulling on my bra and underwear. She turns and hisses when she sees my leg.

"How y'all got into so much trouble while I was sleeping, I'll never know. So am I poisoning the fuckers so that they think they had food poisoning? Or are we burying them in the backyard so no one finds them? I need to know what kind of retribution is needed for making my bestie cry."

I laugh, shaking my head as I grab my dark blue jumpsuit. I'll have to get naked to pee, but I need a power outfit after this morning's fiasco. I sit down and put it on, wiggling into it. It's quarter sleeves and the neckline shows off my collar bones.

"We can't kill them for this, Tesa. Most of it isn't their fault, but that asshole who lives with them. It just made me realize though that I don't need to be around them. They make me react in ways that aren't me." I cough in embarrassment as I say this because Miguel is her brother and she rolls her eyes.

"And I'm not a whore. That's how I felt when I shrugged off the haze of lust. You said yourself that they're not relationship guys, and I'm a little bit broken right now. I went for a run because I used to love running...before. And I wanted it to be mine again."

Tesa stares at me for a beat and hands me a mimosa.

"Definitely the food poisoning then," she says without skipping a beat. "*Mija*, I have a lot of questions, but I'm gonna let you sort yourself out first. They had better not come around looking for me to cook them dinner, or they will see that I don't fuck around when it comes to my bestie. I don't need to know any more to know that you're hurting and confused. They need to stay away and not contribute to that. You've been through enough. You deserve to grow into the bad bitch that you are."

I finish putting on my peep toe pumps and she grins.

"Oh I see her now...yassss. Go on with your bad self!"

I laugh because I know she's trying to make sure I walk into the rest of my day in a good mood.

"Let's eat this amazing breakfast. To besties!" I toast to her and sit on the bed with my food.

"You better believe it." She grins, and sips her mimosa.

———

WELL, so much for today looking up. I found my voicemails blown up when I arrived at work, and the day has been crazy. The plot hole that one of my authors was trying to close hit a snag, and she's panicking. I video call her even though it's nine in the morning, and we work through it. After two hours, she's happy with how it reads now, and tells me that she'll finish up and send it to me by the end of the day. This means that I'll be working late because I'll need to finish editing it today as well.

I grab my phone and text Tesa.

ME: **I have to stay late tonight. I have a Hail Mary edit that needs to be done today, and I don't have her final copy yet.**

Tesa: **I can stay, I have a mountain of work that I can get a jump on. Want to grab takeout from that place that does amazing steak salads?**

Me: **Omggg with the really amazing ranch that I could eat by itself?!**

Tesa: **LMAO 😄. Yes, *mija*. I'm taking this as a yes. Get your butt back to work!**

. . .

KNOWING that we will both be eating at our desks for lunch, I turn towards the next emergency that needs my attention. I hit each item on my to-do list, send out my emails about edits as I go through each one, and then do another video call.

I came up for air around three, shocked that I worked through lunch. I am starving, and I know that Tesa won't break for dinner until at least six. I get up and head for the break room, where my lunch is waiting for me to heat it up. I pop my food into the microwave and stifle a moan as I smell my turkey chili as it warms. I hear a cough and I roll my eyes.

Dammit why do I do this to myself?!

Forcing a smile, I turn. Tom, my other manager, is standing there, struggling not to laugh.

"Really hungry, I take it? It's kind of late for lunch."

Taking the out that he's giving me, I nod.

"Yes! I know, I had an emergency with an author this morning, and then today has been just crazy. I have to stay late tonight to finish the *Storm Rises* novel."

Tom's eyebrow rises. "Okay, tell me about that."

I explain as I grab my food. He follows me back to my office and patiently listens as I take bites in between, at his insistence. God, I love this man!

I have finished my lunch by the time I finish with my shit show of a busy morning. Tom leans back.

"Honestly, this is why you're on the fast track for this promotion. You just went for it, figured out how to accommodate this author, and helped her with her vision. That's what a solid developmental editor does. The author that you're interviewing with on Thursday-"

Shit, no one told me that this was happening Thursday!

"He's...kind of prickly. He's hard to work with, and he has a dark and painful past. He took that history and turned that into inspo for his book, think True Crime, but he changed the names in the book. It's going to need a lot of work to get it ready to publish, but his writing is solid.

This will be his debut, but he wants to find the right person to work with. If he chooses you to be his editor, and you can help him, without killing each other, then you have the job. You'll be able to choose what books you edit after this, and who you work with. He's friends with someone at the publishing house, so we feel obligated to help him."

That's a lot to unpack, but I want this job. I just have to figure out how to work with this author and have him choose me. Piece of cake, right? Urgh, I can totally do this.

I nod at Tom and smile.

"Can I ask how many people he'll be interviewing?"

Tom approves of my question because he cocks his head to the side, assessing me. "Eight. Why do you ask?"

"I wanted to see how steep the competition was," I say, winking. "I appreciate the back story of this author, and I can be respectful of what he's gone through, and this story is a part of him. I just want a chance to show him that."

Tom slaps his thighs and stands up. "And that's exactly what you're going to be getting. Happy editing, Tori."

"Thanks, Tom! Have a great day." I call out as he walks out the door.

I wash my dish in the staff lounge, and then put them away in my lunch cooler before going back to work.

"Piece of cake," I mutter to myself again.

ten

I went for a longer run tonight than I expected to alone. After we teased Tori, I've felt pretty shitty all day. She's absolutely gorgeous. I wouldn't mind licking up her body and making her eyes roll back while she screamed my name...but Tesa did warn us that she had had a bad break up recently. It explains how skittish she is, and the mood swings where she's fine one moment and then the next, she can't regulate her breathing, and she's panicking. These all point to things that make me want to murder her ex-boyfriend. He obviously didn't treasure that girl the way that she deserved.

Listen to me though, I think deprecatingly, as my shoes pound cement beneath my feet, like I know what I'm talking about. I've never been in a relationship. My parents were poor role models, and now they may as well be dead for all the attention I throw their way.

I don't deserve a girl like this, so I treated her like a play-thing, teasing her with Miguel, seeing how far I can push her out in plain sight. Gah, I feel like an asshole. She obviously isn't ready for anything, but damn if she doesn't smell amazing even after running hard. Her scent of coconut and jasmine. The perfect combination of fresh and sweet. What I wouldn't have done to take that gorgeous mouth with mine.

It's what I really wanted to do before Link so rudely interrupted. However, he doesn't know Tori, and he's super protective of Tesa. He hasn't made an effort to go over, scared that he would make an ass of himself and then Tesa would ban him from her food. The girl can throw down in the kitchen, and damn if I don't miss her meals too.

My stomach growls and I sigh. If I ever want some good Latin or Southern cooking, I'm going to have to apologize to Tori. And then when she fell on the stairs in her hurry to get *away* from us, my heart dropped uncomfortably.

I don't know what to do with this girl. I can't fuck her, I can't date her, what's left? Friendship? Ugh.

Friends with this beautiful, five-foot-two, red-headed beauty with a mouth built to suck my cock and a body to tempt me. When I saw her running this morning before she stopped at the house, she looked so beautiful.

Her hairline was sweaty, she looked happy, free, and gorgeous. I wish that I could see her like that more. Fuck, I have to apologize to Tori, and hope that Tesa isn't on hand to cut off my balls. My honorary little sister is savage.

Ending my run, I stomp up the driveway, glancing at the house next door. It's empty, not a light on. I dislike that they're working such late hours lately. It's eight pm, and they're still not there.

I'm in a foul mood now, having realized how much I screwed the pooch this morning. I went about everything wrong, and Miguel and I tried to bulldoze through her defenses by force. Even if my asshole roomie hadn't interrupted us, it still probably would have ended badly.

I use my phone app to unlock our front door, intent to grab a beer before hopefully unwinding with the football game.

Atlanta is playing, and it'll give me an excuse to yell at the television.

I close the door and reactivate the door lock and house alarm. I know everyone is home for the night, so I make sure the place is secured. Pocketing my phone, I move to the kitchen for that beer. Link and Miguel are bickering at each other. I roll my eyes. For fucks sake, the world would be a better place if they just fucked already.

I know that sounds insensitive or weird, but the sexual tension, if you're looking for it, is off the charts. They hide it well under testosterone and joking, but before Sheila came into Link's life, I thought they were a done deal. They always had their arm around the other's shoulder, were touching each other, and I know there was a hot make out session in a hot tub while they were very drunk, one night six years ago. Then that she-bitch came and her actions are still having repercussions to this day.

I swear, if I were to ever run into her, I wouldn't be able to keep myself from tearing into her. She single-handedly tried to destroy one of my best friends. Scowling, I take my beer into the living room.

The boys look up, grinning.

"Dude, you do not look more relaxed. You look even more pissed than when you walked out earlier. I know that y'all are both mad at me for this morning," Link says.

I snarl in his direction.

"Okay, a *lot* pissed, but I thought she was a plaything that the two of you had together. You're lucky that I didn't suggest stepping in to fuck her mouth or that perky ass of-"

Miguel does what I can't get close enough to, and punches him in the stomach.

"Fuck me!" He roars.

"Absolutely not, you don't deserve it," Miguel says with a grin.

Link rolls his eyes, nursing what I'm sure is going to be a bruised stomach and some ribs. Miguel has power behind his punches, but I don't feel bad at all for him right now.

"Look, she's not a fuck toy," Miguel says. "The look in her eyes before she closed the door, ugh. I feel like shit. You should have seen her man, those blue eyes confused and filled with tears. We are not going to be able to eat anything in that house without worrying that Tesa is going to poison us, for one. And second of all, I need to apologize to her. I pushed too hard, and I know she had some sort of shitty relationship with her ex. Tesa mentioned that he ran them out of the parking lot, screaming at them when our little *gringa linda* left the apartment. It's a shame because I think he really got into that girl's head."

Miguel turns to Link.

"Something that I know you have a history with, dick. Give her a break. We need to try to be more friendly with her, because I don't think she'll be going away anytime soon. I want to see my sister and know that she's not going to use the butcher knife on me one day and bury me in the backyard under her bluebells. I'm her brother, we are her people, but so is *la gringa linda*. So we need to do better."

Link and I look at him slack jawed. If I didn't know that he seriously liked her before, I do now. He's not much for speeches, especially not over a girl. Link looks at Miguel curiously, both respect and a little jealousy creeping over his face.

"Alright, man. You're right. When she fell as she ran away from us, I knew we had fucked up. She didn't deserve that from us, and she's sweet. We will *all*," I glare at Link, "do better. I'm looking at you, kid," I growl to make my point and take a sip of my beer.

Yeah, yeah, so I'm only nine months older. I still hold it over the grumpy fucker when he's seriously wrong, like now.

"Then we're in agreement. We need to apologize to her after your interview at the publisher. That's this week, and I want to make sure that you're focused on that, so we'll deal with our misguided fuckery later, yeah?"

Link chuckles at Miguel and nods.

"Yeah, I'd hate for Tesa to take me out while I'm talking to the str- urm the girl before my meeting," he fumbles.

"That's settled then, let's watch the game and quit the therapy time, yeah?" I joke, uncomfortable with all the feelings talk, but knowing that it was completely necessary.

The guys grin, head to the kitchen for more beers, and then drop to the couches. We settle in for a night of yelling at the television, and my brain feels quieter and less chaotic finally.

eleven

TORI

I still feel unsettled today, and I know that Tesa can tell that something is going on with me. It's now Wednesday, and I've been working long days in order to get ahead of work. My interview with this author is tomorrow, and I need to make sure that I'm on my A-game so that he picks me as his editor.

I push back from my desk with a sigh. I need a change. I've been working in silence for hours, and as weird as it sounds, it is starting to chafe. I grab my phone and my AirPods, and select a playlist. I make sure they're synced, pop them in my ears, and turn back to my computer, bobbing my head to the music.

Lose yourself by Eminem starts to play and I feel myself relaxing into the beat. I've been wound too tight and surprisingly the harsh rap song is motivating me to work again. I've been so lost and caught up in *him* and then the drama after my run with Greg and Miguel, that I haven't had any kind of stress release. I haven't had sex in ages either, and as much of jerk as Anthony was, when it was good it was *really good*.

Shivering, I shake my head. *No, Tori! No thinking about sex during work*!

I obviously need to go shopping for a vibrator later,

because a girl has needs. My needs require a rechargeable boyfriend that won't talk back. Feeling better about that decision, I throw myself into the song and my work.

Life is so short, and I have lived so little of it. College was fun, but I got together with my ex at the end of sophomore year. Slowly, he had reshaped my life completely by senior year: who I was allowed to hang out with, what I wore, what I was allowed to do. I never realized how completely I had changed until I walked away.

I have no friends outside of Tesa. When my parents died my junior year, I was in such a haze of pain, it all got out of control really quickly. I leaned really hard on him emotionally, and he reveled in it. He couldn't have planned it better if he had tried.

I dash away a tear and shake my head. No more. From now on, I'm going for what I want. This promotion for one, and I have to deal with all of these emotions that I have when I think about Miguel and Greg.

We need to talk about what happened at some point, because I'm pretty sure that Tesa is plotting their deaths. She was in the backyard forever yesterday, and I'm not sure why. Her garden looks as gorgeous as it always does.

There's a knock at the door, and I turn off of the music.

"Come in!"

"Hey girl!" Tesa says as she comes in with a grin.

I genuinely smile back at her, one because being grumpy at this bouncing ball of energy is impossible, and two because I've made a little bit of progress on myself.

"Are you ready to get out of here for lunch? I need *out,* and I don't want to eat at my desk again. It's too pretty of a day, and it'll be getting cooler soon."

I nod eagerly. The time has flown by and it's already one in the afternoon. As if in agreement, my stomach growls.

Tesa laughs. "Yep, your stomach agrees. It's time to feed you before you get hangry and turn into a gremlin. Proper care of your bestie one-oh-one!"

"Well, how could I possibly disagree with this?" I giggle and grab my things.

We head out for lunch, determined to relax and enjoy the day. We eat outside at a new restaurant that just opened up called *Blunch*. They serve breakfast and lunch all day, and their food has received great reviews since they've been open. They have an enclosed garden and patio area in the back, and we choose to sit there.

"Oh my goodness, I need their breakfast scramble in my life," Tesa whines, looking over the menu.

"That sounds good, but I really want this omelet with sausage, mushrooms, and feta. I can taste it already. I'm starving, and my little gremlin ass needs this in my life," I say, rubbing my stomach as it growls again.

"We definitely waited too long to eat," Tesa agrees.

The waitress comes up, and we order.

"Oh, and two cappuccinos, and two glasses of water, please," I tell the waitress. She nods and walks away. Tesa turns to me. "Okay, we both look cute today, and we should take a picture as a part of *Operation Taking Back Tori*," she says happily.

Tesa has been doing this everywhere we go lately, to show me photos of myself without the running commentary that I'm fat, not pretty, etc. So now, we take photos of us lounging in the living room, having lunch, etc. She's calling it *Operation Taking Back Tori*. I'm for it, and it fits in with everything else I've been doing for myself.

I love her so much, so we take cute selfies as we wait.

Our food comes, and we dive in. I swear we both moan into our meals because it tastes so good. When we had paid the check and were walking out someone called my name. Tesa is leaning in to talk to me, and we both turn.

Standing there, is my ex's secretary and she's taking a photo of us.

"When I heard you broke up with Anthony, I didn't believe it. The little perfect girlfriend, quiet as a mouse. But now, it's completely obvious! You're a lesbian, and working in that hobo publishing house turned you into one." She grimaces.

There are so many twisted and wrong things in that statement that it's not even funny. So, oh well when in *Blunch...*

"Hey babes, this is Veronica, my ex's secretary," I start, wanting her to know that she was free to be as mean as she wanted to be.

Tesa winks at me. "Oh! That douche canoe? I'm so glad you are with me now, baby. I'm gonna take such good care of you. You know those moans you were making during lunch kind of gave me ideas for when we get home..." Tesa flirts.

She's a flirt on the regular, and this isn't even the most outrageous thing that she's ever said to me. But, because it's me, I still blush.

"I also want to see how far that blush goes," she says, directly quoting her brother.

Gah, now it's just mean and weird!

"Tesa, don't make me turn your ass red." I snark, trying to get my blush under control.

"You know you love it!" Tesa cackles as she turns to Veronica and says, "Love is love, how dare you twist something that you don't understand."

I grin because she's right: she does love me, just not like that.

Veronica looks like she's about to become apoplectic, angry that we are both making fun of her and that I'm not more embarrassed that she 'caught' me. *Well, his spies all over the city definitely backfired on him on this one!*

Tesa grabs my hand, and walks out of the patio, using the side gate to get back to the sidewalk.

Tesa and I look at each other and burst out laughing. "That could have gone so much worse. Thank you for playing along on that."

"Bitch, you are my ride or die. There's not much that I wouldn't do for you. And fucking with that woman was just plain fun. Now I can envision her and cackle while I'm at my desk the rest of the day. It's gonna be awesome!"

I throw my head back and laugh, because half the marketing department is gonna think she's insane and the other half will be worried for their safety. Yeah, that's just a normal Wednesday for her. Linked arm in arm, we walk back to the office. Today definitely doesn't suck.

———

HOURS LATER, I'm finally done for the day. Looking around my office, I grin. I'm here late, but I accomplished everything that I needed to. I'm on track to finish editing the last manuscript that I have by the end of the week, and then I can start next week fresh.

Standing up, I stretch out my back. Everything cracks and I groan. I'm so stiff from sitting for so long. It's seven pm, and instead of ordering in, Tesa and I are picking up a pizza to eat at home with some wine.

Grabbing my phone, I made a note to make an appointment with my chiropractor, because these long days at my office are making me really sore. I also need to make sure I continue to run regularly.

I pick up my purse and throw everything in, and then text Tesa:

ME: **Yo! Your bestie is about to turn into a gremlin. I'm dying! You about ready to head home?**

Tesa: 😂😂😂 **Yes, bitch. Meet you in the lobby. We can't have you getting** 🔪🔪 **on me!**

I AM the only one on this floor right now, so I let out a cackle and lock up my office. It's kind of creepy, but I had to get everything done today. I hit the down button to call the elevator and wait. Leaning against the wall, I'm suddenly too tired to hold my own weight up. Yes, I'm dramatic but dammit I'm tired and hungry. The doors open and I peek my head in, making sure no one is hiding in the corners. Tesa and I watched a couple of slasher movies last night and I'm still jumpy today. I step inside and hit the button for the lobby. Sighing, I tell myself I'm being ridiculous.

Everything is fine. There's the guard at the desk, and-

The elevator hits the ground floor and the doors open. I walk out. Tesa grabs me and yells, "Boo, bitch!"

I scream bloody murder and jump about twelve feet in the air. "Don't fucking do that! Gah!"

Tesa laughs wildly and I can't even get mad at her. Heart beating out of my chest, I laugh with her.

"Girl, now I really need that wine. Holy shit."

The guard on duty runs up to us, asking if we're okay. I sigh.

"Yeah, sorry, I think this place is a little creepy after hours and I got a little freaked out."

He grins, and nods. "Happens to the best of us. Y'all be safe now."

I still feel embarrassed as we head out to the car. We've been carpooling since I moved in. It seemed silly to take two cars.

We hop in, grab our pizza, and before I can get too hangry, we're home. We get out of the car as Miguel comes out of the house. Not wanting to get caught into conversation, like a chicken, I walk quickly to the door.

"You're just getting home? What are they, slave drivers?" Miguel scowls at us, as it is almost nine by now.

"Busy day," I murmur, stepping up the steps to our porch.

Tesa gets the memo quickly, hustling after me with our pizza.

"Don't be like that! I miss my sister! Let's make up, baby!" he coos.

Baby? Ha! What the hell is he on?

Tesa stops, drops the pizzas on the outside table and hangs over the side of the porch railing to yell at him. Here we go...

"Maybe if you weren't such an asshole to my best friend, you'd be allowed over. Eating our amazing pizza with us. If you hadn't ganged up on her, made her cry, maybe I'd spend less time in my garden plotting my vengeance. But no! You and Greg had to be dicks, and now she doesn't want yours! So go the fuck away!"

I can't handle it anymore, and I start to choke on my laughter. I know it sounds like I'm crying but I'm not. I open the front door, cover my mouth with one hand, and grab the pizzas with the other.

"Oh, shit. She's stealing the pizza, later bro." Tesa dashes into the house after me and I hear Miguel yell forlornly.

"Gah! Please don't cry!!! She's gonna kill me in my sleep! I know it!"

I can't breathe now from laughing so hard and drop to the floor, gasping. Tesa closes the door behind her and locks it, meeting my eyes worriedly. And then immediately bursts out cackling at how red my face is from laughing.

"Oh...My...God. Is he always so dramatic?!" I gasp out in tears, in half a scream, half laugh.

Tesa falls next to me crying from laughing so hard.

"Yes! Always, oh my god, you really had me going, I thought you were crying too."

"No, no! I was losing it, but didn't want him to see. Oh, random but, can we go vibrator shopping this weekend?"

Tesa looks at me and bursts out laughing again.

"Yes, *mija*, we can. Oh my god, life is definitely so much more interesting with you in it."

Her phone buzzes and she pulls it out. Nosy bitch that I am, I lean over her shoulder.

Miguel: *There are weird noises coming from the house, do you need help? Do Greg and I need to come over and eat pizza to establish a balance of sanity?*

Tesa angles the phone so I can see better and I shake my head.

"Say what you want, but that man is *not* a quitter," I say with a laugh.

"Ugh, he's really not. He gets super annoying and won't back down. You know you're gonna have to talk to them eventually, right?"

I sigh. "Yes. I do, but I want to get through tomorrow first. Tell him that I'll talk to him and Greg tomorrow over ice cream after work. Let him know that I like chocolate mint fudge."

Tesa grins and texts back.

***Tesa:* You can talk to her tomorrow night after work. She wants you to bring ice cream: chocolate mint fudge for**

her, and you know my favorite treat. Don't come over empty handed when you grovel, Miguel.

Miguel reacts with exclamation marks over her message and she giggles.

"Ok, that's about as much of an answer as he'll give me, let's go eat. He'll be here tomorrow."

We get off the floor, plate our pizza, and settle in the living room with wine and background music. We don't really talk, fully comfortable with food, alcohol, and happy dancing, which is our normal routine.

"Fuck, this week has been crazy and its only Wednesday." Tesa groans once she's full.

"I know, and if this author is as prickly as Tom said, my week is about to get a lot tougher. It's hard to prep when they refuse to give you a name so you can't social media stalk them."

I sigh, pretending to be put out by this.

Tesa knows better, and grins. "Stop it, stalker. You'll meet whoever this is tomorrow, and you'll be the charmer I know you are. You know your shit. You're the author whisperer for a reason."

"No one calls me this." I disagree with her.

"Ha! Um, yeah they do. Just not to your face." She winks at me and I throw a pillow at her. This leads to a forty-five minute pillow fight before we clean up and head up to bed.

twelve

TORI

I'm calling today D-Day. Miguel may be rubbing off on me, because I know I'm being dramatic. I dress in a purple pencil skirt and black cap sleeved shirt. My makeup is on the natural side, with brown and gold eyeshadow and a nude lip. I pull my hair into a fishtail braid, then put on my most comfortable peep toe pumps. As a nod to fun, I slip on a pair of cute fairy earrings too, and grab my purse to meet Tesa for breakfast in the kitchen.

"Look at who looks gorgeous today! You look like you're ready to throw down. Do you have flats so you're not in heels all day?" Tesa is sipping her coffee and watching me knowingly. I will not survive all day in these.

"Yes, mom. Thank you. They're in my bag." I tease her, but I'm really grateful that she reminded me anyway. It's against the dress code to go barefoot at work, no matter how much your feet may hurt.

I made my coffee, some avocado toast, and grabbed my lunch. We game planned for our day while we ate. Neither of us needed to stay late tonight, so we decided to make dinner after work before the boys came over. All of these late nights have been wreaking havoc on our routines, and we need time to decompress from the crazy week.

I check the time, and bite my lip.

"We gotta go so we make it on time, Tesa."

She nods. "You're right, let's get this all put away. Thank god we're close."

"Ma'am! Miss McAllister?" Someone calls as we cross the lobby. I glance to my right and see a guard striding over to me. *What could he want?*

"Hey! I just wanted to let you know that that guy, Anthony, tried to come by with flowers right before you came in. We escorted him off the property, and made sure he got in his car and left. He was not happy, but he's also been made aware that he's not welcome in or around the building."

My eyes widen and my breath hitches. I would have run into him if we hadn't taken our time today. *I'm fine,* I remind myself. *He doesn't control my actions anymore, and he can't hurt me here.* Taking a breath to steady myself, I smile at the guard, though by his face I think it wobbles just a little.

"Thank you," I checked his badge, "Peterson. I really appreciate you taking the time to tell me. I didn't think he'd come by with flowers, but he regularly surprises me with his actions. I'm just glad Tesa and I didn't run into him today."

Peterson nods, "Yes, ma'am. Me too. I doubt it'll deter him completely, but for now, if you're working late, I would like it if one of us walked you out please."

I can't believe I didn't think about that. I nod profusely.

"Yes! Yes, please. That would be amazing. I've been working crazy hours, and we've both been walking out after five every night."

"Y'all work hard. It's all good. We just want to be sure you get home safe too, so you can do your jobs in peace. I didn't like the look of that Anthony guy, or the names that he called you when we escorted him out."

I cringe, because I'm sure he was really loud during that ordeal. I'm really glad I wasn't here for that.

"Thank you again, yeah he's not a nice guy. It just took me a little longer than I'd like to admit to realize it."

Tesa and I walk to the elevators and wait for it to come down to our level.

"Holy fuck, he can't catch a clue," my bestie gripes to herself.

I nod, again happy that I talked to the guard station the other day. We get on the elevator, and part ways on our floors.

"Knock 'em dead, bestie!" Tesa yells at me when she steps off.

I grin. "Love you! Have a great day, babes!" I call after her. A few people turn at our silliness, not that I care.

My interview with this author is at eleven, so I throw myself into my day. I take a call, work on an edit, and check the time periodically. I have to go to the first floor conference room to meet with him, since it's one of the bigger ones that we have. I'm not sure why we need one that large, since I assume it'll just be Peter, Tom, the author and I. However, there are a lot of things that I don't know about this guy.

It's fifteen minutes to eleven when I shut down my computer, grab a notepad and my phone, then head down-stairs. Stepping off the elevator, I move towards the large conference room down the hall. I find the door closed, and check the time. It's five till, so I'm not late.

I knock on the door and wait for someone to tell me to come in. Opening the door, I walk in, to find that Greg, Miguel, and another man are staring at me in shock from the confer-ence table.

"What the fuck is the stray doing here?!" the man says, and

it hits me that the guy I don't recognize is their other roommate.

Breathe, girl, breathe. It's obvious that the universe has jokes today. It's fine. I have survived worse than this asshole.

I pick my jaw up off the ground, and glance towards my boss, who is looking at me with concern. Not every day that his fast track person to a promotion is called a 'stray', I'm sure. I hear more than see the *thwack* and grunt that follows.

"Ugh, what the fuck was that about?!"

"She, *come mierda*, is apparently your interview!" Miguel growls at the man. I still don't know his name, and Peter didn't tell me.

"Is there a problem, gentleman? I am not in the habit of allowing my employees to be called names, especially not one as special as Tori." Tom is starting to turn red in anger. I know that he has a soft spot for me and he's starting to get mad.

"Tom, it sounds like there's been a misunderstanding and I may know our author. How about some introductions to clear up some of this confusion?" I'm praying that he'll give me the out that I'm giving him.

Please, please. I beg him with my eyes. Tom growls, holy fuck, I didn't know the normally mild-mannered man had that in him, and nods. I know I'll be answering a lot of questions later, but never in my wildest dreams could I know that this man would be who I'm meeting with. Also, why are Miguel and Greg here?

I've never prayed for the floor to swallow me up more than now. So much for wanting to lose my shit, I can't do that till later. *Get it together!*

"Tori McAllister, I would like you to meet *Link Anderson.* I apologize for all of the cloak and dagger, and not giving you a lot of information about who you are meeting with today. I wanted both of you to meet each other with a clean slate, and not be able to cyber stalk each other."

Tom chuckles, "I'm starting to realize, based on your reactions though, that that may have been a mistake."

I give a weak smile, and sit next to Peter, across from the guys, and take a deep breath. Miguel is looking worriedly at me and looks like he may punch his friend. Greg is smiling like he doesn't have a care in the world, but there's a slight pinch to his eyebrows, so I wonder if this is a front for something else.

"Tori, why don't you explain to me how you know the men across from you?" Tom says.

"Sir, Miguel is Tesa Rodriguez's brother, she works in marketing and she's my best friend. As of two weeks ago, we are also roommates now. The guys live next to us. Uh, the guys didn't really like that I moved in, but as you know, my ex-boyfriend is on the list of people not allowed on property. Things didn't end well, and that's all I feel comfortable saying at this time. If you want to know more later for my safety, we can schedule a meeting after this."

Maybe I shouldn't have mentioned my safety because now the guys are sitting rigidly, and Tom and Peter have weird looks on their faces. Oh fuck it all, I can't take it back now.

Miguel can't hold it in anymore and growls, "What about your safety, Tori? Is this why you're so skittish?"

I sigh, "Can I tell you over ice cream tonight? I don't really want to get into it when this is the difference between a promotion or not."

Meh, maybe I shouldn't have said that either, but fuck my life, there's too much testosterone in this room. It's messing with my head. There's a glass of water on the table in front of me, so I take a deep sip, hoping it'll settle my nerves and lack of filter. I've just about had it with everything that's happened the last couple of weeks. I deserve something good, dammit. His eyes soften a little and he nods.

"Well that's not any less pressure or anything," Link grumbles.

"No, Tori is right, you should know what's on the line for her and everyone else that you're going to be talking to. We are giving you a chance to share your words, Mr. Anderson. I was told that you can be difficult to work with, but this is ridiculous. I almost don't want to subject one of my best editors to your bullshit," Peter says.

I bite my lip to hide a smile. His protective side is definitely out to play today.

"Okay, st-erm, Miss McAllister," Link stresses.

And fuck, I press my thighs together. Why did that half growl, half exasperated tone work for me? *That's it, I am buying a vibrator on the way home. Now pay attention, bad vagina!*

"Tell me why you're the best person for my book?"

"Honestly," I huff in exasperation and then reel it in. *Stay professional.* "I'm the best at this publishing house. I have great attention to detail and I don't have a problem staying late to make sure that a book is ready."

Link has his finger pressed over the right side of his mouth like he's trying to keep himself from smiling. Dick. Gah, taking a second to actually look, I admit that he's a semi-gorgeous dick on legs.

Link tosses his blond hair out of his green eyes, and my fingers twitch to touch it. *Bad, Tori.* I must be broken. I can't possibly want all three of these very biteable men. Nope.

"Okay, so you're an editing badass. What can't you do?"

"Work with you." It comes out of my mouth before I can bite it back and my eyes widen. Nope, no taking it back now. I also find that I mean it.

I turn to Tom apologetically. "I'm sorry Tom, Peter. I know

that you wanted this to work out but I don't think this is going to. He calls me stray at every turn, and I find myself hoping that my roommate may actually poison him one day. I know that you said that his book is about his past, and that it changed him into *this*."

I pointedly rack my eyes down Link, turning them before they can appreciate his very muscular chest and abs in his tight dress shirt

"However, I think this is a conflict of interest. I love my job, and working with Mr. Anderson would make me want to die a slow death. I want to continue to enjoy my job, and I'm afraid that a consequence of taking Mr. Anderson as a client would be hating it."

I take a breath, and feel a twinge of regret when I see a touch of pain in Link's eyes. But no, life isn't easy, you have a choice on how you treat people.

"Tori-" Tom begins, but I have already started standing because I'm done.

There go my plans to advance from my position. I officially feel like crying, but I won't take it back. I meant every word. I look at him, my eyes widening a touch to keep myself from crying. Fuck this day, y'all.

"You're right. You two seem to have history, but I don't want this to impact your career. You work too hard for that, young lady... Mr. Anderson, meet your new editor."

I gasp. *What the hell is happening?*

Link surprisingly releases the grin that I thought he had been hiding. Ugh, officially fuck my life.

thirteen

LINK

I can't help the smile that's on my face right now. This whole 'interviewing the editors' has taken a turn I didn't expect, but I'm not mad about it. I have really enjoyed provoking this gorgeous girl. It's true what they say about the anger of a redhead, but I also don't want to die any time soon, so maybe I'll focus on trying to rile her up in the bedroom instead.

Fuck, where did that come from? My best friends are clearly interested in her, and this girl hates my guts. Oh shit, Tori is *fuming*. See, I can be taught. I can use her name. It fits her, I wonder if it's short for something. People always ask if my name is short for something, but really my parents are hopeless romantics. They always said that I linked them in love and completed their little family. I'm an only child.

Shit, how can I diffuse this?

"Tori, I'm really sorry. I only kept calling you a stray because we don't know you. Tesa is practically my little sister, and we are super protective. She adopted you and didn't tell anyone else. It was just kind of sudden is all. Miguel is the one that's a bloodhound around his sister, so the name stuck. I didn't even know your actual name until a second ago. The guys' interactions with you have been disastrous and I'm the resident asshole of the group. I was afraid to even try to get to know you because I tend to say the wrong thing."

Miguel and Greg look at me in shock. I never talk this much in front of people I don't know well. I'm more likely to grunt one word answers at you. I also never apologize. I am more likely to tell people to fuck off. However, if she's the best, and we are stuck together, then we have to make this work.

I'm a walking poster child that domestic violence creeps up on you, and it's easy to ignore warning signs until it's too late. Sheila ruined me, made me doubt myself, and I almost lost everything and everyone. I almost lost the guys and Tesa with my lies about what was happening with her. To this day, my parents still have a hard time talking to me after I sunk so low into my depression that I tried to kill myself.

Sheila ruined my life. It started with trying to control where I went and who I talked to, and then escalated to her holding a knife to my throat one night, saying 'no one would be able to have me because we'd both be dead'.

Then, she decided to have mercy and keep me around, by stabbing me in the thigh instead. That's why I need this book to be published. If my book can reach one person going through what I did, and reach them in time, then the book is worth the heartache of writing it.

Tori doesn't know any of this, and looks less than impressed.

"You have the ability to control how you interact with the outside world. You choose to be an asshole. Do better. Be better, or it'll affect my ability to be your editor."

Tom, her boss, clears his throat. Tori gives a movie star-worthy evil laugh. Fuck if it isn't throaty and delicious. *This girl.*

"Oh, I didn't say I wouldn't do it, Tom. Just that it would affect my ability to be at my best. Is there anything else you need from me?"

Her voice has gotten super aloof and indifferent and I find myself wanting to change this. I would rather her be raging mad than indifferent. Indifference means that she doesn't care, and I find myself wanting her to care.

It doesn't make sense, but for the first time in a long time, I find myself wanting the attention of a woman. *Does this mean I'm not broken?*

Intrigued, I lean forward to push her buttons again, just to see her pushed to anger, but Miguel grabs my arm and shakes his head sharply. Huh. Well there's more to this girl that I'm not seeing then. Maybe this blank, indifferent tone is a defense mechanism? I need to find out more about her so I can learn to read her like Miguel can.

I find myself jealous that he's had more time with her than me. It's an irrational feeling, yet it's still there. Her day has been pretty shitty, so I'm going to let this go. But I do need to learn her ins and outs so I also know when to push and when not to. I don't like that Miguel knows more about her already.

Tom sighs. "Yeah, this is about as good as it's gonna get today, folks. Link, send her your manuscript, here's her email."

He slides her card across the table, and I see that *all* her contact info is on here, including her cell phone. Yahtzee!

"Schedule a time tomorrow during business hours to go over any concerns you may have with your work, or anything you want to make sure comes across. I know this is important to you. Please do not reach out to her about this while she's off work. I know that y'all are neighbors, when she's off the clock, she's off the clock. This girl is here more nights late than any of my other editors. She works hard, and deserves to be done when she walks out the door."

I nod in assent. I am interested in other things from her besides work when she's off the clock anyway.

———

WE ARE WALKING out of the building and I brace for impact. It comes from a place I didn't expect, and Greg punches me in the ribs. Fuck why does everyone go for my ribs?

"Dude!" I yell.

"No, fuck you. I get we were all surprised that Tori was your interview, but I watched you goad her. What the hell?"

All of a sudden Miguel stops and pushes Greg away a little.

"You like her, don't you?" Miguel says in awe, getting in my face. "I don't know the last time you flirted with a girl that wasn't..."

He means Sheila. We both ignore the elephant on the sidewalk there.

We continue walking, and he's silent, and Greg looks like he's about to have an aneurysm. He's holding onto his questions so hard. But, we are a united front until we get into the car. Then I'll have some hard questions to answer.

We hop into the car, and I sigh. "Before you blow a gasket, Greg, out with it!"

Greg sputters.

"Do you like her because you want to fuck her, or because you want more. I want her because there's so many layers to her. I want to get to know all of her. I still feel like shit for what happened on Monday morning. Miguel and I pushed her for something that she wasn't ready to give. She just got out of a relationship that really fucked her up. All of the signs are there: she's jumpy, she has panic attacks, her emotions are all over the place, and it doesn't sound like she feels like she's safe after what she said today. That's something that we need to discuss with her. How dangerous is her ex? I don't need every detail if she doesn't want to give it to me yet, but the signs that her relationship wasn't a healthy one are all there. I can see the signs because we saw some of the same ones with you. *I* want her, Miguel wants her, and I don't know how it'll work, but having her in our arms as she came apart felt right."

Greg is glaring at me and breathing hard. Wait, share? For real?

"Are you saying that you both want to date her? What happens when she has to choose, Greg? Like this doesn't happen in real life."

"We date her with the understanding that we are a package deal. Listen, I don't know if that's something that she'll be into. But I want to help her figure out who she is, as I learn the ins and outs of this girl. Tori is a breath of fresh air, and I've never met anyone that is this feisty, passionate, and smart. I have never dated anyone. I never wanted to, and I know that Tesa calls us fuckboys. We hit it and quit it and move on. We have quite the reputation and I'm tired of it. So, Miguel and I are going over to talk to her, apologize for being idiots, and we are bringing over their favorite ice cream."

Greg blows out a breath before continuing.

"I don't know how long Tesa will be there for the conversation, but I'm certain that she'll want to make sure that we aren't going to upset her. I have never felt like a bully until recently after seeing those gorgeous blue eyes fill up with tears. I wanted to punch myself for putting them there. Link, she thought that she was a plaything, and I distinctly heard her tell Tesa that she was no one's whore. *We* made her feel that way. This beautiful girl who blushes so easily and has obviously been hurt. I want to fix it. So, I need to know: are you in or are you still a fuckboy?"

Fuck I hate that term so much. I get that I've been allergic to dating after Sheila, so I've kept most of my interactions to sex only. However, so do the boys because we said we'd never let another woman get between us...

I feel like I had the combination of a light going off over my head and being hit by a two-by-four. If we share the same woman, we'd be less likely to have an issue because she'd have to be perfect for all of us. I can, however, admit that I'm still really fucked up after my abusive relationship. I sigh.

"Can I say that Tori intrigues me more than any other woman that I've met? I want to get to know her, I want to know what makes her tick. I want to know when to push her and when to back off. I'm jealous as fuck that Miguel knows this, but not because I want her for myself. It's because I want to get to know her too."

I turn in my seat so I can make eye contact with both of my best friends.

"But here's the deal. I have a lot of concerns. Am I ready to think about another relationship? I share everything else with you fuckers, why not her too? But, I'm an asshole. A pretty broken asshole if I'm being honest here. She deserves a whole person, not someone that struggles to keep it together."

The guys' jaws drop. I know we don't talk about our feelings very often, but they know how bad the aftermath of my relationship was, the suicide attempt, and my downwards spiral into depression. It took me a long time and help from them to pull me out of it. I never thought I would be interested in anyone else again, well any other woman. Miguel and I have always been different.

Miguel blinks. His mouth opens a few times and closes. I think I broke him. I can't help myself and chuckle. Miguel reaches over and smacks me over the head. Yep, he's officially back.

"Okay, *idiota*, let's unpack some of that. First off, you're a little bruised, but not broken. Second of all, I don't know what Tori is ready or not ready for. So this is a little early to be worrying about. However, the fact that you are thinking about her needs and what she deserves already says a lot about where your head's at. So, I'm going to be proud of you for that, even if I'm shocked too."

"There's something about this girl. She makes me smile when I see her, and she's in my head for hours after. So, let's get the ice cream that we promised her, and see how tonight goes. Tori has been burning the wick at both ends. Let's help her relax some tonight, apologize, and see what happens. Whatever *this* is. I'm just glad that we are all reading from the same book, and working towards being on the same page." Greg says, relieved.

I nod and relax back into my seat. All we can do is see where things go, even if that kind of scares the shit out of me.

fourteen

TORI

Holy shit. Who would have thought that Link and the guys would have been in that conference room? I'm sitting in my office still in shock that I had basically flounced out of the room, and surprised I still have a job. I know my bosses love me, but I've also never defied them quite like that before, and I don't know what got into me.

There's a knock at my office door and I breathe deeply, then croak out, "Come in!" *Still not getting fired,* I mutter to myself. I have to survive helping Link with his book first.

The door opens and there stand Peter and Tom. My eyes widen and I whisper weakly.

"Hi guys. I'm really so-"

Peter shakes his head. "Nope. No. Absolutely not. One, I know you're not sorry and two, you have nothing to feel sorry for. You defended yourself and your skills, and Mr. Anderson clearly hasn't been house broken yet."

My jaw drops and then I giggle, slightly hysterically because today has been a shit show. My nerves have been stretched so tightly.. Peter turns to Tom.

"Can you do me a favor and grab me a soda for her please? I

can tell someone may be about to have a much deserved break down."

Tom glances at me and nods, walking out and closing the door behind him.

Oh shit, yep, he's right. Cue the tears. God, this is so embarrassing. Peter smiles kindly at me, and sits across from my desk.

"So, it seems like you have some stuff to tell us. You've had a hell of a day by normal standards, and it has been crazy for a while, right?"

Appreciating that he's not mentioning the tears while still being sympathetic, I nod as I wipe away the tears that are coming faster than I can dash away.

"Yeah, you could say that. I've had some major changes the past few weeks. I haven't had time to process them, and then the guys being there was the final straw."

Tom knocks and walks in with a Coke. He closes the door behind himself and strides into the room. He opens up my soda in front of me, and hands it to me.

"Drink." This is all Tom says before sitting down next to Peter. Okay then. I take a sip and immediately feel the shakes start to pass. The stress and adrenaline have been taking a toll on me. I meet Tom's eyes and he grunts again. Apparently this brought out the cave man in him. "Talk."

Yep, he's mad at me.

Peter interjects. "What the caveman means is that we are worried about you. It's one thing to be busy and stressed and then have an emotional breakdown. That's normal, fuck I have them, and I'll be the first to admit it. The company has been really busy as we've started to expand. However, you mentioned your safety and that worries us. I also checked with the guards' desk, and they mentioned that your ex was here this morning trying to gain entrance to the building. So, what's going on?"

Taking a steadying breath, I sigh, eyes bouncing between them.

"This won't go past us, right? I don't want my drama to be spread around the building."

Tom rolls his eyes. "Of course not. This isn't a locker room or high school. Now your safety is more important to Peter and I than your secrets. Time to spill, Tori."

I nod. He's right. I've just held onto this for a long time. I focus on Tom and take another steadying breath.

"So, two weeks ago I moved out of my apartment. Peter," I said gesturing towards him, "saw me when I told him that I had an emergency and had to leave early. It's because I had finally decided that I wanted out of my emotionally and mentally abusive relationship."

I sigh, hating that I have to tell these men this.

"I didn't want to be this person anymore. The person who makes excuses as to why she can't go out with friends, is exhausted in the mornings from forced morning runs because I'm 'fat and gross', and need exercise, and has to give up things that I love to do. I don't-"

My voice breaks and I close my eyes as the room spins from the stress so I don't lose it completely.

"The afternoon that I broke up with him, he threatened me like he always does. I don't want to talk about the threats, but they center around isolating and controlling me."

I open my eyes, and look at my bosses, worried I'll see pity when I do. They look at me, waiting for the rest of the story, with empathy in their eyes. Relaxing a little, I nod to myself. *Just keep going, you're fine.*

"So I went to pick up my things with Tesa. She offered to have me move in with her, and I accepted. However, Anthony knew that I was getting my belongings from the apartment. He," I shiver, remembering the cameras and lack of privacy.

"He has cameras in the apartment, and he must have been watching as I packed with Tesa."

My eyes flick between the two of them again and my leg is starting to bounce as well with nerves. Tom starts to look a little red after I mention the cameras, and let's be honest, that's only one on a long list of messed up things that my ex has done to me.

I continue to tell them about how Anthony had reacted when he found us in the parking lot as we were getting into the car and yelled at me, but Tesa sped away before he could do anything. I bite my lip, watching them as I finish.

"And... that's what happened with my ex. I've blocked him from all forms of communication, but he still has his co-workers watching me. His secretary saw Tesa and I when we went to lunch, and I know she was spying on me. Georgetown isn't a huge place, and I've always known on some level that he was watching me. It just took me a while to realize that he had his friends and co-workers reporting back."

Tom and Peter glance at each other and silently communicate. They then turn to me and both start to talk at once.

"You can't-"

"Please don't-"

It seems to be what was needed for the tension in the room and I giggle. Tom rolls his eyes and Peter laughs.

"Okay," Peter says. "So, what we mean to say is: we want you to stay safe. Can you accept having a guard walk you out to your car after work?"

I nod effusively and then wonder if I look like a bobble head.

"Yes, the guard requested this of Tesa and I earlier today and I feel dumb that I didn't think of it before. I don't know what to expect from him now. I was so used to him that I never thought of him as dangerous. That was before I left though, and he's not happy that I did."

Tom nods, "I would consider him dangerous. I would say that I'd like you to go to the police department, however as terrible as everything has been, I don't think they'll allow you to file a restraining order without some sort of physical abuse."

I figured this would be the case, so I'm not surprised by this. I sigh.

"This is what I thought. It's kind of frustrating that this is the law, but I'm also happy that I left when I did. Without Tesa there that day, seeing the messages that he was sending, I honestly don't know if I would have."

I'm looking at my desk as I say this, eyes welling with tears and shame.

"None of that." Peter barks.

I look up, blinking away the tears in surprise.

"None of this was your fault. I do think that you've been going through something rather traumatizing and now that you're out, you should look at finding someone to talk to. What are your thoughts on this?"

I love that he gives me the choice. I haven't had a lot of choices in a long time.

"I think that that's something I may be open to. I've been having panic attacks and sometimes nightmares," I admit.

Peter nods. "It's totally understandable that you would. If he shows his face around here again, I'll have him arrested for trespassing. I won't have him hurting you again if we can help it."

"Thank you, Peter. God, this has been the longest day."

Peter chuckles. "It definitely has. Do you want to cut out early? We wouldn't hold it against you if you wanted to."

I shake my head. "No, I have work to do, and Tesa and I

carpooled. I'll suck it up, and promise myself wine when I get home."

I grin and my bosses chuckle, then they get up, and tell me to take it easy today, and to let them know if I change my mind.

Best bosses ever.

————

"THE GUYS JUST TEXTED ME," Tesa says. "They'll be here in a few minutes. You sure you're ready for this? Even Link?"

We've just finished dinner and a couple glasses of wine, where I told her about the unexpected turn of the day. She had no idea that Link had a meeting at the publisher today. She had been, however, the person who had requested management to help him.

I smile and take another sip of wine.

"Yeah, you did say that we should talk, and now is as good a time as any. It's a long time coming, and the guys are kind of upset about my slip up about Anthony and not knowing if I'm safe."

I shrug. "Honestly, I wasn't expecting him to show up at work, even though I should have. Tom and Peter want us to get walked out to our car from now on, which is why I stopped by the guard desk today. They understand why I didn't say anything earlier about Anthony, but wish that I had. But, really what was I going to say?" I laugh deprecatingly. "My boyfriend doesn't hit me but is kind of an asshole?" I shrug.

Tesa shakes her head. "No, it's a series of super fucked up things that made this relationship unhealthy. I think that one thing could be ignored as a red flag, but because you tried to brush it off, it turned into a runaway train. Don't brush off his insanity now or when you talk to the guys. They need to understand how bad it is if they want to have anything real with you."

I blink owlishly at her, surprised by the change in conversation. *How much did I drink?* "Um, say what?"

"I'm not an idiot, babes. Miguel wants you something fierce, and I think Greg may too. I saw him prowling his front yard talking to himself yesterday as I was watering my flowers on the porch. That man is feeling like shit about how he treated you. Trust me, none of those guys apologize easily, and you have managed to get all three of them here tonight with ice cream and promises to grovel. So with that being said, I am going to take my ice cream up to my room while y'all talk. I just ask that y'all please not fuck on our couch."

I gasp indignantly and she cackles. "You did say you needed a vibrator, and we have not had the time to go shopping. So protect your heart, and enjoy the orgasm induced endorphins. Now we shall not speak of this anymore because ew." She winks as there's a knock on the door and I laugh.

Tesa answers and puts her hand out. "Gimme," she says. Miguel smirks and hands her her own pint of ice cream; mocha chocolate and a spoon. Tesa rewards him with a big smile. "Okay, here are my ground rules for entrance: if you upset her, you will lose all food rights to this house."

I have walked beside her by this point, propping myself up against the door frame. "Hi, guys." I wave with a smirk.

"Hey, gringa linda."

"Hey, baby girl."

"Hey, pretty girl."

Miguel, Greg and Link chorus respectively.

My smirk turns into a full blown smile. Tesa giggles. "Okay, look, just be nice to my bestie. She's an amazing person, and she deserves good things. If you do not provide those things, I have a selection of vibrators being delivered to the house later.

Love y'all, bye!" Tesa turns and runs up the stairs, laughing with her ice cream.

The boys' jaws drop, and Greg shakes his head. "I shouldn't be surprised anymore by what comes out of that girl's mouth, but for some reason I continue to be." Greg turns to me and smiles. "Okay baby girl, how was the rest of your day? We have ice cream and more wine depending on the answer."

Feeling sassy I step further into the doorway and put my hands on my hips. "Well, right now my day has been okay, so the ice cream should work. Depending on how this conversation goes, will determine if I need wine or snuggles." Sobering, I cross my arms.

"Guys, this isn't going to be an easy conversation for me." I bite my bottom lip, eyes bouncing between the three of them.

Miguel steps forward and cups my face, pulling my lip from my teeth. "I know it's not, but we need to know." Miguel smiles and brushes his lips against mine. "Fuck, you taste good," he sighs into me. "We want to be able to help. Whatever it is. We survived some pretty bad shit with Link and his ex, too. So let us in? We have guaranteed cuddles too, gringa linda."

His hands circle my waist and his thumbs draw circles on my stomach. It makes everything tighten and I shiver as my eyelids start to hood. Greg chuckles. "None of that yet, baby girl. Soon enough, if you're very good and tell us all the things."

I scrunch my face and step back with a huff. "That's if I feel like it after this." I trust them to close the door after themselves, and walk back to the couch. I have blankets and pillows in the corner waiting for me to sit because I wanted to be comfortable. I'm wearing an off the shoulder gray shirt with a bralette and blue sleep shorts. I can feel the guys eyes on me as they follow. I sit in the corner of the couch and tuck my feet under me, covering my legs and lie back. The boys are staring at me, and Link may have a little drool collecting.

I smirk and hold my hand out. "I believe I was promised ice cream?"

Miguel shakes himself as if out of a fog, and opens the container, placing the spoon in it before handing it to me. It's perfectly thawed. Nice. I slip the ice cream laden spoon into my mouth and moan. God, I love ice cream so much.

The guys cough and I realize that I also closed my eyes. Fuck, I didn't mean to tease them this much. My eyes pop open as I eat my bite of dessert, and the guys are staring at me hungrily.

I clear my throat. "Okay, so I guess I should tell you then, yeah?"

The guys sit around me: Miguel next to me, Link across from me on the love seat, and Greg on the coffee table to be closer to me.

Miguel pulls my legs out from under me and into his lap. "I have to touch you," he murmurs with a shy smile. *When is Miguel ever shy?* He's usually so confident and smug. Interesting.

I stick my spoon into my ice cream container and say, "So up until two weeks ago, I don't think I have had ice cream in two years." The guys weren't expecting that and their jaws dropped.

"What the fuck?" Greg growls.

I smile sadly. "Yeah, so I may enjoy this more than normal."

"Tell us why?" Link practically demands before sighing, "Please."

I scoop more ice cream out and stare at it, willing my eyes not to fill with tears. It should be just a frozen treat, but really it's freedom for me too. "So it started with little things after we began dating. For about six months, everything was amazing.

Dates to the beach, telling me how beautiful I was, introducing me to his friends as his girl. I had never had so much attention from a guy before. Then the comments about my weight started," I hear a growl but I'm staring at the spoon like it's my lifeline.

I take the bite as if to say fuck you Anthony, and continue. "Then he was asking me to go on runs before class, because he wanted to make sure that I wasn't a 'college statistic' from too many late nights eating pizza. It seemed weird but sweet that he cared, right? Then, my parents died my junior year of college. We had been dating since sophomore year, and my parents had been making comments at the beginning of my junior year, that I should make sure that I enjoy my college years, and not get pulled into a long term, serious relationship so fast. I mentioned it to Anthony, and we had our first really bad fight."

I feel Miguel start to rub my legs and I smile, but I won't move my eyes from the ice cream. It may seem silly, but I don't think I can do this and look at them. A single tear runs down my cheek and I shake my head angrily at it.

"Anthony told me that they wanted to break us up, and that I couldn't do better than him. That I was short, my boobs were too big, and slightly lopsided, but that he loved me so he didn't care."

I take a vicious bite of ice cream as if to quiet his voice. I chew thoroughly, thinking about my next words. "There were more talks like this, and then he forced me to suck his cock 'like a good girl' because it was my punishment. So I believed him, that I made him do these things, and I stayed. This was two weeks into junior year of college." I hear a strangled grunt and it does what nothing else did. My eyes fly up and meet Link's.

His hands are fisting his hair and his eyes look red rimmed but there are no tears.

"Pretty girl, can I hold you? I'm okay, I just need to hold you, please."

I find myself nodding my head before I realize that I am, and turn to look at Greg and Miguel. Miguel looks worriedly at Link, and then smiles softly at me. "Yeah, baby, let him hold you. I'll put away your treat."

I hand him my ice cream, stand up, and walk towards Link slowly. He leans back, off his elbows that were supported by his thighs and opens his arms. I crawl up onto his lap, and his arms go around me. He tucks his head into my shoulder, breathes deeply, and relaxes. "I needed that, pretty girl," he murmurs into my ear, his entire body shuddering as if in relief.

"What did you need?" I whisper. Miguel is putting the ice cream into the mini fridge that we have in here for movie nights and sits back on the couch.

"I needed to remind myself that you're here, with us, and safe. That you're not with that dick that had to exert control and terror over you. You got out."

I have tears flowing freely down my cheeks and I smile. "Yeah, I did. Because of Tesa. She helped me realize that it's not okay to have to give up dancing, friends, my favorite clothes, and foods because a man told me to. A man that was supposed to love me. She helped me see through all the fucked up things that he was doing to me." I shrug my shoulders. "And now I'm here."

I allow myself to snuggle into his arms, figuring the conversation is over. I feel warm hands on my thighs that are draped over Link's lap, and Miguel is kneeling by my feet. "Hey, there's more though, right?" I swallow hard and nod. "Tell us?"

A simple request, but I think of the early morning runs in the last year, the cameras in the apartment, and the last time we had sex. I gasp to catch my breath. "Hey." Link lifts my head up to meet his eyes above me. "Remember. We are here and he's not. You're safe, and we've got you. All three of us." I nod my head, as he leans down and kisses me hard. I press into his kiss, letting him lead, and I'm still very aware that Miguel is rubbing my thighs with one of his hands as he's slowly climbing up my thighs.

Link breaks away and stares at me intently. "Make me a promise?"

I want to promise him anything at that moment. "Yeah?" I breathe.

"If we ever do anything that you don't like, you're not comfortable with, that triggers you, you tell us. I don't want us to ever be a problem for you. We won't not be assholes overnight, but I need you to use your words with us, okay?"

I nod. I can do that.

Miguel makes himself known by pushing my legs around so he can hook them over Link's legs, and I turn so my back is now against Link's chest. Then, Miguel kneels so he's in between Link and my legs. "Words, Tori. Use them."

I look at him, and sigh. Shit. "I promise," I say.

"Good girl," Miguel growls and leans in to kiss me too.

Fuck, why was that so hot?! I shiver as the echo of the words wash over me. Link chuckles darkly in my ear, "Did you like that, pretty girl?"

Miguel leans back and I whisper, "Yes."

Miguel grins, "Tell us more and then we get to play." Ugh, why don't they play fair?

"Fine, but it gets worse." I pout.

Link grins and shakes his head. "Such a brat," he murmurs, adjusts me in his arms to make me more comfortable, and Miguel is still kneeling at my feet, rubbing my legs. Greg smiles, then moves from the table to sit next to Link. "Tell us."

Well, it looks like they can't be distracted anymore. "So we graduated from college, and I thought for some reason that things would be better, but they weren't. I moved in with him into an apartment, and I found that he had installed cameras. I found the one in the bathroom because of the red light that showed it was recording. It hadn't been hidden correctly. So I covered the lens with my black eye liner, and then found him and lost my shit. He told me that they were for 'security'" I make bunny ears with my fingers to show what a crock that was.

Greg's eyes widened. "Holy fuck," he breathes. "That's why you freaked out when we came over, talking about security and cameras."

I nod. "Yep, I wondered if I had traded one hell for another. I obviously know better now. About two months later, Anthony started waking me up at a quarter to five in the morning to go for a run, because all of my time in my little office job was making my ass flat and flabby. It wasn't a suggestion. He yanked the blanket off me, then pulled me out of bed, pushing me towards my closet to change. He'd smack my legs while we ran if I couldn't move fast enough. I never could, because he was so much taller than me. His stride would always be longer than mine. It's a lot of things that made me realize enough was enough."

I sigh and focus on Miguel. "Before I danced with you at the club, Miguel, I hadn't danced since the end of senior year. Anthony became jealous of people looking at me, and told me I couldn't dance anymore or he'd punish me. His punishments by then had amped up to spanking me with his belt while he held me over his knees as I screamed. I'm sure people just thought we were having super kinky sex."

I rolled my eyes. Miguel looks both livid and slightly sick. "I finally decided that I couldn't deal with Anthony anymore when he threatened to take Tesa from me. I know," my voice breaks. "I know that she and I don't know each other well, but she saved me. And I would *never* hurt-"

Miguel's eyes get huge and he shakes his head. "No, *mi vida*, no. Shhh. I know. God, I'm so sorry that I made you doubt your friendship with my sister. Seeing you together, how pissed off she was for you, how hard she fights to protect you. Yeah, that can't be forced. Y'all are ride or die. I'm sorry. I was a dick. An overzealous dick that needed to realize that y'all are good for each other. It's just been us and the guys for so long that I didn't understand. She *knew* that you were destined to be her best friend from the moment she met you, and I thought she was insane when she told me this," he sighs and hangs his head. "Did I mention that I'm a dick?" Greg and Link burst out laughing and my lips twitched.

"Yes," I said. "I believe you did, several times."

Link rubs my arm, and I twist my head up to meet his eyes. "Anything else we need to know?"

I'm drained and I can't think of anything else, so I shake my head.

Miguel grunts, "Words, Tori."

I giggle because I had forgotten, and say, "No, nothing that I can think of right now."

Link sighs, "Good, because there's something that I've been dying to do." He dips his head and gently kisses me. I feel Miguel's hands move my legs wider to completely hang over Link's legs and they travel in small circles higher and higher until they're skirting my pussy. Omg, they did promise me orgasms, didn't they?

fifteen

TORI

Miguel's lips come up to my ear and he whispers, "*Querida*, do you want those orgasms now?" I whimper into Link's mouth as I nod.

Greg chuckles, "I'll allow that for now. Miguel, take her bottoms off. I need to see that gorgeous pussy. How about you?"

Miguel groans, "Fuck yes. I've needed to see this pussy since Tori first danced with me. Speaking of." Miguel's hands are on my waistband and then slowly pulling down my bottoms.

I break my kiss with Link and breathlessly turn to face him. He continues to pull my shorts down and I lift my hips for him, letting my legs slide off Link's lap to fall between them. Link bands his arm around my waist and then grinds his cock against my ass. My pussy clenches on nothing so hard I swear I see stars and my thighs rub against each other.

Miguel continues as if I'm not suffering, "I'm taking you out to dance at my club this weekend. I need to dance with you again. The guys are decent dancers too." He tosses my shorts away and lifts my legs, opening them wide, staring at my panties. I had put on a thong without thinking about it and he licks his lips.

"Fuck, I can see where you're wet already."

Greg gets up, bends closer, and his face is in front of my pussy. "She smells amazing. Fuck me." He nuzzles my pussy and then bumps my clit with his nose.

I mewl, and Link quickly covers my mouth. "Pretty girl, you have to be quiet. Can you?" I helplessly shake my head. I haven't come in so long and I'm already so keyed up. I'm going to orgasm embarrassingly fast. They'll barely even have to touch me.

Link chuckles. "Pretty girl, I'm not above stuffing your mouth with something to keep you quiet." Fuck, now I'm thinking about his cock. So, like the brat I am, I rub my ass against him. Link groans into my neck. "Fuck, you don't play fair."

Greg chuckles and nonchalantly slips his hand under my underwear at my thigh. He then wraps one of the straps around his hand and pulls. Both straps snap and he tucks it into his pocket. "It's a good thing that I don't either. The spoils go to the victor. Miguel, now make our girl come." Miguel grins, and moves forward again, his hands still on my thighs. He slides his palms under my ass so I'm completely presented to him and Greg. Miguel then licks me from my ass to my clit and my hips jerk forward. Or they would have, but Link is holding me tightly to him. I have nowhere to go.

"So delicious, so responsive, so fucking *mine*," Miguel growls and then he's devouring me. He flicks my clit in circles, then sucks. He's eating me like he would his last meal, making sure to taste every drop. I'm gasping and moaning behind Link's hand. He's effectively gagged me. Miguel sticks his tongue into my slit and flicks in and out.

God why does that feel so good. He groans and then moves

back a little, slipping one thick finger into my pussy. My pussy spasms and holds on tightly. Miguel looks up at me with his face glistening with my juices and grins. He slips a second finger into my hole and pushes his way in to start fucking me with them. It feels so good and my body shudders.

Greg tugs my shirt down my shoulders and pulls out my breasts. "So fucking gorgeous. What I wouldn't do to come all over these." He leans forward and puts as much of my nipple and breast into his mouth as possible and sucks. Gah, it shouldn't feel this good.

Miguel has slipped a third finger into my needy pussy and is sucking and biting my clit, too. God, they're making me crazy. I know Tesa can't hear me and I'm grateful for this because I can't be quiet. Link's hand is tight against my mouth. My pussy is so wet, that I can hear the sounds it's making as it squeezes Miguel's fingers.

"Will you be a good girl, and come for us, pretty girl?" Link growls into my ear.

Fuck, why is that so hot? And oh my god. Miguel has just started to twist his fingers as he thrusts and my eyes roll into the back of my head.

My head drops back onto Link's shoulder. I feel tingles that begin in my toes and start racing up my legs, and I know I'm about to come. My toes are curling because it feels so good. Greg is alternating between biting my nipple and sucking it, going back and forth between both, as Link is licking, and kissing down my neck. My legs are shaking, and Miguel starts fucking my pussy harder. Making eye contact with me, he licks the index finger of his other hand and grins. He goes back to eating me out, and I feel his finger enter my ass. That's it, I'm gonna die. I come all over his face just like he wanted me to and I'm a puddle. I never knew that sex could be like this, and we haven't even gone all the way yet.

My thoughts are drifting, and Link has lifted his hand from my mouth. He turns me so I'm snuggled into his arms. The guys sit on either side of me, stroking my arm or thigh.

Miguel smirks and says to me, "So we learned something new about you, beautiful. You are gorgeous when you come, and if oral is done just right, your pussy showers me in appreciation."

My jaw drops in shock as I turn my head slightly to look at him. "I need to make that happen as often as possible. And I need you to let me." Miguel's eyes heat before he kisses me. I can taste myself on his tongue, and strangely it's even hotter. I arch my back to kiss him harder, and arms wrap around his neck.

Greg trails his hand down my side, and says, "Fuck, anyone else not want to sleep without her tonight?"

"Me," Link says immediately.

I break my kiss with Miguel to look at them both. "*Gringa linda*, we are in no way done with you. Come home with us. I need to play some more, and I'm sure Greg and Link both want to spend some time between those luscious thighs. Plus you don't have to be quiet. I want to hear you scream when you come for us again."

The guys nod and I'm half tempted to. I'm naked on Link's lap, and there's work tomorrow, and…

The guys see me starting to talk myself out of it, and Link shakes his head. "Miguel will pack everything that you need to spend the night and go to work. I'll wrap you in a blanket and walk you right to my room, and I even promise that you'll get to sleep. We won't do anything you aren't ready for, but I do need to make you come."

I squirm in his lap, wanting all of that. I look at the three of them and bite my lip, thinking. "Okay, yeah. I kind of don't want to sleep alone."

Link whoops and then mutters, "Oh shit, apparently I can't be quiet either." I giggle because I'm still fueled by orgasm endorphins.

Link grabs a blanket and wraps it around me, just like he said before standing up. "Out we go, is there anything you absolutely need?" I mentioned a couple of things from my bathroom, and Miguel nods, then quietly runs up the stairs to my room.

Greg and Link are hustling me to their place. The nights have a little chill to them now and Link breaks into a jog as he crosses into their yard. Greg pulls out his phone and unlocks the door from an app.

Man, they weren't kidding when they said that he ran private security. Greg smirks at my slightly dropped jaw. "Baby girl, this is what I do. This house is buttoned up tight once everyone is home, so I'll walk you out in the morning. I need to make sure you get home in one piece anyway, from one yard to the next." He wiggles his eyebrows to show that he's being extra ridiculous. I release a peel of laughter, hiding my face in Link's shoulder to stifle it. I can't control it after the face he gave me.

"Fuck if I wouldn't do anything to hear that again." I raise my eyes from Link's shoulder to see Greg looking at me in awe.

Miguel has caught up to us as we are stepping into the house. Their place is bigger than the one that Tesa and I share. It's two stories, it looks like, but there are more rooms.

Link walks me right up the stairs, not bothering to put me down. They aren't trying to be quiet either, and it sounds like a herd of elephants are stomping up. I release another giggle and the boys release that low masculine laugh that just makes everything tighten. Fuck, my pussy is a hussy. I shiver remembering the orgasm.

Link leans down and kisses me as he opens the door to his

room. The guys walk in and start undressing. Oh, I guess we are all staying here together. Good, I didn't want to sleep without any of them. Does this make me needy?

"Stop thinking so loudly, pretty girl." Link tosses me gently onto the giant bed so I bounce into the middle. He grabs his shirt by the back of the neck and I lick my lips as he shows me that toned stomach and chest that I had been eyeing earlier today.

Miguel leans into my ear next to me, "Isn't he just a work of art?" he growls. Oh god he is, but, hmm what is happening here?

Link glances at us as he shucks off his shoes, pants and underwear. I give a little moan as I take all of him in. "Like what y'all see?" Link asks, including Miguel in the statement.

"Yeah, I think we do," Miguel grunts as he stares at Link as well with hooded eyes.

Greg grins like he has a secret and lays next to me on the bed, slowly stroking his cock. My eyes are drawn to it because it's so thick, with a bead of pre-cum already at the tip. And... there's metal on his cock. I lick my lips as I see that it goes all the way down the underside of his dick like a ladder. One of the guys chuckles, and my eyes jerk up to look at them.

"Enjoying the view, *querida*?" Miguel asks. He's upgraded me in pet names I notice and I nod with a smile. "He was such a baby when he got those done," he chuckles. "Remind me to tell you about it one night. For now, you want to taste that juicy cock of his, don't you?"

My eyes widen, because I never thought that Miguel was capable of dirty talk like this and I decide to go with it. Consequences are for tomorrow's Tori, today I want to enjoy the guys.

Remembering that the boys want my words and I want to be good for them, I say, "Yes, I really want to taste his cock.

That bead of cum is taunting me. I want to lick him like a lollipop." My eyes travel back to where Greg's hand is as he touches the bead and I watch as it stretches. God, I really want to taste him.

"Baby, lay on the bed with your head hanging off the side. That way, Greg can have your mouth, and Link can eat that pretty pussy of yours," Miguel suggests.

Suddenly I very much want to do that and I look up into Greg's eyes and say, "Can we?"

Greg smiles. "Well, because you asked so nicely, yes you can have my cock while Link eats that gorgeous wet pussy."

My thighs press together for friction and Link grabs the blanket he had wrapped me in and pulls it away. "Nuh-uh, pretty girl. You are gonna come on my face or not at all, understood?"

I must be dick-drunk and I haven't even had their cocks yet. Yes, yes, because I need them after seeing them. "Yes, please," I say in a needy moan.

Link pulls me around and kisses me hard. "Scream for me as you suck Greg's cock, okay baby?"

I can't even say anything, because I'm laying back and my head is hanging off the side. Greg is standing, looking down at me with a smirk, stroking his cock, and I sigh. He paints my lips with the tip of his penis, and fuck yes I need it. I lick my lips and then the tip of his cock. *Mmm yes I need more of that.* I reach my hands back to his ass and pull hard.

"Fuck yes, baby. You're gonna take every inch, aren't you?" Greg says. I moan around his cock as it slides into my mouth.

I feel Link's big hands on my thighs, opening them. I can tell that they're his because I noticed the calluses. They provide a roughness that I can't help but love. I squirm and get a smack on my ass in return. I yelp and then moan as he massages the sting. Greg pushes further down my throat. The piercings are initially cold as they slide down, but are already starting to warm with the heat of my mouth.

"Mmm. Make her scream around my cock, Link, will yah?" Greg groans as he lazily pumps himself in and out of my mouth.

His hand wraps gently around my throat and squeezes. My pussy is a hussy and clamps down on nothing. *Link, please, I need you.*

As if Link can hear me, he blows hard on my pussy, right over my clit. Gah, such a fucking tease. "I got you, pretty girl. I need you all over my face. You gonna see how it's done, Miguel?"

I can hear the sounds of Miguel stroking himself as he chuckles. "Yeah, big man, give me some real life porn to stroke to. See if you can make her squirt again and shower us in her juices."

Link chuckles and then attacks my pussy. *Fuck me, game on.* Link sucks my clit into his mouth and does this thing with his tongue that makes my back bow, inadvertently also taking Greg the rest of the way down my throat. I gag a little and moan.

"Fuck yes, baby, I wish I could see those pretty eyes water for me right now. If it gets too much, tap my thigh, okay?" Greg is sweet to worry.

I tighten my hands on his thighs and he echoes my thoughts. "Game fucking on, baby girl." He starts to fuck my throat a little harder and I drag my tongue down his shaft.

"She looks so good taking your cock," Miguel pants, and I know he's enjoying the show.

Link inserts two fingers into my pussy hard and I scream. It's exactly what I need because I'm squirting all over his face a second later.

"So keyed up, so fucking beautiful. We aren't done with this pretty pussy by a long shot, though," Link murmurs.

He licks around my clit, teasing me and I keen. "Yeah, baby. I'm not even sorry. I know you had to be quiet before, but I want to hear you around that cock that you're taking so well."

Link lifts my legs up over his shoulders and continues to fuck me with his fingers. The change of angle means he's hitting my g-spot now. He runs his nose along the inside of my leg and kisses it as he slowly moves towards where I really want his mouth.

My pussy clamps down around his fingers, and I want to come again, but it's not enough stimulation and I can tell he knows that by his dark chuckle.

Deciding to focus on what I control, I grab Greg's ass and push him back, then forward to tell him that I want him to fuck my face harder. Greg gasps and gets the memo.

He begins fucking my mouth harder, and squeezes my throat too, to feel himself as he slides down.

"Fuck, yeah. You're so good at taking my cock. It's like you just know what I need. I'm not gonna last, baby, because your mouth is like a fucking hoover sucking me down like your favorite ice cream." Greg praises me.

I groan because fuck yes, he's exactly my favorite treat right now. Salty, and slightly sweet, I need to taste his cum right now.

Link gets with the program and starts to nip and suck on my clit. The scrape of his teeth as he nips does it for me in a way that I didn't know could. I feel the tingles start in my toes and I curl them.

"Link, she's so fucking close. She's doing that toe thing before she blacks out. Fuck yeah. Make her do the thing I like," Miguel says.

I would smile if I didn't have a mouth full of cock. It's nice that he was paying attention earlier to my tells.

Link slips a third finger into me and then starts to thrust and twist. Fuck, its like they downloaded the *How to Make Tori Come* manual. I'm not mad about it though.

I want to finish with Greg, so I hollow my cheeks and suck harder.

"Argh, Tori!" Greg yells, and starts to cum.

The tingles are stronger in my legs, climbing to my thighs, and I struggle to swallow him all before I explode so I don't choke. *Multitasking is hard y'all.* I enjoy every swallow that is uniquely Greg and know I am completely addicted to him.

I can tell that I'm gonna come and I smack Greg's thigh. He steps back quickly in a panic, and his jaw drops as my head falls back and I scream, "Link! Fuck yes!"

My body writhes but he holds tight as he continues to fuck me through my orgasms as I whimper. Link pulls my body down a little so that my head slides back up onto the bed. I stare down my body as he continues to slip his fingers out and then swirls his tongue over my slit to mop and suck up my juices. His thumb firmly presses on my clit and I think *oh fuck* as he starts to work me over.

"Fuck, again," Miguel growls.

My head drops over to my left where he's working his cock, staring as his best friend eats me out.

Greg reaches over me and hands something to Link, but my eyes are on Miguel. Miguel smiles evilly and I wonder what on earth-

A buzz starts and Miguel says, "As I was leaving, there was a UPS delivery in your name. I remembered my sister had said there would be a vibrator delivery, so I took a chance that this was it. Your bestie was good to you. Now scream for us, *querida.*"

Link puts the toy on my clit and I gasp. *Fuck that's intense.*

He lets my legs fall open on either side of me, and Greg gets on the bed to widen my thighs. I've never owned a toy before, but I have a feeling this is gonna be amazing.

Link slips three fingers into my pussy, and I feel it pulse around them. "Yes, take it all baby. These fingers are gonna fuck you into oblivion again. Just scream for me once more when you do it. I'm addicted to your noises."

I writhe and gasp and then Greg is next to me, laying beside me and kissing me. I pour all of my moans into his mouth as I am surrounded in sensations from the toy, Link finger fucking me, and Miguel's grunts and groans as he fists his cock watching us. When I come next I scream, my eye sight blackening around the edges and my body shuddering.

"Fuck," Miguel groans and I hear him come.

"Mmm. So fucking hot," Link groans, kissing the inside of my thigh.

I start coming back to myself and glance over to Link and Miguel. Miguel came all over his stomach and hand. Link is staring at him hungrily. I remember the looks that they've been giving each other and decide to push just a little.

"Link," I moan needily, turning my body to face them.

Link tears his eyes from Miguel to me. "Yes, baby, you sound like you need something."

"Yeah, Miguel made a mess all over himself and I'm too far to help. Will you taste him for me, clean those gorgeous muscles, please?"

Greg snorts and says, "Holy fuck, about time."

Link glances up tentatively, Miguel grins as he says, "Hey, you up to the challenge? You are responsible for some of this." Link crawls over to Miguel and I give a small moan, completely into what's about to happen.

Greg slips his lips up to my ear and growls, "God, I owe you orgasms for making my best friends happy. They've been circling around this for years." He slips his hands between my legs and grinds his cock into my ass. Oh fuck, he meant now and he's most definitely ready to go again.

Link puts his hands on either side of Miguel's waist and looks up at him as he takes a long lick along his stomach, thoroughly cleaning him up.

Miguel's clean hand tangles into Link's hair and he groans, "*Si, carino*, just like that, fuck."

Link smirks and lets his tongue follow the ridges of Miguel's abs, cleaning and then nipping at him. Miguel is quickly hardening again and Link chuckles.

"Do we like that?" he teases.

Miguel's hand tightens on his hair and he growls.

"Be a good boy and take care of this."

He feeds Link his cum covered fingers, and Link is a very good boy. He sucks them into his mouth to clean them, as my pussy tightens on Greg's fingers, while he finger fucks me lazily.

"Fuck she's so wet, guys. And needy. Does this pretty pussy need to be fucked by a thick cock, baby girl?" I whine, because yes Greg I need that now! He chuckles and kisses my neck.

Link turns to me, drawing his hand down Miguel's body with his finger.

He moves over to me with some of Miguel's cum, and says, "Suck, first. Then we fuck."

I writhe against Greg's body, lean my head back and open. Link feeds me the cum laden finger as I suck it clean. They are all so delicious.

Speaking of, I look at Link's cock, thinking that he hasn't come yet. I lean against Greg's chest as he works me up. I know I'm going to come again and I arch in his arms, moaning while staring at Link.

He grins and says, "No."

I gasp. What the hell? "N-no?"

Greg takes his hand away and licks his fingers. "No, huh?" Greg says.

"Yep." Link grins. "You said you wanted to be fucked tonight, right?"

"Yes, please. Right now!" I'm super enthusiastic about this. I don't think that I can sleep before this happens.

"Turn and face the headboard on your hands and knees. Present that pretty pussy for me, pretty girl," Link commands.

Wondering what he has planned, I get on my hands and knees, facing the headboard as asked. He puts his hands on my ass, opening me up to them.

"Goddamn, she listens so well," Link growls.

I look over my shoulder and the three of them are staring hungrily at me.

"Greg, lick her from slit to ass for me, get a good taste." Link directs.

Greg grins and does that, lazily sucking on my clit on the way. I moan, then get my ass smacked for my efforts.

Link chuckles. "So fucking pretty," he says as thumbs my asshole, gently pushing and I tense. Link clicks his tongue. "We'll work up to this, pretty girl, okay?"

I nod because I do want that...with him. Anthony and I had but it had always hurt, and it was always tied to degradation.

Link hums. "I'm going to fuck Tori's greedy pussy, who wants their cock sucked?"

Greg grins, "Whatever happens, I wanna watch. Since we've opened the Miguel and Link box, Miguel can eat her pussy, and Tori can suck his cock. Then, if anything else slips into his mouth while Link is fucking her, he won't cry about it, huh?"

Miguel growls, "Gimme. Now."

I laugh as Link moves me up and Miguel slides under me,

head up. This way I can also suck his cock too. Best day ever. Miguel grabs my hips and massages them from underneath me. Hearing a condom wrapper tear open, I glance over my shoulder. I open my mouth to tell him I'm on birth control, and Link smiles, a little sad.

"Baby, we were kind of man whores before you, so the three of us are going to get all checked out, and then you can have all the bare back sex you want, yeah?"

I grin and nod enthusiastically.

Greg lays next to me against the headboard and reaches over to make me look at him.

"Baby, he really wasn't taking care of you, was he? You're fucking insatiable."

I give a small, sad smile in return and shake my head.

"Well, never again, baby. Starting now," Link says as pushes the thick head of his cock into my pussy without warning and my eyes roll back.

Miguel sucks on my clit and I shriek in surprise.

Greg grins and directs, "Told ya, now show Miguel how you're gonna rock his world."

I grin, looking down at his cock. It's thick and gorgeous, the tip already red and angry as if it's been waiting. I stick my tongue out and lick him from bottom to tip. Miguel groans and his cock jerks. He's eating my pussy so good and I shiver thinking about how he may be licking Link too as he pushes in and out of me.

Greg follows my train of thought and grins. "Miguel, you're in the perfect position to do all of the things I know you've thought about. I suggest you take advantage and suck the base of Link's cock while you're down there."

Miguel groans, "Fuck yes." And then I hear slurping, and Link gives a strangled groan as he stops moving and slaps my ass as if he's reprimanding me, instead of Greg for giving

Miguel ideas. I slip my mouth off Miguel's cock and give into the laughter bubbling up.

I look over at Greg and he grins as he lazily fists his cock. "Oh baby girl, we're gonna have so much fun. I love to laugh and fuck."

I can't respond because Link is moving again and he's somehow changed position so that he's hitting every one of my nerve endings from opening to g-spot.

"Oh my god, what, oh fuck that feels good," I groan.

Link laughs and says, "Suck Miguel's cock so I can pretend it's me, pretty girl. Does he taste good?"

I sigh, "So good." I go back to licking Miguel up his cock slowly and then fist him hard. There's no way I'll be able to swallow him all down at this angle, but I can use my hand on him.

Miguel moans, "Oh fuck me, *querida*," as I open my mouth wide and lett saliva drip down his cock, then sliding down as if following it.

Greg hungrily watches me suck Miguel, as he fists his own cock. "Fuck me indeed, baby girl. You suck dick like it's a sport. Make him scream, feel how much you love sucking his cock down."

Miguel is grunting and moaning as he sucks and nips at both Link and I.

My body is all sensation. Between Miguel eating my pussy like it's his job, Link fucking me so he can wring out every orgasm, I am close to coming again.

Link's hands tense around my hips and I moan. "Oh yes, baby, I need to know that I'm not gonna break you as I fuck you harder. I need to fuck you into this bed and Miguel's mouth."

I am all fucking about it.

Greg grins. "Link, she knows how to tap out if it's too much. Fuck her how you want to. I think she's into it."

Miguel seems to agree. I can hear him sucking the base of Link's cock and Link groaning like a porn star. I mewl and suck Miguel farther down my throat. "Argh!" I hear Miguel gasp as he continues to suck.

Link groans, "Fuck my control around you is gone, pretty girl." He drives his cock harder into my pussy, and Miguel must have grabbed the vibrator because he presses it hard against my clit. I scream around Miguel's cock and come, knowing I'm drenching Miguel's face and Link's cock.

"Fuck, I'm coming!" Link groans and I can feel his cock pulsing inside of me. I pump the base of Miguel's cock hard, knowing he has to be close too. Miguel thrusts up into my mouth and I gag but continue to suck him harder.

"God, you're so fucking perfect," Miguel says on a strangled scream and then he's coming for me too. I swallow every drop.

Breathing hard, I rest my head on Miguel's thigh. Looking over at Greg, he's grinning at me, with his abs splashed with cum. He must have really enjoyed his live porn.

I'm turned onto my back and see Link looking at me. "You feeling good, baby?"

I grin goofily. "So good," I murmur.

He slips my arms under me and grins, picking me up. "Good because we have to get clean now, pretty girl."

The guys follow us into the bathroom. I look over my shoulder and my jaw drops. The shower is huge, with varying ledges and a waterfall showerhead .

Miguel chuckles as he turns on the water. "When we built this house, Link insisted on having a huge shower and soaker tub. I can't say I'm mad about it now."

We all get in, and Link puts me down. My legs are a little shaky and he chuckles. He holds me as Miguel soaps up my body. I noticed he grabbed my shower products from the house and I smile.

Miguel and Link make sure I'm directly under the rainfall so the water washes my body off. Lifting my hand to move my wet hair off my face, I see that there are other spouts around me too so we can get clean at the same time. Ooh fun. Greg is rinsing his body off too and I can see the soap washing down.

Finishing, he steps into me and drops to his knees. "Mmm, Miguel, you do give the best presents. She's all cleaned up and ready to get dirty again."

Miguel laughs and starts to lather up where Greg was before. "She's delicious," Miguel says. "Make her scream for us."

Link is holding me and Greg lifts my legs up onto his shoulders so I'm supported between them. Greg looks up at me and laughs. "This is gonna go a little different. Link, you're not getting any extras from me, so don't ask."

I giggle and Link growls in my ear, "Soon I'll be able to slip into your pussy without a condom and fuck the giggles out of you. The guys and I are gonna fix this little problem tomorrow."

Fuck, this man. Why is this so hot?! I shiver.

"Oh, baby girl, I haven't even touched you yet," Greg says, then moves to stare at my pussy.

The water is still gently running over us and it serves to stimulate my skin even more.

"So pretty. I need you all over my face." Greg gets to work and licks me lazily, around my clit, sucking on my labia.

I mewl and his chuckles vibrate up to my clit. Then he's there nipping it. He slips his thick fingers into me and I'm riding his hand as he teases me with his teeth. I never knew how amazing the hint of them would be, pushing me slowly over the edge. Link kisses and sucks down my neck, telling me how amazing I am, asking me to come for them. Who am I to say no when he asks so nicely?

I start to tense up and moan, "Greg, I don't know if I can again."

"Fuck that, yes you can," he growls into my pussy and I whine. He changes the angle of his fingers and curves them, and I'm done. I writhe and gasp as I come on his face.

"That's our good girl," Link growls into my ear and I moan again.

Miguel comes forward and grabs me by the waist. I wrap my arms and legs around him and he smiles into my neck. "Hey, *querida*, I need you after watching just now. This is gonna be hard and fast. Can you handle coming all over my cock for me?" *God, yes please.* I moan and rub myself over his erection. "Good fucking girl." Miguel growls and I sigh.

He perches me on one of the ledges and I gasp.

"Cold!" I squeal.

Miguel has an arm around my waist still as he grabs a condom. They must have stashed some in here as we came in. I raise my eyebrow and Miguel laughs. It had started as a chuckle when I squealed and now it's the laugh I love most. He throws his head back, shaking his head. I grin at him, wondering what set him off.

"*Querida*, you're the only one that's been to the house. We did hope you'd come home with us, so there's condoms all over the house as prep."

I grin. "Oh really."

He tears the wrapper with his teeth and pulls it out, slowly rolling it over his cock one handed, he says, "We were hopeful, not assuming."

I nod, not realizing how much I needed to hear that. He nudges his cock along me, drenching it with my arousal.

"*Querida*, every time you allow one us to worship between your legs is a fucking miracle and we know that, okay?"

I smile wider, looping my arms around his neck. "I hear

you loud and clear. Now make me scream, baby." He lifts me and drops me over his cock. "Oh, fuck!" I scream, getting used to his girth. Miguel laughs again and the boys chuckle darkly, moving to watch as he impales me on his cock. He slowly pulls me down, watching my face for pain. I gasp out, "I'm good, I promise!"

"Fuck, you're perfect. Tap out if you need to, baby," Miguel says.

Not a chance, I think to myself.

"I think she's good, Miguel." Greg smirks, lazily tugging at his cock as he watches.

I nod profusely and Miguel says, "Let's fucking go then." He sits me on the edge of the ledge and growls, "Hold on, *gringa linda.*"

He pulls his cock out slightly as I wrap my legs and arms tighter around him, then slams forward. Soon he's got a punishing pace going and I'm sobbing, and coming around his cock. I don't even have words, my eyes rolling and my eyesight darkening around the edges. I don't know if I can come again, I'm so overwhelmed by sensations. Link slips his hand in between us and pinches my clit hard. I shudder and scream, coming once more.

"There she goes," Miguel growls as he comes hard with me.

He picks me up and walks me back into the rainfall shower, kissing and praising me. I cuddle against his chest as he ties off the condom and the guys step out of the shower to dry off. My eyes are closing and I sigh. I barely notice as Miguel turns off the water, stepping out and drying me off without letting me go. My eyes close completely.

"Mmm fucked to sleep, come here baby." My eyes are closed so I don't see who lays me down, because I'm already slipping into sleep.

sixteen

MIGUEL

I wake up feeling a touch too warm, with a hard body up against my back and a soft body snuggled against my front. I smile and crack open my eyes. Tori's gorgeous red hair is curled all over and I gently move it so I can see her face. I snuggle into her neck and breathe deeply. It'll never get old smelling her unique scent of coconut and jasmine.

Last night was amazing. Hearing the details of her relationship with her ex was hard, but I know that it triggered Link more. He hated knowing that she had been going through her own personal hell.

The man in question kisses my back and snuggles against me with a sigh. His breathing is still measured and deep, so I can tell he's asleep again. His cock, however, hasn't gotten the memo and is rock hard against my ass. I snigger, making sure I don't wake up either of them.

Link and I have been flirting and fighting for so long that Greg has joked that fucking wouldn't be far behind. I had often wondered the same, but after Sheila and how broken she left him, I worried that it wouldn't happen. Link was so closed off, even with us. It would figure that we'd need this beautiful, fiery angel to break through some of his walls.

I'm lost in thought as I gently rub my fingers along Tori's hip. "What are you thinking so hard about?" Link startles me with his growl against my neck. I smirk.

"You, me, her." I grunt.

"You're lucky I speak caveman," Link chuckles, kissing my neck.

I shiver. Fuck, this is another thing I'll never take for granted either. I let Link have access to more of my neck with a small moan.

"Get a room, you two," comes a chuckle from the door.

I look up to Greg coming in with three coffees in his jogging shorts and T-shirt. It must be later than I thought it was.

I glance down at Tori before meeting Greg's eyes to say, "First, we have a room. Second, are you here to wake her up for work?"

Greg nods and puts the coffees down softly. His movements are exaggerated, slow, and extra soft and I get the impression that our girl is not a morning person. Struggling not to laugh, I raise my eyebrow in question.

Greg grins, "Tesa warned me that our girl is not a morning person. She gave me very specific instructions on how to wake her up. First, coffee and low voices until she's had at least four sips."

Link chuckles as he slowly sits up against the headboard. "Oh shit, she knows her bestie well. Apparently she approved of us stealing her away for the night, too, if she made a point to tell you, instead of having us find out how growly our girl is on our own."

"Yeah, apparently it's not pretty," Greg murmurs. He gets on his knees with Tori's coffee where she will see it first and gently rubs her arm. "Hey, gorgeous. It's time to wake up for work, but I have coffee just the way you like it."

Tori moans softly. "I know, baby girl. Mornings are the devil," Greg croons and I sit up and put my hand over my mouth to stifle my laughter. I don't think I have ever heard Greg talk like this before. He glares at me and then continues to coax Tori awake.

Tori reaches out and takes the coffee. She takes a sip and moans again. God if it doesn't sound like her sex noises and make my cock punch up. Link chuckles darkly, as if echoing my thoughts. He squeezes his hard on through the blanket to alleviate some of the pressure.

Tori pushes her hair back and slowly sits up to join us. Her eyes are still half closed and we watch as she takes another sip. She sighs and lets her head drop back on the headboard.

Greg holds up two fingers to show two sips and hands out coffee. He slowly backs out of the room and salutes as he walks towards the bathroom to shower.

I smile into my coffee as I take a sip. Yeah, I could get used to this. *We just may need a bigger bed.* Tori takes a third sip in silence and I lift three fingers so that only Link can see. Link's right side of his lip kicks up, but that's the only sign that he'd seen me. He takes another sip of his coffee and enjoys sitting with us.

There's something really nice about enjoying some time in the morning with Tori. I can see what Tesa was on about when she said that she was claiming her. There's just something about her. She's vulnerable yet fierce, gorgeous yet down to earth. She's completely unique from anyone else that I know.

Tori takes a fourth sip of coffee and I can feel her completely relax. She snuggles into my shoulder and murmurs, "Good morning guys." Man, it really is like magic.

I wrap my arm around her waist and give into my chuckle. "Good morning, *querida*. Feeling a little more yourself now?"

"Mmm. Yes. Coffee good."

Link snorts. "Baby, you are not a morning person are you?"

"Uh-uh. Takes some caffeine first. Your sister wakes me up with a cup every day." Tori giggles. "I think I scare her in the morning."

I guffaw. "Ya think? She gave us strict instructions on the proper way to wake Tori McAllister up."

Tori's giggles turn into a snort and a hiccup. Fuck she's cute. "She's not wrong. It just takes me a bit to get moving." She takes another sip of coffee with her head propped up on my shoulder. "We were up late last night. What time is it? I'm trying to figure out how much time I need to be ready."

Link grabs his phone. "It's fifteen after seven, baby girl."

Tori smiles. "Sweet. I have an hour before I have to be a badass," she says.

Link and I glance at each other with a grin. "Baby, you're a badass all of the time." Link says., "You're just the cutest badass I've ever seen right now." I agree.

Tori drinks the rest of her coffee and then places her cup on the side table. She pulls down the blanket over us and tosses it towards the bottom of the bed. Then she straddles me and grinds her pussy on my cock.

"Oh sweet fuck, Tori." I groan.

"It will be once you're inside of me, Miguel," she croons.

I hand my cup to Link and say, "Well, there's only one thing to do then..."

Link grins and puts the cups to the side, grabbing me a condom. "How wet is she? You need to work her up a little first, Miguel."

He bites his lip as he hands me the condom and I can't

fucking help myself. I grab the back of his head and kiss him. Link gasps into my mouth.

Tori murmurs, "Oh fuck yes." She grinds herself against me and moans, then kisses down my body and I groan in protest. Then I'm moaning as she takes as much of me as she can in her mouth and down her throat.

"Our girl loves to suck our cocks," Link growls.

"Yes, oh fuck, Tori, baby," I moan unintelligently as I thrust into her as gently as I can.

I grab Link by the back of his head and make out with him, slipping my tongue in his mouth and grabbing his cock, to fist.

"Urgh!" He groans in surprise and I smile as I kiss him. Link breaks the kiss and says, "Fuck her, so she starts out the day seeing stars and coming on your cock before we run out of time."

I grab our gorgeous girl and pull her up my body. I rip open the condom and slide it down my cock. "Ride me, beautiful. Teach me what you like, and come on cock. You up for it?"

Tori positions herself over me and grins. "Totes in," she says before pushing herself down my cock with a gasp.

"That's my girl," I growl as my eyes roll back.

"Fuck y'all are sexy," Link moans as I hear him start to fist his cock.

I guess we are all getting a happy ending this morning. Greg'll be sad he missed this. Tori holds onto my shoulders and uses her knees to push herself up and down on my cock, inching more and more into herself. She's dripping wet from sucking me and watching Link and I kiss. I didn't know that would do it for her. She tightens along my shaft and moans.

"Tori, fuck you're so tight, wet and perfect," I sigh, grabbing her ass and bouncing her up and down slowly. She mewls and digs her fingers into my shoulders. "Tell me if it's too much. You know how to tap out if you can't use your words," I remind her.

Tori gasps and shakes her head. She cries out again, coming on my cock. Okay then, she's good.

I notice her eyes are slightly crying and I kiss up her neck. Link moves behind her and reaches between us, working her clit as I fuck her.

She leans her head on his shoulder. "Fuck, I feel so much and not enough and fuckkk." She screams as she comes again, and I grin.

I haven't seen an incoherent Tori until now, and I need to make her do this more often. Her tits are bouncing in front of my face, and I lean forward and catch her nipple in my mouth to play with. Link grabs some lube from his bedside table and pours some between her ass cheeks. I reach out for some because I'm still worried about not having prepped her enough, lifting her a little, I pour some on my cock. She slides easier up and down, and I feel confident enough to thrust into her.

She screams and I swallow them down as I kiss her. I question for half a second if it's a good scream, but her eyes are blissed out and I know we are all on the same page. Link is now thrusting between her ass cheeks and continuing to play with her clit, while kissing her neck. I want to make her scream again. I nibble and bite along her breasts, listening to her moans and repeating the things that give me the biggest reactions. I just want her to feel good. I fuck her hard holding her hips to work her over between Link and I. She keeps pushing herself back down on my cock, riding me hard as I fuck up into her.

She's not breakable and she isn't afraid to show it. I feel her toes start to curl by my thighs and I grin. *Fuck yes, here comes an epic pussy shower.* I kiss her mouth, fucking her with my tongue like my cock is her pussy. She tightens more and more around me. Link gasps and his rhythm starts to stutter. "*Querida,* Link is close. He's gonna blow all across that gorgeous ass and your back. Gonna paint you so pretty with his cum. Come for us, yeah?"

Tori's eyes roll again and she moans, "Yes, yes, close, argh!"

Link chuckles and meets my eyes as he gasps, "Close?"

"Yeah, I just need her to come again," I grunt, concentrating on holding back.

"Done," he promises.

Link reaches between us again and strokes Tori's clit hard before pinching. Her entire body shudders and she's gone. She screams his name and comes. I sigh happily, fucking her through her orgasm and coming myself. Link paints her with his cum on the other side and we collapse. Tori falls onto me and Link turns at the last minute to lay next to me so that he doesn't crush her. We are all breathing hard when Greg walks in.

He chuckles darkly. "Well that's one way to wake our girl up." He's dressed for the day in a black shirt and black tactical pants that have all the pockets. He shakes his head in amusement. "Make sure she's showered and ready soon. No time to fuck in the bathroom, so no funny business."

We chuckle, and as if in agreement, we chorus, "Yes, Daddy!"

Greg looks aggrieved as he drops his jaw at us. "Ugh, just no. I can't handle the three of you ganging up on me. I already have to go to work with a hard on, baby girl. This isn't fair!"

Link, Tori, and I laugh uncontrollably as he throws his hands up and walks out.

Fuck, that was fun. He's hard to fuck with usually. We get out of bed, and shower. True to our word, we do make sure she's showered and dressed. She braids her hair in a way that looks complicated, but looks amazing on her.

She gives Link and I both a kiss, and walks out with her hips swishing in the dark blue dress I picked out for her, to meet Greg downstairs so he can walk her out. He won't be the only one walking around with a hard on. She looks absolutely edible.

seventeen

I smile as I step into the house. Greg was true to his word and walked me up the stairs of the porch. He gave me a lingering kiss, then said he'd see me later. He made sure to watch as I walked into the house before turning away.

"Hey best bitch, you look much more relaxed and well fucked. Did they treat you right? Wake you up the way you like with coffee?" Tesa has a grin on her face as she asks, but she has small lines around her eyes in worry.

I laugh before saying, "Without going into a lot of details, yes they were wonderful. I think you may have scared Greg with your instructions, because he was super soft and soothing when he woke me up this morning."

"Good, because I told him not to fuck it up and make the rest of us suffer because you were cranky the rest of the day." Tesa smirks. I roll my eyes. This girl. I'm *not* that bad in the mornings, I swear.

I grab my bag, as Tesa hands me a muffin and my lunch. She is super organized this morning. We won't even be late. I appreciate how efficient she is today.

Tesa grins. "I figured you'd be running a little late and

they'd distract you. I see your talk went well and the delivery of vibrators went missing..."

I rolled my eyes at her. "Yeah, your brother found that package on our way out. They were very much enjoyed."

"Lalalalalalalalala!" Tesa crows as we walk out the door. I can't breathe because I'm now laughing so hard.

"Good morning ladies!" Greg says as the guys walk out their door at the same time. "We gave Tori back in one piece, are you already breaking her, Tesa?"

Tesa waves her hand in her face to say no and is also dying laughing. "No! No, I swear I'm not!"

Greg is amused and shakes his head. "Y'all are crazy."

Tesa and I step down the stairs giggling.

Miguel grins from his side of the fence, "Good morning! Have a good day, be safe...are you sure you locked the doors? I see an awful lot of laughing first thing in the morning."

"Yes, Dad!" Tesa replies, rolling her eyes, and walks to the car, but I can't remember if she did or not as I follow.

I open my mouth to mention it but Link says, "Hey, pretty girl, Tom emailed me to tell me that I'll have a meeting with you later next week to go over the book once you start reading and editing."

Distracted, I look over at him and smile. Man, he looks good today in a pair of jeans and dark blue button down. I don't know what he's doing today, but he's edible. I realize that I don't know what he does for work, and make a note to ask at another time.

"That's fine, I'm starting to read today. I'll do a full read through and then start editing. I'll email you or call depending on the importance of my questions," I tell him.

The guys nod and say their goodbyes as we get in the car to drive to work.

"It's nice that my people aren't sniping at each other," Tesa says as she climbs into the car.

I nod. "Yeah, it is. Miguel mentioned wanting to take me dancing this weekend, but I don't have any plans outside of that. It's odd that they aren't jealous or anything. I keep waiting for the other shoe to drop," I confess.

Tesa frowns and glances at me as she drives. "No, you don't get to do that. My brother and his friends don't date because they never wanted to have another Sheila situation. They also worried that they would grow apart or something if they dated. They share everything. So it doesn't really surprise me that they all managed to fall for the same girl. Is it unconventional? Meh. They don't do anything the 'normal' way."

"I know you're right, but I'm having a hard time trusting this yet," I mutter.

For some reason, I have trouble throwing off my worries. The last twelve hours have been amazing, and I haven't had a lot of good moments that have lasted.

They aren't Anthony. Not by a long shot and I deserve good things.

Tesa is waiting for me to say something as she pulls into the parking lot. Fuck. "You're right, but this is all new. I want to trust what the guys and I have, but I think it'll take me some time. Plus, Anthony is still Anthony. I feel like it's only a matter of time before he finds a way to see me or does something."

Tesa nods. "Yes. The douche canoe will probably try something. But you have people in your corner and you're not alone anymore."

Tears prick without me realizing it and I blink furiously. I had forgotten how freaking lonely the last couple of years had been until she said that. I do have people now, and I'm not used to that. Breathing deeply, I decide to go with it, even if I'm not sure what I'm doing at times.

"You're right. I do. I'm going to try to be more positive, and to trust things a little more." I tell Tesa as I get out of the car with my bag and lunch.

She follows me in, and we head up the elevator to our departments. I smile at people as I walk to my office, unlock my door and feel uneasy. I forgot to ask Tesa if she had locked the door. I kind of wish we had Greg's fancy door lock now. Maybe I'll ask him about the cost of getting one. Apparently, we can't be trusted to lock up because we get distracted.

I roll my eyes and shrug. *What's the worst that could happen?*

————

WORK IS BUSY, but that's normal on a Friday. Authors get nervous, knowing that the office will be closed for the weekend. I start Link's book around one in the afternoon, and eat my lunch while reading. I need to make sure I get through as much of this as possible because I have a meeting at three.

Link changed the names in the book, but I know that he leaned heavily on real life events. I feel my eyes prick with tears as he talks about how helpless he felt that the woman he loved was hurting him. I can feel his emotions as I read.

IT STARTED SLOWLY, *fights instigated because I wanted to go out to dinner with my best friends, which led to her screaming 'that I obviously didn't love her if I wanted to spend time with them instead of her'. Then she manipulated me into moving into her apartment a month before our wedding, even though we were going to look for a place together after our honeymoon.*

It continued on to her saying my friends were mean to her, and she'd burst into tears after starting an argument with one of them when I walked into the room. She gaslighted me at every turn, and I thought I was going crazy.

My friends kept asking me if I was making the right choice? Why she couldn't chill and always picked fights with them? However, I never saw her pick the fights, just that they were fighting. What was I supposed to do? I always thought that my girl and my best friends would get along. *I hadn't done a lot of dating before starting a relationship with 'Sheila', and my only example of a healthy relationship was my parents.*

It got to the point that I went to see my parents a few days before the wedding, and they told me that I was throwing away my life by marrying her, and that they were disappointed that I wasn't making better choices. I felt blindsided, and we got into an argument. I didn't understand where this was coming from. They didn't come to my wedding a few days later, either.

I HAD FINISHED EATING a while ago and didn't realize that I was crying until there was a knock on the door. I dash my tears away. This isn't the first time that my emotions have caught up with me when reading for work, and I doubt it'll be the last. *Poor Link.*

"Come in!" I call out and Tom enters. He notices my tears and frowns.

"Are those from working, or did something happen?"

He knows I'm a big softie and I grin. "I'm reading Link's book, and I hit a sad part."

Tom smiles sadly. "Let's be honest, it's not a happy tale, and you may want to read with time in between to process. If it's going to trigger you too much, please tell us."

I shake my head. "No, it's okay. Our situations were a little different. I think even without my experiences with Anthony that his story would affect me. This woman was awful."

Tom nods. "I just wanted to make sure you were ready for the staff meeting. It's almost time, and I know you get sucked into your work."

Panicked, I glance at the clock. Shit, it's almost three. Wide eyed, I blink up at Tom.

He chuckles at me. "That's what I thought, Tori."

I grab my notepad and my phone. I open my camera to selfie mode to make sure that my mascara isn't smeared, and then grab a pen too. I stand up and start moving towards the door.

"I totally lost track of time. Thank you for checking on me," I tell Tom.

Tom backs up with me into the hallway and says, "Peter suggested I come to remind you. Our meetings aren't usually on Friday and it was sure to throw you off."

We start walking to the smaller conference room and I shake my head, embarrassed. "I thought about it this morning and then I was pulled into my day. I seriously appreciate the reminder before I was late."

I slip into the meeting, and get lost in the details of it. It's only an hour long, reminding us of events coming up and our deadlines.

At the end, I'm the first to slip out. I sit in my office chair just as my video call box pops on my computer. I sigh when I see it's one of my authors that has ghosted my last few calls to her.

"Hey Judy, thanks for your call..."

The rest of the day flies much the same way, until it's finally half after five. I am *not* staying late on a Friday. I finish everything that couldn't wait until Monday, and excitedly grab my things. I open my door and Tesa is outside of it.

"Girl, you look like the fires of hell are chasing you!" she says with a laugh.

"I'm trying to get out before something happens!" I close my door and hear the phone in my office ring.

"No! The door is closed. You're officially out of the office. You're done, babes."

I stare at the door and sigh. Fuck. Technically she's right...

"Go home!" Tom calls as he passes by me. I sigh in relief and nod. They're right. I'm done. I lock the door and step away.

"Done!" I yell with an excited whoop.

Tom shakes his head, muttering about crazy girls and Tesa and I laugh. Her arm goes around my waist and pulls me towards the elevator.

"The guys want to come over for dinner now that they've made you come and I'm not threatening to poison them anymore." Tesa says nonchalantly once we are in the elevator alone and the doors close.

I snort in disbelief, wondering how long she had been holding on to that.

Tesa giggles. "Come on, you know that was perfect. So are you good with cooking for a few more with me tonight?"

I nod. "Yeah, that sounds like fun. What do we want to make? Tacos? Fajitas? Lasagna?" I shoot off options that can feed more people without a ton of extra effort.

"Mmm fajitas sound good with margaritas!" Tesa exclaims. I grin. Fuck yeah, it really does.

The guard at the desk walks us to the car, and we head home. I walk up to the door and see a package. Huh, maybe Tesa ordered something. Reaching out for the door, I find it open. I step back and look over my shoulder. "Hey babe, I forgot to ask. Did you lock the door this morning? Because it's unlocked right now."

Tesa screws up her face thinking. Her eyes widen. "Oh fuck, I should have checked this morning when Miguel said something. I guess I didn't. Let me see if one of the boys is home and available. Don't go in yet."

She calls Greg first. "Hey, you available? I need you to check the house. Miguel was right, I didn't lock the door...Hey Tori, did you order anything?"

I feel a pinch of dread and take a breath that feels like sludge moving through my lungs. It could be anything, I tell myself, willing myself to calm. I shake my head because I can't say anything.

"And there's an unknown package here." She finishes.

The door next to us slams open as Greg rushes out. Wow, he really doesn't fuck around. That settles me for some reason, knowing that he's coming to help. Greg is on his phone, locking his own door, and he walks over.

"We are changing your locks to match ours," he announces as he crosses our yard and walks up the stairs.

Tesa sighs, "Greg..."

"Nope, it's not just you anymore, and her ex is a wildcard. Suck it up buttercup. I also texted one of the guys at my office, he's coming up to check the house with me and change your lock right now," he growls.

Tesa and my eyes widen. *Well then.*

I feel a little more settled with Greg in professional mode. He looks over at me and his eyes soften a little. "You doing okay, baby girl?" He traces my jaw line, lifting my eyes to his. "I'm sure that this is all overkill. However, I need to protect the people that I care about, okay?" I wonder if there's a story there, I think and nod. "Good," he murmurs.

I'm rewarded with a smile, and kiss on the forehead, then he slips into the house. Tesa grabs my hand and walks me to the swing.

"Tori, I'm so sorry. I should have locked the door. I fucking know better and I wasn't paying attention." Tesa is worrying her lip, glancing over her shoulder as Greg walks through the house with his gun pulled.

Someone pulls into our driveway and jumps out. "Is Mr. Fox here?" I have no idea who he means. I glance at Tesa.

Tesa just nods and points behind her. "Yes, Greg is checking out the house to make sure we don't have any unwanted visitors."

The man nods and follows to help Greg. A half hour later, Greg walks out grimly.

"Umm...find anything?" I ask.

Greg sighs. "Yeah, but you're not really gonna like it."

I jump up, alarmed. "What do you mean?"

"I need you to come see," Greg says, and grabs my hand. I shiver and go with him. Tesa is hot on my heels as she follows me to my room.

He and I enter and there's a photo album. The pages have been ripped out and they're all over my bed and the floor. I look at the photos as they're strewn around and see they're pictures of Anthony and I. Tesa gasps and I make my eyes focus. In the middle of the photo album is a knife pinning it to my bed.

Fuck me, I must be in shock because I missed that when I walked into the room.

I take another step forward, I can't help myself and there's so much drawing my eyes. My bed and the floor are a mess. The photo album is open to a smiling photo of Anthony and I, but the knife is right over Anthony's face.

What? He wouldn't have done this to his own photo. He's much too vain...

Greg grabs my hands, which were reaching out. "No, babe we have to call the police, have this documented. Okay?" I shiver and nod. "Come on, let's get you a soda to combat some of this shock. I don't know what the fuck is going on, but I don't like it."

Tesa looks around the room and her lip trembles.

"Uh-uh. It's done, it can't be undone. Now all we can do is change your locks, and make sure that the new alarm system is also armed. The app will be on both your phones. So even if you forget to lock it, you can do it from wherever you are. However, I want y'all to get into the habit of making sure it's locked. Yeah?" Greg asks sternly.

We nod and I feel unsteady on my feet.

Tesa looks hard at me and says, "You're safe. You're good. Let's go sit and get something to drink, okay? Too much adrenaline is happening right now."

"K..." I whisper.

They hustle me out of the room and into the kitchen, where they sit me down and hand me a can of Sprite.

I slowly sip, watching Greg call the police and ask for someone to come out to the house. I feel like this is all happening to someone else and shiver. I blink and the guys are here.

Miguel is crouched in front of me. "Hey, *querida*. I'm not gonna ask how you're doing cause I can see it's not great. Can I hold you?" he asks.

I nod, blink again, and all of a sudden I'm cuddled into his lap and he's sitting in the chair.

The police come in a moment later. It's an older male with silvering hair and a younger female. The male looks at me cuddled into Miguel's arms like I can hide from everything there and smiles kindly.

"I'm Detective Reynolds. I went up to your room, and saw the mess. Your roommate confirmed that the knife is one from your kitchen. We took photos as well. Do you know of anyone who would be stalking you? Want to hurt you?" He's asking rapid fire questions and I am having trouble following.

I clear my throat and one of the guys grabs me water. I look up and see it's Link. I smile weakly and take a sip.

"I moved out of my apartment a few weeks ago after I broke up with my boyfriend. We didn't end on great terms. But the knife was on my ex's face from what I saw. So I don't know if this could be him. I don't know who else I could have pissed off. This is all just really creepy," I tell him.

The detective nods. "Agreed. Here is my card too. We don't have any real evidence to talk to your ex, but just in case, what is his name?"

I answer the detective's questions, and he seems disappointed in my answers. I just really don't know who could have done this, unless it was Anthony.

"Yes, well Mr. Fox has informed me that you will be changing your locks so that should help keep people out." Oh, hmm well I guess I deserved that since we didn't lock our doors to begin with. "Please be sure to stay vigilant, don't walk to your car alone, and let us know if you think of anything else."

I nod and thank the detective for coming out. I'm lost in thought as Tesa crouches down. "Hey, we are just going to order pizza and hang out, okay? Do you want ice cream or tequila?"

I give a hysterical giggle and Tesa smiles. "Tequila it is!"

"Umm." Greg starts.

"Shut up! It's been a long fucking week and this is the cherry on that fucked up sundae. So...tequila it is." Tesa reprimands him and Greg sighs.

"Fine, but I call 'not it' on holding your hair back when y'all get sick," he mutters.

I enjoy the chaos, not bothering to tell him that I rarely get sick when I drink unless I mix alcohol. I could also probably drink him under the table. I snuggle into Miguel's arms, happy to just drift as I listen to Greg and Tesa bicker. At least I'm not having a panic attack.

Link slips his hand into my hair and tilts back my head, searching my eyes. "Hey baby."

I sigh, "Hey..."

"The locks are being changed now on the entire house," Greg reports on what he's been doing. "You'll be safer. No one will be able to get in that isn't supposed to. We are also wiring the house with an alarm, but no cameras, okay?"

I sit up straighter on Miguel's lap and nod. That caught my attention. "Yeah, okay." I'm only slightly aware that I sound out of touch. I struggle to focus. Link bites his lip worriedly, watching me.

"I'm fine. I'm just...a little overwhelmed. I don't know what to think, and I'm a little scared. So yeah, tequila and pizza sound like something that I need tonight. Y'all don't have to stay if you don't-" I start.

Link's hand tightens and then relaxes in my hand as if it was by reflex. "No, that's not what I want," he growls and my eyes widen.

Miguel sighs. "*Querida*. No one is leaving. We are just worried because someone was in your room. We need you to go up later and see if there is anything missing. Link is growly because he wanted to hold you instead and I called dibs."

I look over at Miguel and give him a real grin. "You speak caveman so well."

Link rolls his eyes and kisses me hard. I gasp, then melt into him. Link starts to relax.

Tesa coughs. "Ahem. Cough cough ahem! No porn in the kitchen please. At least not with my bestie and my brother,

Link. I am very happy that y'all figured out your shit. The unfulfilled sexual tension was becoming a problem."

Miguel groans, "Tesa!"

Link gasps and turns his head towards her wide eyed.

Tesa rolls her eyes. "Did you really think I wouldn't notice? I was just waiting for you to get your heads out of your asses. Figures, it would take my bestie to do that."

Link stands up and rubs his face. "Can we talk about this never? Why aren't you still in diapers?"

"Weird kink for someone that you think of as your kid sister," Tesa lobbies back.

I let a peel of laughter out and squirm, hiding my face in Miguel's neck. "Oh my god, I have to pee! I'm gonna run up to my room and change too. Enjoy the crazy."

Miguel chuckles and then grabs my hand as I stand up. "Wait, do you want me to come with you?"

I know he's worried, but I remind myself that the knife is gone and it's just us now in the house. I smile and deflect. "I'll tell you what. I'll be fast. If I'm not back in fifteen minutes, you're welcome to send the search party."

Miguel growls, not happy, but his attention is being drawn to the boys and Tesa, where Link is giving her a noogie.

"Hey, serves you right, little girl! Link, defend my honor!" Miguel cheers.

I shake my head at the chaos. They're insane.

I bounce out of the room like everything's fine, and then sigh as I look up the stairs. *Fuck, I'm fine, its totally fine...just go pee and change, Tori.*

I force myself up the stairs and walk to my room. Stepping in, I see that the photos have been picked up and laid next to the photo album. The knife is no longer in the room that I can see either. I go to the bathroom, have what feels like the world's longest, most satisfying pee, then wipe, flush and wash my hands. I look at my reflection and wrinkle my nose.

I look a mess. No wonder the guys and Tesa keep checking on me. I wash my face, then use a little blush so I don't look so pale. I unwind my braid and fluff out the waves. Okay, that's a little better, but my eyes are still a little blown from the shock.

I step out of the bathroom while pulling my dress over my head. I already closed the door to my room, and everyone in this house has already seen me naked. I snort, shaking my head at my thoughts. Pulling my bra off too, because fuck bras right now, I open my closet. I find a soft long sleeved hooded shirt, and throw it on over my head. It's long, and easily works as a dress on my frame.

Perks of being a tiny pixie.

I glance at the bed and frown. I really don't want to leave that on my bed. I'll just throw it in a dresser drawer to look at later.. Picking up the album, I hear something hit the floor. What was that?

I get on my knees, hand searching for what I discover has fallen under my bed. I pick up and look at it. Is that...

The necklace is a plain silver chain, with a silver medal of St. Benedict, protector against temptation and suffering. My parents had given me one when I went to college for spiritual protection. I always wore it, because it made me feel close to them. I had lost mine my junior year, right before my parents died, and had frantically searched for it. Anthony half heartedly helped me search, but told me that it had probably fallen off when I was walking and that it was gone forever.

There are others that exist of course, but only one...I turn the medal over and shiver. Around the edges of the back is inscribed, "To Tori: To protect you when we aren't there to. Love, Mom and Dad."

My eyes well in tears...*how? How did this get here?!* I'm so confused. I lost it years ago. I know now though, that I'm not letting it out of my sight. I check the clasp, in case it did fall off junior year of college, but the clasp is intact. *So weird.*

I put on the St. Benedict medal, and its weight settles something in me that I didn't know was missing. *Love you, Mom and Dad.* Sighing, I look over my shoulder at the album and photos in disgust. Good riddance. I toss it in my dresser and close the drawer. I open my door and stop. Miguel is there. I guess I ran out of time.

"Time. I came to find my gorgeous girl," he says softly, touching my face with a smile.

"She's right here...and hungry." I pout.

Miguel laughs, "Brat. Food just got here too." I cheer, and he pulls me into his arms. I promptly forget everything else as we walk downstairs.

eighteen

I'm worried about our girl. There are shadows in her eyes and her fingers twitch when she doesn't think anyone is looking. She took two bites of pizza, and then threw down a shot of tequila without a problem. I may still be pretty impressed by this. *Who the fuck is this girl?* There's still a lot that I don't know about her, but I want to get to know her.

Tesa tries her best to distract her. She watches the bites that she takes and frowns a bit but doesn't push her. I take my cue from Tesa and don't say a word either. Greg opens his mouth to say something but Miguel shakes his head at Greg to stop him. Tori looks up and bends back to look at him, and Miguel meets her lips from upside down.

"Is that what you wanted, *querida*?" he says with a smile.

"Mmm," she sighs. "No, but it'll do." She smiles at him with a big goofy grin.

Fuck, she cannot be drunk already or this'll be a long night.

"Tori, come make margaritas with me!" Tesa orders her around and Tori seems totally fine with it.

"Yay!" She squeals and jumps up.

She's in this hooded sweatshirt that barely covers her ass,

taunting us. She rolls her hips as she walks away and I bite my fist. Goddamn, the things I could do to her.

"Am I the only one that wants to bite her ass?" Miguel whispers in my ear.

"Fuck no," I mutter and pour myself a shot of tequila, knocking it back.

Miguel chuckles and murmurs, "Make sure to leave me some, baby." He then leans my head back to kiss me, making sure his tongue lazily explores my mouth as he does. "Yum. That really hit the spot, Link, thanks."

My lips part in shock as he walks away. *No one noticed that?!* Greg has a faint smile on his face when he glances at me, but the girls are making margaritas and not paying attention at all.

Latin music starts to play on the speakers and Tori grabs Tesa's hand with a grin. Tesa lets Tori lead her as they start to dance bachata. Miguel claps his hands, and Tori doesn't miss a step. I remember vaguely that she told us that she used to take dance lessons. She hasn't forgotten anything it seems.

Our girl needs to move, have fun, enjoy herself, and that's exactly what we're going to do. I stand up and stride over to the margaritas, taking over to finish. I grab the bright pink margarita cups and begin filling them. I enjoy the cat calls as Greg whoops at the girls twirling and dancing in the kitchen, and Miguel teases Tori about how well she can dance the male lead. Regardless of how we got here today after this shit show of an afternoon, it's nice to spend time together. *Now, if I can get her to eat a little, soon...*

The girls come up to grab their margaritas and we all cheers and drink. I wrinkle my nose, fuck me there's a lot of tequila in these. These girls will be wasted in no time.

Tori starts singing to a song that comes on that I don't know in Spanish and Miguel's jaw drops. *Holy fuck, does she sound amazing.*

"Oh, you didn't know my bestie speaks fluent Spanish?" Tesa giggles. "Tori took Spanish in college, and she picked it up really well. Now, my new favorite thing is when people think the red-headed gringa doesn't know what's going on."

Sneaky girls, I chuckle to myself. Listening, I recognize the song as an older Carlos Vives song. I only know it because Miguel went through a phase where he'd listen to these tracks non stop.

Miguel is clearly turned on, and wraps her in his arms with a growl. He starts to dance with her, singing in her ear as they dance together. They look so good. Miguel catches my eye and winks. I had asked Miguel once about the lyrics to this song and what the words meant.

He told me that it was a song about loving the woman who was made for him, wanting to marry her and never straying from her side. Suddenly I know exactly why he had such a visceral reaction to our girl singing this to him. Goddamn she really is perfection in that gorgeous body, with a gorgeous voice, and incredible dance moves.

I take another sip of my margarita, leaning against the counter. "I thought Miguel was going to fuck Tori against the counter when she started singing," Greg teases.

I snort, "Fuck if I'm not tempted to do the same right now."

Tesa comes up and rolls her eyes. "She's not a piece of meat y'all. I know you can dance just as well as Miguel can. My bestie needs to forget for a little while. Don't knock it, just do it. Or I'm kicking you out."

Greg rolls his eyes, "Yes, ma'am."

Greg is six- feet tall and the shortest of the three of us. His dark hair is buzzed close to his scalp, and he has a short, well kept beard. The beard is newer, but Miguel and I would tease him for his baby face without it, so he grew it to shut us up. He's very muscular even though he runs every day. He also hits the gym, and spars for work. He and I will spar at least once a week, so I know he's quick on his feet, too.

Greg reaches out as Miguel lifts Tori's arm with perfect timing to turn her. Greg grabs Tori's hand and pulls her into him, settling her into the cage of his arms to dance. Tori grins, swinging her hips to salsa dance with him. Miguel walks up to me and bumps his hip into mine.

I chuckle. "Fancy moves there, *cariño*." I tell him, mimicking his accent.

Miguel snorts, winding his arm around my waist. "I'll show you my moves anytime you want." I shiver, happy to let him drag his nose up my neck. "Speaking of, come dance with me," Miguel whispers in my ear and I nod.

The music changes again to Truth Hurts by Lizzo and I snort. The girls have a very eclectic music selection to say the least. Greg is grinning dancing behind Tori, while Tesa grinds her ass against Tori with a laugh. Miguel rolls his eyes and pulls me to dance with him. He's taller than me by two inches, so I dance in front of him, and he uses this as an excuse to grind his cock into my ass. *Fuck me*, this man drives me crazy.

Miguel kisses up my neck when no one is looking, so to be a brat I grind my ass harder against him.

He growls. "Fuck, I'm not against taking this ass. You're such a cock tease."

I snort, because I've only ever been a brat around him. For years we've teased each other, and it was never anything else. Now though, well we have the green light to do whatever we want with each other, and it's nice that Tori was so nonchalant about finding out that Miguel and I were exploring our feelings.

Hmm. We should talk to her at some point and make sure she's good...

Eventually we get tired of dancing, and Tori grabs a bottle

of water. She drinks it like she's been without for years, and Miguel teases her about it. I take a sip of water too, and I grin. It's fun to see them tease each other because Tori isn't afraid to push back and tease Miguel too.

"Anyone up for a movie or a game?" Tesa asks.

We all agree that a movie sounds good. Tesa makes popcorn, leaving the tequila in the kitchen, and Tori is content to snuggle between Miguel and I. Tori quickly falls asleep, snuggled between the two of us. Her legs are in Miguel's lap and he's massaging her feet while I play with her hair.

Tesa lowers the volume on the movie, and turns on a lamp, sighing.

"Are you as worried as we are?" I rumble softly.

"Well, yeah. But I didn't want her to shut down completely, because she was really close to it. We have no idea who could have left those photos, and I feel like shit that I basically let whoever it was into the house. I can't believe I was so dumb," she says, rubbing her face angrily.

Greg shakes his head. "This person was obviously biding their time. This could have been worse, and now we have safety measures in place and a police report on file, as much as that can help us. Unfortunately, no we don't know who's doing this, but we are all here to make sure she's okay. I don't feel comfortable leaving y'all in the house alone tonight, so we are probably going to crash in Tori's room. Thank fuck there's a king sized bed."

Tesa snorts, "Y'all are giants, as it is, you'll struggle for space."

Greg shrugs. "We'll make it work. I'm not worried about it."

"Lalalalala," Tesa covers her ears and I guffaw.

She's so ridiculous, I swear. I am pretty much the same way with her. When Miguel told me that she had fucked the bouncer in the bathroom at the club a few months backs, it took everything in me not to beat his ass. The bathroom of all things?! For fucks sake.

We agree to make sure to give Tori the support she needs, and to try to coax her into talking. Miguel suggests that we have her over for dinner tomorrow before we take her dancing. She needs normal, to blow off steam, while still being as safe as possible. We can give her that so that she doesn't get reckless and go off on her own. I just wish that I knew who was doing this.

Miguel gathers Tori into his arms and gets up to take her to bed. She can sleep in her shirt, it looks soft and comfy. We get her up to her room, settle her into bed and all strip down to our boxers. Tesa has extra toothbrushes for everyone, and we get ready for bed. Greg snuggles Tori on one side, I snuggle her on the other, and Miguel is the big spoon this time. I chuckle to myself as I get comfortable.

Miguel kisses my neck, grinding into my ass. "My turn to be the tease," he whispers and I shiver.

Yeah, I definitely want to explore that more soon. My mouth waters, and I wonder what his cock would taste like. My cock thickens and I roll my eyes. *Why did I start something I can't finish?* Miguel's hand brushes over my hard on and he sighs contentedly.

"Is that all for me?" he whispers.

I nod, biting my lip. I hear Greg lightly snore and I grin. He always has been the first to fall asleep.

I turn and face Miguel. The room is dark, and we can't really see each other.

Miguel grabs the back of my neck and kisses me hard. "I want to try something," he growls, "but we have to talk to Tori first. We need to solidify how much we want her and talk to her about how we feel about each other too. I want to be able to touch you whenever I want, but I don't want her to worry that it means we want her any less. I don't think she would, she seems excited every time we kiss...but I don't want to fuck anything up."

These are things that I've considered too. I want to explore things with both of them, but I don't want to assume anything. That shit gets everyone into trouble, and there's too much already happening for hurt feelings because something was misunderstood.

I agree with Miguel and I can see the flash of white teeth, but only because I'm so close to him. "Good. Now this means it's gonna be uncomfortable to sleep while I'm hard as fuck..."

"What are y'all whispering about?" Tori says softly as she turns and snuggles me from behind.

I chuckle. *Of course she wouldn't stay asleep if someone isn't snuggling her from both sides.* My bad. I turned onto my back and pulled her into my chest. "Hey baby, Miguel and I were just talking. We, uh, wanted to make sure that we are open and honest with you about how we feel about you and how we feel about each other..."

Miguel picks up hurriedly, "So that there's no misunder-standings, *querida*. We want you and we also want each other. Are you opposed to us sometimes being together without you? It doesn't mean that-"

"Oh my god, guys. I love that y'all are exploring your feel-ings. And it would be selfish of me to expect to have to be around for every little thing. I've had time with you and Link without Greg, and I didn't think that that would be considered cheating..."

Greg wakes up with a start, "Huh? Cheating?"

Miguel snorts. "We may as well just talk about this now." He turns on the light and I sit up against the headboard.

Greg groans and sits up too. "What are y'all going on about right now? Who's cheating?"

I laughed, shaking my head. "No one, Greg. We wanted to talk to Tori about how we want her, but Miguel and I are also-"

"Interested in making out in dark corners and messing around alone too? Y'all have been making eyes at each other for years. I think Tori can kind of figure that out. It doesn't lessen what we are all starting too," Greg interrupts smugly.

"Yeah, that." I finish lamely.

Tori giggles. We all know each other so well that we can still finish each other's sentences.

"Y'all. I mean, I could tell that there was something special between Link and Miguel. And I think it's amazing and I love seeing you guys together. I think you should also be able to kiss, hang out together, hell go on dates. I don't need to be there."

I tip her head back and kiss her hard.

Greg chuckles darkly, "I want some too." He turns her and kisses Tori too.

Miguel laughs. "If we are passing Tori around, I want her too."

Tori giggles, not minding at all as we manhandle her like cavemen. "No, if we give her to Miguel, we'll never finish talking," I laugh.

Tori grins, the minx. She snuggles back into my arms and reaches out to hold Miguel's hand. "Honestly, I watched you guys make out when we danced, and it didn't feel odd. I didn't feel any jealousy. I want you guys to be able to kiss, fuck, date, do what you want, and it won't affect what we are doing. I... I don't want you all to date anyone else though..." her voice goes small and uncertain.

I smile down at her. I struggle not to laugh, because this is serious and I don't want her to think I'm laughing at her. Fuck, this is hard.

I take a deep breath and struggle to wipe the amusement from my voice. "Pretty girl, there's no other girl for us. I don't want to get too heavy for you too fast, but you have to know. We don't get involved with women. Tesa calls us 'fuckboys' for a reason. It's because we never fuck the same woman more than once. So, you really don't have to worry about us dating anyone outside of this bed. In fact, we all had appointments to get tested, and the three of us are clean. So from now on, we can do whatever we want together."

Tori giggles and then her eyes widen. "We already need a bigger bed I think."

Greg grins "No, baby girl. We're good. No one's ass is falling off the bed, so we all fit perfectly. And, I'm glad Link remembered to tell you we had our tests. I want to feel your wet, tight cunt strangling my cock fully the first time we have sex. So, are you good with everything?"

Tori yawns. "So good. Sorry to do this so late. I woke up and it felt like we needed to talk about this right now."

The plus side of this conversation is that my cock is no longer harder than steel. I kiss the top of Tori's head.

"Time for bed, pretty girl. I adore you." I bite my lip to see her reaction and she kisses whatever she can reach and wiggles to get comfortable.

"Mmm. Me too," she says and I chuckle.

She's so cute when she's sleepy. Miguel turns out the light and we all get comfortable. That talk was so much easier than I expected. I listen to everyone's breathing start to even out as they fall asleep and I follow, feeling more at peace than I have in a long time.

nineteen

TORI

I wake up startled, and for some reason my hand reaches for my necklace out of some long forgotten reflex. I feel it and relax. *It wasn't a dream. I really did find it.*

The guys shift around me, and I know that it's because I moved. I glance at the time and roll my eyes. It's only four-forty-five. Even Greg is in bed still and it's a Saturday. Fuck, can I go back to sleep? *What the hell, Tori?* I feel twitchy, like I can't get completely comfortable and I immediately decide to go for a run. Maybe one of the guys will wake up and come with me when I get up.

Thankfully I'm not pinned by anyone, so I wiggle slowly out of the pile of sexy men. I've just crawled out of the bed and am walking across the room with my hooded shirt going over my head when I hear a deep voice say, "Goddamn baby girl, you're sexy, but why are you out of bed?"

I smile secretly because of course Greg would hear me first. I turn, only wearing underwear and he bites his fist. "Fuck, come here now. I need to worship between those gorgeous thighs."

God, these men!

I ask myself...run or fuck, run or fuck...*fuck whyy.*

"I, um, kind of have all of this excess energy and wanted to go for a run. Come with me? And then we can do the other thing, um, after?" I blush, and he follows the blush down my chest, where my nipples are darker, with his eyes.

"God, you really do blush everywhere..." he mutters.

Completely embarrassed because I do, I bury my head in my hands, and turn quickly. I drop my hands, and walk to my closet to change.

"Woah," Greg says, jumping out of bed to run and grab me around the waist. "Slow down there, baby. No reason to get embarrassed. You're absolutely gorgeous. You have to know that."

He kisses down my neck, and keeps one arm wrapped around my waist as the other tweaks my nipple. I moan and gasp in his arms.

"There's my girl. I love it when you moan for me. Now, tell me...are you upset because I complimented your blush?"

"No," I wiggle against him as he grinds his cock into my ass. God I can't talk to him like this. "It's just...I can't control it and it's embarrassing for everyone to know how you're feeling all of the time."

Greg chuckles against my neck. "We aren't everyone. I know that I want every one of your blushes, your moans,." He pulls hard on my nipple now that it's pebbled for him and I gasp. "So responsive, so fucking gorgeous," he growls into my ear. "I want to learn what makes you crazy, and what makes you explode. I want to know your favorite color, dreams, favorite food...and for that to happen, I want to take you on a date."

My brain must be melting. Did he say that he wanted to date me? I must have been quiet for too long because Greg turns me around and tilts my head up.

"Did I do that wrong?" he asks.

He looks worried and I remember that he's never dated before and holy shit this is a huge deal. Before he hyperventilates because he thinks he asked me out wrong, I smile.

"No, you didn't do it wrong. I've never been asked out on a date in a more romantic way. I would love that. I don't know why I was so surprised." I bite my lip, looking up at him, and hop into his arms.

Greg grins and he grabs my ass to support me. My legs wind around his waist and I kiss him.

"Honey, you deserve the world," he murmurs against my lips.

He's never called me honey before and I shiver in pleasure. He squeezes my ass and kisses me again.

"And if you don't believe that yet, that's okay. The three of us are gonna spoil you rotten. Will you let us?"

Light snoring erupts from the bed and I giggle, looking over. Miguel has his leg wrapped around Link's waist and they are zonked out. Greg rolls his eyes.

"Always stealing my thunder," he chuckles.

Remembering that he asked me a question, I put my hands on his face. "It's been a long time since I've had anyone spoil me, Greg. I may not be very good at it."

Greg gives me the biggest smile. "Oh baby, that'll just make it even more fun. All you have to do is agree to come along for the ride." He grins suggestively and I toss my hair like a brat and grind on his cock.

"Fuck, do we really have to go for a run right now? I'll do it, but are you really sure?" he groans.

I giggle. "Yes, while I have the energy and motivation too. Plus, I'm not very quiet and Tesa is next door to my room."

He groans. "Well, fuck. Why can't you be our roommate instead of hers."

I freeze, because no this man did not just insinuate what I think he did. Breathe, Tori. Nope, not having the move in conversation this early. No matter how fancy his peen is and how dickmatized he makes me.

Taking a deep breath, I answered him as if he was completely serious. "Well, she did ask me first, so it was only fair." Then I give him the toothiest, brattiest grin. He growls good naturedly and I giggle. "Down please?" I ask because he is holding on too tightly to me to drop down easily. He sighs and sets me on the ground. "Thank you!"

I step into my closet and throw on my running clothes. The mornings started to have a colder bite to them, so I put on a pair of leggings, sports bra, and hooded long sleeved crop top. I grab my socks and shoes to put on once I'm out of the closet. Greg is standing in my bathroom brushing his teeth. I smile at how cute he is, and I sit in a chair to slip into my socks and shoes. Before walking into the bathroom to also brush my teeth. He glances at me in the mirror.

He spits the water out that he's rinsing with, and his eyes widen. "That's what you're running in?"

I bite my lip, looking down. "Um, yes?"

"You look edible, baby girl. I can't wait to strip you down in the shower and fuck you clean."

I giggle because what? This man is crazy. I grab my toothbrush and he moves to the doorway to watch as I brush my teeth.

"Fuck, you're so sexy. Finish up here and I'll meet you on the porch. Please don't leave withoutme, K? I need to change into running clothes."

I promise not to leave without him, and he kisses my forehead, then books it out of the room. Shaking my head, I finish brushing my teeth, put my hair in a ponytail, then wash my face. I don't know why, it just wakes me up when I wash my face first thing in the morning. Ready for my run, I move to my room and decide that I'll stretch on the porch while I wait. I have the new app on my phone that'll lock the door so I'm good to go there too.

I glance at the bed as I walk to the door and giggle. Link is now cuddled into Miguel's chest and their arms are wrapped around each other. They are so cute. I'm glad that we talked last night, and I want them to explore their relationship. They've ignored their feelings for each other for so long, and I feel tingly and happy watching them together. Turning, I remember to grab my arm band and AirPods for my music to run to.

With a smile, I walk downstairs, grab my water and I'm ready to go. I unlock the door, knowing that if Greg went to his house the alarm isn't armed. Opening the door, I step outside, then grab my phone to lock the door.

It's my first time doing it, and I'm worried that I'll screw it up. I grab the door handle and try to open it just in case. Nope, it's locked. I breathe a sigh of relief.

I put my phone and water on the table on the porch and started going through stretches. A thought pops into my head a few minutes later. Did I ever open that package that was at the door? We all had forgotten about it with the excitement of the day. I tell myself to check later as I watch Greg jog up to the driveway.

"Hey, beautiful, need to stretch more, or are you ready to run with me?"

Grinning, I grab my things, slip my AirPods in my ears, and put my arm band on with my phone. I make sure I have my water too. He kisses me hard.

"Let's do this so I can fuck you in the shower after, baby girl." I shiver and look at him with hooded eyes. "Fuck, baby, we have to go because exhibitionism isn't one of my kinks and I'm about to fuck you on the porch," Greg laughs.

With a giggle, I let him pull me with him to run. The air is slightly chilly, but the early morning is still gorgeous. I turn on my playlist, and *Drivers License* by Olivia Rodrigo comes on. I love this song!

Greg and I run through our neighborhood streets, and I lose track of time, just my feet pounding on the sidewalk, not thinking about anything else. I love how free running makes me feel, and I needed it after yesterday. *Nope, not thinking about that right now.*

Greg slows down, so I follow his lead. I need a water break, and I'm breathing hard. Turning off my music, I open my water, and take a sip. I let loose a small groan. I freaking love water on a normal day, but after a run it makes me extra happy.

Greg finishes his own drink of water and chuckles. "You make me think of sex in everything you do, baby. You're unlike anyone that I've ever known. You're so free in your reactions."

I smile, because for the Tori post-Anthony, yeah that sounds about right. I didn't much like who I was when I dated him, because I always had to worry about laughing too loud, what I wore, being...perfect for him.

Greg palms the right side of my face, and I shiver because his hand is cold. His smile is a little sad as he looks into my eyes. I frown, wrapping my arms around his waist.

"What's wrong?" I ask.

He kisses up my neck, plucking my AirPods from my ear to press his lips against it. "You sometimes get these shadows in your eyes when you think about things. It makes me want to burn the world down when I see them," he says protectively. He sucks on my neck and bites down a little and I moan softly. "Fuck, baby, I may be a little addicted to you."

Feeling a little like a brat, I smile, feeling lighter.

"Good," I say. "This makes us even, because I can't get enough of you either."

Greg growls in pleasure and kisses me hard. "We're close to a local coffee shop. Let's grab coffee, and then walk back. We ran hard today."

"Mmm, coffee. Yes please!"

I bounce on my feet with a smile, my arms still wrapped around him. Smiling, he drops our AirPods in a pocket in his shorts and zips it closed. *Why do guys have all the best pockets in their clothes?*

"You're like an energetic pixie temptress after a run," he laughs, throwing his arm over my shoulders.

We are hot and sweaty, but he still smells delicious. We walk across the street and down to the coffee shop that he had been talking about. We had run in a different direction than I usually do, and I haven't been to this place before. *The Java Spot*, the sign proudly says and I smile. It's adorable. Walking inside, I sigh happily. It smells amazing in here. Coffee beans, caramel and fresh pastry surround me.

"Baby girl, I know you're in your happy place," Greg chuckles.

I nod excitedly. "I love trying new coffee places, so..."

The shop is busy, and the line is long. Greg absently trails his hand down to my waist and he massages just above my back. His hands are amazing. I need to ask him for a full body massage soon, I bet it would be incredible.

I check out the menu and decide on a warm specialty drink with caramel. Yummy. My tummy growls and I'm reminded that I'm hungry. Crap, did I eat yesterday?

"Please get breakfast while we're here, baby. We can bring back muffins for the guys and Tesa, too," Greg murmurs as he looks at the menu.

Appreciating that he didn't nag me for not eating yesterday, though I didn't miss the worried look when he glanced
down at me just now. I decided on a breakfast wrap that I see
they have with sausage and egg. Sighing happily, I snuggle into
Greg's side.

A woman walks up to us and huffs in a pair of joggers and
tank top. She looks vaguely familiar and has brown pin
straight hair, tall, and is currently looking at me with disgust.
Somehow it's the disgust that makes it click: this is my ex's
secretary, Veronica. I didn't recognize her outside of work
clothes. Ugh, fuck my life.

"Seriously, Victoria? How many people are you fucking,
anyway?" She accuses me. I wrinkle my nose. Ugh, now I know
Anthony is talking about me, he's the only one that calls me
that.

Excuse me? Oh, yeah, I can't help myself and laugh. Tesa
may have insinuated that we were sleeping together when we
last saw her. Ooops...

Greg stiffens, and his hand comes up to squeeze my
shoulder.

"Excuse me? What did you just say to my girlfriend?" he
growls.

Oh fuck, girlfriend. I want to melt, but I have to deal with a
meddlesome bitch first.

"Girlfriend? Are we using this term loosely for whore
instead?" She snorts. "I saw her at *Blunch* with some girl not
too long ago, and that girl said they were together."

I look up at Greg and flutter my eyelashes at him. He
snickers because he realizes that she means Tesa.

He leans into my ear to whisper, "You two have been bad
girls, haven't you?"

Playing up the brattiness, I grin and turn my head to nip at
his lips.

"Are you gonna punish me later, daddy?" I was totally kidding, but he growls. Oh fuck, did I just wake up the beast?

"We'll talk about the spanking you'll be getting later, baby girl." Fuck me, these panties are totally destroyed right now.

Smirking, he looks at Veronica. "Haven't you learned by now that it's 2022, and slut shaming is overdone? I don't care who my girlfriend loves, as long as she loves me too."

I know that he's playing up to Veronica, but fuck if his protective tone doesn't do it for me.

Veronica's jaw drops. "But, she probably has a million STDs!" she screeches.

Ugh, okay, now I'm embarrassed. Not because it's true, but people are starting to turn around. Fuck my life. Maybe I don't need coffee or food that badly?

My feet start to move of their own accord and Greg wraps his arm around my waist. "Just wait, baby girl," he whispers into my hair. I'll give him another minute of this shit before I'm out.

"What the fuck is happening out here?" A tall, gorgeous, blonde woman storms around the counter towards us. Oh shit.

"Hey, Grace. Sorry for the drama. This woman apparently has an issue with poly-relationships, and is slut shaming my girl." Greg looks super smug at the moment.

"Well, then...what's your name?" Grace turns and glares at Veronica.

"Uh, Veronica Trace, why do you care?"

"I'm the owner here, and you're officially banned from *The Java Spot* for fucking with my friend, and one of my best customers. Scoot! Bye!"

Veronica sputters, and everyone in the coffee shop yells, "And another one bites the dust!"

Apparently, she's not the first person to be banned. This

day looks like it's just gonna be weird and I'll roll with it. I laugh in Veronica's face. She growls and stomps her foot.

"Dammit, and I never got my coffee." Veronica complains. "I don't care what anyone says, Victoria, you're still a whore. Anthony has always been way too good for you. Just wait till I tell him about this!"

Fuck, that's the last thing I need. I go to say something and Greg says, "You may as well get the story straight when you go to tell him. There's two other men, and we will do anything to protect her. Tell him to fuck off."

Veronica looks apoplectic. Okay, well that makes it slightly worth it. I wave at her.

"I believe you were leaving," I tell her. She stomps out of the coffee shop as everyone cat calls and whoops that the trash took itself out. Okay, I am kind of in love with this place.

Grace grins. "You rang?" she says with a grin.

Greg rubs the back of his neck with a chuckle. "I knew you wouldn't stand for that shit, so I just waited for her to get your attention. I could have taken care of it, but it wouldn't have been with your flair."

Grace throws her head back laughing. "Yeah, I definitely have flair. Now introduce me, silly." Greg pulls me in front of him. I usually care more when I'm manhandled, but I don't with him.

"Grace, this is my girl, Tori. Miguel, Link, and I are dating her," he chuckles. "Contrary to what Veronica thinks, Tesa is her best friend, and isn't dating her."

Grace chuckles again. "Alright then. Well, I am Grace Tamry, and I own *The Java Spot*. I may be well known for banning assholes from my place, so now it's a thing. I'm sorry that she was harassing you, and I'm sure there's a story there. Greg is amazing, and he helped me a few years ago when I needed it. Now, he's a silent partner here, and I refuse to let him pay for anything. He'll grumble, but it's part of his charm don't you think?" She's a whirlwind of spunk and I kind of love it.

Grinning, I let myself get carried away in her energy.

"I'll see you up front for your orders, I'm off now that I've rid my shop of the wicked bitch!" she says with a wave.

Twirling, she rushes back behind the counter. I can do nothing but shake my head and giggle. I can feel the vibrations of Greg's chuckle through his body as I lean against him.

"Grace is the best, huh?" Greg grins as he leans over me and hugs me.

"Yes, she's amazing!" I look over my shoulder with a smile.

"Hmm," he kisses my temple. "My company and I helped her with a sticky situation, and we've kept in touch since. Then when we were catching up one day, she told me about the concept for her coffee shop, and I told her I was in before she was finished." Greg shrugs, "She's done an incredible job, and the food and coffee are always amazing. She will also make sure that this is a safe place for you to come hang out when we aren't around. They make great sandwiches and salads. It isn't far from your office, either. Tesa mentioned that you tend to run into people your ex knows or works with and then it affects your appetite. I want to make sure that you get to enjoy your lunch with your bestie, without any issues."

Gah, don't cry, Tori. Even now, this is him protecting me.

I turn in his arms and kiss him hard. He must be watching the line because he picks me up and walks forward two steps while still kissing me. I giggle.

"I didn't want to stop kissing you," he murmurs.

"Good call," I say.

We chat as we wait, and then it's our turn to order. I spin to face the counter and grin when I see that Grace is at our register. My face has been non stop smiling today, despite the run in with my ex's secretary.

"Alright, love birds, what can I get for y'all?" Grace bounces behind the counter with a smile.

We order, and then wait for our coffee and food. We ordered extras, and Grace made sure to package it so that it would stay warm on the way back.

We snag a table so we can eat first, because my stomach is officially trying to eat itself. I unwrap my sandwich and take a huge bite, moaning. Greg grins and takes a bite of his whole wheat bagel sandwich. It looks amazing, and just sinful enough after all of our running that we did. The coffee shop is busy, but not so much that we have to yell to talk to each other.

"I know you have to be hungry, Tori," he chuckles. I nod and take another bite.

"Mm-hmm," is all I can give him at the moment and he snorts laughing.

I shrug. I can't talk until my tummy is full. I'm not responsible for what I say before coffee and I'm slightly hangry. He doesn't take offense, and eats his food. I think he enjoys watching me eat. I feel bad that I worried them yesterday, but I just couldn't stomach anything. My stomach is finicky since dating Anthony, and any anxiety or strong emotions turns it. After that, my appetite is ruined.

My breakfast sandwich inhaled, I take a sip of my coffee and sigh happily.

"Life complete?" he asks with an indulgent smile.

"Hmmm." I respond happily. "Coffee good."

Greg nods with a chuckle. We clean up, and start walking back. I take another sip, and relax, completely happy.

"And...four," Greg says.

"What? Four?" I ask, wondering if he's losing it.

"Yes, it takes four sips of coffee in the mornings for you to be able to have a conversation if you're not running," he says.

Oh fuck, they actually timed it. Ugh, I want to argue, but it's true. It does take me a little to get going, especially once the running endorphins start to fade.

"You're right. I'm kind of a bear in the mornings." I concede, blushing slightly.

Greg shakes his head. "You're really not. It's adorable. Tesa warned us, and we all have our quirks. Yours is easy to work around."

I smile happily, because Anthony never got it. He'd bully me into moving in the mornings. I'm glad that they aren't annoyed by my lack of motivation until I have coffee in me.

We walk back to the house, enjoying each other's company, and chatting about some of the things that Greg had wanted to know about me. His favorite color is lavender, and mine is royal blue. His pet peeves are clothes on the floor and dishes left overnight in the sink, and mine is when clothes get folded inside out. They're things that are totally manageable, and not deal breakers for us.

"Hey! You're finally back. Did you bring us breakfast?" Link is leaning over the front porch, watching us walk up with a lazy grin.

"Yeah, coffee too, babes," I say.

"Mmm, best girlfriend ever," he says. I giggle and blush. I'm not used to hearing them say that yet.

"You're so damn cute, baby girl," Greg says with a chuckle. I stick my tongue out, and his eyes heat.

"No time for that!" I giggle.

"Mmm, we'll see, baby girl. That tongue of yours and I have a score to settle!" Greg winks at me, licking his bottom lip. *Game on, Greg. I can't wait!*

We move inside with the food, and Tesa grins. "You're alive and caffeinated, I see! Everything good?"

I smile. "It's excellent. I watched Veronica get her ass handed to her, and then banned from *The Java Spot.*"

Tesa grins. "Soo what you're saying is that we have a new lunch spot without the bigot secretary reporting back that I'm your new favorite snack." Tesa licks her lips suggestively and Miguel looks alarmed.

"What the fuck? I need an explanation immediately. Also, please don't look at my girlfriend like that again!" Miguel grabs me and pulls me into his arms.

Wow, I just realized that all three of them have used the 'g-word'. Yes, please.

"Mine!" He growls.

Mmm I've never been into alphas before until now...

Tesa laughs maniacally and explains. Miguel looks slightly mollified.

I giggle in his arms, gasping for breath. "Miguel, you should have seen your face!"

Miguel shakes his head. "You're supposed to be on my side, *gringa linda.*"

He starts to tickle me and I squeal. "Oh my god, Miguel I have to pee! Miguel!"

Miguel rolls his eyes. "I'm not afraid of a little pee in my quest for vengeance. Bah. Go pee." Miguel chuckles, shaking his head.

I run to the bathroom on the first level, sighing happily as I relieve my bladder just in time. That was way closer than I'm comfortable admitting. I'm going to have to double time my kegels if they're gonna tickle me like that.

I wash my hands, dry them, and walk back out to the kitchen. Link calls dibs, and cuddles me into his arms after pulling me onto his lap.

"Oh. Yesterday was so crazy, did you ever check that box that came in?"

Oh shit, that's right. I shake my head. "No, that's on my to do list today. I can go grab it."

Greg shakes his head. "I got it, where is it, baby girl? You're comfy."

Smiling at how sweet he is, I tell him it's probably by the front door. He finds it, and it is where I thought it was.

He puts it on the table and I bite my lip. I open the package, and the first three items are books. I pick up the first book, and see that it's a signed AK Graves book that I had won in a give-away. *His Atonement* is the novel, and a very sexy demon is staring up at me. Yummy. I can't wait to read this book.

I guess Anthony had forwarded my mail. I mean, that's kind of nice of him. The next items are book swag: a key chain, shirt that says, *"Demons like Sex toys too,"* and a bookmark. I snort at the T-shirt because fuck yes. I think I'm officially a fan too after the other night.

The last thing is a note. I bite my lip and open it.

TORI, **I am forwarding you your mail until you decide to stop this nonsense and stop shacking up with the lesbian. Remember that you enjoy cock and come home.**

Anthony

I ROLL MY EYES. I mean he got one thing right. I do like cock. None of it is threatening, except that he knows where I live. Ugh, why. Link growls behind me. Couldn't I have one non-drama day? Or an hour?

"Well, we all have established that my ex is a douchebag..." I begin.

"Is that who the box is from?" Tesa asks.

"No, he forwarded a book and swag from a giveaway that I won. But, he did drop a note in the box," I reply, and hand the note to her.

She snorts after she reads it and then reads aloud for those that haven't read it. She takes a photo for herself, then lights it on fire and drops it in the sink.

"Bye, fucker!" She yells.

Have I mentioned how much I love her?

"Okay, so now that's over, tell me about this book," Tesa says, as she watches the paper burn.

Tesa is determined to have a good day, and I'm grateful for that. It wasn't really threatening, and she has a photo for proof if we ever need it. The boys look on in slight disbelief as I gush about the book I received.

They're just going to have to learn to move on, because we certainly have, I think to myself as Tesa turns on the faucet to douse the paper.

twenty
GREG

I watch Tori closely as she acts like it's not a big deal that she has an ex-boyfriend who is determined to remind her that he exists. I can't prove that he also had something to do with the photo album, but it is clear that he isn't willing to let her go.

Too fucking bad. He needs to move on, because she's free now, and she's with us. We won't let anything happen to her.

"So, what do we want to do with our day?" Tori says brightly with a smile.

She takes a sip of her water, and leans back into Link. Like the caveman that he is, he pulls her tightly into him, and lightly bites her shoulder.

"Link, Tori isn't food. Stop trying to eat her. If you're hungry, here's a muffin." Tesa hands him one and I snort.

I just can't with her.

Tesa smirks at me and rolls her eyes. "Why don't we all get ready and go to the Harborwalk? There's a few museums that Tori and I have been talking about going to see near there too, and then we can go have lunch?"

The guys and I look at each other and shrug. That sounds

really nice. We rarely get out and experience Georgetown, because we are so busy or decide to be lazy at the house.

"I'm in, we'll go get ready next door, then meet you in the driveway," I say, already planning what we'll do in my head. The girls nod and we walk back to our house.

"Guys, do you really think that our girl is doing as well as she says?" Link asks with a sigh.

I unlock the front door and disarm the security system with a shrug.

"No. I think that Tori is really good at compartmentalizing. She just shoves it into a corner and thinks about it later. She's been through the shit this week, and it hasn't stopped."

I tell them about the run in with her ex's secretary as we move upstairs. They shake their heads at how awful she is, but it makes sense that her ex is getting intel from others. Especially after the note Tori got in the box.

Miguel shrugs. "We are just going to have to follow her lead right now. Greg, you and I have seen her have a panic attack and that was scary shit. She is easily triggered, and I've noticed that she can't eat when she's upset. Her relationship with food is crap, and I feel like a lot of that is her ex's fault. That *pendejo* has a lot to answer for. What did Tori call him? A douchebag. It fits him perfectly."

I chuckle. "If we are going to follow her lead, let's get ready and prepare to give our girl a good day. We haven't done many of the museums in a while or just gone out and enjoyed our town. Hanging with the girls today will be fun, too."

The guys nod and disappear into their rooms.

Sighing, I hunch my shoulders and go into my room. I'm putting up a front of my own with the guys. I feel like our girl is headed towards a melt down, and I'm worried about what that will do to her. She's so fucking strong, yet there are times where I see the shadows in her eyes. She's been through a lot of bullshit, and she deserves good things.

Stripping in my bathroom, I turn on the shower and head in. Just being in the water, even though it's my bathroom and not Link's, reminds me of the last time I showered with Tori.

Her skin was slick with beads of water and she had the most gorgeous secret smile as she watched us. All that red hair, I just want to wrap it around my fist and pull. Speaking of cavemen, I feel like I turn into one around her.

My dick bobs against my stomach and I groan. It's been hard for hours, and I didn't get to fuck her this morning. I loved our time together, and while I'm glad I didn't end up fucking her on the porch, I wonder what it would be like to fuck her tight, wet cunt. I fist my cock and my eyes roll slightly. Fuck, now I'm just torturing myself.

My cock is extra sensitive with the piercings. I had gotten them for myself as much as I had for the pleasure of those that I was with. I loved to force as many orgasms as possible from the girls I fucked, even if I was a one and done.

May as well send them on their way with as many good memories as possible before it was over. Yeah, I'm kind of a dick.

But that's over, I think as I rub and tug on my cock. The sensations of the water flowing over hit the piercings just right, and feel so good. Smoothing my hand down to my balls, I tug on them, and imagine it's my gorgeous girl on her knees for me. She's putting them in her mouth and sucking hard as she wraps her hand around my shaft and jerks me off.

I shouldn't be doing this. I should really just finish showering and get on with my day, but I can't. I need to come, or I'm going to steal Tori away the second that I can to fuck her in a closet or something. That's not what today is about though. Today is about relaxing...my hand travels back to the base of my cock and pulls, and I lose track of what I was thinking about. Fuck it. I need to come if I'm going to enjoy today.

I lean against the wall with my head on my arm. Pulling harder, I gasp and know I won't be able to last long. I imagine that it's Tori's tongue running up the base of my shaft before sucking on the tip. My hand mimics what I wish she would do. Tugging where she'd be sucking. Fuck, do I miss her right now. Her mouth would be going down on me, her hand tugging at the base of my cock. She'd choke on my cock like the good girl she is, and tears would stream down her face. I'd watch for any true discomfort, but she'd look up at me with her gorgeous blue eyes that can't hide anything and I'd know she's okay.

My balls start to tighten and I groan again. I pretend that I'm cumming all over her tongue and face, and my knees buckle. I don't think I've ever come so hard, my dick is still twitching, and only my arm against the wall is holding me up. Shuddering, I push myself up to stand, watching as my cum that painted the wall, washes away. She makes me crazy, and she most definitely owns my cock, and is working her way into my heart.

Yeah, I think, I know it's super soon. I wash my hair thoroughly, thinking. I don't really know her, and I want to go slow, but then she'll tell me something that makes me want to bundle her in my arms and never let go. She makes me feel protective of her, and I have only ever felt this way with Tesa and the guys.

I bounced from foster home to foster home from the ages of five to ten. When I turned ten, I went to a foster home to live with the Foxes. I don't remember my real parents, so the shuffle from place to place didn't really bother me. The Foxes couldn't have kids, and I hit it off with them. They asked if they could adopt me, and I agreed. I was excited to have a family. I met the guys our first year of middle school, and we became instant friends that first day at lunch.

As much as Miguel teases Tesa about claiming Tori, he claimed Link and I. He said, "we're gonna be friends, anyone have a problem with that?" Neither of us did, and that was considered that.

I chuckle, because we have gotten in and out of more trouble that I can remember. My foster parents retired to Florida when I turned nineteen, and I visit them once a year.

I grab my body wash and wash cloth and clean the sweat from my body. I know that I've been in the shower entirely too long now, and the guys are gonna give me shit. I finish quickly, and grab my towel. I walk into my room while drying my hair naked.

"Ya know, your cock isn't Miguel's size, but it's still pretty impressive with all the metal," Link comments from the bed next to Miguel. Fuck me, I knew they'd be ready to go.

"Yeah, yeah. I will be ready in a couple," I grumble.

"Oh come on, I know that you've been jerking off to Tori, you can't still be grumpy after that." Miguel hides his smile behind his hand.

I roll my eyes, because of course they'd somehow know. Fuck, they could have been in my room listening to me for all I know.

"I'm not grumpy, I was just worried about making y'all wait," I tell them.

I grab a light blue crew sweater, boxers, and jeans. Today is supposed to be colder, and fall is finally making its appearance. Miguel rolls his eyes.

"The girls are probably not ready yet. I figured we'll go walk, check out a museum or two, and then have lunch. I want her to have a relaxing day, so she'll actually eat."

I pull on my clothes nodding. "Yeah, she had breakfast this

morning, but only because we ate at Grace's place. Otherwise, she may not have wanted to. I never noticed because she has such amazing curves, but she is a little skinny. I can't help but think that Anthony may have been making her over exercise and then starve. Even when she does eat, she doesn't eat a lot."

Link growls. "Yeah, I notice that she grazes. I'm thinking that she's been eating small amounts for so long that her stomach has shrunk. So, we'll have to offer her snacks throughout the day. Fuck, I feel like I'm talking about a toddler, but that's really how she eats."

Miguel snorts. "No, she's not a toddler, but she definitely forgets to eat and then ends up hangry. Finish up, I'll go pack some snacks for us all and bottles of water."

He jumps from the bed and I listen to him run down the stairs to get started. I grab my socks and shoes and sit on the edge of the bed to put them on.

"Do you find it odd that Tori is so perfect for all of us?" Link asks.

I grin as I tie my shoes. "No, man. It's not at all. She's perfect for all of us. I've never dated, so I asked her to go on a date with me, just the two of us. She loved it. I think we should all make sure that we do things like that. We can get really busy, and sometimes I need to travel for work, so this way she always has one of us. She also has Tesa too, and that girl will fight for her girls only nights."

Link rolls his eyes. "If it involves dancing in their underwear and singing at the top of their lungs for stress relief, I agree that they need that time." I stand up and Link follows, continuing, "I can't help but feel like she's keeping things from us. I don't know if it's because she's protecting us, if she's embarrassed, or being secretive though."

I shake my head as I step off the last step to turn towards the kitchen. "Nah, man. She still doesn't know us well, and we are protective. It's natural that she would be keeping some things to herself. Plus, Tesa didn't seem overly worried about it. So, I'm going to take my cues from her bestie."

Link shrugs. "Yeah, you're right. I just want to be able to be there for her. And then other times I want to lock her in my room so the outside world can't hurt her."

We've entered the kitchen by now and Miguel snorts, hearing us. "Kinky, man. Maybe we should work our way up to bondage, yeah?"

That has us chuckling, but fuck that may be fun too, maybe we should ask her about it. Fuck, and now I'm hard as stone.

Link groans. "Is anyone else thinking about asking her if we can tie her up now?"

"Fuck yeah." We chorus and chuckle again.

We grab the cooler with water and snacks and head out. I make sure to arm the security system and lock the doors as we go. The girls are chatting and laughing on the porch.

"Before you ask, the house is armed and locked up!" Tesa chirps with a smile.

I grin. "She can be taught, folks!" I crow and she shoves me.

"Hey, hey! No breaking my men!" Tori teases and then blushes.

Tesa snorts. "Yeah, that's never not gonna be weird, babes... I guess," she sighs dramatically, "they'll just have to work to deserve you."

"Hey!" We all chorus. Tesa and Tori chortle. Ribbing each other and teasing, we all get into my car that's parked on the street. It's the biggest, since it's an SUV and will be the most comfortable. As I turn the car on and wait for everyone to get settled, I sit in awe of how well Tori fits in with us. It's like she was always meant to be with us.

I look behind me as I pull out into the street because I have precious cargo with me. My most important people are all in one place, and I'm super excited to spend the day with them.

———

I PUSH BACK from the table, laughing so hard my sweet tea almost shoots out my nose. We had spent the day walking around Harborwalk and going in and out of the shops. Tori has lived here for a few years, but hadn't had time to do a lot of sightseeing, and her ex hadn't seen the point once they had moved in together. I can't tell you the last time that I had this much fun though.

Tesa had made an ill-timed joke just as I had a big sip of sweet tea. Now I'm coughing and laughing. Fuck, I don't know how we all survived growing up with her. She has absolutely no filter, and Tori is blushing hard, hiding her face in Link's shoulder.

"Aye, Tesa! Not while we're eating. You almost killed Greg," Miguel laughs.

We are getting looks, but we chose to eat outside because we know we are loud as fuck when we are all together.

Today has been the best day, and Tori has been relaxed all day. We stopped at a restaurant that sat on the water that had really good seafood. Tori went to town on a seafood platter, and I don't think I've ever enjoyed watching someone eat as much as I have her. I'd feel like a creeper, except that I also can see that Tesa, Link, and Miguel are casually doing the same thing. I'm glad I'm not the only one that's noticed that our girl doesn't eat enough.

Tori sighs happily. "Oh my god, that was amazing. I'm so happy that we stopped here. I was starving. Everything was so good."

Miguel grins slyly. "Good you're gonna need your energy tonight when-"

"Lalalalala. Miguel!" Tesa snorts, covering her ears.

"Ha! And that's the beginning of the payback from fucking my bouncer in the bathroom, *hermanita*." Oh fuck, not this again.

"Guys." Tori laughs. "Why am I going to need my energy, Miguel?" She pushes with a saucy grin. Fuck, she's so cute when she's a brat. My fingers twitch and I close my fist with a chuckle. Now, all I can think about is spanking her.

Miguel shrugs innocently. "The four of us have a date at the club, and I know how much you love to dance. This'll be a night to just go with the flow and let loose. I also want to make you scream later, so you're staying the night with us, if you're good with that?"

Miguel cuts his eyes to Tesa with a laugh, where she is dramatically throwing her hand over her eyes. *So ridiculous,* I chuckle. She acts super innocent, but I'm sure she teases Tori about us too when we aren't around.

We finish up, pay the bill, and stroll out of the restaurant. I throw my arm over Tori's shoulder and kiss her forehead. She sighs happily.

"Good day, baby girl?"

She tilts her head up and smiles. "The best. It was nice to get outside. I think it's exactly what I needed today. I'm glad y'all suggested it."

"I think we have 'a Tori's favorite things theme' going on today." I chuckle.

"Mm. I'm about it. I could totally take a nap before tonight though." I can hear the happiness in her voice as she wraps her arms around my waist.

She continues to walk with me, snuggling.

"Lucky bastard. I see someone is cuddly after a day of fun and food." Miguel chuckles as he walks beside us.

"Our girl has requested a nap if possible," I relay to him.

"Mmm. Well then our princess will get her wish. I could totally go for a nap, but I have to check on a few things at the club. I'll have to meet you there. Link, you in for a nap?"

Link shakes his head sadly. "No, I also have to go in and check on some contracting stuff. I'm a contractor and own *Dream Builds, LLC.* I actually built Tesa and your house and ours. I got a text that one of our permits may have hit a snag, so I have to call in some favors."

"Wait? You built those houses? They're gorgeous." Tori exclaims.

Miguel smirks. "Why do you think he gave himself the bougie bathroom?"

Link bursts out laughing. "There's so much that I would say if your sister wasn't right here-"

"Lalalalalala! Ughh, you guys. I know Tori has a magical pussy, and I am super happy that she is getting all the peen." We groan in unison and she cackles in glee. "But," she stresses. "I would rather hear the details over wine and pretend that it isn't happening with y'all. Thank you for coming to the Tesa talk." She bounces over to the car in the parking lot.

"Your sister is next level, dude." Link shakes his head. "Who the fuck says peen?"

Tori raises her hand. "I do! Here it is used in a sentence. Peen: Greg has a fancy peen, and it hits places in my pussy that I never thought possible. Peen."

She has the tone that the moderator during a spelling bee would have and I look at her in disbelief with the guys. She then realizes what she says and blushes.

"Okay, so my vagina is also a hussy. Forget I said anything."

Ducking her head, she joins Tesa and jumps in the back with her.

I shake my head. *Fuck me, great job fancy peen.* I've never been happier for these piercings. I really can't wait to get her to myself soon.

"Anyone else want to spank her perky, gorgeous ass right now?" Miguel growls. Link and I raise our hands, and he snorts. "Cool, remind me later of this conversation when we are making her scream for us tonight."

"Fuck, and now I'll be hard at work," Link whines.

Miguel chuckles. "If you're a good boy, I'll suck your cock later." Link's jaw drops.

I snort, completely amused. "Y'all are even more fun now that you're finally fucking."

Link blushes. "I mean, not quite." Now that's adorable.

"You know what I mean. It's only a matter of time." I laugh.

Miguel shrugs. "You're not wrong. It'll happen when it happens." He slings his arm over Link's shoulders and talks softly to him as they finish the walk to the car. I open the driver side door with a grin. Yeah, I'm pretty happy with life right now, and now I get to snuggle my girl and nap too. Best day ever.

twenty-one

TORI

I stretched in Greg's arms with a yawn. We did get a nap in his bed, and it was amazing. I feel so much better. Greg kisses along my neck and then touches the necklace around my neck. I'm surprised that he's the first to really notice it, since I've been wearing it since yesterday.

"Hey, when did you start wearing this?" he murmurs.

We are both feeling lazy and don't want to get out of bed yet. His entire body is surrounding me.

Snuggling into his arms, I sigh. I will later blame my brain not being completely awake for saying, "My parents gave it to me when I left for college. They gave it to me to protect me. They were nervous about me moving two hours away for school. But, I thought I lost in my junior year, and never saw it again."

Greg grunts, "Then how are you wearing it now? That doesn't make sense, Tori."

I jerk in his arms, realizing what I said, and that I hadn't told him about finding the necklace. I sigh, sit up and turn towards him.

"It's weird. I thought I had lost it, but somehow I found it yesterday. It fell out of the back of the photo album when I picked it up." I tell him, biting my lip.

Greg sits up as well. "What the hell! You didn't think to tell us this? That's kind of a big deal. Necklaces don't mysteriously show up somewhere that you've just moved in."

"I mean, I know that. I don't know how it would have ended up in that photo album. It was a newer album of photos of Anthony and I. It shouldn't have even been in there. I asked Anthony to help me look for it when I initially lost it, and he blew me off."

I shrug, not knowing what else to say. Maybe I should have told them, but I'm used to doing things on my own. I also was just so grateful to have found it, that I didn't want to think too much about the logistics of it showing up.

"You really are clueless, aren't you? Like is it a lack of self-preservation?" Greg frowns at me, and he looks...disappointed.

I flinch as if slapped, and blink my eyes. Shit, I will not cry. Nope. Blinking madly, I shake my head. "No, you don't understand. This is the only thing I have from my parents before they died. It devastated me when I thought it was lost."

Greg sighs. "Baby girl..."

"*No.*" I gasp and jump to my feet.

I'm shaking right now. I'm so angry and sad. I thought he'd be different, but are all guys like this? I know that I should have mentioned the necklace last night, but he's acting like I'm an idiot for accepting its return at face value.

"You...you don't get to do that with me. You basically called me dumb, and then you want to act like I'm overreacting? Fuck off with that nonsense. Maybe I should have mentioned it, but I didn't think to. I was so excited to have a piece..." I hiccup a sob and shudder. "A piece of my parents back, that I just wanted to hold onto it."

Greg leaps up off the bed, jaw dropped. "Baby," he says in horror. "I didn't know. I'm so sorry. Of course you're not dumb, I'm just worried about what it might mean that this lost jewelry is back. You don't think he may have taken it back then?"

I wrap my arms around myself, keeping my distance. I'm in a T-shirt and panties and I feel exposed as he looks at me. My skin feels too tight and the edges of my eyesight are starting to dim. Fuck, no I refuse to be this vulnerable with him. I force myself to breathe and his eyes narrow as he watches me.

"Tori..." he says in warning.

"Fine," I gasp out. "No, I didn't think that he may have taken it, but I am now. There's nothing I can do about that now though. I'm not gonna let him taint my memories of my... parents."

Dammit, I was doing so well breathing in and out, and every breath just hurts now. I take another step back and somehow feel lighter. That's it...I need space.

"I gotta go..." I whisper.

"Baby, don't I'm so sorry," Greg whispers.

I shake my head. "I just need space or I'm going to fall apart and I can't do that with you right now."

Greg blinks his eyes hard. "Fuck, fuck, I fucked up. Honey... Tori, how can I fix this?"

I stare at him and shrug. "I don't know. I just need Tesa right now."

I turn and leave the room. I'm still not dressed, but fuck it. I can't be here right now. I walk down the stairs quickly. I hear silence for the first eight steps, and then Greg roars. Fuck. I walk faster and jump off the last step.

"Tori, Tori don't leave. I need to fix this, please." He is panicking and yelling, but it fuels my own panic.

He's barreling down the steps and I face him, walking

backwards. Somewhere in my head, I know that he won't hurt me, but I'm not feeling very rational.

I hit something hard and arms are wrap around me. I scream.

"Fuck, Tori. What is going on?! Baby, it's me...it's Link."

I shudder again. "I just need to go," I moan. I know that it doesn't make sense, but I feel hurt and alone. I'm desperate not to head down the path of abuse again.

"Tori, I won't make you do anything that you don't want to do. But will you turn and look at me? Please?"

I turn and stare. I don't say a word.

Link looks at me and sighs. "In one word, tell me how you're feeling right now."

The tears drop down my face. "Betrayed," I whisper.

Greg mutters, "Oh fuck."

Link holds a hand up. "Why?"

"Because my feelings matter," I whisper.

It's like Greg isn't in the room and it's just Link and I. Link bites his lip and nods.

"Yes, they do. Tell me why you felt like they don't, pretty girl," he says softly.

I take a breath and a sob escapes. I wrap my arms around my body and hug myself.

"Tori, who are you protecting yourself from right now?" Link asks.

I sob again. "Everyone. Eventually, everyone I care about hurts me." Link shakes his head sadly.

"I think Greg made a mistake that he's paying for right now." I turn my head to look behind me and he shakes his head. "Talk to me right now, okay?" I nod, still crying. "Okay. Can you tell me why you felt that your feelings didn't matter?"

I wrap my hand around my necklace and sigh. Clearing my throat, I struggle to talk through the tears.

"My parents died two months before my twenty-first birthday, driving to see me. We had been fighting, and I was mad at them. This is the last thing that they ever gave me. It went missing after they died. I thought I had lost it. I found it yesterday when it fell out of the photo album that was on my bed. I don't know how it got there, and I didn't think to tell anyone. I was just happy to have it. But..." I sigh. "I guess its dumb." I shake my head and look down, shrugging.

"No, its not dumb," Greg says. He's in front of me, and he raises my head with his index finger under my chin. "I didn't know, but I didn't ask about its importance either. It isn't dumb to miss your parents and to be excited to find something that you thought was lost. I'm on edge that someone came into the house when you were at work and destroyed a photo album in your room. The fact that that person stopped first at the kitchen for the biggest fucking knife that Tesa owns scares me even more. That's what I meant earlier, but I did a shit job of explaining my fear."

I blink at him, because I didn't think about all of that. "Maybe I am an idiot..." I whisper. Link growls.

"No, Tori, you're not an idiot." Greg says. "My brain will always go to the worst case scenario. What if you were home, what if things had ended differently. My brain is wired that way, because of all of the bad shit that I've seen while working. A normal person wouldn't think this. I was out of line in how I spoke to you. I made you feel unsafe and unwanted and I never want that for you. I want to be your peace, but I get that I fucked that up just now."

I swallow hard so I can talk over the knot in my throat. "I have had to second guess everything that I've ever said for years now. If I said the wrong thing...bad things happened. I felt like I was right back where I was with Anthony."

Greg's eyes are red, and I want to hide. I don't want to be

the reason this usually sweet, protective man is sad. "Maybe I'm just too broken..." Link pushes Greg out of the way.

"Absolutely fucking not, Tori McAllister. You stop that shit right now." For some reason what Link says breaks through and my tears start to dry. I straighten and nod.

"It sounds like y'all fucked up on both sides, and I'm sorry that you felt unsafe and unwanted. You are so wanted, and Greg will just have to work extra hard to fix what he broke by not thinking. Okay?"

I nod with a sigh. "Now were you really going to go out there in your underwear in sixty degree weather?" Link asks.

I giggle because I was. I also realize that I'm no longer having a panic attack. I hug Link hard, and he wraps his arms around me.

"Can you do me a favor, pretty girl?" I nod and look up at him. Link smiles. "Don't you want to know what the favor is?"

I shrug. I feel tired after everything and can't bring myself to use my words.

"You give your trust so implicitly, even after everything you've gone through. Trust me, that's not a trait of someone that's broken. You're a little emotionally banged up. Honestly, most people are. Just, keep putting one foot in front of the other, okay? That's my favor. Don't give up." I nod hard and he smiles. "Good," he murmurs, then kisses me hard and I moan. "Mmm you taste good. Now, do you think you're up for giving Greg a hug? He's suffering right now, honey. But between you and me, you're within your rights to make him work for it." He winks at me, and despite my better judgment, I giggle again.

Link smiles wider and nods, stepping back. I walk over to Greg and he looks at me sadly.

"Sometimes I suck with people," he says softly. "I'm really blunt and I can be an ass. I don't want to be an ass with you, but I can't promise that it won't peek out here and there. When it does, I promise to make it up to you. I'm really sorry for jumping down your throat earlier."

"Thank you," I tell him. I should be mad, but I'm not. I reacted so strongly because his tone reminded me of Anthony's. I vaguely wonder if that's some kind of trauma response...

Greg brushes my hair out of my face. "You're thinking awfully hard there, baby girl. Penny for your thoughts?"

I shake my head. My thoughts don't make sense right now and are jumbled. I feel Link's warmth against my back as his arms go around me.

"Tell us, even if you don't think they make sense," he says to me, kissing my hair.

I let myself lean against him. "I'm just thinking that I reacted so strongly because of the tone that Anthony always used with me. I felt small when Greg said that I was clueless. It was like I was right back in that apartment with him. I don't want to go back there. I don't like who I am with him. I don't want to be helpless anymore."

Greg palms my face and kisses my forehead. "Something tells me that you won't let yourself be helpless ever again. You called me out today, and nothing bad happened. We talked, we figured it out, and everything will be okay. Now, do you still want to see Tesa?" I nod that I do. "Tesa is gonna kill me for making you cry," Greg sighs. "I'll run you over."

I thought I'd be getting dressed to go next door, but he picks me up in a bridal carry. I giggle, shaking my head at him.

"You'll be warm enough if I carry you," he decides.

Link rolls his eyes and opens the front door.

He carries me over, but Tesa isn't home.

"Are you sure you want to be home alone right now?" he asks, settling me on my feet and handing me my phone.

I nod. "Yeah, I'll set the alarm," I tell him.

I need to figure out how I feel. Greg brushes his lips along mine.

"I am really sorry, baby girl. I just didn't think when I said that to you. I worry about how safe you are a lot lately. I'll be happier when we figure out who was in the house." His tone is filled with sorrow as his thumbs pulls on my lower lip.

I unlock the front door with my phone and sigh. "We haven't known each other for very long, and you couldn't have known. As for the house, it could have been Anthony or someone he knows. I wouldn't be surprised if he was fucking people at work. He was always working late, or he was on his phone and hid the screen from me. There's probably a lot that I don't know about him, and he enjoyed that he kept me guessing."

Greg's eyes darken. His naturally teasing green eyes are now angry. "He's fucking delusional if he cheated on you."

I smile sadly. "Nothing that man has ever done has ever made sense. I don't want to spend any more energy today trying to figure him out."

I open the front door and go inside. I make sure to lock the door and set the alarm, then walk upstairs.

All of the emotions from today and the adrenaline leaving me is making my body twitch. I decide to take a shower, and walk through my room, into the bathroom. I strip off the T-shirt that I had borrowed from Greg to sleep in and push my underwear down, letting them drop on the floor. I'll pick it up after my shower.

I turned on the water, wait for it to heat, and step in. Feeling the weight of the world on my shoulders, I sink to the floor with my back to the wall. I wrap my arms around my legs and let the water wash over me. I know now that I may have overreacted with Greg, but he was also really mean. I need to be in control of how I let people treat me.

I know that I'm one breakdown away from losing my shit, I just don't know how to stop it from happening. I feel like I'm on a runaway train, and the train is my life. Could Anthony have been behind the photo album being massacred? Maybe.

The photos had been ripped and it looked like someone had been pissed off when they destroyed it. I just don't see Anthony getting that emotional and it felt like something a woman may do to their ex. I just don't know of a woman that I've pissed off enough to do that to me.

My thoughts drift as I sit on the floor of the shower. I don't know how long I've been here when I realize that the water has gone cold. I shiver and sigh, cutting off the water, and step out of the shower.

Drying off, I walk out of the bathroom with the towel loosely around me. I glance at the time and see it's around eight o'clock. I wonder if our plans are still on or if my argument with Greg has changed things. I feel excess energy under my skin and unsettled. I need to dance or run, and either one will do right now. I check my phone.

Miguel: Gringa linda, **what do you need? Yes, I'm well aware that you understand your nickname lol.**

I roll my eyes.

Me: **I have all of this excess energy and I need to do something with it.**

Miguel: **Fuck or dance?**

I'm so surprised that I laugh. This man is incorrigible, but if I wasn't feeling so mixed up I would probably choose sex.

Me: **Dance.**

Miguel: **I'm in. Be sure to eat something before the guys pick you up at nine-thirty.**

So bossy. I am actually hungry though. I wonder if Tesa's home yet. Feeling bratty, I text back:

Me: **Yes Daddy.**

Miguel: **No.**

I throw my head back and cackle that this is all I get in reply. This man isn't boring, that's for sure.

There's a knock at my door, and I'm pretty sure that can only be Tesa.

"Tesa?" I call out so she'll hear. The door opens and my bestie peeks her head around the corner.

"Why are you laughing like a witch over her cauldron? And why wasn't I invited?" she asks with a grin.

I giggle. "Your brother is being ridiculous as usual and I'm being a brat."

"Oh so like the normal witchy things," she teases. "Are you still going out tonight?" I nod, securing the towel around me as I sit.

"Yeah, I am. Today has just been kind of weird and Greg and I had a fight? It wasn't really a fight though, so I don't know what to call it." I tell her, wrinkling my nose.

"Okay, so how much time do we have?" She checks.

"Link and Greg are picking me up at nine-thirty."

Tesa glances at the clock. "Meh, we have time. Cliff notes version and go."

I smile weakly and quickly explain what happened and show her the necklace. She purses her lips and nods when I'm done.

"Well you didn't even tell me about the necklace, so it sounds like you just didn't think to. Which, I get. Having people that you count on is new to you, so I understand." Tesa doesn't look mad, and instead shrugs.

My body relaxes and I realize that I had been preparing for

her to get mad at me, too. She smiles gently at me and I know that she noticed.

"What are you wearing tonight? Dress and talk or you'll end up going naked, and I doubt that'll go over well with the guys." My bestie smirks.

I laugh because she's right, and I grab a long sleeved black mini dress, heeled boots with a small platform for comfort, and thigh highs. Tesa nods in approval, and I grab a thong, bra and drop the towel to get dressed.

"I honestly was just happy that I found the necklace. The only thing that I can think of is that Anthony did take it. He didn't like my parents, and they were pushing for me to break up with him before they had their accident." I adjust my bra straps and then put the dress on. Making sure my ass is covered, I shrug. "It would make sense since he isolated me from all of my other relationships that weren't him. He wanted me to be completely dependent on him, and constantly wanted me to quit my job."

I sit on the bed and start putting on my thigh highs. I dressed partly for comfort and partly because I need to remind myself that I'm the badass that Tesa reminds me that I am.

"It all tracks from what I know about Anthony. Did Greg overreact, oh fuck yeah. He does that a lot because he worries. And I get it, I've been on the receiving end of his security lectures often. He reminds me all the time to make sure that I'm aware of my surroundings. He means well, but he's very blunt and he's hurt my feelings more than once. It's different though when he's talking to you. It has to be. Y'all are in a relationship, and he has to temper his inner possessive alpha asshole."

"I don't want to be that girl that insists that people change for them..." I start.

She shakes her head. "No, that's not what you're doing or

asking. You're asking that he take your past and possible triggers into consideration. It does no one any good if you're thrown into a panic attack because Greg went full alphahole on you. I can tell you exactly what I need to without being a bitch about it. He can learn how to use his words like a big boy."

I chuckle because what she's saying is making a lot of sense. As we've been talking, I've finished putting on my boots and lacing them.

"Gorgeous. Finish up and do your hair and makeup. I'll get some dinner for us. Pizza or adult grilled cheese with tomato and bacon?" Tesa asks, starting for the door.

My stomach growls and I giggle. Apparently it votes for grilled cheese.

"Grilled cheese sounds amazing," I confess to her.

"And it's fast for me to make too. Scoot! Go finish."

I hadn't washed my hair in the shower and it is looking a mess. I sigh, detangle it and start drying it. I purse my lips as I look at the mess that is my hair. Shrugging, I decided to pin it up. I braid my hair into a crown, tuck and smooth it all out. It looks much better and adds a touch of femininity to the outfit. I add bobby-pins where I need to, then wash my face before makeup. I decided to go with a gold highlighter on my cheekbones with browns, golds and purples for my eye shadow.

Tesa comes into the room with food and I decide to wait on lipstick until after my sandwich. I'm already wearing my necklace, because I don't want to take it off. It works with the outfit and means I just need earrings to finish.

Tesa's jaw drops as I come out. "Fuck me, babes. Every time I think you can't be any more beautiful, you show me a different side of my bestie. The guys are gonna have their hands full tonight."

I grin as she hands me my plate. Tesa gives the best compliments and they're always so genuine.

"Thank you. My hair was a mess and I didn't know what else to do with it. I tried something new and I love it. It'll keep my hair out of my face tonight too. I'm just trying to figure out what color lips to do."

I take a bite and moan. There's nothing better than adult grilled cheese. She added bacon and tomato to it and it's absolutely perfect. She grins and takes a bite as well before disappearing into the bathroom. She comes back out with a tube of liquid lipstick. Taking it from her hand, I see that it's a deep purple. I had bought it on a whim one day and hadn't worn it yet. I nod because it's perfect.

"Fuck yes, this is the one."

We eat our food chatting and laughing. The doorbell rings before it opens. Tesa rolls her eyes.

"Neanderthals, I swear," she grouses.

Greg did set up the locks, I'm sure he copied all of the passwords.

Taking our empty plates, she jumps up. "Finish up, I don't want them to see you until you're totally done getting ready."

I head to the bathroom with my lip color, wash my hands and brush my teeth. I put on the lip stain and then step back. I admire the look and smile. Yeah, that's exactly what it needed. I make sure that I didn't get any on my teeth, because that's the worst, then grab a pair of tear drop blue earrings. They match my eyes perfectly, and finish the outfit.

I grab a clutch and throw in my phone, ID, and a credit card before rushing out the door.

"I'm coming!"

I walk down the stairs and then around the corner where everyone is at the front door. Link and Greg's jaws drop.

"Can we stay home? Is that an option?" Link asks.

I grin and walk up to him, running my hand over his chest. He's in a buttoned down black shirt and nice jeans. He also smells amazing. In heels, I'm still tiny, but I can lean up and kiss his lips. The lipstick is the smudge proof kind, so I don't have to worry that it'll transfer. Though, it would be pretty smeared all over his cock...

Bad Tori, I think and my lip twitches. "God, I wanna know what you're thinking so bad right now," Link growls.

Tesa grins. "No fucking in our hallway. Go have fun. Out!"

I turn to face her. "What are your plans tonight?"

"I'm reading one of the books that you recommended, and then I have a date with a bubble bath and ROB." She winks at me and I blush.

"Wait? Who's Rob? And why is Tori blushing?" Greg asks.

It's official. This is how I die of embarrassment. ROB is her rechargeable boyfriend, and I'm not explaining this to the guys. Nope, not today!

"Let's leave Tesa to her fun," I say as I glare at her. She cackles and shoos us with her hands.

"Fuck, I hate you so much," I growl as she grins.

"Love you too bestie!"

Shaking my head I open the door and stalk out. The guys trail behind me confused.

"Wait, I want to know! Link, do you know?" Greg insists.

Link shakes his head and throws his arm over my shoulder. "So, baby girl, will you tell us so that we know who to sic Miguel on?"

I giggle. Because I tried to deflect, they'll bother me forever if I don't tell them.

"*ROB* is what Tesa calls her vibrator, Link." I look at his face as this sinks in and giggle again.

"Oh for fuck sakes," Greg groans.

"One, you wanted to know and two, you told me not to

keep things from you..." I sing song back at them and they both groan at me as we get into the car.

"Tori!" They yell at me.

I stifle another giggle. Fuck yeah, pay back is a bitch and I'm loving this. Tonight will be fun.

twenty-two

Work has been so busy. I had three people call out sick this afternoon on one of our busiest nights. I had to beg and plead for people to come in. It's been one thing after the other, and now I'm officially done for the night.

I have three managers on duty now, which should suffice since I'm planning to dance and enjoy our girl. The guys should be bringing her to me in the next few minutes. Link texted me earlier in the day to tell me that Greg had triggered Tori without meaning to, and that they'd had a fight.

I'm not really sure what kind of mood she'll be in when she gets here, but I'm determined to do whatever she needs. If she needs to dance, we'll dance. If she decides that she needs shots of tequila, I'll take them with her. I'm even down for teasing her to the point of madness, and then making her scream in my club. It's nice to be the boss. I know all of the private alcoves.

I check my phone impatiently, and see that Link had texted that they were walking in. Fucking finally. Bouncing on the balls of feet, I roll my eyes. I definitely also have excess energy today. Seeing them across the room, I start walking in their direction. Tori looks edible in that black dress, and she looks like she's up for some trouble as she grins and walks towards me with an extra sway in her step.

I scoop her up into my arms and bury my nose into her neck. She smells amazing. I kiss her neck and then lightly bite her. She shivers and gives me a small moan, blushing lightly, and it just makes me want more. Mmm yes. She's perfect.

"I missed you," I murmured into her ear. "Do you want a drink?"

She nods and smiles. I can't help myself and kiss her hard. I pull back and spot that her lipstick didn't budge. Oh, that'll be a lot of fun. I'll enjoy testing how well it stays on later.

Taking her hand, I see Link beside her, smiling. I grab him around the neck and pull him into me, staring at his smile.

Leaning to his right, I ask, "Ready to get into some trouble tonight, baby?"

He shivers and nods. It's too loud for much else in this part of the club. I place an open mouthed kiss on the side of his neck, and then start walking towards the bar with Tori in tow. I didn't miss his jaw dropping though, and my mouth twitches.

Link's a lot of fun now that our relationship talk has happened. I don't really give a fuck what anyone else thinks. I only hesitated because I didn't want to push after Sheila and his epic failure of a marriage. I absolutely plan to dance with my boyfriend and girlfriend tonight.

Arriving at the bar, I nod at one of my bartenders. My staff knows that I'm here tonight, but I'm not working. Her eyes widen and she rushes over to me. "What can I get for you, boss?"

"What should we all start with?" I ask Tori.

Eyes sparkling, my darling girl grins. "Tequila please!"

Oh yeah, tonight is gonna be interesting. Raising four fingers I say, "Tequila shots, please."

Nodding, she pours me four top shelf shots of tequila. Thank fuck. Tesa had cheap tequila at her house and it burned going down. I need to upgrade her alcohol if I'm going to be drinking with her.

Passing out the shots, we toast. "*Salut!*" I say, then we all take our shot with salt and lime.

Link shudders. I chuckle, shaking my head. He's always disliked tequila after a particularly brutal night where we overdid it, and made out in the hot tub a few years ago. I don't even know how much he remembers.

Shrugging off my memories, I ask, "Dance or another shot?"

"Another, because I'll probably be on the dance floor for awhile with y'all." Tori grins.

Ah, a woman that knows what she wants. My girl does love to dance, and tonight is a good night to let loose. I plan to fully enjoy this.

We take another shot, and then head upstairs to dance. I know that she really likes this DJ, and it'll still have a good crowd even though it has a smaller dance floor. The three of us surround our girl and dance with her.

Link pulls her back to his front and grinds his cock into her ass before starting to move with her. His dancing has improved a lot over the years and the way his hips sway with hers makes me think of all kinds of things that I can do to him.

I am rock hard as I move in front of her and turn her into a Tori sandwich. Lifting her chin, I kiss her, putting my hand on her hip, pulling her into me as Link rotates her hips to grind against her again. Before long she's mewling into my mouth.

Dragging my lips down her neck, I whisper, "Need something?"

She blushes and Greg brushes his hand down the side of her breast as if it's an accident as he cages her in on her right side. We are surrounding her on all sides and I'm well aware of how overwhelming one of us can be, much less all three of us.

Link whispers in her ear, "Maybe I can help, pretty girl."

He drags his hand up her dress and brushes her panties. She throws her head back into his shoulder with a soft cry. Since I'm still grinding into her, he brushes my hard cock too with the barest of touches. Fuck, this man.

As if he knows I'm thinking about him, he meets my eyes with a grin and winks. Fucker totally knew what he was doing. Gah.

I step in closer and kiss up Tori's neck, making sure that Link strokes my cock as he plays with the scrap of material that Tori calls panties. Link starts to pant. I glance at Greg and he looks amused and not at all turned off.

Link slips her underwear to the side and drags his finger through her folds. Tori's eyes roll back.

Grabbing Link by the back of the neck, I ask, "Is she wet for us? Check for me."

Link bites his lip and nods as he slips two fingers into her tight, wet hole. Every thrust has the back of his hand stroking me. It feels amazing, yet it's not enough to get me off. That's okay though, because I want to see our beautiful girl explode in our arms. I kiss Tori hard as she gyrates her hips, and Link finger fucks her. He brushes his thumb against her clit, and she shudders.

I wish I could pull her dress down and suck on her tits, but I don't want to expose her to all of these people. It makes me stabby just thinking about it. So I brush my hands over her body and Greg palms her side before dragging his hand up, and twisting her nipple hard through her dress. She jerks in our arms and comes with a cry.

Link helps hold her up as I grab her ass and grind into her. She must feel amazing strangling his fingers with her tight pussy. Greg pulls her face to him and kisses her through her shivers, as she enjoys the aftershocks of her very public orgasm that no one notices in the dark, crowded club.

Link growls, "That's my pretty girl, you're so gorgeous when you cum."

He makes sure she can stand–ever the gentleman. She grins and we help her adjust her dress, taking turns dancing with her, moving her around in our little circle. Greg pulls her to him as Tinlicker & Helsloot - *Because You Move Me* comes on and he pulls her close and kisses her. She wraps her arms around his waist and they grind their hips together as they dance.

Link wraps his arms around my waist and kisses my neck. "Fuck, they look good together. I'm glad they're moving past what happened today."

Distracted from Tori and Greg dancing, I wrap one arm around Link and grab him by the back of the neck with my other hand.

"I still don't know all the details to that," I growl into his ear, and lightly bite his lobe.

I enjoy the hitch in his breath and grind my cock against his.

"Fuck, Miguel, I can't think when you do that."

"So don't think and dance with your man," I order. Link grins at me and we dance.

We switch between dancing together alone and with Tori and I have to agree she looks so much happier and freer. Maybe there is something to my sister's 'dance it out stress relief' weekly ritual. I'll need to make sure that I remember this.

We break to drink water, because I know that Tori will forget to hydrate, and take another tequila shot too, as Tori stands between my legs looking like the absolute vixen that she is. I crowd her with my thighs on either side of her as I sit on the stool. I massage her hips and her eyes glaze in pleasure. I've barely touched her. I decide to push her a little.

I kiss up her neck and she sighs. "Your noises drive me wild, but I suspect you know this."

She bites her lip and squeezes her thighs together and I chuckle darkly.

"Baby girl, are you feeling needy?" Greg chuckles behind her and kisses up the other side of her neck.

She lets her head fall back on his shoulder. He splays a hand around her stomach and pushes her ass back into his erection. Her eyes roll back and she whimpers.

"*Amor*," I growl in her ear and she shivers. "Are your panties ruined for us yet? Are they flooded with your desire for us?" Her eyes widen and she nods. "Good girl," I praise and she blushes in pleasure. Interesting. "Will you show me? Show me how wet you are?"

Her breath hitches and she whispers, "How?"

"Let Greg pull them off. He'll pretend to drop something and give them to me. You won't need panties soon with what I want to do to you."

"What-what do you want to do to me?" She's stuttering in her need and my lip twitches.

I need inside that beautiful pussy, and I want her bare. I'm so excited that I can do that now and my dick twitches. If we weren't in my club, I'd already be balls deep inside of my gorgeous girl.

Greg chuckles darkly in her ear and grinds against her ass, again. She gasps. "Miguel wants to fuck your gorgeous, soaking wet pussy. Will you let him?"

Greg turns her head back and kisses her hard. I listen to her noises and growl. Fuck, I've been hard all day and I've been teased between dancing with Link and Tori...I don't know how long I'll last.

Tori looks shocked and I grin. Our girl is still so innocent and I can't wait to corrupt her. Her head whips to me.

"Where?!" I don't miss that she also looks intrigued.

I tug her between my thighs again and kiss up her neck. Link has been watching and turns her head and kisses her hard.

"I'd take you against a wall, in one of the recessed alcoves. They're like little spaces in the walls for privacy. If I had to guess, that's where Miguel wants. Are you game, pretty girl? I would understand if you weren't..." Link's lip twitches as he speaks and I think, asshole, he's teasing her.

Tori doesn't realize what he's doing, and she inches up on her toes and kisses me. Fuck, she's gonna kill me.

"You don't have to," I start, worried that what I suggested was too much for her. I just need her so badly.

She shakes her head. "No, I need you. I'm so needy and you promised me dancing or fucking. We already did one of those things," Tori teases me.

I stare at her in shock. I can't believe she said that. "Give me your panties, I want to make sure you're ready for my big cock to fill your needy hole," I growl into her ear.

"Fuck me..." she whispers.

"Mmm, yes, well that's the plan." Greg teases her.

She laughs in surprise and nods. "Yeah, I'm in."

Greg slowly moves his hands up her legs and under her dress. She shivers and sighs. I wrap my arms around her and kiss her. Greg, sneaky asshole, must be teasing her, slipping his fingers under her scrap of lace because she moans into my mouth. So fucking perfect. Greg squats down, and Link crowds us so you can't tell that he's divesting Tori on her underwear. Thank god it's dark in this corner.

I feel her underwear get pressed into my hand and I grab it. I rub my thumb along it and it's completely drenched. Yeah she's ready for me. I shove them into my pocket. "Come with me, darling girl," I say standing up, then kiss her hard again. Greg chuckles.

"Make her see stars," he says.

I grin. "Consider it done." I grab her hand, and pull her to me.

She bites her lip and blushes. She's so beautiful and doesn't even realize it. I walk with her, whispering things in her ear that make her squirm. Someone steps in front of us and I blink. Who the fuck...

It's a girl with long blonde hair and she smiles coquettishly at me. Tori is gonna kill me if I don't get this nipped in the bud.

"Can I help you...?"

"Trish!" she says with a smile. "We met a couple of months ago, and you showed me an amazing time. I was wondering if you wanted to spend time together again? Oh...I mean I don't mean sharing..." she glances at Tori with a smile. "You're gorgeous and I'm sure you know all about Miguel's stamina."

I never knew my male whore fuck boy ways would bite me in the ass until this moment. Why did I have sex in my club? I internally groan. My mouth opens and closes like a fish as I'm struck mute for one of the only times in my entire life. I look pleadingly at Tori and clear my throat.

"*Carino*," I finally get out. "This is apparently Trish, and Trish this is my girlfriend, Tori. She doesn't share outside of my best friends. So as nice as that offer is..."

Fuck, she's gonna castrate me. I've never felt so awkward in my entire life.

"Miguel has one thing right, I don't share. You should find your own man, Trish was it? Mine is taken. Have a great night! We have plans." She tugs my hand and I remember...Yes we do have plans!

Waving awkwardly, I walk past her and then turn Tori and

grab her ass, picking her up so she has no choice but to put her legs around me. Tori laughs and wraps her arms around my neck.

"You're the most beautiful woman I've ever seen, and I love that you just staked your claim. I'm sorry I just didn't..." I start.

"You didn't think that fucking in your club would come back to bite you in the ass, *mi amor*?" She croons.

I stop suddenly and my jaw drops. "Say it again," I growl.

"That you're a fuck boy? A male whore... I won't slut shame but-" she giggles.

"I'm all of those things. I was. But now I'm yours," I growl. "Fuck, I either need to fuck you or spank this perky ass of yours. You're making me feel indecisive."

I start walking again and she cackles. Rude. Maybe I will take her over my lap and spank her. See how wet she gets for me. Mmmm. This woman makes me crazy.

"I'm sorry I think it's so funny," she croons.

In her defense, the giggle she releases is really small. The entire thing is laughable, and embarrassing as fuck. Gah. Yeah, I need to be inside this gorgeous pussy. I'm squeezing her ass and am reminded that she's not wearing any underwear. I head down a hallway, and step into one of the recessed alcoves that can be found all over the club. I'm aware that people are drunk and horny, this gives them a place for a quickie.

This is a hallway that people rarely use, so she can be as loud as she wants. No one will come to investigate, and my girl can get lost in her pleasure. I did promise that she'd see stars. I push her dress up and groan. There's just enough light to see how beautiful she is bare.

I drop to my knees and she gasps. "I need you to cum before I stick my fat cock inside of you, baby. You know my rules."

"Ummm. No sex related injuries?" she asks cheekily.

I chuckle. "Exactly."

And then I've pushed her up so her legs hang over my shoulders and kiss her clit. "Scream for me, baby. No one will hear you, and I need to apologize for my past."

"Miguel-" she starts and then I am eating her out like she's my last meal.

She moans and I enjoy her sounds, but it's not the screaming that I promised her. I slip my right hand in between us and play in her folds as I suck her clit.

"Please..." she whines and I slip two thick fingers inside of her pussy, curling l them.

And then it's game on. I finger fuck her pretty, wet hole and nip her clit, she's so close to giving me I want.

Gasping, I lift my head and say, "Show me those gorgeous tits, *gringa mia*, and then pinch them hard."

"Miguel..." she gasps.

"Nope. I need to see them. I've waited long enough, Tori."

She pulls down her dress and slips them out of her bra cups.

"Mmm. Now show me what I want, baby," I growl, my breath blowing across her pussy.

Her hands drift up and then she's playing with her breasts, pulling on her nipples, and writhing. Fuck yes, I know what my girl needs. I resume eating her out while finger fucking her and I hear the change in her breathing. She's close. Her voice is higher and I know she's about to come. I push a third finger in and she gushes, clamping down.

"Argh!" she screams and I growl on her clit, making her buck on my face and cum harder. She's still spasming when I stand up. Moving her legs from my shoulders to my waist, I kiss her.

I pull my cock out, slipping it through her folds to coat myself in her arousal. "Beg me for my cock, baby."

"Miguel, I swear to god if you don't fuck me with that monster-"

"Good enough," I mutter and push my way in.

She gasps, "Oh my God, yess."

I chuckle darkly. She'll be screaming my name soon. I suck hard on her nipple and bite as I fuck her against the wall. Is it the most romantic thing I've ever done? No. But being able to fuck her tight, wet cunt and enjoying as she...there she goes. She's comes all over my cock, and I plan to have her drenching it multiple times. The slap of our bodies together as I fuck her seems loud, but I know we are the only ones in this hallway.

"Baby, I need to change positions, if I put you down, can you stand?" She nods eagerly at me and I kissed her hard. "Such a good girl. You're so fucking perfect for us. Here we go, *mi amor.*"

I put her down and groan at the loss of her sweet body. I whisper in her ear, "Turn around and show me that beautiful ass. I need to fuck you rough and deep."

Her eyes widen and she blushes. Her nipples turn dark with pleasure, and I grin evilly. Tori likes the dirty talk. We are going to have so much fun. She turns, bends over at the waist and pushes her ass out. I kick her legs apart and she whines.

"Shh, baby I'm gonna give you what you need I promise... but first." I bite my fist and growl.

I look at her gorgeous ass and dripping pussy, and crack my hand across her ass. She cries out and then moans. Oh yes, my girl likes it rough too. I wasn't sure if she would. I massage her ass as it's light pink with my hand print, then slide my hand up and draw my fingers through her folds. She's drenched. I really want to taste her again, but there isn't time. I suck on my fingers and moan.

"Tori, I could eat your sweet pussy for breakfast and before bed every day, and never get tired of it."

Tori struggles, wanting to rub her thighs together for relief, but they're spread too far apart.

"It's gonna be okay. You don't get to come again, unless I'm inside you. So, without further ado..."

Like the asshole that I am, I push hard into her pussy. It's still wet from her arousal, and it glides right in. She cries out because I didn't give her any warning. Reaching around, I decide I'll make it up to her. I glide my fingers up and down slowly on her nub and she rewards me with a guttural moan.

I may have her screaming gibberish soon, and that's my goal. I fuck her hard with long strokes, feeding her pussy all of me. I'm not small by any measure, and I want to take her by a mirror at some point soon so I can watch myself fuck her. I pinch her nipple hard, playing with it and enjoying as they bounce from our movement.

"Miguel, baby, uhhh, I'm so close, please please..." She's not above resorting to begging, I see.

I pinch her clit hard and fuck her deeper so that my nuts are pounding against her sweet pussy. I feel a tingle in my balls, and I know I'll be coming soon. One more, I tell myself, I need her to come again with me.

"Tori, I need you to come again! Come with me, can you do that?"

She cries out and there's the sound I wanted. I wanted her to forget where and who she was, speaking gibberish as she tries to promise me that she'll come again.

Fuck yes. Deciding to be evil, I slap her pussy hard and her walls clench. Grinning I pinch her clit again and she screams as I fuck her through her orgasm. I come with her, whispering how much I adore her, and how tight her pussy strangles my cock. I lay my head on her shoulder, breathing hard, spent. I kiss her shoulder where my lips can reach.

"I'm unalived. Your sweet pussy has killed me, *mi amor*," I grunt.

She giggles sweetly around her gasps to get her breathing under control, and I know that she's perfectly fine.

After a few minutes, I pull out, and I know that I've left a mess inside of her.

"Baby, do you want to clean up in the bathroom? I didn't think this through when I decided to fuck you bare tonight."

I chuckle because I'm not all that sorry. I love that she let me have my way with her at my club, and that we both saw stars tonight. Tori chuckles as she straightens up and pulls her dress down. She turns and rolls her eyes at me as I straighten my clothes and zip up my jeans.

"Didn't think it through, huh? You're a riot, Miguel. Yes, the bathroom would be wonderful. Show me the way, please?"

Grinning happily, I kiss her hard and she moans into me. "I'll walk you there. It's just around the corner, *mi amor*."

I wrap my arm around her waist, feeling very much the caveman at the thought that my cum is slowly leaking out of her right now. I know I'm addicted to this girl, and I'm never letting her go.

twenty-three

Stepping into the bathroom, I giggle. I can't believe that I had sex with Miguel against the wall, but at the same time, I'm glad. I was so keyed up, I needed him. The three of them kept teasing me, and I can't wait to tease them back. Maybe I'll spend the night with them again.

I can't completely fault Greg for our fight earlier, I muse as I walk into a stall to clean up. He doesn't understand that I'm not used to having people in my life to lean on, and he didn't know that his tone would affect me so badly. I felt like I was crawling out of my skin, and I just needed to feel safe. I'm glad that Link was there to help me through my emotions, because I felt like I was drowning.

I pee first, and that helps a lot with cleanup, then I wipe away the rest of his cum. I know that the only way to get completely clean is to shower, but at least he's not running down my leg anymore. I roll my eyes at how proud and smug Miguel was. There's a little bit of caveman in the three of them, and I really do love it...most of the time.

Finishing up , I straighten my dress, and step out of the stall to wash my hands. Miguel said he'd see me back out at the bar area that we were at, making sure that I could see it from the bathrooms. He also worries about my safety, and that makes me feel safe in a nightclub this size.

I'm so involved in my thoughts that I jump when I hear someone clear their throat. A very male someone. My eyes don't believe what they're seeing, and I stare in horror as I see Anthony. What the hell is he doing here?

"You- you can't be here," I stutter, shaking my head.

"Why, Tori? Is it because it's the women's bathroom, or because your newest fuck boy owns it? Really, fucking in the hallway where anyone could see you? Are you really that much of a whore these days?"

I shake my head, because in my eyes, having sex with my boyfriend is not 'whore like' activities, even if it was techni-cally very public. He walks towards me and grabs me around the neck, walking me back until my spine hits the wall. He's so close to me that I can feel his erection, he's caging me in with his body, and I shudder in revulsion. My breath quickens in fear, knowing that I can't get away.

"I watched every bounce of your tits as that asshole fucked you like the whore you are. What the fuck are you wearing? You may as well be a streetwalker for all of the care that you're putting into your appearance."

Feeling bold, telling myself that there's nothing that he can do to me, I say, "I like the way I look. They're just clothes and I'm out with my boyfriends having fun."

Anthony shakes his head and squeezes my neck until I'm gasping for air. He isn't squeezing enough to leave bruises, he's always been too smart for that.

"Girlfriends, boyfriends...how many people have you been screwing these days? Does it not matter anymore? Have you ruined that perfect, tight cunt of yours?"

He tugs up my dress slowly and I try to fight him, but he

tightens his hand around my throat until my eyesight starts to darken around the edges. I can't risk being unconscious with him, so I stop struggling.

"No panties...have you not been wearing any all night? Or did he take them from you, in preparation for your whoring?" He sneers at me.

Feeling humiliated and powerless, I feel tears slide down my face.

"Leave me alone!" I scream, hoping that someone will hear me.

"Scream all you want, Tori...no one can hear you with how loud this club is. Though, that club owner douchebag may be coming back for seconds, so I will make this quick. No one touches what's mine."

He has an evil glint in his eye as he lowers the hand that pulled my dress up to my pussy. "I wonder if you're still wet, and if it'll be for your fuckboy or me. Does your pussy still weep for me the way that your eyes do?"

To my horror, he drags his cold fingers through my folds. I shudder with the change of temp, but Anthony thinks that I want more. He forces a thick finger into me and I whine. I don't want this. Why is he doing this? My body is still primed from my time with Miguel and it accepts the second finger that he forces in as well.

All I feel is revulsion, no longer recognizing that man that I thought I loved. He's staring at where his fingers are disappearing into my pussy, mesmerized. I'm pinned beneath him. Just as I try to scream, he squeezes hard, and I know that he no longer cares who sees the marks around my neck.

"No, Tori, I'm talking now. You be quiet and enjoy our chat," he says as he lazily plays with my past arousal. "I have removed people in your life that threatened to take you from me before, and I won't hesitate to do it again."

Leaving my dress up, exposing me to the cool air, he keeps me pinned one handed to the wall. His fingers slip from my body and he stares into my eyes as he sucks hard on his fingers, cleaning them off. "Even knowing what you did earlier, you taste amazing. You taste sweet, even when I know that you're rotten inside. You'll need to be retrained once I get you back."

He must be losing it. There's no way I'll ever be his again.

Humming in thought, he reaches out to touch the necklace my parents gave me. I flinch and release a strangled scream, but his hand and body keep me pinned. I don't want him to take my necklace.

"I see you found the present I left you. I couldn't deliver the photo album to you personally, as I was in a meeting. I needed an alibi, you see. But...the person who did, sent me proof that they left my warning to you. You don't listen well, though, do you Tori? You've never listened well, which is why you always made me punish you," He sighs, shaking his head.

His thumb strokes the column of my neck almost lovingly, as he glares at me.

"I took this necklace from you three years ago, and then you never saw your parents again. Coincidence? Or was it divine justice because they wanted you to break up with me? I knew they didn't like me, and they were right not to. However, when they took steps to get you to end things, I knew that I had to nip that in the bud. I can take anyone from you at any time..."

The weight of what he just told me, has me unable to breathe even if I had wanted to. Could he have hurt my parents? Taken them from me?

"Now, now, Tori. Don't get all emotional. They've been gone a long time, it just seems that the circumstances around their death may be a bit different than you thought. I will not stand for your defiance. You will end your whorish behavior and come back so that I can make you into who you should have always been."

I force air into my lungs and gasp out, "Nooo. I will never go back to you. I...can't be that person again!" I scream.

There's a knock on the door. "Miss! Miss, are you alright?! Please open the door!"

Rolling his eyes he pulls me to him and kisses me, squeezing my throat even tighter. Apparently he's yanking off the kid gloves today. I keep my lips closed and try to scream against him. He chuckles.

"I never thought I'd like it when you fight me, but that may be something to explore. Think of what I said, Tori. Remember, don't tell anyone about what we talked about. Oh, and I won't be so forgiving next time to those that play with my toys."

He shoves me hard against the wall and I gasp, knowing that my back will bruise. He walks toward a large window that is across from us and opens it, jumping out. I cry holding myself around the waist and there's a banging on the door.

"Tori!" Miguel roars on the other side of the door. "Are you okay? Let me in if you can! Otherwise I'll kick in the door!"

Walking on unsteady legs, I unlock the door, and step to the side. Miguel bursts into the room and sees me crying and shaking. "What the fuck happened, baby? Someone said that she heard screaming! Who was here?!"

Today has been a lot and I can feel the walls closing in. I can barely breathe, and there's suddenly more than one Miguel in front of me. My breath is coming out in sharp pants, my blood roaring in my ears. It's fine though, because maybe they'll be able to protect me better together. I open my mouth to tell him what happened, but all I can gasp out is, "Anthony..." before I feel myself start to fall, and the room goes dark.

twenty-four

MIGUEL

I rush into the bathroom, catching Tori when she passes out. She said her ex's name and her dress is shoved up to her waist. What the hell happened? I know that there's a lot of things that I should worry about, but I have to carry her through the club to my office to stay with her until she's awake, and I don't want her exposed when I do that. I pull her dress down so it's covering her and the vice around my heart loosens just a little.

I'm terrified that she's hurt and I can't physically see it. I'm terrified that her piece of shit ex may have just sexually assaulted her. There are fingerprints on her neck and she sounded so afraid. The marks are an angry red, and I can tell that they'll bruise on her pale skin. I'm livid that someone would hurt my sweet girl like this and that I wasn't there to stop it.

I pick her up into my arms in a bridal carry and stride out of the room. Security closed off this bathroom and is now holding the door open for me. Thank fuck that this was after I had fixed Tori's dress. No one gets the privilege to see her like that, except me and my friends. I need answers as to what is going on, but I won't get them until she wakes up.

I walk down the hall, talking to one of my security guys.

"She said her ex's name. Ask the security that's outside if they saw anyone that looked suspicious. Also, please tell Greg and Link, who are at the bar, to meet me in my office. They'll want to check on Tori as well."

Bear, one of my security guys that has been with me the longest, nods his head. "I noticed that the window in that bathroom was open. If it was her ex, he must have jumped out and took off. I'll have people look to see if he may still be skulking around, but without a photo it'll be hard to find him."

I nod. "I understand, just do your best. He may have hurt my girl and I won't tolerate people getting hurt inside of my club. We need to do better." My voice is barely a growl, I'm so angry.

I'm vibrating in rage and I'm grinding my jaw. The bouncers and security here pride themselves in profiling for sketchy people. I feel like we failed Tori here.

I walk down to my office, open the door, and flip on the light without jostling Tori. She looks pale and she's wheezing slightly in her sleep. It sounds like she's running from someone. I sigh and sit at my desk, cuddling her body to me. I'll wake her up when the others get here. *What the fuck happened to you, baby?!*

I hear a crash and look up. The guys must have raced here and they're fighting to get into the door first. I roll my eyes. If I wasn't so worried, I'd laugh at them. They finally get through, and Link closes and locks the door behind him.

"What the fuck happened?"

"Is she okay?!"

The guys ask rapid fire questions, and I raise my hand, silencing them.

"This is all I know right now, guys. Take a seat." I nod to the couch in front of my desk, and they sit down eagerly.

"I noticed that Tori had been gone longer than expected while I was sitting with you, and I went to check on her." I start and the guys nod.

They had teased me initially, but had been eager to see her, so they had waved me on. "When I got to the hallway, there was a woman yelling at the bathroom door, which turned to screaming and banging on the door. I knew Tori had gone to that bathroom, and I ran down the hallway towards her. I banged on the door too, yelling for security to come and open it. I've never wished I had a radio on me more than that moment," I sighed.

Fuck, I had just wanted one night off.

"She managed to unlock the door and if she hadn't moved over, I would have plowed into her. I was frantic. She was alone in the bathroom and she whispered 'Anthony', before passing out. There was something wrong with her voice though. It sounded hoarse and was super soft. I caught her before she would have hit the ground. But..." I grind my teeth together, and kiss her forehead.

I'm so angry and I feel tears prick my eyes. *She's fine, she has to be*, I tell myself. Taking a deep breath I say, "But what's worse is that her dress was pushed up to her waist and I don't know what happened. I didn't feel any wetness on her legs, she had gone into the bathroom to clean up after we had had sex. I just...I can't say for sure that he didn't rape-"

Yep, the boys yell. Fuck.

"What the fuck, do you think she was...fuck!" Link roars, and that's what startles Tori awake.

She screams and starts to fight me and I hold her tightly. "Tori, it's me. It's us. You're safe, *mi amor!*" I speak forcefully, because I need her to hear me.

She looks around the room, seeing everything yet nothing. She's completely terrified. Link and Greg stand and lean over the desk so they see her.

"We're here," Link says.

"You're safe," Greg growls.

Tori sags in my arms, then bursts into tears in a combination of relief and sadness. I swear, if we ever get our hands on this guy, he'll pay for trying to break our beautiful, strong girl.

I hug her tightly, then tilt her head up so her eyes will meet mine.

"Hey..." I say softly. Gasping as her tears slow, she stares at me like I'm her savior. "Baby, you're scaring me. Can you tell me what happened? Can I get you a drink first?"

Link jumps up and goes to my mini fridge, grabbing a bottle of water.

Tori nods, croaking out, "Water, please." The fingerprints are starting to darken around her neck and I see red. Taking a deep breath, I don't want to scare her.

"Link's got it for you, *mi amor*. Take it." She turns her head, hissing slightly. Oh this fucker is so dead. I have to know what happened. It's killing me, but I also have to go at her pace, remind her she's safe without going all caveman. She opens the bottle and her lip twitches. I know that she finds a strange satisfaction in being the one to open a bottle, makes her feel safer that her drink hasn't been tampered with. I know that she knows that we wouldn't, but I have a feeling that she needs every comfort that she can get right now.

After taking a small sip, she winces.

"Is your neck hurting you, Tori?" I ask gently.

"A little," she says but her voice comes out very raspy. Motherfucker. She puts her head on my chest, and I gently rub her back, shooting the guys a look of fury. Link nods and takes the lead.

"Tori, can you tell us what happened when you went to the bathroom? You and Miguel had fun together, right? Our man took care of you?" My lip twitches at the fact that he called me his man.

Tori nods her head. "Yes, Miguel always takes care of me." I kiss her head, happy at the use of always. Damn straight I do, I just need to know that I protected her enough tonight. That I got there before...I stifled the shudder threatening to shake my body.

I clear my throat, telling myself that I need to keep going. "Okay, so you walked to the bathroom, and then what happened?"

"I cleaned up, because I was kind of a mess." She seems to have a touch of humor to her voice, and I smirk. Yes, my cum was proudly running down her legs, I think to myself.

"And that was fine, but when I got out I was in my head. I should know better, and be more aware of my surroundings..." she starts and Greg shakes his head.

Link and Greg had both sat down so that they wouldn't crowd her.

"No, Tori. I mean, yes, I'm gonna teach you to be more aware of your surroundings, and if you're comfortable with it, some self defense. But not one second of this was your fault, baby girl," Greg says.

Tears soundlessly trail down her face and she takes a deep breath. Too deep apparently, because she starts to cough.

"Motherfucker, I'll kill him with my bare hands," Link mutters just loudly enough for me to hear.

I catch his eye and nod, before shaking my head not a second later and staring meaningfully at Tori.

Link sighs, "Baby, your throat is gonna be a little sore. Try to take a sip once the coughing passes, and then continue telling us what happened when you can."

Tears are streaming from her eyes because her throat has to be hurting her right now. She nods and the coughing dissipates. She takes a small sip of water and shudders as she swallows.

"Feels...like...glass going down," she rasps.

"I wish we didn't have to ask, but it's killing me not to know. And this is unfair of me, I know it is and I'm sorry for being a dick. I just...I need to know," I whisper.

Nodding, she snuggles up to me. She doesn't say anything for a moment, but if she wants to touch me, then I hope that means that she forgives me for my selfishness in insisting she tell us.

"I walked out of the bathroom stall," she starts again, with her arms wrapped around herself. I put my arms around her again, and she holds onto me for reassurance. "Like I said, I was in my head and walking to the sink to wash my hands, and he started talking to me. He... was watching us in the hallway, Miguel, and he called me a whore."

I growl. I knew that it was possible for someone to see us, but for it to have been her ex makes me incredibly angry.

"What happened then, baby?" I ask as calmly as I can.

"That's when it all went to hell. He pushed me into the wall and choked me. My neck must be a mess. He threatened you all and Tesa...and he said that it wouldn't be the first time that he's taken someone away from me that I love," she sobs, and I wonder what she means.

How could he have taken people from her? She was so isolated already, did he intimidate people to stop talking to her?

"And then, he pulled my dress up," she cries.

The guys and I go rigid and she stiffens. I force myself to relax my body. No matter what, she's done nothing wrong.

"What did he do then? Did he hurt you?" I ask calmly.

"Yes but no? I don't know. He's so good at mind games. What matters is I did not give him permission to touch me the way he did. I need you to know-"

"Honey, Tori, baby, I know. We know. You're ours now. Not his."

She nods frantically, looking up at me. Her eyes are blown wide in fear and horror.

"You're safe now. You're with us." I tell her again.

"You'll hate me when you know," she sobs.

"Never." Greg growls. "Tell us, please, baby girl. Will you trust us?"

"Yes..." she whispers. "He was so close against me, so... excited to see me. He made comments about if I would be wet for him and I swear I-"

Fuck, he really got into her head. She's terrified, there's no way she'd want him, I muse.

"Small breaths, baby. I don't want you to hurt yourself again." I remind her.

She takes small sips of air in, and reaches out to grab her water on the desk. She takes a small drink, shaking her head.

"Just the facts..." she whispers so softly that I would have missed it if she wasn't on my lap.

"He..he shoved his fingers into me while saying how he now thought that he liked when I fought against him, and choked me so hard that my ears rung. I didn't want to pass out. I tried to scream and fight, but he pushed his fingers in deeper and it hurt. He had me pinned and I couldn't get away." She shudders and my eyes prick with tears again.

I glance at the guys. Greg is staring at her in horror, and Link has tears trailing down his cheeks as he sniffles.

"He... he told me that there would be consequences for telling anyone, and I can't be responsible for people getting hurt because of me. When he realized that his time was short, he pulled his fingers out of me and told me that I would be his again." She shudders once more. "He kissed me, but I didn't want him to. I can't believe that person is the same one that used to say that he loved me. I don't know if I can trust my judgment on anything for a while. Someone was banging on the door and I screamed through the kiss. Or, I tried to, but I didn't have the air to. Then he shoved me into the wall and my back kind of hurts, so I'm sure there is a bruise from that too."

The emotion has leached from her voice by now and she's staring at a point on the floor. "There's a big window on the far wall, and he unlatched it and jumped out. We were on the second floor...I hope it hurt. I heard your voice Miguel, and I opened the door. Everything gets really hazy from there..." she finishes.

"You passed out, probably from the adrenaline and the shock. I managed to catch you, and then pulled your dress down and came to the office. I was scared to death. I didn't know how badly he hurt you, clearly it was awful."

She seems to twitch slightly, shivering and my forehead furrows. That looks like...shock. I'm an idiot. "Greg, I have blankets in the closet. They're clean. Can you pull a few out for me?"

Link's eyebrow quirks but he doesn't ask. Fuck me.

"Sometimes I sleep on the couch...alone. If it's late, I don't want to drive home. So I stay here," I explain.

He nods. We all usually have off schedules and won't run into each other until dinner.

Greg brings me the blankets and we cover Tori.

"Wh-at-" she stammers. She's chattering and I'm sure she's unsure as to why.

"Shock, Tori. You're going into shock. That's why you're shivering and your teeth are chattering. Snuggle into me, you're safe and we've got you."

"How...why...how could you want to hold me after what happened?" she asks.

Link, Greg, and I freeze. What...the...fuck? What does she mean?

"Tori, none of this was your fault. You didn't ask for it, you didn't want it. Your ex-boyfriend decided to stalk you, watch you have sex, and then attacked you. Where is this your fault?" I ask her seriously, staring into her eyes.

I hold her tighter, rubbing her body to warm her. "We adore you, *mi amor*. This changes nothing for us, except that we have to protect you more. Please let us take care of you, okay?"

She shudders and starts to cry. "I'm sorry," she cries out, burrowing into my chest.

I can do nothing but hug her to me, eyes wide staring at the guys while I whisper that she's done nothing wrong.

Greg grabs his head and curses, shaking his head. The tears are getting to him too because he blinks hard. Our girl is so strong, but Anthony, the bag of dicks, tried to break her. I can only hope that we find him in a dark alley one day so we can show him what happens when he fucks with our girl.

Link wipes his eyes and stands up. "Gimme," he grunts, walking over to me.

I stand up with Tori in my arms and transfer her into his arms.

"Hey pretty girl, you're gonna be okay. You're gonna understand real soon that the three of us are wrapped around your pretty finger and there's nothing that you can do to change that. We lo-adore you." Link's eyes widen and he mouths, fuck...

I'm about where he is too and I shrug. I sit down and watch as he goes to the couch and cuddles her.

"You know, people who abuse the people that they're

supposed to love are the worst kinds of people," he murmurs softly, his voice thick with tears. Oh fuck, is he gonna...

My eyes cut to Greg and he is also looking at Link in shock. He sits on the edge of my desk and watches them. I look back over at Link and Tori. He never talks about Sheila, outside of when he cut himself open to write his book.

"It is hard to understand why those people will call you awful names and hurt you. It's never your fault. But, they like to make you think that it is. If you did or said something differently then they wouldn't have had to hurt you. Once, Sheila, my ex wife, backhanded me across the face, because I opened the door for someone. It made no sense. Why wouldn't I be polite? She was angry because that person was a woman, and she accused me of staring at her for too long. I only looked at her to make sure she was through the door before I went through. It starts innocently enough, until you believe that you're a shit human, and that you're not good enough. You want to be, so you do whatever you can to change what you feel is their opinion of you. It is never enough, pretty girl, and I don't want you to take on that burden. You're free of him, and you can't take the blame for his actions." He kisses her forehead and she sobs.

He hugs her tighter as tears continue to run down his face.

I feel wetness on my cheeks. There's so much that he never told me, and I hope that being with Tori helps him. Sheila systematically tried to break the man I love, and I've always hated her for it.

Do I love Link? Hell yeah I do. I think that I've loved him for years, but I couldn't show him the affection that I wanted to, until now. I stand up and walk over to the sofa, sitting down next to Link, I hug them both, laying my head on Link's shoulder. Greg follows soon after and he sits on the other side of us and joins the group hug. This feels strangely right, and the three of us cry for lost innocence together.

Slowly, Tori sniffles and sighs. Her body is much more relaxed, and she's no longer twitching or cold to the touch. We sit in silence, rubbing her back, a leg, her waist, to feel connected to her.

"Can we go home?" she whispers softly.

Link grunts. "Pretty girl, I really want to tell you yes. Are you sure that you don't want to call the police?"

Her head whips back and forth so quickly that she whimpers.

"Babe," Link groans. "Honey, okay. Fuck, your throat is gonna be tender for awhile."

She cries and I want to burn down the world for her in that moment to make it stop.

"We're going home." I tell the guys.

Link looks at me beseechingly and I shake my head. "No, she's getting whatever she wants right now. Do we have arnica cream at the house?"

"Yeah," Link grunts, kissing her forehead.

"I'm with Miguel," Greg says. "If she doesn't want to press charges, then she's better off at home. I need to check and see how bad the bruises are, and I would rather do that at home. Tori, you're staying with us, is that okay? I want to give you the option. I want you to feel safe."

His words echo from what he learned during their argument. He can't force his will on her, she needs to know that she has the option.

Tori sighs, "I love that you made sure to ask," she says softly.

I automatically feel like a dick that I didn't make sure she felt like she had a choice. I wince. I just want to have her with me.

"Of course, you have the choice, *mi amor*. I'm trying so hard not to beat my chest and be a dickhead caveman...but I need you with me if you'll let me. Let...us." I amend.

"Yes," Tori rasps. "I want to go home with you. But...can someone make sure that Tesa is okay? He...It just would make me feel better."

I nod and grab my phone from my pocket. It's one am, she should still be awake. I dial Tesa's number and listen to the rings. One...two....three...I almost hang up when she picks up.

"*Hello?!*" She answers both panicked yet sleepy. Shit, she went to sleep early.

"Hey, Tesa. It's Miguel. Tori is going to spend the night with us, but wanted to make sure that you're okay before we head home."

I wince, and wait to be busted. "Tori? Yeah, of course that's okay. Is she okay? Why didn't she call me?"

Thinking fast, I said. "Well, she left her phone in the car, and she was taking a break from dancing in my office to hydrate." Fuck if I'm not the worst liar on the planet.

Tesa chuckles. "Yeah, if you don't make her drink water, she'll forget the entire night. Okay, you can have my bestie tonight. Be sure to caffeinate her and feed her before you bring her home, please." I snort. Yeah, that would be cruel and unusual punishment to do anything else.

"You got it, sis. I'll bring her back later in the morning. Let her sleep in if she can."

Tesa yawns. "K, Miguel. Love you. Night."

"Love you, too. Sweet dreams."

Tesa grunts and hangs up. I chuckle. She definitely enjoys her sleep.

I look over at Tori who is looking at me with wide eyes. "We aren't going to be able to hide this from her, and you shouldn't. But, she's safe and was asleep when I called."

Tori releases a breath. "Okay, thank you. No, I know that I need to tell her. I'm just so tired all of a sudden."

"Us too, pretty girl. Do you want me to carry you to the car?" Link asks and kisses her forehead.

"I can walk," she says.

Hmm, I'm a little worried about her walking, but I also want to see if she's dizzy. I don't know if he hit her head or not.

Tori slips out of the blankets and Link holds her by the waist as she stands up. She seems pretty steady and I shove my phone in my pocket, offering her my arm.

She gives me a small smile and murmurs, "My hero."

I wish, *mi amor*. She is a treasure. I haven't known her very long, but she's helped to heal Link, and Greg is completely wrapped up in her. Somehow she's healing us all in ways that we didn't know we needed.

She threads her arm through mine and I feel better knowing that I'll be able to help her if she feels dizzy. We have one set of stairs to go down before we can head outside. The four of us walk out of the office and I lock the door behind us. We move down the hallway, out to the main club, and then down a flight of stairs. As we walk out of one the side doors, Bear sees us.

Tori recognizes him and offers him a small smile. "Hey, Bear," she rasps. She's been screaming and strangled...yeah her voice is a bit rough right now.

Bear double takes and his shoulders deflate. He must have just realized that she had come in with Tesa a couple of weeks back, the night she met me.

"Hey, you're Tesa's friend, right?" Bear says. Tori nods and true to his namesake, he growls. "Well now I'm even more mad that no one saw him, boss. We searched the outside of the club and inside, just in case he came back in. No dice. I'm sorry this douchebag hurt you, Tori. No one will allow him entrance if you can give me a photo."

Nodding, Tori reaches for her bag. It had been tossed on the floor and one of the bouncers had made sure to give it to me on our way out. She grabs her phone, and pulls up a photo of him. Greg, Link, and I memorized his face so that we can recognize him again. Tori sends the photo to Bear, and we head to the car. Tonight has been a shit show, and I just want to cuddle my girl.

twenty-five

TORI

My entire body hurts. My voice sounds like I smoked three packs of cigarettes and swallowing hurts.

Getting out of the car makes me whimper. The drive home was a blur. My back has to be black and blue from when Anthony slammed me into the wall. He's got fifty pounds of muscle on me. It's one of the reasons that I always did whatever I could to make sure that he never hit me. I knew that being knocked out and vulnerable with him wasn't a smart idea.

Greg had opened the door and growled when he heard me make a noise. "Baby girl, can I pick you up and carry you? I don't want to hurt you, and I need to see where you're injured when we get inside, okay?"

I nod because I'm suddenly exhausted.

I didn't hit my head, right? I don't remember but I shouldn't have a concussion. At least that's one thing to tick off of my long list of aches. Greg bites his lip and bends carefully over my frame. He doesn't even jostle me as he picks me up in a careful cradle. I put my head on his shoulder and sigh. This leads to a shudder because fuck my throat hurts. *Maybe I can work from home Monday.* I don't know if I can push through this, or if I want people to see me like this.

Greg starts walking with the guys flanking us, and my thoughts drift. I just want something to drink that won't hurt my throat, and a shower. I need to wash Anthony off my body. I shudder again in revulsion.

"Shhh. Honey, I'm sorry if I'm hurting you," Greg murmurs as he walks into the house.

One of the guys must have opened it, I think idly. *Wait, hurt?* No, Greg is far from hurting me.

"No," I rasp.

"Baby girl-"

Link growls. "Stop hushing her, Greg. Baby, what do you need?"

"Not hurting me," I whisper. "Thirsty, though."

I can't see him from where my head is lying on Greg's shoulder, and I'm not motivated enough to lift it right now. Everything feels so heavy and so much harder to do.

"Miguel, can you make Tori some chamomile tea please? Not too hot, though. And I need a cold pack for her neck while you're in there, babe."

My lip twitches hearing Link call Miguel *babe*, and I belatedly realize that at least my ability to feel humor is still there. I definitely feel broken in a way that I never did when Anthony and I dated, regardless of all the bullshit that he put me through.

Greg lays me carefully on the couch and grabs a blanket to wrap me up in for now. I'm not feeling as twitchy, but I know that he's still worried about me going into shock. Greg sits on the coffee table to look at me intently.

"Can you point to where you hurt, baby girl? I want to take

care of the bruising on your neck first... Hey, Link can you get the arnica cream from the second floor main bathroom, please?" He turns his neck to address him.

Link nods and takes off. I take a catalog of my injuries and point to my neck and back. Honestly there's a throbbing between my legs too, but I don't say anything about that. I just want to shower off Anthony and then sleep for a million years.

Greg stares at me intensely and I shift uncomfortably. I think he knows that I'm not telling him everything. He stands up and kisses my forehead.

He whispers in my ear, "It's okay if you don't want to tell me everything. I think I have a rice bag that I'll heat up for your back too. We have it for Tesa when she has her period and just wants us to feed her junk food and pamper her." He snorts in humor and then sobers. "Please let us take care of you, okay? We don't want to smother you, but we need to take care of you. Let us know if we get to be too much, yeah?"

"Yeah..." I whisper.

He grunts and goes to the kitchen. I can hear him rummaging through drawers. Miguel comes back out a second later with tea, and I know then that this can't be a coincidence. They really don't want to leave me alone.

"Okay, *mi cielo*. I have a warm tea and a cold compress for your neck. Are you thirsty?"

I nod and he hands the tea to me. I take a few sips, and sigh. It's soothing my throat. Then we switch the cup for a cold compress to help with the swelling. My neck has to be a mess, and I will be avoiding mirrors if possible. I give a small moan because the cold feels amazing on my throat.

Miguel startles and then smiles when he realizes it wasn't because I was in pain.

"Feel good?" he asks softly.

"Hmmm," I reply and he nods.

Link and Greg come back in and I shift up for the warm rice bag. I notice it's shaped like a pillow and it really does feel amazing. My body starts to relax and Greg's eyes pinch in before relaxing himself.

Grabbing the arnica cream, he carefully applies it on my neck, then checks me over, growling when he sees the fingerprints on my upper arms that are bruising now. I didn't even notice them, and it hadn't registered that he'd been holding my arms that tightly before slamming my back into the wall.

He professionally and carefully rubs the arnica cream into the bruises. I continue drinking my tea, and feel more relaxed. My head is still processing and overwhelmed, but the bruises don't hurt as much.

"Tori, can you take some Tylenol for me please?" My eyes fly up to Greg and I nod.

He shakes out two, and I open my mouth.

Greg rolls his eyes and mutters, "Just this once." And pops the pills into my mouth.

I swallow them with my drink.

I can barely keep my eyes open and Miguel takes the tea from me. "Tori, did you hit your head at all? I just need to know before I can let you go to sleep. I know you're tired."

"Uh-uh." I tell Miguel, and my eyes feel heavy.

"Okay baby girl, off to bed we go..." I hear Greg say and then he's very carefully picking me up.

He doesn't jostle me at all and my head settles on his shoulder once more. I vaguely hear a door open and then he's settling me on the bed.

I open my eyes again and give him a weak smile. The side table lamp is on and Greg's looking at me worriedly.

"Let's get your dress and shoes off, okay? I need to get

cream on your back and check out the bruising. You can sleep if you want through that," he says

"Okay," I murmur sleepily.

Greg gives me a small smile. "You're so fucking cute, pretty girl. Alright, foot please."

I lay back on my elbows, careful not to arch my back and put my heel in his hand. He sniggers and rolls his eyes.

"Such a brat, Tori."

He unzips my first boot and carefully pulls it off without yanking on my foot. Then the next shoe is unzipped and slipped off. Tears prick the corner of my eyes at the care that he takes with me. I'm so lucky to have the three of them.

Next, he slowly slides his hands up my legs and slowly pulls down my thigh highs. Again, he's really careful, and I would be super turned on under different circumstances. I remember that I'm not wearing underwear and I try to close my legs.

"Nuh-uh. Don't hide from me. I've seen every side of your perfect body. No reason to be shy now. I'm just helping you get undressed. It's just you and me, and I'm taking care of you." His voice has lowered to a growl and I shiver.

I'm so glad that I'm not broken because *that* definitely turned me on. I give a small shudder that has nothing to do with being cold and he smirks knowingly.

My boots and thigh highs are gone and he takes a step back. "Sit up, darlin'. Dress is next."

I listen and lift my arms. He pushes my dress up my body and I lift my hips so that he can continue to remove it. The dress moves up my stomach, skims my ribcage, my breasts, my neck, and then it's over my head. He pulls it the rest of the way off and tosses it over a chair. I should really unbraid my hair, but I don't have the energy to. I'll have a pretty plaited crown until tomorrow.

"Bra off, and then lay that gorgeous body face down for me," he orders.

So bossy. My lip twitches and then falls. I'm kind of worried about what my back will look like. I carefully remove my bra and toss it towards the end of the bed, then lay down on my stomach, with my head turned away from him.

Silence. There's not a gasp, no curse, and somehow that scares me even more.

"Greg?" I ask softly. My voice is still all fucked up and raspy.

"Yeah." He clears his throat. "I'm here, baby. I'm just gonna, ah, put this cream on. Relax into my fingers and close your eyes, beautiful."

Huh. *Am I still beautiful?* I take a deep breath, and slowly release it, happy that it doesn't lead to a coughing fit. I feel Greg's hands on my back as he's slowly massaging the cream into my skin.

"Less thinking, pretty girl," he murmurs and I roll my eyes.

Yes, sir, I think secretly. I don't think I'm ready to tease outside of my head right now.

Tears start to slide from my eyes and onto the pillow without a sound. I fucking hate this day so much. I'm suddenly very mad. I'm angry that this is my life, that I ever said yes to that first date with Anthony. He was so charming then...

I gasp out a sob and try to stifle it.

"None of that, sweet girl. If you're gonna cry, I'll hold you. Don't wait for me to walk out of the room because I thought you fell asleep." Greg slams the jar down on the table and I wince. "Up," he grunts.

I sit, and he picks me up carefully. He tosses the blankets aside, and I belatedly realize that I'm in his room. Why am I here?

He lays propped up on the pillows where I was and carefully situates me across his body. My legs are now tangled in his, with his arm around my waist, beneath the bruises, and my head is on his chest. He had shocked me out of crying and I now lie staring unseeingly at the wall.

Greg starts to gently pull out the pins from my hair and places them aside. I shift so my eyes look at him and he shakes his head. "It's gonna bother me, knowing that you have all of these in your hair. It'll make your head sore and you'll wake up with a headache. Just close your eyes and let me do my thing, baby girl."

"Hmm...k." Is all I can say as my eyelids start to droop.

It actually feels really good as he rubs my scalp and pulls the pins from my hair. My thoughts drift as he slowly unbraids it.

How did Anthony find me at the club? I knew he had little spies at work, but did someone tell him that they saw me? God, I can't believe that he saw me with Miguel...

"You're safe, Tori," Greg says softly. "Feel my arm around you, my fingers digging into your hair, playing in these gorgeous red waves. You are the most perfect woman that I have ever seen. You're sweet, kind, and sassy. You're Tori Motherfucking McAllister, and there's no one like you." His voice is low and soothing. I release a small sigh and he kisses my forehead. "That's my girl. I got you. I'll be here when you wake up, and then we will all face the day together. Until then, sleep. That's the best way for your body to heal."

My eyes feel heavy, and as I drift off, I hear, "I'll keep away the nightmares and I'll slaughter the boogeymen, sweet girl. I love you."

———

GREG

Fuck, I think as my fingers slide through Tori's wild, curly hair as she sleeps. Today has been a shit show. The marks on her neck, the bruises are dark purple and I can see the deep fingerprints on the thin column of her throat. Her voice was hoarse from screaming, and her back was one huge bruise. She said that he slammed her into the wall once, but she's so damn fair...

I was stunned when I saw her back. I knew I should have said something, but my voice was stolen. I wanted to scream, but my throat had a huge knot in it. I didn't want to scare her, I knew that she'd feel self conscious about it, and I didn't want to bring attention to it. So I said nothing and then rubbed in the lotion. I snort at the *Silence of the Lambs* reference and then worry that I disturbed her. Tori's breath is even and her body is relaxed.

I promised Tori that I wouldn't move, and that I'd be here in the morning, and I'll keep that promise.

My thoughts drift to texting the guys, who will be waiting for me to come back down. I blink hard. Holy fuck, I told this girl that I loved her. Did she hear me? Did I mean it?

I don't know, I haven't known her for long, but tonight made me realize that she was made for us. She fits, and yes, I do love her. I am angry that she was assaulted by her ex. I also know that she's hiding things from Link, Miguel, and I.

I don't know what this guy, Anthony, told her, but she was terrified. Her reaction when she asked Miguel to call Tesa to check on her said a lot. She was worried that he would try to go after Tesa. Just who is this little shit anyway? And why does he terrify her, outside of what happened today.

My phone dings. I had put it on the nightstand, so I reach out my arm to pick it up. Yep, the guys. It's our group chat.

Miguel: **You climbed into bed with our girl, didn't you?**

You're such an opportunistic fucker. You napped with her today too.

I grin. Getting more comfortable on the bed, I message back.

Greg: **Snooze you lose. She needed me more than you. Trust me, you wouldn't be able to handle what her back looks like, dude. It's all purple splotches from when she hit the wall.**

Link: **Fucker. Did anyone else get the sense that he said things that made her even more scared than she already was of him?**

Yep. As always, we are on the same wavelength.

Greg: **Y'all may as well come up, as long as you can keep your voices down. She's passed out sleeping.**

Silence reigns, and then I hear footsteps coming up the stairs and moving down the hall.

My door opens and the guys come in. Her back isn't facing the guys, and I'm happy for small mercies right now. I also fixed the blankets at the first shiver and covered her up.

Miguel's lip twitches as he looks at her, then grabs a chair to sit next to the bed. This bed is a queen and not as big as Link's. Link sits between Miguel's legs on the floor, as if he's been doing this for years.

Fuck if these two aren't adorable.

"Okay," Link starts. "Elephant that is in the room right now is that the douchebag did touch her against her will. He didn't rape her, but he did hurt her. I'm proud as fuck that she was strong enough to tell us but...I worry about what this will mean for her, too."

Link sighs and rests his head on Miguel's thigh.

"I think it'll take a little time, but she and I joked a little when I was undressing her to get her ready for bed..."

"Yeah? What do you mean?" Miguel growls, moving his

hand and playing with Link's hair as if he can't help himself. Fucking adorable.

"I mean, she had some heat in her eyes when I undressed her. And her, erm, she was...wet by the time I was done taking off her stocking things." I wave my hand up in the air because I can never remember what they're actually called. "She's still not wearing panties because someone is a caveman and kept them."

Miguel snorted proudly. "Soo...she's not wearing any now," I continue. Now Miguel is glaring at me. "Anyway, her legs were wide open on the bed after I took off her boots and stockings, and her gorgeous pussy was glistening. She almost looked shy and uncomfortable once she realized that she was wet. I think that we'll have to help her work through her feelings, because she's confused as fuck."

Link nods against Miguel's thigh. "That would make sense. Get ready for her to go through being pissed off and then sad," Link sighs. "It's how I felt for a long time. I'm so fucking angry that he shoved his dirty fucking fingers in our perfect girl like that." Link shakes his head angrily. "People who take what isn't freely given like that are the worst pieces of shit."

I sigh and we all agree. "There's other things that I worry about. Does anyone know if Tori can work virtually for a couple of days? Her throat is gonna look worse before it gets better. She's also going to be sore for a few days."

Miguel pales all of a sudden. "My sister is gonna kill me." I arch an eyebrow at him because I'm confused. "I didn't tell her that her best friend was strangled and is now laying here, bruised to hell, Greg." He stresses.

"When were you going to tell her? Besides, Tori didn't want you to. We'll deal with the fall out in the morning. It'll be fine. Promise." Even as I say that, I feel a little uneasy. Tesa may very well kick our asses.

Link sighs, "As for what you were asking before, Greg. I'm sure her bosses will let her work virtually for a couple of days. They'll want to know why, though. I get the feeling that they're super protective over our girl. I need to be available for questions for her, so she can ask me them while she's here. I don't want her alone if she's home working. Someone already got into their house one, and granted there are better security measures now, but I don't want to chance it. We can arrange our schedules so that one of us is working from home to be in the house with her."

Miguel and I grunt yes. There's no way that our girl will be alone for a while. She'll be lucky after she was accosted in the bathroom, if we let her go alone again.

I roll my eyes. Yeah, that'll go over about as well as a hole in the head, but I'm not taking any chances with her.

"Okay, let's all see about getting some sleep, guys. Unfortunately my bed isn't big enough..." I start.

"Mother trucking conniving asshole. You planned it like this," Miguel growls.

Link sighs and stands. "Come to bed with me," he says and reaches out for his hand.

Miguel snorts and says, "This is about the only other thing that will make it okay."

I cave and give them a triumphant grin. "Y'all are just the cutest. Keep all noises to a minimum please. My girl needs her rest and doesn't need to hear y'all fucking."

Link grins and shakes his head. "No, the first time any fucking between Miguel and I happens, I want Tori to be there."

Miguel throws his arm over Link's shoulders and kisses his cheek. "Yep, the first time I take his tight ass will be while he's fucking her tight pussy. You're welcome to be there so she can suck your cock, Greg." He winks and my jaw drops.

He's even more insufferable now, I think to myself. And then I get uncomfortably hard, shifting Tori a little so she's not laying across my cock.

Now, why am I thinking about this, but also wanting to be there for our first real foursome as the guys solidify their relationship too?

twenty-six

I breathe in the scent of sandalwood and vanilla that tells me that I'm lying with Link. I snuggle into his chest, and breathe him in. Link snores softly and I grin. I watch him and he looks so damn edible. We had both fallen asleep in our boxers and the blankets had been thrown off in the middle of the night. We both give off a lot of body heat, so we were warm enough snuggling together. Trailing my hand down his chest, I see that his boxers are tented. I lick my lips.

Taking my knuckle, I drag it firmly down his cock. His cock jerks up and he releases a small whimper from his pouty lips. My mouth waters, and I decide that I need to give my first blow job while Link is sleeping. I sit up and pull his cock out. It's already leaking pre cum, and the head is red. I lick up the bottom of his cock with the flat of my tongue like my favorite ice cream. I may have never done this before, but I know what I like.

Link gives a deep groan, throwing his arm over his face. Link sleeps hard, so he'll probably be asleep until he's cumming down my throat. *Fuck. Yes please.* I swirl my tongue around the tip of his cock, lapping at the pre cum.

He tastes sweet, yet salty and it's officially my favorite kind of dessert. *Fuck, baby, you taste delicious.* Well, let's see how well I excel at swallowing cock...

Link isn't as big as I am, but his head is thick. I grab him by his base and open wide, relaxing my jaw. I lick the tip again, and then take him into my mouth, sucking hard as I continue to let him slip down my throat.

"Uhhh," he whines, deep asleep as he tries to push his hips up. But he's not in charge today, I am.

I make sure to dribble spit down his length as I take him down my throat. I gag, and fuck if I don't have even more respect for Tori when she does this like the queen she is. Not to be bested by her, I fist the base of his cock, smearing my spit over his shaft. I pull up and twist my hand firmly around the base and work to get more of his length down. The more I slowly bob my head up and down, the more my throat relaxes.

You'd think Link would have woken up by now, but he's passed out, thinking he's in the throes of a sex dream.

"Gahhh," he moans. "Miguel," he grunts.

My eyes shoot to his face as I drag my tongue up the underside of his member. My fist follows around his cock as I come up off him to see if he's awake. Nope, his breathing is just a little more erratic, and I grin. I wipe a bit of drool off my chin and go back to the job at hand. If I wasn't so determined to get him back into my mouth, I'd have chuckled at myself. I'm a fucking riot.

I take my time, lazily jerking him off at the base of his cock before tasting him, licking him from bottom to top before sucking him down my throat. I bob and enjoy his noises.

"Miguel, what, oh god."

I grin as much as can with my lips around him and then sink further down, letting myself gag. Sleeping beauty woke up.

My eyes are tearing up but I continue to bob and look up at him as his back bows and his fingers sink into my hair.

"Fuckkkk, baby, I didn't know you could suck cock like this. Yeah, just like...ughhh."

Glad to know that I can make Link lose the ability to speak.

I decide to push a little more and am able to swallow Link all the way down. He's large enough that I can't take a full breath, and I can't wait to swallow his cum. He already tastes delicious. I need all of his salty sweetness.

Link is breathing hard and moaning. His feet are flat on the bed and he's struggling not to thrust. That just won't do.

I slide 'til I'm midway up his cock, lock eyes with him and then tap his hip and wink.

"Fuck, I can't even bring myself to ask you if you're sure when you have my cock in your mouth. I'm not gonna last much longer."

I shrug and he grabs my hair and starts fucking my mouth. All I can do is hold onto the bed sheets as he unleashes control. I need friction so I grind on the bed to come with him.

"Fuck yeah, Miguel," he grunts. "Make yourself come with me, baby. Uhh, god your mouth is so hot, your throat so fucking mine..."

His dirty talk does it for me. I was already super keyed up and I'm cumming in my boxers. I groan and I feel his cock swell.

"Fuck, I'm..."

He's coming in thick streams down my throat and I swallow it all up. He lets go of my hair and I pull my mouth off his cock with a pop, breathing hard. We are both sweaty messes. I wrap my arms around his waist and lay my head on his stomach, trying to get my breathing under control.

"Fuck, you were amazing, Miguel. Have you ever-"

I shake my head against his stomach and look up at him. "No, *carino*, only you."

He grins and pulls me up his body to kiss me hard. "Shower with me? And then we can check on our girl."

I grin, sitting up and hear banging on the door and the bell ringing like crazy. What the hell?

I grab my phone and check the camera at the door to see my sister is flicking me off with both hands. Motherfucker. I glance down at the mess in my boxers and then the phone helplessly. I don't want Tori to have to answer the door to the pissed off hellion that is my sister.

Link glances over my shoulder and winces. "I got it. Go clean up and don't leave me with her for too long, yeah?"

I nod with a sigh. I hear the door open next to mine and I hustle to the bathroom. This morning started off awesome, but it's about to get messy, and not the fun kind.

————

LINK

I DON'T BOTHER PUTTING on a shirt, only going so far as to tuck my dick back in my boxers to answer the door. I glance at the wall clock as I trudge down the stairs and roll my eyes. It's only eight am. Fuck my life, we barely slept.

I hear someone walking lightly behind me and I turn my head. Tori is there, yawning and rubbing her eyes. She's so cute and so sleepy still.

"Hey baby, I think your bestie is coming to break you out of our plans to lay about and have us worship at your feet," I joke.

Tori giggles. Her voice is still raspy and I can see the moment that something clicks for her. "Fuck, no one told her."

"I know," I sigh. "It was late and we figured we'd tell her in the morning and now..."

"It's the morning." She finishes, biting her lip and then darting around me in the hallway. My hands clench and if she wasn't as sore as I know she has to be, I would have lunged and grabbed her around the waist to stop her.

"Tori, baby let me get the door, it'll be better..."

She scoffs and walks faster. "Better? Really?"

I sigh. "Okay, we'll do it your way, baby."

"Like you had a choice, lover boy." She shoots back with a wink.

Good, at least she can joke. Our girl is bouncing back well, not that she should have had to with all the bullshit that keeps coming for her.

Tori blows out a breath and then winces. I make a note to talk her into seeing a doctor to make sure that she doesn't have any permanent damage.

She goes to unlock the door and I clear my throat. "Alarm is still armed, baby." I reach around her and put in the code. "Go ahead now."

She nods her thanks to me and unlocks the door.

"Why are you breaking down this door, Tesa?" she asks.

She's going for levity, but then Tesa sees the marks on her neck in the long tank top that she borrowed from Greg.

"What the fuck happened?!" She breathes. "I know they didn't do this, so talk."

"There's more," Tori whispers, tears clogging her throat.

I feel tears of my own again and tell myself to get it the fuck together.

I clear my throat roughly. "Pretty girl, why don't you come inside with Tesa and I'll get coffee started and some tea for your throat."

"Tea?" Tesa says disbelievingly.

"Yeah, her throat is pretty bruised up. I want her to have tea today and she can maybe go back to coffee when she doesn't sound like she's smoked a couple packs of cigarettes," I say and then turn towards the kitchen.

Tesa sighs and follows with Tori, closing the door behind her. "You went to the club. It was supposed to be safe! What the fuck happened?!" She repeats desperately.

I can sympathize, but I need to get some caffeine into my girl before she gets stabby.

"Tesa, caffeine first. We didn't sleep much last night," I sigh and start moving around the kitchen. I brew coffee, get water boiling for the tea, and then gesture to the table. "Sit. Tori, I'm grabbing you a pillow." I wince.

Her back is towards me, and I can see the bruises that are peeking over her tank top that hint at the tip of the iceberg. Tesa hasn't seen them yet.

"Pillow...Link you aren't usually this accommodating," Tesa yells after me as I hustle over to the living room for a pillow.

Walking back into the kitchen, Tori has started leaning against the counter forgetting about her back, and I wince for her right before it makes contact. She hisses. She's been trying to create space between herself and Tesa, since she's swinging between being snarky and annoyed that she's not in the loop.

"Tori? What, okay you're officially scaring me right now. What the fuck is going on?!" Tesa has tears in her eyes.

The kettle goes off and my body jerks. I put the pillow on the back of a chair and grunt, "Sit," before I go and make her tea. "Tesa, if you want coffee, make it yourself. How's that for accommodating?" I bite out.

Tesa is looking between us helplessly. Tori sighs, steps forward and turns around so her back is facing Tesa, pulling her hair off her back and over her shoulder.

Tesa gasps. "Oh, honey!" And then she growls, and I glance over, convinced that her brother is there instead. "Who the fuck did this to you?"

Tori turns to face her best friend and sighs. "So the guys and I went out together last night, and we had the best time. We just wanted to be together, the three of us out in the open, dancing and doing couple-like things."

She sniffs and I swear I want to kill someone. I busy my hands with her tea, and then take it to the table and mutter, "Fuck this. Ladies, let's take this to the couch, okay? Tori will probably be more comfortable there."

Tesa nods and gently takes Tori's hand, tugging her to her. "Come on and tell me in there." Tori trails after her, wiping away her tears.

Tesa looks on helplessly as Tori curls up in the corner of the sofa and I take pity on her.

I wrap her in a hug and murmur in her ear, "You can hug her if you're careful. Our girl is strong, just a little sore right now."

Tesa nods and Tori scoots over on the couch, patting the cushion next to her. Tesa moves towards her and I tighten my arms around her and say, "Don't squish her, okay? And make her drink her tea. She hates Earl Gray."

She snorts and gives a watery giggle. "Okay, go," I grunt and let go.

She lays next to her and puts her arms around her waist, squeezing her carefully. Nodding in approval, I pick up her tea and hand it to Tori. She makes a face and takes the mug and sips carefully. I chuckle and sit in the loveseat across from them.

"Spill, girl," Tesa says.

"Okay, so the guys and I went to the club and we were having fun. We joked and flirted, and did um," she coughs, "things."

Tesa giggles. "Dirty girl. I approve, while pretending that I haven't known them my whole life."

Tori snickers. "Okay, um so keep thinking that because it gets worse. So I was super turned on and the guys wouldn't stop teasing me." I can see where this is going and I cough.

Tesa looks at me and rolls her eyes. "Nope, this is bestie time. Deal or go."

Like fuck I'm leaving, so I nod and lean back, crossing my arms. I hear footsteps behind me as Greg and Miguel walk into the living room, freshly showered. I'm jealous, because I'm still in boxers and a T-shirt.

"Welcome to the day your little sister finds out that you defiled her best friend in your club, babes," I say to warn them and to be a dick.

"What? What the fuck...oh." Miguel sees the girls snuggling on the couch and sighs, rubbing his face. "That's just perfect. I need coffee for this shit." He promptly turns and Greg follows him sniggering.

"Yo, I made it so bring me some!" I yell after them.

"Yeah, yeah, *mi amor*. Keep your boxers on!" Miguel yells over his shoulder.

Tesa looks at me shrewdly. Oh shit. "Why are you just in your boxers, anyway? Were you sleeping with Tori and couldn't be bothered?"

Deciding to be equally evil, I nonchalantly grin. "No, your brother woke me up with my cock in his mouth this morning, Tesa."

Her jaw drops and she looks at Tori who smirks. "Good job, Miguel," Tori says.

"Stop teasing her, motherfucker!" Miguel roars from the kitchen and I lose it laughing.

"I'm sorry! Okay, I'm done baby, you happy?"

Miguel stomps back into the living room and glares at me.

He puts two mugs of coffee on the table next to him and rolls his eyes. "Not even close, *carino*." He grabs me by the back of my neck, leans over and kisses me hard. "Now I'm slightly happier," he grunts and drops down next to me.

"I'm never gonna get used to that," Tesa murmurs. I look over wide eyed, worried that we overly flaunted our relationship, and Tesa shakes her head. "I mean I kind of expected this to happen at some point. It's just surreal."

"Yes, yes we are all very happy for them." Greg comes in with his coffee and rolls his eyes. "Did you tell her yet, or is Link being a dick to deflect?"

I wince and shoot him the bird for both psychoanalyzing me and being right.

"Mm-hmm. Tesa's head may explode if you don't tell her," Greg says.

"Yeah, I don't know what to think and I want to kill them all for not telling me when Miguel called me."

Tori sighs and lays her head on Tesa's shoulder. "So we're at the club," she starts again, "and I'm all hot and bothered and Miguel suggested that we go into a hallway to have sex in one of the little alcoves."

"Uh-uh. I know of them..." Tesa says.

"Lalala. Blech." Miguel sticks his fingers in his ears and pretends to retch. I slap him over the head and roll my eyes. "Behave, naughty boy," I mutter. This earns me a little giggle from Tori and I smirk.

"So we went, and we had amazing sex. That's all I'm saying unless we change names for the protection of your brain," Tori says. "Then I walked to the bathroom just down the hall to clean up-"

"Mother-fucker." Tesa throws a pillow at Miguel's head. "If you give my bestie an STD I'll cut it off."

"We're all clean." Miguel rolls his eyes.

Tesa nods and goes back to snuggle Tori. They're adorable, I swear.

"But..." Tori says. "Anthony was in the bathroom when I came out and did all of this. He threatened me, you, and everyone I lov- uh cared about. My back is bruised, my voice box isn't happy, and it hurts to swallow still."

"Drink your tea and take a breath, Tori," Tesa says calmly and Tori nods.

Tesa sighs. "Did he do anything else?" she asks. Tori shudders and inhales too fast and starts coughing. "Fuck, I'm an asshole."

Tori painfully gets a hold of her coughing and starts to cry.

"He-" she clears her throat and then takes a much smaller sip of tea. "He pulled my dress up and I still wasn't wearing panties. He decided to call me a whore and show me how much of a whore I am by shoving his fingers inside of me to see if I was wet."

Greg, Miguel, and I physically flinch. We didn't protect her and those are scars that we're going to be carrying with us for a while.

Tori has tears running down her cheeks as does Tesa and they hug each other. I rub my hands down my face. I can't cry or I'll never stop and I have to be strong for Tori.

I clear my throat. "I want Tori to go to the doctor today or tomorrow to make sure that she doesn't have any injuries that we can't see. I also think that she should work from home for a few days. Do you think your bosses would allow for that?"

"Home? I mean, yes, but that asshole is still out there. I don't think Tori should be alone."

Greg nods his head. "I agree. One of us will make sure that they're with her this week so that she can work safely. Once she's healed, I also want to offer her self defense lessons. I don't know why I didn't think of it before, and it wouldn't have changed what happened last night but-" his voice breaks and he clears his throat. "I still think that going forward she should know how to defend herself."

Tori's voice is full of tears as she nods her head. "He's just so much bigger than me. I fought him, but-"

"No, baby girl. This wasn't your fault." Greg shakes his head. "It's no one's fault but his." Greg has a tell—his right eye twitches when he's lying—and it does it now. I know that he blames himself and us for not being able to keep her safe. "We have the rest of the day to ourselves. Let's relax, watch movies, eat ice cream," he bribes, "and enjoy each other for now."

Tori nods. "Yeah. I want to shower and get some comfortable clothes on, but otherwise I'm game. Oh, and I need to email Peter too to tell him I'll be working remotely." Tesa nods and squeezes her hand before standing. "I'm going to grab you a comfy hoodie and shorts that are loose. Any other requests?" she asks.

Tori nods. "I'm kind of hungry. I'm craving ramen from that place on fourth street that we like."

Tesa grins. "Oh my god, yesss. We'll send one of the guys out for it." She arches her eyebrow at us like it's a done deal. Fuck if she isn't right. We will do whatever we need to for Tori. We make a game plan and I head out for food. Thank goodness they're open earlier on Sundays. I also needed some space after that talk.

twenty-seven

TORI

I can't. I kept it together with Tesa and the guys, but my skin
is starting to feel too tight. When Tesa came back with
clothes and my toiletries, I scurried upstairs, went to Link's
bathroom, and locked myself in.

I take a deep breath, and then turn and face the mirror. It's
wild, but I hadn't seen myself yet. I gasp at the bruising on my
neck. I put down what's in my hands, and then slowly pull off
my shirt. There's purple bruises in the forms of a clear hand
print around my throat, just another way that he wishes that
he could collar me so I'll obey him. Fuck that though, I'm not
following his orders ever again.

I mutter, "Fuck you, Anthony." Feeling like if I open my
mouth again, I'll start to scream this, I start to feel short of
breath. Dammit, I thought I was doing so well. I pull off the
boxer shorts that I had also borrowed from Greg, and turn my
back towards the mirror. I know it hurts, I know that it has to
look awful, but I haven't seen it and I have to now.

I pull my hair to the side and glance over my shoulder at
the mirror. I wince because my back looks like it feels: one big

bruise. Anthony really threw me against the wall for this to look as awful as it does.

My breath shudders and my eyesight starts to darken. That's a big fat nope. Anthony has taken enough from me, I am not letting the guys or Tesa find me passed out on the floor. *You're still a badass bitch, Tori.* I think to myself as the tears come faster. *You're just a little broken right now.*

I sigh, the break in my breathing helping me slip out of the panic attack. My hands shake as I grab my shower toiletries and turn on the water. Thank god for the little ledges, because I feel really unsteady at the moment. I check the temperature, then step into the shower. I put my shampoo, conditioner, body wash and face wash on one of the ledges and then walk farther into the water. *Is it crying if there's water running down your face too?* I gasp a breath out, still able to feel his hands on me, his lips on mine, and his fingers inside of me. I shudder, biting my tongue to keep from crying out.

I walk to the ledge, grab my body wash and pour some onto my hand. If I could just flay the skin where he touched me, I would. I turn the water temperature up and watch the steam. I scrub my shoulders, arms, stomach, between my legs, and the rest of my body. I don't scrub my back as hard though because I'm on a mission to not pass out in the shower. Swaying on my feet, I grab the ledge. I open my eyes, realizing that I had closed them at one point, and then walk back into the water. I barely feel the heat as my teeth start to chatter.

My legs go out front under me and I land on my ass hard. I release a soundless sob, and then a silent scream. I'm gasping, crying, and my arms are around my legs as I hold tight. *Just a few more minutes to be broken, and then I won't think of it again,* I promise myself. I'm great at compartmentalizing, but the things that he said, what he said about my parents...

I can't dwell on if he could have taken my parents from me

as I break down. The medal my parents give me lays heavy between my breasts as I cry. I try to let the thought of them give me solace, and then I start to think about if maybe they hadn't meant to leave me alone so soon.

The water pounds around me as I let myself feel everything. Shame because I wasn't strong enough to get Anthony off of me, anger because he tried to take something from me that wasn't his. *My body*. Mine. He can't have it anymore.

My thoughts wander as I watch the water swirl down the drain, taking me down a darker place. My presence in the lives of the people that I care about, that I *love*, if I'm being honest with myself here. My presence in their lives is dangerous. Anthony will continue to come for me. I don't know how he always knows where I am.

I cry for everything that I've lost; the friendships that I lost because of him, and the lost opportunities that he made me turn down. I wanted to travel my senior year, and he told him that it would be too hard on our relationship. He told me that I couldn't be trusted to travel without him, because I was weak, and that that was to be expected of someone like me.

My values were weak, and I realize now that this was him calling me a whore without saying it. The name calling, calorie restrictions, and forced exercising didn't really start until we moved in together.

I missed so many red flags. I trusted him, I believed what he told me, and more importantly, I only had him. I was alone outside in the world, so I made him my world.

I gasp. Am I doing it again? Can I love? Do I even know how?

I cry in earnest, no longer caring if anyone is upstairs. The hot water is pounding all around me, and hopefully purging me of my past mistakes as well as my stupidity. There are so many words that go through my mind.

Those that Anthony called me, and the ones that my inse-curities go to town on. *Lonely, dumb, needy, unloveable, slut, whore, and why am I still here?*

My tears slow and shudder. It's time to woman up. I promised myself I could have this time to be a mess, but now it's time to pretend I have my shit together. I really lost it there, letting my thoughts go to dark places. I wipe my face, stand up and wash my face. Then I go to town and wash my hair, scrub-bing as I think.

Who would miss me if I was gone? Tesa would miss me. Hell, she threatened to kick the door in if the guys didn't open up. Miguel...he saved me. He would miss me...I think.

I'm washing my hair as I mutter to myself when the door is thrown open. I scream and then see that Link is standing there breathing hard. "What-" I start.

He tears off his shirt angrily and then pushes off his boxers. His cock pops hard against his abs and I lose my train of thought.

He walks into the water with me and curses. He fixes the temperature and then grabs my hair tightly, mashing his lips on mine. I grab him around the waist for balance and I am pulled forward, wondering what the hell is happening. The shower washes away the soap in my hair and I blink through the water running off my face.

He puts his head against mine, breathing heavily. He sounds like he's run a marathon.

"You, don't get to leave us, Tori McAllister. You don't fucking get to check out, listing all of the reasons why you're less than perfect."

My eyes widen and then I whisper, "Oh shit..."

"Yeah, oh shit. Did you know that you talk to yourself? I've been listening to you cry and talk to yourself, and I was going to let you until..." He gasps hard like I've hurt him and I realize that he's crying.

"Until?" I whisper.

"Until you started asking yourself who would miss you if you were gone. I would fucking miss you. You're the reason my heart beats again. You're the reason that Miguel and I are even a possibility. My heart stopped the day that I took a razor and slit my wrists, took a bottle of pills, and sent off a goodbye text to my best friends. I don't think that it really beat again until I met you." Pulling back my head, he kisses me again, but it's more of a punishment. He licks the seam of my lips and I stare at him from under my lashes, opening my lips to him.

He kisses me hard, his tongue slipping into my mouth. I moan and whimper, feeling a tightening between my legs. I'm reminded again that I am not broken, and right then I tell myself that I won't let myself be defined by my nightmare of a past life with Anthony.

"You like that, pretty girl? That one moment doesn't define you, honey. Your relationship with that asshole..." he kisses down my face and whispers in my ear, "...doesn't define you."

I shiver as he runs his hands through my hair to make sure it's rinsed out. Then he grabs my conditioner and tugs me out of the spray of the water.

"Spin," he grunts. It shouldn't be such a turn on that he's such a growly caveman, but my lip twitches because it is. I turn and he conditions my hair, kissing my neck as he goes. He plucks at my nipples and I whimper.

"You were a bad girl, and I shouldn't want to reward bad girls," he growls, pulling me back into the water gently, and massages my scalp as he washes out my hair, then kisses me sweetly. He looks me in the eyes and sighs.

"We all have dark moments, trust me, I know. But, you crashed into our lives and now we need you. You can't go anywhere that we can't follow you. Promise me that you won't hurt yourself...and that if you need to talk, you'll tell one of us, okay?"

He stares at me intensely and tears are building behind my eyes. "I...I just feel like I've brought my past with me. Anthony is trouble. He wants to burn my life to the ground so that I have no choice but to go back to him. He wants to turn me into the perfect, abused Stepford wife. And I'd rather-"

"Don't say that," Link growls. "It won't get to that point. We love you."

My eyes widen. I had almost said it when I was talking to them, but I thought it was too early to tell them that I loved them. Each growly man had taken a piece of my heart, but that was crazy, right? Link runs his nose up my neck and kisses it. The water is gentle and keeps us warm in the shower, instead of the punishing heat that I had been subjecting myself to earlier. It's peaceful and intimate, and feels like it means so much more.

"What do you need, right now? Don't overthink it," he demands.

"I need to feel, yet not feel. I want to get out of my head. Not feel his hands on or inside of me. Every time I think about it..." I gasp as the tears I had been keeping at bay start to slide down my cheeks again. "I want to not feel him anymore," I whisper.

Link gives me a wicked grin, puts his arm around me and lifts. I gasp and wrap my legs around his waist. His cock is hot and trapped between our bodies. I mewl and he chuckles. "Want to feel good, instead?" he whispers, then kisses me hard.

"Yes," I gasp. He thrusts against me and rubs me up and down against his cock. He walks to the wall with me and frowns. "I don't want to hurt you, so tell me if I am and we'll adjust. I want to be careful-"

"Don't be careful," I tell him. "I mean, do but don't. I don't make sense anymore," I sigh. Link chuckles. "I actually really love when you contradict yourself. It means your thoughts are moving so fast that you can't decide what you want or need. It just means that I'll have to figure it out. We'll figure it out together," he amends.

He lifts me and angles me so that I'm cradled in his arms, the tip of his cock is at my entrance and teasing. He kisses me, his cock thrusting through my folds, and I cry out. "I want to be the only one in your thoughts, so I'm gonna fuck him out of you, would you like that? Is that what you need, pretty girl?"

Fuck, yes that's exactly what I need. "Please," I beg mindlessly.

I'm unable to writhe like I want to because he's holding me tightly. He kisses down my neck, enjoying my flush of pleasure as it turns my nipples a deep pink.

"Fucking sexy," he grunts sucking hard on my stiff peak.

He gently lays my back on the tiles, then releases my legs from around his waist. It's only for a second though, because he hooks my legs over his forearms. With a filthy grin, Link leans forward again and bites down on my nipple. As I scream, he thrusts his hips hard, sliding so deeply that he hits my cervix. At this angle he feels so big and I gasp. Every nerve ending feels super sensitive. His thighs are slapping against my ass as he fucks me and all of my thoughts are consumed by Link, and how big his cock feels inside my pussy.

He swivels his hips just a little as he thrusts and my eyes roll into the back of my head. Holy fuck, this man is a god during sex. Link kisses down my neck and sucks on the outskirts of my bruises.

"God!" I cry out as I start to come.

Link pulls almost all the way out and thrusts hard until he's balls deep inside of me.

"Fuck, yes. Your orgasms are mine. My name is Link, though, baby. Let's try it again, and use it," he growls.

I gasp out a laugh. "You're such an asshole."

He grins, kissing me as he fucks me towards another orgasm. "Yeah baby, but I'm your asshole."

He reaches between us and rubs my nub, then lifts me just a little and drops me so I sheathe him at a new angle to the hilt. I gasp, feeling full. He has his hand on my ass as he bounces me up and down, kissing me, and hitting my G spot perfectly. I start to feel my toes tingle and I drop my head back.

"Link! Fuck me, that's perfect."

Link gives me a grin and I squeeze around his cock as his eyes roll.

"Fuck, you don't play fair, pretty girl. I like it."

He continues to pinch and rub my clit until I fall off the edge, screaming as I come. Link fucks me through my orgasm like the gentleman he is before painting the inside of my walls with his cum.

Breathing hard, I hug him to me as he drops my legs, trying to regulate my breath.

Link drags the flat of his tongue gently up my neck and kisses my ear. "I love you, pretty girl. Let's go pretend you weren't just screaming down the house and watch movies, yeah?"

I laugh breathlessly. "I love you too. Yeah, let's do that."

We rinse off quickly, and I feel lighter somehow, leaving my darkness behind from earlier.

twenty-eight

TORI

The rest of the weekend was spent watching movies. We watched comedies, Harry Potter, and no one commented when we watched Sleepless in Seattle and I cried. I swear they agreed to watch it, just so I'd have an excuse to let a few tears leak through.

It's now Monday morning, I have coffee on my table next to me in the guys' living room, and my laptop. I never went home from the weekend, because they knew that I would be working from home this week. All of my documents are stored on a company cloud server, and I can get remote access to it with a password. Shit happens, and sometimes we have to work from home. I am clearly the poster child for this.

Tom and Peter asked questions, but all I said was that I had had a run in with my ex that wouldn't allow me to come into work. They were legitimately worried and asked if I needed to move my video call back a few days. I love that they did, because I can't hide these bruises very well in anything less than a turtleneck.

Today, Miguel is spending the morning with me while Link and Greg are at work, and then Link is switching so that I can ask him any questions about his book. I am finishing the rest of his book today, clarifying things, and then helping him add anything that may need to be fleshed out. I also asked Miguel for tissues, and he nodded, then left to get some without batting an eye. He hasn't read it yet, but I'm sure he suspects it's hard to read, knowing that Link went through a lot of this.

Taking another sip of coffee, I finish my cup, then set it down, and curl up in my corner of the couch that I've taken over. I open my laptop and get to work. Emails are answered, I use my cell phone to return some calls as well. I had been able to redirect my number to show up as the office's number. My calls are also being directed to my cell until I am done for the day. I am ready to make this Monday my bitch.

I never made it to the doctor, mostly because I told them that I was feeling better. Instead, Greg had a doctor come to the house to check out my injuries that often made calls for his team. I am getting the feeling that Greg is some kind of super-hero, especially when the coffee shop owner said that he had helped her out of a bad situation. I kept this to myself though, just side-eyeing him when he brought in the doctor.

Thankfully, nothing is broken or damaged. I'm just going to be super sore for a bit. The doctor was very thorough. I declined a rape kit, but agreed to let him run an STI panel. I didn't think I had anything, but I had a suspicion that Anthony may have been cheating on me. The doctor then gave me pain medication in case the pain kept me from sleeping, and oddly enough an antibiotic.

I had started having to pee a lot more often on Sunday, and Tesa pulled me aside and mentioned that Anthony may have given me a UTI. I shuddered and almost gagged, agreeing to an antibiotic immediately. Blech.

I made a note to make sure I ate some yogurt as a snack so the antibiotic didn't affect my body and then went back to work. I let Link's True Crime story completely take over, editing as I went.

Sighing, I get comfortable in my chair. I know that he wrote it from a True Crime lens, but I can't help but read it and then think about what he went through.

Sheila was a piece of work. She degraded Link when they were alone, telling him that he didn't love her enough, and didn't spend enough time with her. Two years into their marriage, they had gone out to Miguel's club for drinks, and to hang out with Greg and Miguel and their friends. Link bumped into a woman and apologized, and Sheila lost her mind; accusing him of looking at other women.

She then slapped him so hard she cut his lip, before storming out of the club sobbing. Miguel and Greg watched it all happen with dropped jaws, asking what the hell had happened. Link said that it was his fault, that he deserved it, before running after her.

She also purposely didn't give him important messages that family and friends would leave with her over the phone or in passing. He was starting to think he was going crazy as he started missing meetings because the time had changed for family outings. He would swear he was never invited, and then apologize for missing it. Sheila would swear that she told him or left a sticky note on the coffee maker.

One night, she told him that his friends hated him because he loved her more, and his parents never bothered to give her a chance. She called him lazy, dumb, and good for nothing. He almost lost his job a few times because she had manipulated him so often. She then stabbed him with a pen knife.

Link sat bleeding on the living room floor and called Miguel, asking him why he couldn't be a better lover and friend? He asked Miguel why he was such a fuck up? Then started to apologize. Miguel didn't know what to think, and had pleaded with him to let him see him. Sheila had banned his friends from coming to the apartment, and it wasn't worth the trouble it caused.

Link wanted to see him, but it would lead to a black eye that he would have had trouble explaining away. He had actually taken up boxing as a hobby while he was married, to help with his anger, helplessness, and to hide the bruises. He would make sure someone caught him in the face at least once.

Link spiraled the next day, and found himself in the tub, with a bottle of vodka, pain medication, and a razor blade. He drank a quarter of the bottle, contemplating his shit show of a life, swallowed a bunch of pills, and then called Greg.

He had called Greg because if he heard Miguel's voice, he would have asked for him. He'd had feelings for Miguel for years, but it was too late to entertain them by then.

I'm sobbing as I'm reading, no longer editing. I vaguely hear the door open, but I'm too invested in the story.

"Hey. Tori? What's wrong?" Link is crouched at my side, gently brushing the tears from my cheeks.

"I'm fine..." I croak. My throat is dry and clogged with tears.

He glances at my screen and scrunches his face. "Fuck, that part of my life sucked and wasn't my finest moment."

I give him a weak smile. "I'm really fine, I just hate that you hurt so badly. I just need to finish this, and then I have questions for you."

Link nods and bites his lip.

"What do you need, honey?" I ask him.

"I need to hold you while you read. Could we do that?"

I nod and stand up with my laptop. He catches me around the waist and frowns when I sway. "What time is it?" I ask. I have a feeling I may have read through lunch if Link is home and he's switching with Miguel.

"It's two o'clock, pretty girl," he murmurs, frowning harder.

"Oh shit. Um, I think I forgot to eat lunch. I got sucked in. It happens to me a lot, so Tesa will usually knock on my door or call me to remind me to eat."

Link's phone beeps, and he keeps his arm wrapped around me while he digs it out. "It's Tesa," he sighs. "She says that she just realized that it's two and to remind you to eat. We are already fucking up this taking care of you thing."

I giggle and shrug. "I don't make a good adult. I'm super scatterbrained and I need a lot of supervision. Even my bosses will remind me before a meeting because they know I'll forget. Not on purpose, but because I easily lose track of time."

Link kisses my forehead and carefully pushes me back until the backs of my knees hit the couch and I sit. I arch my eyebrows and he shakes his head. "Lunch first. Miguel is about to walk out the door. I'm going to go yell at him."

I giggle. "Most people don't realize that their girlfriend has to be poked to eat," I tease him.

Link rolls his eyes. "I'm texting Tesa for a cheat sheet on the proper feeding and care of Tori McAllister. Be back soon. If *that*," he points at my computer that's back in my lap, "gets to be too much, take a break, okay?"

I nod and lift my legs onto the couch, resettling myself into my nest of pillows and blankets. Link shakes his head and chuckles, leaning forward to make sure I'm covered and kisses my forehead.

"I'm gonna come and fuck up your work nest a little later," he growls into my ear.

I sigh happily, because I know it's because he'll be snuggling with me. "I'm totally okay with that, babes."

He nods and strides away yelling, "Miguel! Dude, why are you not feeding our girl?!"

I hear a grunt a moment later and I look over my shoulder. "What the hell?" I yell.

Miguel calls out, "Link punched me for not feeding you, *carino*! I'm sorry I suck. I'll make Greg make you dinner tonight since I'll be working later. Text him what you want, yeah?"

I roll my eyes, muttering, "Neanderthals."

I grab my water bottle and take a small sip. I decide to take a break from editing to answer emails. I'm on a call when Link brings in an adult grilled cheese sandwich and salad. I grin at him and blow him a kiss, before returning to my call with Nicole Hawthorne. She has some questions about the edit that I sent her, and I'm going through them on my laptop.

I finish up with her, put aside my laptop, then grab my plate and Link comes back in with his own sandwich. We eat lunch together and chit chat.

"Miguel says you've been buried in work all morning," Link says.

I nod. "Mondays are always crazy. I'm catching up on everything sent over the weekend, prioritizing new manuscripts sent to me, and scheduling phone calls. I love it, but it usually means that I eat at my desk or forget completely."

I blink and bite my lip. "Hey, will you grab my birth control in my purse, please? I usually take it around one, and I want to make sure I don't forget." Link nods and goes to grab it. Tesa had brought me the things that I couldn't live without this morning. I sigh. *Did I take my birth control yesterday?* Yesterday had been such a whirlwind that I can't remember. Link brings me my pills and I check them. Ummm nope, definitely did not take it yesterday. I pop two of them out and take them. Maybe that'll help? Is that a thing?

Deciding it's a problem for another day, I go back to my lunch and finish.

"All good?" Link asks with a smile.

I nod. "Yeah, I just have to pee and then I can finish up your book."

Link rolls his eyes. "Do I need to ask if you've gotten up to use the bathroom today?"

I grin and stand up. "Nope," I say and then dash for the bathroom on this floor because my toes are tingling and I definitely have not peed since I woke up this morning.

"Brat!" He yells after me and I giggle.

Breathlessly, I slam into the bathroom and yank down my panties. I worked in a comfy off the shoulder cute shirt and no pants. Business up top is what it's about, right?

I sit on the toilet and sigh happily. My toes curl with how good it feels to pee. Maybe that's why I ended up with a UTI too. I roll my eyes. I'm the world's worst adult.

I finish up, wipe and fix my underwear, then I wash my hands and dry them. I open the door, and Link is leaning against the wall opposite the bathroom with his arms crossed.

"I swear, you need a babysitter, Tori."

I grin cheekily and shrug. I've always been hyper focused and tend to forget everything else when I'm working. Link pushes off the wall and grabs me around the waist, swinging me over his shoulder.

"Link!" I squeal. He swats my butt and I gasp, before rubbing my thighs together.

"Nuh-uh. None of that until you're done with your antibiotics," he chuckles at me.

Thank God it's only a seven day cycle. I may be able to survive...maybe.

Link carefully picks me up and swings me onto my feet. He kisses me hard. "So I have the Tesa approved list of things that you need."

God, I thought he was kidding. I roll my eyes so hard, I'm almost worried they'll stay that way.

"Hush, none of that. She also mentioned that you should have yogurt as a snack later because you're on antibiotics. I don't get why, but there's probably a complex girl reason for this, right?" he asks and I snort.

"Yes, antibiotics can throw off my body, and the probiotics in yogurt will help," I explain.

He nods and doesn't ask for further explanation. He sits in my work space on the couch and hooks his arm around my waist. Toeing off his shoes and socks, he lifts his legs onto the sofa. I then climb between them and get comfortable. He covers my legs up with my blankets, then hands me my computer. I go back to reading and he answers emails on his phone as he snakes his arm around my waist, to play with the patch of exposed skin between my shirt and underwear. I can't think of a better way to read this than a cocoon of blankets, with my head on his chest, and surrounded by Link's scent.

I pick up reading where I left off, starting at Link's call to Greg from the bathtub. Needless to say, it wasn't as easy as just saying goodbye. Miguel had been hanging out at Greg's apartment to watch the game, and not working at the club. When Link had realized that Miguel was there too, he started crying about how sorry he was that he couldn't do it anymore. The guys yelled at him, asking him what had happened. Link had started to feel woozy and dropped the phone. His head lolled to the side and he caught sight of the razor blades. In his drunken wisdom, to hasten his death, he decided to slice his wrists, but had passed out after using the blade on his right wrist.

He had always been adverse to seeing himself bleed. The guys had broken into his apartment and found him bleeding in the tub. They called an ambulance while pressing on his sliced wrist and yelling at him.

When Link had woken up, the guys were waiting at his

bedside. They ignored Sheila's calls and she didn't know where he was. She had come home to find a bottle of vodka on the floor of the bathroom, blood and water everywhere. She had thought the worst, and the guys weren't inclined to tell her differently.

The guys had questions, and Link told them everything that he could. The abuse, how bad it had gotten, and how Sheila said that she wouldn't let him go unless he died. When she had found the blood, vodka bottles, and half empty bottle of pills, she thought that he decided to leave her through death and freaked out. She wasn't completely wrong in her assumption.

Miguel growled in frustration after Link had told them everything, and suggested Link leave Sheila and to get a restraining order now that she didn't know where Link was. Link had agreed, but wanted to know if most of the legwork could be done while he was in the hospital. Link had been under a seventy-two hour observation after his suicide attempt, so the guys talked to Greg's contacts at the police department about how to get a restraining order against Sheila.

While a police officer had gone to see Link and taken his statement, Greg and Miguel broke into Sheila and Link's apartment, packed up his things during his stay and moved him into Greg's apartment.

Greg's contact then helped get the restraining order pushed through once Link was out of the hospital, since he could now prove he had a permanent address. Greg's connections had gone a long way towards making sure that everything went smoothly.

A month later, the guys had decided to live together, and that was when they decided to design Tesa and their houses.

I finish reading Link's story with tears running down my

cheeks and sniffling. Link simply presses tissues into my hand and kisses my head, happy to hold me as I read. I grab my notepad and start organizing my questions, things that need to be explained more, etc. I have personal questions for him too, so I write them down on a separate piece of paper, but I wont abuse my professional capacity as his editor with girlfriend questions.

I sigh and Link murmurs, "I can hear you thinking, pretty girl."

"Yeah, I'm sure you can. I am just organizing my questions for you so I can make sure that it reflects that in your writing." I yawn, suddenly exhausted by the rolling emotions that have been wrung from me as I read.

"Baby, hand me your questions, then come snuggle and close your eyes for a little." My jaw drops, and I lean my head back to look at him.

"But I'm working," I whine.

"You shouldn't even *be* working after this shit show of a weekend," he growls. "So I'll write out my answers while you sleep. Actually." He grins ruefully. "I'll type them out and email them to you because my handwriting leaves a lot to be desired."

I chuckle and feel my eyelids droop. "Okay," I murmur, turning a little and snuggling into his chest. "I'll have to make it up when I wake up though..."

Link chuckles, and I can feel the rumble through his chest. It makes me feel safe, and wrapped up in his love somehow. I smile sleepily. "You can have coffee now, so I'll make you some when you wake up." I nod and fall asleep quickly.

———

I OPEN my eyes and yawn. I hear light snoring behind me, which makes Link's chest rumble. I smile, happy to let Link sleep. Brushing against my phone in the blankets, I pick it up, and unlock it, to find that I have messages.

TESA: **Hey are you surviving with the alphaholes? Did they remember to feed my bestie?**

**   *Me*: Ha! Yes I ate, Mom.**

**   *Tesa*: Chickie, you didn't answer my question...don't make me come over there.**

**   *Me*: Link made me grilled cheese and a salad. Your brother kind of sorta forgot and I was knee deep in edits.**

**   *Tesa*: Shit. I'm coming over and making dinner. I also have a date tonight so I can't stay long. I need your help getting dressed though!**

MY JAW DROPS, and I check to make sure that Link hasn't woken up yet. A date? Well shit.

ME: **Holy shit! Yes I totally want to help. When do I get to meet him?**

**   *Tesa*: ...Ummm tomorrow night? We can do dinner at our house and you can do all the bff grilling.**

I BLINK, touching my neck. Maybe stage makeup? It's now purple and black: it looks like I should be in a horror film. I sigh.

**   *Me*: Tesa...I don't know. My neck is a spectacular black**

and purple today. I don't know if I should. I'll probably scare him.

Tesa sends me a photo of her begging and huge eyes. Fuck me. Way to make me feel like an asshole.

***Tesa*: He's a detective, babes. I promise it won't scare him. He works on lots of homicide cases. It'll be fine. Please?**

I bite my lip harder, then make myself stop, because that last thing I need is a bleeding lip. I really don't want to go, especially if he's a cop. Fuck, fuck, a duck...

***Me*: Okay, fine.**

I throw my phone like it offended me and sigh. "Tori, what's wrong? Are you okay?"

I force a smile and look over my shoulder at Link. I don't want to get into it with him, and I want Tesa to be able to go on a date without the guys getting growly. "Yeah, I'm good. Just an insistent author. I need to get back to work." I lie. I don't know why I lie, but I really just don't want to get into it.

Link frowns and then shrugs. "Okay, pretty girl. Do you want to go over my notes? I sent it to your email. I'll make you coffee."

I give him a real grin and sigh happily. "Have I told you that you're my favorite today? Cause you are, baby."

Link chuckles. "There's my girl." He dips his head and kisses me slowly, exploring my mouth with his tongue. "Mmm. Yum. I'll be right back."

I nod, and scoot forward so that he can get his long legs out to stand up. Scooting back I grab my laptop to continue my work. Taking a sip from my water bottle I bring up my email. As I dive back into them, I hear Link in the kitchen and the coffee machine starting up.

I remember that Greg was going to make dinner before I get too far, and fire off a text to him, letting him know that

Tesa is making dinner. Then I throw my phone back down and go back to working.

Link walks into the living room and puts my coffee on the table. "More client stuff?" he asks.

"Hmm? Oh! No. Tesa is coming over to make dinner tonight. Greg was going to make dinner I think, and I just messaged him to let him know." I grin. "Is that coffee for me?"

Link is still looking at me funny, and I have no idea why. He slowly nods. "Yes, of course it is."

He hands it to me and I do a small happy dance, drinking happily. I go back to my emails, going between screens and getting sucked into my work. Link walks out of the room, but I barely notice.

An hour passes before I'm done. Holy shit! Link wrote a book and it's all edited and pretty. I grin. "Link?" I yell, trying to see if he's around.

I get up and climb out of my nest of blankets. I walk through the house, then go up the stairs to his room. Biting my lip and then shaking my head to stop, I knock on the door.

"Yeah?" he calls out.

Ummm...okay?

"It's me! Can I come in?" The door opens quickly and Link shakes his head. "Of course you can come in, silly. You don't have to ask. I didn't even think about it when I closed the door. What's up?" he asks, grabbing my hand and pulling me into his arms.

I must be tired, because I feel like I'm getting mixed signals. Weird. Did I do something wrong? I wrap my arms around his waist and his body is relaxed. Deciding I'm reading too much into things, I tell him that his book is fully edited and ready to go.

"Do you want to do a final read through? See what I added?" I ask.

He tilts my head up and kisses me. "You're such a badass, Tori. Fuck yes I want to see what you did. Want a snack while I do that?"

My stomach growls and I laugh. "Yeah, I should eat some yogurt. Do you have granola?"

He nods. "Yep, let's get you set up. You can eat and finish what you need to for the day."

I practically skip out of the room and he follows, shaking his head as he laughs at me. Food just makes me happy!

Before I know it, Tesa is at the door, ringing the bell. I'm really excited to see her and hear all the things about her date. I run for the door, checking the peep hole like a good girl, and then open it with a grin.

"Bestie!" Tesa yells, hugging me with her arms full. I giggle and see Greg behind her, rolling his eyes. "Tacos and margs, chick?" she asks.

I sigh happily. "Yes, please!"

Greg snorts, stepping forwards to help with the bags. "Why did I just have some major deja vu happen?"

Tesa giggles, letting Greg help her with the bags. "Stop, we aren't that bad. It's a work night, so we promise to keep it to one. I have plans tonight, so I will be drinking while I cook."

Greg side eyes her as we walk into the house. "You driving?"

"Nope! Griffin is picking me up," she says, then walks quickly to the kitchen.

"Who the fuck is Griffin?!" Greg roars, taking off after her and I giggle my ass off, making sure that the door is locked before racing after them. Never a dull moment over here.

twenty-nine

LINK

Tesa and Tori are up in my room and I can hear them giggling from downstairs as they listen to music. They decided to use my room because apparently my bathroom had better light for makeup or some shit. They are welcome to hang out there, since I have nothing to hide or anything that I don't want them to see. I don't really like that Tesa is going on a date, but apparently it's illegal to keep her locked in her room so she never grows up. I snort because I sound like an overbearing father. I can't tell you the last time Tesa went on a date. Honestly, she doesn't really date. I'm interested to see who she gets in the car with later.

I rub my face, my skin feeling a little too tight. I just feel kind of unsettled. I've been trying to shake this feeling since waking up from my nap with Tori, and she deflected when I asked her if everything was okay. Tori is keeping something from me. Why would she be answering client emails on her phone when she had been working all day from her laptop? My logic makes sense to me, but I'm not comfortable calling her on it or straight up asking her. I can't prove it either, but she turned her phone away from me when I asked her about who she was writing to.

Now, I know that she doesn't need to tell me everything. I also know that not everything is about me, but shit. I hate not knowing things. I growl and Greg looks over at me and rolls his eyes.

"Why are you being such a growly asshole right now?"

I glare at him and sigh. "I think Tori is keeping shit from us." I drop my head back because I know he's going to yell at me.

"Don't be a controlling asshole," Greg hisses. "Don't fuck this up for us. You're better than this. She's not a liar, and she's allowed to keep things to herself. I'm sure there's a reason for whatever you're worried about that's way less nefarious than what you're working it up to be."

"Fuck off, now you're going to be the practical one?" I sigh.

"Yep. You hear that upstairs?" Greg asks. Tori squeals and giggles. "That's the sound of our girl having fun. She hasn't had a whole lot of that for a long goddamn time. Let her be twenty-four and carefree."

Twenty-four. Fuck, she's five years younger than us and I tend to forget. I'm a dick. The three of us don't deserve her, or at least I don't deserve her. It doesn't mean I won't fight to keep her though. She deserves to have her fun, and I'll try not to be so grumpy about it.

"Sometimes I forget how much younger she is than us," I say out loud. "She's tiny, adorable, and absolutely gorgeous. I love how innocent she is, and finding new experiences to do with her. So yeah, I don't want to fuck it up either. I just don't know how to do this whole relationship thing yet, and I'm figuring it out as I go. I think I need to make an appointment with my therapist. It's been a while, and there's been a lot of changes since."

Greg nods. "It couldn't hurt. I also think we should take her out on dates, treat her like the queen she is. All of us being able to hang out with her one on one is nice, but she's still working. I feel like we're more guarding her. And Miguel fucking forgot to *feed her*!" Greg rolls his eyes and throws his head back into the pillows. We've been hanging out in the living room to give the girls space to be, well, girls.

I snort. "Yeah...I may have punched him over that. Not one of my finer moments, but dude. She forgets to eat. Tesa says that she has to remind her, or pop in and drag her away from her work. I also made her send me a list on *'How to take care of Tori.'*"

Greg's eyes widen. "Fuck off, you didn't. Did she send it to you? Cause I need it."

I laugh, open my phone to the text and throw it at Greg.

Greg reads them out loud.

THE PROPER CARE *of My Bestie*

1- Coffee as soon as she opens her eyes. She can have coffee again, so don't mess this up, boys. She needs at least four sips or she's not coherent and hormonal.

2- She's working from home, so remind her to pee. She'll work until her toes tingle because she's that focused. Chickie already has a UTI, let's not make that worse.

3- No sex until she's off the antibiotics. Keep your peen away. Even your fancy peen, Greg. Yes, I heard.

I CHORTLE at this and Greg rolls his eyes.

"That's completely unfair," he growls.

I laugh harder, because he's the only one of us that she

hasn't had sex with yet. "Just keep reading," I wheeze, continuing to laugh. It really does get better.

4- MAKE *sure Tori has time to read smut. It'll give her really great ideas when she can have sex with y'all again.*

5- Make food available to her, but don't push. If you're too pushy, she will get anxious about it and then not eat. So don't be a douche-nugget about it. Her favorite comfort food is ice cream. If she's stressed, she likes to cook. Let her do what she wants.

6- Don't push about Anthony. I know you want to know. I do too. But it isn't our place. Be there if she needs you, don't let her spiral. She's one panic attack from losing her very artfully compartmentalized shit.

NO SHIT, pretty sure she already lost that the other night. Greg stares hard at me.

"Something happened, didn't it?" he asks.

"Yeah, but she's fine now," I sigh.

"Fucking motherfucking piece of shit ex." Yep, that about covers it.

7- SHE'S GOING *to have so much energy soon, that she's going to need to go for a run. It'll probably be tomorrow. Go with her, and don't try to keep her from it. If you let her bottle it up, she'll explode, and it'll just be all around bad.*

8- Don't fuck her up. She's adorable, but she's not an adult. Take care of her.

Xoxo,

Tesa

. . .

GREG LOOKS up at me and rolls his eyes. Tesa isn't subtle in the least. I'm just glad that Tesa is letting Tori stay with us. I am pretty sure it's only on a short-term basis, and she'll demand her bestie back at any time. At least while she's working from home, she'll stay here. Thank fuck, because I really love knowing she's in the house with us.

————

TORI

I SIT on the bathroom counter, watching Tesa get ready, laughing at her antics. "Okay, so I met Griffin through Greg. Greg and Griffin have worked together in some capacity, but they're both really tight lipped." I let a giggle slip out as I remember how I thought he had superhero characteristics. Tesa side eyes me as she releases a curl from her wand.

"Your brain just went to a weird place. Spill the tea, sis. I miss your weirdness."

I grin and tell her. "I sometimes think that Greg has super-hero powers, or is some kind of spy. He doesn't talk much about his security company, he helps people get out of bad situations while being really sketch about the details. Even the owner of the coffee shop just said that he helped her from a bad situation and that was it."

Tesa nods and smiles. "Exactly. He does remind me of a superhero or a spy. I know that he went into the military for a few years after they graduated from high school and then he came back and they never talked about it. He is really well trained, he taught me self defense and how to use a gun. So, he'll be a good option if you want to learn."

I nod. "Yeah. I want to. I don't want to get caught like that again. I was so unprepared for the force that is my ex." I shudder, shaking my head.

Tesa reaches out and squeezes my fingers. "We can't let that happen again. That's why I want you to meet Griffin."

"How long have y'all been dating?" I ask, genuinely interested.

"So we ran into each other when I was grocery shopping last week, and we got to talking. This led to a lot of late night calls, which led to a video sexting session with R.O.B. the night you went out with the guys."

I snort. "Already having a threesome, are we? I'm so proud." And then I realize what I said and cackle.

Tesa shakes her head. "Yes, I'm following in the footsteps of my bestie. Oh...okay maybe not really..." she wrinkles her nose and starts 'Lalalalalaing' and I can't breathe because I'm laughing so hard.

"Stop! Ohmigod...okay. Oh shit...so what else happened, and how were the orgasms?"

Tesa snorts. "That's the most important part! This man is fine, like all alabaster skin, and gorgeous eyes, and girthy cock. Like fucking yum. And the orgasms were amazing. R.O.B. never leads me astray, but it was so much better with him watching, as I watched him stroke himself." She shivers and I grin knowingly. I'm so happy that she's happy.

"Anyway," she says, going back to finish curling her hair. "So he called me the next morning and I told him that I had this weird feeling and that you hadn't called me yet. Nothing wrong per se, and you usually wouldn't, but I don't know. I had this awful feeling when I woke up. He told me to pay attention to my feelings, so I came over. We obviously spent all day together, and then he called me that night to see how I was, and I just fucking lost it. Seeing you like that," she sighs and puts down the wand because her hand starts to shake.

I hop off the counter and go over and hug her. She wraps her arms around me, taking a deep breath. "So, I completely unloaded on him. I told him about what happened, and how awful it was. I told him that Anthony is a douche canoe, and I can't believe he's not in jail too."

"Yeah, I know. When I talked to the police though, they told me that he had to hurt me before..." I shudder when it clicks. He *had* hurt me. "Oh, Tesa. I'm a fucking idiot."

"No," she shakes her head. "You're not. The guys didn't push it when you said that you didn't want to go to the police, and you're right. The police were really unhelpful when they came over after the photo album incident, which we now know he's responsible for because he sent someone to do it. Griffin said that he wanted to talk to you, maybe take photos of your neck, which is a spectacular array of purples and black fingerprints right now." Tesa winces and I sigh, putting my head on her shoulder.

"So you're saying I don't need to figure out how to cover up my bruises," I say with a small sigh. Tesa rests her head on mine. "Nope. Wear something comfortable that is off the shoulder. This way if he needs to see your back, it's easy. I really want to nail Anthony's balls to the wall. Since Griffin told me that's *illegal*," she snorts and I know that she's rolling her eyes right now, "then I have to settle with him going to jail. Maybe he'll even drop the soap when he goes to prison." We both giggle, but it's watery. We hug each other harder, and Tesa's arms are purposefully around my waist so that she won't hurt me. "So, tomorrow I'll have him come to the house for dinner, and you can ask him all the protective bestie questions. In turn, he's going to figure out how to keep you safe. I can't lose my best fucking friend."

We hold each other for another minute and I nod. "Okay, let's do it."

Tesa sighs in relief and finishes her hair. I take over to do her makeup, and then we spend the rest of the time giggling as we go through the clothes that she brought over. It's now the beginning of October in Georgetown, and it is starting to get cooler. It's funny, because I swear the weather can't make up its mind as the day melts into night. It'll be seventy-seven during the day and then fifty-five degrees by the time the sun starts to go down. Layers are the only way to survive during the fall months.

I pull out a pair of gray jeans, black heeled boots, and a heathered blue sweater with a deep v-neck. Tesa chuckles, shaking her head. "Listen, I'm going for sexy vixen, which I know you can pull off well. Strip and show me what your mama gave ya."

"Tori McAllister! I know you didn't just say that!" Oops. Miguel's home. I snort through my giggle, holding my hand over my mouth. "Oh my god!" I giggle.

"Hush, Miguel! My mama gave me a fine ass!" Tesa yells out the door, and then pushes it closed so we don't hear what he says. I sit on the edge of the bed as I laugh, shaking my head.

"It's good for him to get his blood pressure up every so often," Tesa says, winking. She pulls off her clothes and she's wearing a blue push up bra with blue cheeky panties. She gets dressed in the outfit, and then walks to the closet mirror, and whistles. "Damn. I knew I needed you. My boobs are on point." Her phone pings, and she grabs it. "He's two minutes out," she says as she packs up her things into her bag. "I will see you tomorrow, okay?" I smile, and walk her down. I love her, meddling ways and all.

thirty

Last night, we all slept in Link's bed. He was in a foul mood, and Tori kept drifting off in thought. Greg knowingly looked at Link and kept popping him in the back of his head and dragging him into wrestling fights. I don't know what's going on with them, but I know we are out of sorts after Saturday night.

I have a photo circulating of Anthony at the club, and my employees have been asked to detain him if they see him trying to get into the club. Bear begged to rough him a little and I gave him the green light.

It's fucked all of us up to see our gorgeous red headed pixie look so broken. Tori seems to have bounced back almost too quickly after Saturday night. But, after reading that absurd list that my sister also forwarded to me, I can't help but feel like Tori is pretending to be okay. Link also mentioned that Tori had a breakdown right after but was doing better now.

I am a nosy fucker, but I'm not pushing for answers because it's not my place. I'm grateful that she broke down in front of someone, so that they could help her. She's always so strong and she compartmentalizes so well that it can't be healthy to hold everything in. I'm well aware that I tend to wear my emotions on my sleeve, so most people know what I'm feeling and why.

I trail my hand down Link's chest to his waist with a grin. He catches my hand with a dark chuckle. It's still early in the morning, and I thought he was still asleep. Tricky fucker. Tori's snuggled against his shoulder and her hair is curled over her face. "None of that, Miguel, even though my morning wood has me begging for relief. I don't trust you not to hit Tori with my cum."

I snigger because he's right, and then she'd be super pissed. I'm sure getting cum out of your hair isn't fun. That's why girls tie their hair back when they give head, right?

Tori moans and I make a pained sound. We can't have sex until she's off her antibiotics and I'm trying my best to be good. And then she makes noises like that. "Guys, it's so early..."

Greg sits up running his hand through his hair. "I'm going to go for a run since it's obvious I won't be going back to bed."

Tori sits up too and I tense. *Do not tell her no*...I think to myself. "I'll go with you, Greg," she whispers as if the morning affects her ability to talk. I smirk and sit up. "I guess we are all coming with you this morning, Greg." Greg snorts knowingly, rolling his eyes. Link and I won't tell her not to go for a run, but we'll go with them to make sure that she doesn't push herself too hard.

Tori gets up and moves to the bag that Tesa brought her yesterday. There were running clothes that she packed, knowing that Tori would have some pent up energy to run off at some point this week. The bond that those two share is amazing, and I'm happy that they have each other. While Tori gets dressed, Greg and I go to our own rooms to get ready.

I pull on a long sleeved shirt and joggers because it's so

much colder in the mornings now that it's October. I brush my teeth and wash my face in freezing water because I went to bed late last night. I went over the books for the club in my office at home instead of staying at the club because I wanted to be close to Tori and the guys. I never really cared before, but there's been a lot of shit happening, and I felt more comfortable being around.

Scrubbing my face, I meet Tori and the guys downstairs. We make sure we have bottles of water, and fuck if Tori doesn't look adorable in her sweatshirt and joggers. She gets cold easily, so I'm not surprised.

Greg disarms the alarm and I unlock the door, walking out. Everyone else follows, with Greg taking up the rear as he rearms the alarm and locks the door. Even on the best of days, Greg doesn't mess around with security. Tori glances over at the house next door and I throw my arm over her shoulder, kissing her forehead. "Miss Tesa already, baby?"

Tori smiles, wrapping her arms around my waist. "Yes, but I was also seeing if anyone had stayed over...shit," she says. She looks up at me wide eyed and I roll my eyes.

"Yes, I'm aware of this so-called date. Yo, Greg, thanks for introducing them, by the way, you little shit," I call over my shoulder.

"Me...whoa. Who is she dating, anyway? She wouldn't tell me Griffin's last name."

I snort," Adams. Detective Adams...?"

"Oh shit," he breathes. "No fucking way! They pretty much avoided each other when they met, and Adams was kind of a dick. No way it's the same guy. We've worked together before, but he's not the easiest person to get along with."

I chuckle. "Apparently they found a way. *Gringa linda*, you're going to have dinner with them tonight, aren't you?"

Tori nods warily, unwinding her arms from my waist as she

watches me. We walk to the street and I roll my eyes. "I'm not upset, baby. My sister is going to date at some point, and I know that. I just want to make sure that she's not dating a douchebag. It was one thing when I wasn't dating either, but now I am, and it's not fair for me to lock her in a tower and scare off everyone from dating my baby sister."

Link groans. "I had this same thought yesterday, and then thought it was really fucked up that I wanted to," he laughs. I chuckle. And this is why Link and I have always clicked. We are absolute cavemen about the people we love.

"Okay, fuckers and lady, let's get our asses moving. Tori, I promise you coffee at the end of our run as long as you promise me not to overdo it, okay?"

Tori stares at him for a second, and I wonder what's going through her head. I know that she's had a love-hate relationship with running, but...

Tori smiles and then runs and jumps into Greg's arms, wrapping her legs around his waist. She kisses him hard, and I have to adjust myself because it's so darn hot. "Have I told you today that I love you?" she asks breathlessly. Greg's jaw drops. I know that he's been falling hard for her, but has been avoiding telling her that he loves her. I chuckle. He looks absolutely gobsmacked.

"No," he says hoarsely. "I think that's the first time you've told me that you love me. Do you mean it?" Tori nods and her ponytail bounces around with how hard she's nodding her head.

"Yup, I really do." Greg wraps his hand around her hair and kisses her hard. "Thank fuck, because I love you too. I thought it was too soon-" She cuts him off leaning forward to kiss him hard again. He releases her hair so that she can, dropping his hands to her ass to squeeze it firmly. She gasps, and I can see that if I don't stop this soon, they'll be fucking against the fence.

I clear my throat. "None of that love birds. Let's go for that run."

Greg and Tori laugh a little wildly and she jumps down from his arms. She pops in her air pods and we all start to stretch. Tori is stretching more carefully, and I can tell that her back is still hurting her. I decide to keep an eye on her while we run, and I glance at Greg. He's also watching her and I catch his eye. I raise my eyebrow, jerking my chin towards Tori. He nods and I know he's on the same page as me.

Done warming up, we head down the road. The roads curve as we run, but there's no one around. It's only five am, so everything is still going to be quiet for at least another hour.

We head out of the neighborhood, running towards Tori's promised coffee, and the stores are starting to open. We cross the street, pass the big park that Greg sometimes has us run because it has a huge lake, and I check on Tori. She is keeping pace, listening to music, and in a groove. I grin because even with her short legs, she's keeping up with us, and she's not breathing hard. I'm excited to see how she does with Greg during self defense lessons.

We run up the street to *The Java Spot*, finding that Grace is already open and has a line. Greg holds the door, and the four of us walk in.

Grace sees us as we enter and waves. We wait in line chatting and teasing. I grab Tori around the waist and she looks up at me with a smile. "How are you feeling, beautiful?" I ask, kissing what I can of her neck, since she's wearing a hoodie. It's covering most of her, and seems to be a little oversized. It's swallowing her tiny body.

"Mmm, I'm in a coffee shop where my ex's secretary is

banned for life. I'm fucking fantastic," she says with a giggle. I snort, shaking my head. This girl. I can't.

"Greg wants to teach you some self defense, and I think it's a good idea," I murmur as I drag my nose up her neck. She smells delicious, even after running as hard as she did. Fuck, and now I'm hard as a rock. *Damn gray sweatpants.*

"I think I'd be up for that," Tori says breathily and I chuckle. It seems I'm not the only one affected from snuggling together. Deciding to end our torture as it's our turn next, I kiss her forehead, and we move towards Grace who's on register. "Good morning, Grace-" I start, only to be startled by Grace's face. She's staring wide eyed at Tori with her jaw dropped.

"Who the fuck did that?" she gasps. I turn and see that Tori is uncomfortably pushing her sweatshirt back up. I had moved it just enough for Grace to see her neck under the cheerful cafe lights.

"It wasn't us-" I start, because she might cut us if she even thought that we had hurt a woman.

Grace glances over at me and shakes her head. "No, I know better than that. Tell me the fucker is six feet under at least, Greg," she says and turns towards him. Tori is looking at Greg with a startled expression, and Greg looks between them helplessly. Link and I know Grace's story, and her ex is six feet under thanks to Greg. I don't really want to have this conversation in a coffee shop, and Grace knows better.

I cough to get her attention. "Not yet, Grace. He attacked her in the bathroom of my club." Grace looks at me accusingly and now I feel like shit again. Yeah, I know that shouldn't have happened in my club of all places. "Her ex is an abusive dick, we are trying to work within the law to keep him away from her. But-"

"But, the law isn't always on our side," she says bitterly.

That's exactly what had happened to her, and why she had contracted Greg to kill her ex and make it look like an accident.

"No, no it isn't. I promise, she's never left alone anymore," I tell her.

Grace sighs. "Fuck." She shakes her head and blinks hard. I feel like shit now that I didn't check to make sure Tori's sweatshirt was fixed, and Tori is hiding with her hood pulled up. Tesa may just poison me yet with the herbs she keeps in her backyard.

"I didn't mean to freak out, Tori," she says. "I just hate when assholes take things that don't belong to them, and put their hands on others through force." Tori flinches and Grace sighs. "Motherfucker."

"I'm fine," Tori says softly. "I mean, I'm getting there anyway."

Grace stares at her and says, "I need a photo so that I can make sure he's not allowed to come around either. This town is small, and you deserve to have a place where you can come have lunch when you're at work and feel safe."

Tori nods and shows Grace a photo of Anthony. Grace forwards it to herself to show her employees so they know not to allow him service. She's well known for banning assholes from her cafe. It's also understood not to piss off Grace.

She takes our order, and then gives her number to Tori in case she ever wants to talk. We walk over to a table, and Tori sits huddled in her sweater, drinking her coffee. We had gotten her a pastry, but she looked a little green when we offered it to her, and refused to eat it. I look at the guys and Link shakes his head. I know better than to push food on her but I don't like that she's hiding.

I push the hood back off of Tori's head and her eyes flinch over to me. I can see that she's starting to breathe a little heavier. "Hey, you're good and you did nothing wrong, you know that right?" She shudders and tears escape from her eyes. Fuck me, I hate when she cries. I pick her up and put her on my lap. I don't give a fuck what anyone thinks.

"Hey, have I told you today how amazing you are, *mi cielo*?" I ask her. Her lip twitches and I know that she's starting to pull out of it. Ever since I found out that she speaks Spanish, I've purposely dropped new pet names into my sentences. I think she likes it. "We are absolutely going to figure out how to get rid of your ex. In the meantime, Greg is going to teach you how to be even more of a badass, so that you can get away from anyone that wants to hurt you, okay?" She is still crying but her breathing is evening out. "Now, I only counted two sips, anyone else?" I look at the guys and they smirk. Tori bursts out laughing and I know she's back. She takes another sip of her coffee and snuggles into me. For now at least, the crisis is averted.

———

TORI

THE COFFEE SHOP had thrown me. I didn't really know how to deal with people seeing my bruises because I have been intentionally hiding since Saturday night. I even wore a hoodie on my run with the guys so that it would cover all of them. Miguel's snuggling must have messed with my plan to keep them hidden.

It's now nine in the morning, and I'm back in my 'office', also known as the living room. Miguel is working in the office at the front of the house, and I'm currently returning phone calls. I have about nine calls to return from yesterday. One of them is to my bosses.

I dial them first, and they switch the call to video chat. I sigh, I wasn't expecting a video call. I have my hair in a messy bun, and I'm in a scoop neck blue romper that's comfortable. It unfortunately leaves a lot of skin on view.

I smile weakly, "Hi guys-"

"Don't you 'hi' me, please tell me that whoever did that to you is in jail." Tom is turning red, and I hate that I tend to bring this out in him.

"Well, I wish I could, but he jumped out a window and ran away, so I can't." I am getting tired of everyone thinking that the police are my solution. So far, they haven't been.

"How?!" Tom roars, and Peter rolls his eyes.

"Calm down, before she goes to HR and says her bosses are creating a hostile work environment." Peter winks at me and I giggle.

Tom looks slightly abashed and sighs. *"So he hasn't been found?"*

"Kind of. My last interaction with the police wasn't very helpful. Someone broke into my home, and left a knife embedded in a photo album on my bed. So, it's been a weird week. I didn't know that you'd want a video call, or I'd have worn something where you couldn't see it as much. I've rescheduled all of my author video calls for next week, and everyone's been fine with it. I told them I was sick and was working from home this week."

Tom nods. *"We just wanted to see how you were. We didn't want to make you uncomfortable. Take your time getting better. I saw the edit that you did for Mr. Anderson, and I was impressed, as usual. I also wanted to tell you that you're getting the promotion, effective on Monday. You'll be changing offices and getting a raise. We'll talk details when you're back. Hopefully on Monday, yes?"*

"Yes!" I exclaim. "My plan is to be back on Monday. Thank

you. I'm super excited for this promotion, and everything it'll entail!" I'm bouncing in excitement and my bosses laugh.

"*Okay, then. Back to work it is. I'm glad that we got to see you and that you're mostly in one piece. Don't overdo it, okay? Please listen to your body.*"

I nod and smile. "I definitely will. Thank you!"

We hang up and I squeal. "Yes!" I glance over the couch in embarrassment. I sometimes forget that I'm not the only one in the house. Miguel doesn't come around the corner to ask why I'm yelling and I relax. Time for the next call.

The morning flies by as I return all of my calls. Miguel remembers to feed me today when my stomach started talking. I probably shouldn't have refused to have breakfast this morning, but my stomach had cramped at the thought. I figure it's stress.

The chicken quesadilla that he made me was amazing, and my stomach has been happy ever since.

Miguel went to work and Greg came in, kissed me, and then went back to work in the office. I roll my eyes. I'm sure I would have been fine in the house by myself. Silly guys.

The day continues to fly by, and I have to check my purse for my notebook for a client, where I find my birth control pills. Huffing in annoyance, I thank my lucky stars that I at least remembered to take it at all. The antibiotics I remember because the guys hand it to me in the mornings, but I feel like it's weird to ask them to remind me to take my birth control pills.

Be an adult, Tori. I take the pill, and then grab my phone, setting an alarm to remember to take it from now on.

I go back to editing, and realize that it's almost five. Tesa wanted me over by eight, just in case either of us had to work late.

I grab my phone and send off a text to Tesa:

. . .

ME: **Hey bestie, are we still on track for tonight? I'm slammed, but I can be done by eight.**

    Tesa: **Hey best bitch. Yeah, I'll be here till at least seven. Griffin suggested Chinese food. You in?**

MMM. My stomach gurgles and I roll my eyes.

ME: **Yes! OMG that sounds amazing. My stomach approves.**

    Tesa: **Make sure you have a snack! It'll be a late dinner.**

I ROLL my eyes and another message comes in. It's a boomerang of her pointing to her eyes and then me. I snort, take a photo with my fingers arranged in the scouts honor, and promise to eat something.

I message each of the guys, letting them know that I'll be working late editing in the living room before going over to see Tesa. I need to do a load of laundry while I'm there, and grab extra clothes too.

Sighing, I move back to my computer when my phone pings. I grab it, and see that I've been added to a group chat.

LINK: **Hey pretty girl. I decided that we needed to be in a group chat.**

    Me: **Lol, okay. Hi!**

    Miguel: **Hey, baby. It's fine that you have to work late. Can you grab a snack while you're working please?**

. . .

MY LIP TWITCHES. They're always trying to get me to eat. I know I have an awful relationship with food because of Anthony, but I'm trying to be better about it.

ME: Yes, I'm hungry so I'll grab some yogurt and granola.
   Greg: Nope, I'll grab it, you stay and keep looking adorable working.

I THROW my head back and laugh as Greg comes into the room.

"I know, I'm hysterical," Greg says, leaning over to kiss me upside down.

"Yes, you really are." I think of something and can't believe I haven't said anything. I really do tend to keep things close to the vest. "Oh! Guess what?" I turn to face him with a smile.

"What, baby girl?" He indulges me with a chuckle.

"My bosses called me this morning to tell me I got the promotion! It starts Monday when I go back to work!"

Greg's face looks conflicted. He's smiling and frowning.

"Ummm. Why do you look constipated?" I ask with a nervous giggle.

"What?!" He sputters and I laugh harder.

"You do! You look like you wanna be happy, but you're also upset and I don't really know what to do with that."

He wrinkles his nose and sighs. "Okay. So if it was up to me, I'd wrap you up in bubble wrap and never let you out. But, that's apparently illegal or some shit-" I snort, unable to keep it in, because um, he's being ridiculous right now. "So, instead,

I want to teach you some self defense, have you carried pepper spray?"

I nod, because I'm okay with doing these things. "Yeah, that's fine." His shoulders had been getting higher with anxiety until I agreed. His shoulders drop, knowing now that I won't fight him on this. I'm not an idiot. I know that Anthony is a lot bigger than me, so I need to learn ways to get away from him. If I can learn some way to also kick his ass a little, that would just be the cherry on the sundae. Fuck, now I want ice cream. Shit.

"Why is your nose wrinkling, baby girl?" Greg asks.

"Um, because my brain is a weird and scary place, and now I need ice cream but I can't have ice cream. And I can't have ice cream because I have to be an adult and eat yogurt." I pout and he laughs.

"That was indeed scary, babes."

He heads out to get me my yogurt and granola, while I return to editing. It's already been a long day since we went for a run this morning, but I know Tesa will have coffee waiting for me later. I've missed her and I'm excited to chat and meet Griffin, even though I have a lot of anxiety about talking to him about Anthony.

thirty-one

TORI

I t's now seven thirty, and I'm going to be cutting it close to go over to see Tesa. I leave my phone on the coffee table, knowing that it won't be messed with and head to the stairs to shower in Link's room. I don't see Greg as I walk, so he's probably still working in the office. Link and Miguel aren't home yet either, so I guess everyone is working late tonight.

I slip into Link's room, pulling my shirt up and over my head. I put it by the duffle bag that I'll be taking with me to do laundry before dropping my bra and panties next to them. I've been enjoying living with the guys, but I'm looking forward to being around my things again. We just aren't ready to live together full time.

I don't have time to wash my hair, so I put it up in a bun and get into the shower. I shiver because I'm an idiot and don't want to wait for it to warm up. I feel hot and gross from working on the couch all day.

I make sure to wash thoroughly, but then that also makes me horny and I roll my eyes. Maybe the guys will be up for some fun when I get home. I know I'm not supposed to, but after a steady diet of sexy time, I'm not used to going without. I roll my eyes again at the idea that I need more sex and turn off the water now that I'm done. Grabbing a towel, I dry off, then drop it into the hamper.

I stand naked in front of the mirror and sigh. I know that Griffin will probably want to take photos of my neck, so I forgo makeup. I washed my face in the shower, so I finish up with toner, eye cream, and moisturizer. My skin already seems a little brighter.

I pull out my messy bun and reactivate my natural curls with some water and curl serum. Shrugging, I decide that's as good as it'll get and pull on ripped jeans, with a green off the shoulder sweater because it's chilly now that the sun has gone down.

I still feel cold, so I also pull on fluffy socks and combat boots. I'll take off the boots once I walk into my house, but for the moment they make me feel a little more badass. I'm nervous that I'll be talking about Anthony tonight, but I'm even more anxious that Griffin won't be able to help me.

Dropping to the floor, I repack my clothes into what I'm calling *the laundry duffle*. Ugh, I hate laundry. I stand up and pick up the bag, taking one last look at myself. The bruises are super dark today since it happened Saturday. Shit...what time is it?

Deciding that I need to just suck it up and head over, I run down the hall, then down the stairs like my ass is on fire. I glance at the wall clock and see that I somehow still have ten minutes. Relaxing, I walk into the living room where Greg is with my phone and a pinched look on his face.

"Hey...everything okay?" I ask. I'm not sure why he has my phone in his hand, but I have nothing to hide. Greg gives me a weak smile. "Yeah, your phone buzzed so I was going to bring it up to you. It looks like an unknown number though."

Shrugging, I stick it in my back pocket. I don't want to deal with it right now, especially if it's Anthony from another number.

"I'll look at it later. I don't want to be late. I really don't have anything to hide, so if something is bothering-"

"No, Tori." Greg's voice is gruff and I blink in surprise. He doesn't usually use that tone on me. The room swims and I gasp. Is this what anxiety feels like? Did I eat enough?

I must sway too because Greg is steadying me by holding onto my arms. "Hey, I'm fine. I promise. But, what was that about just now? Are you sure that you want to go see Tesa and Griffin tonight? I'm sure it'll keep."

I don't think it will though. I close my eyes, hoping that my ears ringing, and the room spinning will stop. "I'll be good...in a second I think." My voice sounds nowhere near as confident as I was hoping and I curse my body for being so weird lately. Could I be allergic to the antibiotic? Is that a thing?

"Could I have some water, maybe?" I ask. "Maybe I didn't drink enough." I open my eyes, blinking because they're starting to water. I hate feeling this helpless. Greg grabs my bottle that I still have on the table and shakes it to make sure there is still water. He flicks open the straw and slips it between my lips. I take three deep sips of the cool water and then wait for the room to stop spinning.

"I'm fine now, thank you," I say gratefully. Greg frowns. "Baby girl, I don't like that you're having these spells. Have they been happening a lot?" Well, at least he's back to calling me cute pet names...

I shake my head. "No, not often. I'll take it easy and I'll have Tesa to make sure I don't overdo it too. I promise, I'll be fine."

Greg nods and wraps his arms around me, kissing my fore-head. Wow, his mood swings are a little crazy. One second he was upset, and now he's kissing me. I don't really know what to think. Maybe work is busy?

He pulls back, grabbing my bag and putting his arm around my waist to steady me as we start to walk. I decide to dig a little to see if he's just stressed.

"So, work was busy for you today?" I ask innocently.

"Hmm? Yeah, I was tracking leads for clients, making sure my employees are checking in, and taking client calls all day. We are starting to expand, so it means I'm a little busier." He shrugs. "You seemed pretty busy too?"

This conversation feels a little stilted, so I give him a bright smile.

"I had edits, calls, and returned emails. I also made sure to reschedule my video calls for when I'm back in the office. I told my authors that I was home sick but still working, and they were totally fine with it. While it's getting cooler, a turtleneck will still get noticed," I say, pointing at my neck.

Greg glowers at the marks. "I guess you're right. I didn't realize how much you interact with your clients as an editor. I'm realizing we still don't know much about each other, and I still want my date. Maybe we can go out on Saturday? I have a couple of things in mind, we can decide together, or I can surprise you."

I grin, bouncing as I walk. I used to hate surprises with Anthony, because they were usually awful. Maybe this'll be fun? I'm willing to try.

"Yes! A surprise could be fun!" I say excitedly.

Greg chuckles as he opens the door for me, arming the alarm and locking the door with a quick tap on his phone.

"You're absolutely adorable," he chuckles, then shoves his phone back into his pocket and wraps his arm around my waist again. I want to joke that I can walk, but I kind of like that he's holding me close.

We head over to the house and I break away from Greg to run up the stairs. Tesa opens the door, and I know she watched me walk up. Laughing, we hug and talk a mile a minute.

"Good luck tonight getting a word in edgewise, Griffin," Greg chuckles. "They're used to being together more than apart, so these last few days haven't been easy."

Tesa turns towards Griffin with a grin. "Griffin, meet the bestie! Tori, meet Griffin."

"Her boyfriend," Griffin adds. Tesa blushes and my eyes widen. I don't think I've ever seen her blush.

"Hmmph." Greg grunts.

Griffin shrugs, "It kind of just happened, man. You can't keep her locked away. Besides, wouldn't you rather she date someone that you know is a good guy?"

Tesa waits for an answer, biting her lip. *Don't be a dick, Greg...please.*

Greg sighs. "Yeah, you're right I would. The guys and I are watching. You know we're next door."

I breathed a sigh of relief. Okay, only half a dick! I'll take it.

Tesa rolls her eyes at Greg. "Okay, you dropped off my girl, thank you. I'll text you when I'm ready to give her back."

Griffin sighs. "Is it really bad enough that she can't walk two feet next door?"

Tesa grabs my hand, pulling me inside. "If only you knew, Griffin. It's so much worse."

Griffin waves at Greg, hurrying inside before Tesa locks him out. As much as she's excited for me to meet him, she also doesn't like anyone discounting my safety. So, tonight could go either way for the future of their relationships and I think he just realized that.

———

I SIT BACK from my dinner with a happy sigh. Tesa wanted me to eat first because my stomach was grumbling. I also think that the guys have told her that I haven't been eating as much and she's worried that I won't have an appetite once I start.

I really enjoyed having dinner with Tesa and Griffin, as they recounted how they connected. He remembered meeting her a few years ago at a bar with Greg, but he was clearly told by Greg that Tesa was untouchable. In an effort to not show how attracted he was to her, he had blown her off and mostly ignored her.

They reconnected when they ran into each other at the store last week, and flirted and talked. Griffin had asked for her number, and they've been texting and talking to each other all week before their date.

Watching them interact, I can say that they're cute together. He doesn't stifle Tesa's over the top comments and I've caught her staring at him when he says something. He has floppy brown hair that he pushes out of his green eyes often. He wore a green dress shirt with the sleeves rolled up and I can see a tattoo peeking out on his forearm. Until I get evidence otherwise, I'll tell the guys that I approve of him for now.

It had been dark outside when Greg walked me over, despite the porch light being on, so I don't think that Griffin was able to see my neck. It was much brighter in the foyer, but I was walking ahead of him with Tesa dragging me behind her to get me fed and settled. This means that Griffin didn't see my neck clearly until I pushed my hair off my shoulder after dinner.

I have been having fun and I'm comfortable in this space that I also consider mine now, so I didn't think about it. I hear a sharp intake of breath and look to find Griffin staring at my neck. He snaps out of it when Tesa noisily clears her throat, and his eyes leap to my face.

"We're definitely talking about that, right?" he asks.

I shrug, feeling like a brat. "I thought I was safe enough to walk next door," I deadpan, tilting my head at him. The only way I could be more of a brat would be to bat my eyelashes, but I don't feel like being shanked by my bestie today.

Tesa snorts. "Down girl."

Griffin's jaw drops as he looks from Tesa to me and shakes his head. "I'm an ass. I'm the one who told Tesa that you should talk to me, and then I treated you like every other cop who has ever victim blamed a domestic abuse survivor." He sighs. "Okay...let's try this again? I would really like to hear your story. I think that any man who puts their hands on a woman or takes something that is not freely given is detestable and the worst kind of person."

I flinch at the last part, feeling like I'm reliving this morning. He slowly blinks at me and takes a deep breath. Anthony has definitely taken a lot from me over the years, more than I even completely knew if I'm to believe what he said in the bathroom about my parents. I play with my necklace trying to find a way out of the anxiety that I now feel.

"What do you need to be comfortable as we talk?" he asks, switching gears.

"Ice cream?" Tesa asks, because really that's all I need in life.

I turn towards her. "Yup, you have my favorite?" I ask.

She snorts, "Is Greg an asshole?"

I cackle and roll my eyes. Touché. "I mean, he's gotten better, for the most part." I defend.

"Hmm. That's because you're sleeping with him." She teases.

I stand, shrugging as I head to the laundry room to switch out my clothes. "Not yet," I yell over my shoulder with a chuckle.

"What?! Seriously?!" Tesa screeches. "I need a date without boys, Tori!"

I laugh. "You'll have to fight the guys for it!" I yell over my shoulder as I start pulling out clothes to put into the dryer. I can hear Griffin and Tesa chatting from where I am and I smile. They are really cute together. Once done, I remind myself to run up to my room to grab other clothes. Sighing, I turn and head back to the living room.

"Hey bestie, here you go!" She offers me my ice cream bowl with a smile.

"Yay, yes please!" I sit next to her, sliding my legs under me. I guess I tend to make myself as small as possible when I'm about to have an uncomfortable conversation.

"Okay, Tori, are you okay with me recording our conversation? This is just for me, and if I need a more formal interview, I'll let you know. I want to be able to focus on you, without taking notes." I nod that it's fine.

"Perfect." He turns on the device and leans forward. "Can you tell me about how you met Anthony? Just tell me about your relationship and what led up to the marks on your neck."

I eat some ice cream as I think about how Anthony and I had met and start to tell Griffin and Tesa my story:

IT WAS *the beginning of my second semester of sophomore year, and I was sitting under an oak tree on a blanket. I had a habit of staying outside as long as possible to study until the cold sent me indoors. A shadow fell over me as I was reading and I looked up. I couldn't see his face from where I was sitting because he was so tall. He crouched down next to me with a smile and perfectly straight teeth.*

He wasn't someone that would normally talk to me, I remember thinking. He had perfectly styled wavy dirty blond hair, and I wondered if I saw it in the sun if it would have any highlights. He had this ethereal beauty to his face, and gorgeous gray eyes that I saw when he pushed his sunglasses up onto his head to look at me. His shirt sleeves were pushed up and I remember thinking how muscular they were.

"I don't think I've seen you around. I was walking by, and I had to come say hello," this really gorgeous man says to me. I give a shy smile, closing my book.

"I picked a new place to study today, so maybe that's why? I'm Tori McAllister. Well, it's Victoria, but I don't go by Victoria." I smile as I give the introduction that I always give when I meet someone new.

"I'm Anthony St. James. I think Victoria is a gorgeous name. It's a shame that you don't go by it." Little did I know that he'd use this excuse to call me Victoria instead of Tori, no matter how much I stressed that I disliked it.

We had exchanged numbers when Anthony asked if he could take me to lunch or coffee. I was surprised that he had any interest, so I agreed. This led to two weeks of going on dates, studying together, meeting his friends before he asked if we could be exclusive. He told me that he couldn't imagine seeing anyone else and hoped I felt the same. I did, but I kept waiting for him to get tired of me. I was kind of nerdy, an English major, and had a small group of friends.

If anything, he was more into me, and things progressed quickly. I was a virgin, and he was really excited about this. He said that this instantly made me more attractive to him, and he was already a little obsessed.

I enjoyed being with him, but he'd make comments when we were on the phone that bothered me. It was finals, and I hadn't eaten very much all day. I'd ordered a meatball sub because it sounded good and was about to eat it when he called. We talked and I told him I was about to eat and asked if I could call him later.

He told me that was fine, but that he was worried that I would gain weight with these late hours and bad eating habits. He reminded me that the 'freshman fifteen' didn't only happen freshman year, and that he was just looking out for me.

I looked down at my food and my stomach had immediately soured. I wasn't hungry any more, and I offered my sub to my roommate, who had taken the free food without asking questions.

Pretty soon I was hanging out mostly with Anthony's friends, spending more and more time with him, occasionally running in the mornings with him. In the spring he mentioned that he wanted to take me to the beach, so to make sure I was beach ready. I was curvy, and I didn't know how I could change that or if I even should.

My parents came to see me twice a month and lived two hours away from the university. They started seeing the changes and were worried. Anthony also met them about a month into the relationship, and they instantly disliked him. I went home for a few weeks over the summer to see them because I was also taking summer classes. My mom mentioned that she was worried about how much time I was spending with Anthony, and that it was important to meet more people. She was worried that I was limiting my college experiences and she wasn't wrong.

I had studied abroad my freshman year, and my mom suggested that I look into doing it again. She offered to pay for it, and my dad agreed. I should take some time, see if the relationship survived if I was away from him as well.

I made the mistake of telling Anthony the first week of school, and he had been livid. I ended up having a fight with my parents, and then they died a week later on their way to visit me. I was truly alone after they passed and I became even closer to Anthony.

Junior and senior year continued the same way, but he found a way to drive away all guys that wanted to be friends with me, monopolizing all of my time outside of classes. He quickly became more and more jealous.

What I wore, what I ate, and who I talked to constantly became a fight that made me continually change who I was to appease him.

I SIGH, dashing away some of the tears that started to fall. My ice cream was gone, but even if it wasn't, I didn't have an appetite anymore.

I look over at Tesa, and she's also discreetly wiping her cheeks. She meets my eyes and shrugs. I hug her with a sigh.

"Anyway, I ignored a lot of the red flags that I may have noticed if I hadn't been wrapped up in my grief after my parents died," I tell Griffin. "Then, after we graduated, I moved in with him and things got so much worse."

I sigh again and catch them up on the year that I lived with Anthony. I tell Griffin about the cameras that were installed in our apartment that I found. How he and his co-workers would always appear if I went out to lunch with my coworkers, and how he continued to shame me about food.

By the time I tell Griffin about the club, I can tell that he's unable to keep that perfect, calm professional demeanor that he's done so well with. He shakes his head as I finish, turning off the recording hurriedly before cursing.

"I think Tori deserves a drink after that, love," Griffin mutters, shaking his head.

Tesa shrugs, "Margarita or wine, babes?"

I give a small smile. "Definitely a margarita. On the rocks is fine, Tesa." She gets up with a nod, leaving the room to get us drinks.

"Have you told the police about what happened in the club by chance?" Griffin asks, leaning back on the couch.

"No. I haven't. I just, I didn't want to rehash it for them to tell me that they couldn't help me again. Anthony scares the shit out of me, and I really do think that he was going to rape me if Miguel hadn't threatened to break down the door. Anthony is so angry, and it's made me rethink so much that I thought was an accident."

"You mean the car accident your parents were in?" Griffin asks. I sigh with a shiver and nod.

"He pretty much told me that he killed my parents, and I know I can't prove that. It makes me so fucking angry. He knew how much they meant to me, and it's my fault because he thought he'd lose me so he removed them from my life."

"It is not your fault, Tori." Tesa caught the tail end of our conversation as she brings us drinks.

"Wouldn't they still be alive if I hadn't said anything or if I had been smart enough to see the red flags before they became this toxic?" I wipe tears from my eyes.

Tori hands me my drink and I take a big sip. She sits next to me, handing a glass to Griffin as well.

"We need a game plan. First, we need to take photos of your bruises. We can use your recording as a statement if you are okay with that, and get a restraining order at the very least. I'm worried that he won't follow the restraining order, since he doesn't have a problem using others to do his dirty work. Would you be willing to press charges against him?" Griffin looks nervous as he suggests this.

I snort, taking another sip of my drink. "How soon can I press charges? Like now? I didn't before because I was kind of traumatized and in shock, but I want him as far away from me as possible. If this means he goes to jail, I'm all for it. I'm not in love with him anymore if that's your worry. I just want to know that something will be done. If I press charges and nothing happens..." I shiver, thinking about how unhinged Anthony might get if he knew that I tried to put him in jail.

"You'd definitely have a decent case and the department

would have to listen, regardless of who he may know." Griffin winces and I worry that this may not be as easy as I thought.

"What do you know, Griffin?" Tesa barks at him, never one to beat around the bush.

"When you told me his full name earlier, I had a feeling that I recognized it. He's friends with a lot of people on the force..."

I deflate into my seat. He had made a lot of connections over the last few years, and I've been to a lot of dinners with him. I was introduced, but he never told me what anyone did for a living and I never thought to ask. Shit, this was way worse than I thought, but I need to do something.

"I can't sit on my hands and wait. Something has to give, and he's not the kind of person that'll give up. He wants me."

"Okay, let's take some pictures, and then I'll need to print something off using your printer, Tesa. This way I can have her sign a statement that my recording wasn't in any way coerced, okay?" I'm nodding in agreement to what Griffin says before he's even finished.

The next twenty minutes happens in a flurry of activity, and then Griffin is walking out the door to head to the police station. Tesa and I watch him jump in his car and listen to his tires squeal. I nod my head after him and chuckle, "You didn't have any other plans after I left, did you?"

"Nope. Come have another drink with me and tell me if Greg really has a fancy peen or not."

I sputter laughing. "You're on." We walk back into the house, and I cross my fingers that everything will be okay.

"Let me text Greg that we'll be a little longer," I say, pulling my phone out of my pocket as we go back inside. I hit the home button and see there's a few messages from an unknown number.

My screen cuts messages off though for privacy until you unlock the phone so it reads:

UNKNOWN: **I miss being inside of you baby-**
Unknown: **I know now how rough you like-**
Unknown: **Can't wait to make you my whore**

I WRINKLE my nose because it can only be Anthony. I'm walking and opening my phone, making sure I don't walk into anything. I don't need any more bruises that I self-inflicted because I wasn't watching where I was going.

I follow Tesa into the kitchen. "Fucking cringe!" I exclaim as I read the messages.

"Use your words."

"Yes, Mom." I automatically respond because that's what I'd tell her when she said that to me. Tesa and I both giggle, and I read the full texts to her.

UNKNOWN: **I miss being inside of you baby. You're always so wet and ready, no matter what I do to you.**
Unknown: **I know now how hard you like it, so I'll be sure to mark you up some more. Do you let them hurt you when they fuck you? Learn any new tricks?**
Unknown: **Can't wait to make you my whore, train you up just how I want you.**

I TOSS my phone on the counter, shuddering. "That's him isn't it?" Tesa asks, grabbing for my phone.

"It's an unknown number since he's still blocked, but it has to be Anthony. Why, what are you doing?" I ask as her fingers fly over my keyboard.

"Sending these disgusting messages to Griffin. I know he says that he is going to do everything he can for you, but I need him to be motivated. Do you want to tell the guys?"

I remember how weird Greg was when he had my phone and I lurch my phone to check the time they were sent. Did he see them? Was this why he was so weird before?

"Tori, what-"

The messages were sent at seven-thirty, which was when I was getting ready. He definitely saw them.

"I think Greg already saw them? He was acting kind of weird when I came down after showering and getting dressed to come over. I didn't know why, but the time coincides. What...what if he thinks I wanted these messages?" I whisper, suddenly feeling sick.

"No. There's no fucking way any woman would *want* these kinds of messages. Much less you. You're the absolute sweetest."

I mean we know that...but the guys don't know me well.

"Yeah, no way at all," I say almost as an afterthought.

"Let's go get drunk, do your laundry together, and talk. Let's forget the douchebag for now. I'll have my brother walk you home. He's doing inventory at the club tonight."

Nodding, I decide to just forget about what's happening for a few hours.

thirty-two

I t's midnight when Miguel texts Tesa, asking if I'm still with her. Tesa and I drank three very strong margaritas, did laundry, repacked my bag and gossiped after Griffin had left.

Tesa snorts at her phone, typing something that I can't see, before rolling her eyes. She throws the phone on the bed and grabs my hand.

"Let's go see the mean brother," Tesa giggles. I grin, because she's just as tipsy as I am.

As she tugs me out the door behind her, I bend over and grab my bag.

We carefully walk down the stairs, laughing and shushing each other like there are people that may wake up.

Miguel knocks hard on the front door and we burst into giggles again.

"Tesa Rodriguez, did you get my girlfriend drunk?!" Miguel roars.

This doesn't help her laughter as we half stumble to the door, and Tesa opens it. She pushes me into Miguel's very surprised arms and says, "I'm sure she's horny after all the tequila. She's probably fine to take advantage of. Lalala...love you bye!"

She slams the door closed and I hear the snick of the lock being thrown and then the beep of the alarm being armed. I throw my arms around Miguel's neck and give him a toothy smile. "At least she remembered to lock the door?"

Miguel sighs, kissing my nose. "How drunk are you, *gringa linda*?"

"I almost want to have sex in the porch swing drunk?"

Miguel wrinkles his nose at me in confusion. "What porch swing, baby?"

"Exactly!" I giggle. Damn, it made sense to me. "I'm totally fine to walk to the house, Miguel."

"Mmhmm. And is my beautiful girl a little bit horny too?" His hands run down to my ass and squeezes. Before I know it, he's hoisting me up and my legs naturally wrap around his waist.

"You're not wearing shoes, baby. I can't let you walk home like that." Miguel kisses down my neck slowly, and I moan. "Where are your shoes, *gringa linda*?" Miguel is laughing at me as he meets my eyes.

"They didn't make it on my feet before your sister pushed me into your arms. She said something about me being cranky and needing to get laid," I lie. Tesa totally didn't say any of that, but tequila definitely helps my clothes come off.

I push my hands into Miguel's hair and gently pull. He growls and I sigh happily. I like my caveman a little growly.

My lips meet his and he eagerly kisses me. He squeezes my ass, massaging and then...I gasp as his hand slips down the front of my pants and under my panties.

"Do you want to come? Or do you need me to turn your ass red first for drinking while on medication?"

Miguel traces the lips of my pussy, teasing as I whine.

"Please," I mewl, even though I'm not sure what I'm asking for.

Miguel chuckles as he slips two thick fingers inside of me and starts to thrust. "You're gonna have to tell me *mi amor*..."

"Urmmmm..." I have no words when it comes to this man except... "I love when you threaten to spank me, but," I gasp breathlessly as he starts to rub my nub. I'm riding his hand and I'm not going to last long. "I really need your cock inside of me, please. Just maybe not on this porch. Yours would be better though?"

I moan as he kisses me hard, then sits my ass on the railing and grinds his cock into me.

"You're right." He kisses down my neck and slips his hand out of my pants. "I definitely shouldn't fuck you on my sister's porch." He grinds right against my pussy and I suddenly am rethinking my life choice of wearing pants tonight.

"Miguel..." I whine, trying to be quiet but I know I'm failing.

"Yes, *mi cielo*?"

"Hmmm...I like that one. Call me that more often." I'm apparently also easily distracted.

Miguel chuckles and picks me up. My legs wrap as naturally as breathing around his waist again, but I'm not at the right angle to grind on him, and I huff in frustration.

Walking quickly, he heads down the porch steps and towards his house. "I'm going to fuck you hard and fast over the couch while you scream and I spank your naughty ass, *mi cielo*. I want you to scream the house down. The guys went to bed early tonight."

I shake my head, struggling to get friction as all thoughts go to how good it'll feel.

Then a stray thought finds me. "I-I get to come right?"

Miguel's eyebrows furrow as he hurries up his porch steps

and unlocks the door. "The day you don't come on my cock at least three times is the day I hand you my man card."

I grin. I love when he gets all wound up like this. "Yes, please."

Shaking his head, he closes the door and flicks the lock, then props my ass on the table and leans me back, kissing me again.

"I think I need to start the orgasms early," he growls, undoing my pants and tugging them off. "Ha! Do you get to come, silly girl. Who the fuck would ever deny you orgasms?!"

He throws my pants over his shoulder, shoves his face into my pussy and gives it a long lick. Sucking hard on my clit, he puts his elbows on the table to prop himself up and stay awhile. Shit, I may have made him decide he had something to prove, and my man is slightly competitive.

"Miguel-" I start to say and squeal as he slips two fingers into my pussy. A third quickly joins to collect my arousal before slipping back out and into my ass.

"Unh!" I have no words as I writhe on the hallway table gasping and leaking juices all over his face.

"Give it all to me, baby," Miguel hums as he sucks and licks my clit. I am so overstimulated that I give him exactly what he wants, moaning as I come all over his face.

"That's one," is all Miguel says before picking me up and throwing me over his shoulder.

"What?!" I sputter. I think my brain is broken and my ears are ringing a little from how hard I came.

"I want your toes to curl on the next one," is all he says as he swats my ass.

He strides into the living room, turning on a light before walking to the couch, then slides me down the front of his body, sucking on each of my nipples before placing me on my feet. He kisses me hard before turning me and pushing me over the side of the sofa.

I squeak as I catch myself on my elbows. "You gonna yell down the house for me, baby?"

Miguel undoes his pants and slides his cock into my folds, making me moan.

Swat!

I gasp and everything tightens. That should *not* have been as hot as it was.

I try to rub my thighs together for relief and Miguel runs his hand over my now pink butt cheek with a dark chuckle.

"No, no. You are going to come because I made you come or not at all. Understood, *mi cielo*?"

I huff like a brat.

Smack!

I shiver because it made me even closer to coming.

"I'm learning so much about you right now, baby."

Miguel drags his cock through my folds again this time hitting my clit purposefully.

I whimper as he does it, coating himself in my cream.

"I need your tight cunt wrapped around my cock, baby. I don't think I have gentle in me. Are you good with hard and fast?"

"Yes! Please stick your cock in me!" I half scream at him. He grabs my hips, turning me so I can wrap my legs around his thighs, and pull him into me.

He slips his cock into my pussy, tugging my hips back hard. There's no time to get used to his girth and length and I scream as he fills me. Just like he wanted.

He pulls back almost all the way and I gasp a breath before he pushes back in until he's balls deep. He teases and taunts me as he continues to do this and my eyes roll in pleasure.

It's both too much and yet not enough.

Miguel spins me back around, shoving me over the arm of the couch until I'm kneeling with my knees wide apart. He rocks me hard against him until all you can hear is the slap of his thighs against my ass. My toes start to tingle as I moan.

"That's my girl." Miguel slaps my ass again and that's all I need for my toes to curl and push me over the edge. I'm still screaming when I hear voices.

Miguel doesn't stop fucking me as he shakes his head. "Mine. That was two, baby. Stay or go guys, but our girl needs to come again."

"I just heard her come a couple of times." I push my hair out of my face to see that Link is smirking at us.

Greg looks at me hungrily, and I wonder if I imagined the weirdness earlier before I went to see Tesa.

Slap!

I gasp and Miguel groans. "Fuck, your pussy gets so tight when I spank you."

Greg pushes his sweatpants down low enough to pull out his cock. He lazily strokes himself as he walks around to watch Miguel fuck me.

"Your ass is glowing," Greg groans. "Fucking gorgeous, baby girl. Are you taking all of that cock like a good girl?"

"Fuck, I wanna be good," I groan.

I don't even care what I'm agreeing to as long as Greg keeps talking to me just like that. They are going to kill me with this dirty talk, but at least I'll go happy and well fucked.

Greg walks over to the other couch and sits down to watch us. Link shrugs and plops next to him, pulling down his pants to pull out his cock.

"Do you like watching them? Are you thinking about them covering you in their cum?"

Miguel's words have me gasping and I shudder in pleasure.

"Baby, we are finding out all kinds of fun kinks today," Greg chuckles as he strokes himself.

I close my eyes and Miguel applies pressure to my nub as he fucks me harder. I moan because I can feel my pleasure climbing. I know that this is it. This is where I pass out because of too many intense orgasms.

Tears leak from my eyes and I cry out Miguel's name.

"Fuck, I'm a little jealous that she's not yelling my name like that right now." I hear Greg muttering and I gasp out a laugh.

That's all I can afford to do because Miguel is perfectly hitting my G spot. I feel pressure start to build and I know Miguel is about to be rewarded with an epic pussy shower.

He pinches my clit and a whine escapes.

"I know *mi amor*, I know. I don't think you have a fourth in you, so I want this orgasm to last. Can you hold out a little?"

I gasp and nod. My cheek is pressed against the sofa, my ass is high in the air, and Miguel is fucking me like it's the last thing he'll ever do.

I can feel his cock start to thicken, and I realize that he's close too.

"Miguel, fill me with your cum," I moan.

I want to tease him back and he rightfully punishes me with a hard swat. My eyes roll and I clamp onto his cock.

"Fuck, she's such a brat," Link moans and I can hear him working his cock with his fist.

Miguel smacks my other ass cheek before pulling me hard against his cock.

I squeal because he's suddenly deeper than before and I realize that he was holding out on me.

He rubs my clit harder and I push back as hard as he's pulling me to him.

"Fuck!" Miguel roars as he continues to work my clit.

I don't need more before I'm screaming and coming. I'm drenching his cock as he explodes hard inside of me.

Miguel collapses on top of me, and my legs slip from the kneeled position. Breathing hard, I giggle.

Holy fuck is he intense when he's competitive.

Link grunts and I push my hair weakly out of my face to see him coming hard onto his stomach. He wasn't wearing a shirt, and thank god for that. Link's abs are amazing.

What's wrong with me that I wish I had enough energy to crawl over and lick the cream from his abs.

Miguel is still inside of me as my muscles contract.

"Fuck, baby. Do you need to come again?"

I whimper because I don't have the energy to get up for that. Miguel is still pinning me to the couch.

"Greg, come use that fancy peen for something and fuck our girl. Her pussy is still thirsty for a fat cock."

Greg bites his lip and he looks at me for direction.

Miguel pulls his cock out of me. He's still hard and as he walks past me I can see his cock is glistening with the remnants of my orgasm.

Link's eyes follow Miguel and I grin. I can see he's about to get exactly what he wants.

Greg stands up pushing his pants off before walking to me and helping me sit up. He fists his cock and I lick my lips as I watch.

"Is Miguel right? Do you want my cock, baby girl?"

I roll my eyes up to him and bite my lip. He reaches out, pulling my lip from my teeth. "Words, beautiful. What do you want?"

"I want you to show me what your fancy hardware will feel like inside of my pussy." I shiver in anticipation, because it's not the first time that I've wondered.

Greg picks me up, and switches our positions, so that he's sitting and I'm straddling his lap.

I grind on his cock like I would if I was giving him a lap dance and his eyes widen.

"One day I'm gonna make you strip for me. It's all I can think about as you grind your wet pussy on my cock, baby girl."

He lifts me gently so that his mushroom head rubs against my entrance, then pulls my hips down and I writhe as I feel him enter slowly inch by inch.

There's no possibility for comparison because sex with each of them is so different. Miguel was hard and fast, while Greg is maddeningly gentle and slow.

He slides me down until I am fully seated and I moan. All of my nerve endings are firing, the piercings awakening areas that I didn't know I could feel.

"I need to move," I cry out. I feel so full, I need to take control. I need to see if Greg is capable of losing control and I wonder what that would look like.

I lean forward and kiss Greg gently before I push up on my knees until he almost slips out of me, then I drop myself down again. Greg roars and I give a satisfied giggle.

"So fucking bad. Fuck!"

I grin, licking the seam of his mouth. "I was wondering what you would look like a little unhinged," I whisper.

His jaw drops and he wraps his arm around me before moving so that I'm laying down and he's on top of me. He grabs my hands and holds them over my head.

"Maybe it's about time you found out."

Greg lifts my right leg, putting it over his shoulder before starting to fuck me.

Fuck, he's so deep and there's so many sensations from his piercings.

"Oh...oh my god!" I pant.

Greg kisses me hard, swiveling his hips which makes me arch against him. He kisses up my neck, growling, "Look to your right, baby girl."

I look over, arching again and see that Link is sucking Miguel's cock. Miguel's so big that he can't get him all down, and I sympathize. Link reaches for our man's balls and tugs which makes Miguel throw his head back and curse.

"Mmmm. You covered Miguel in your cream baby girl. Link's gonna lick him like his favorite dessert. How do you feel about that?"

I have no words for how that makes me feel. My eyes roll into the back of my head and the room whites out for reasons other than anxiety.

"Woah, you still with me?" Greg says in awe, still inside of me, but not moving.

"I think you broke me in the best ways," I moan.

"Ha! Best compliment ever. Baby, I'm so close, think you can come again and breathe so you don't pass out?"

"No promises?" I giggle and Greg grins.

"K, I'll do my best."

I think that his best may kill me, but he kisses me while slowly dragging his piercings in and out.

I hear Miguel moaning and grunting encouragement to Link and I sigh happily. This is what I needed in my life. I missed them because of how busy the week had been, and my doctor warned me against having sex with a UTI.

"We've been neglecting you, baby, haven't we," Greg growls as he grinds the piercing at the base of his cock against my clit and I see stars.

I whimper, shaking my head that they haven't. Greg grins.

"We have, but we're making up for it."

I start to feel pressure building and I whimper, telling Greg that I'm close with my body.

He grinds harder on my clit, thrusting deeper until I'm coming with a half scream. Greg follows with a moan, burying his face in my tits as he comes.

I lay there breathlessly with him, turning to see Miguel and Link sprawled on the couch across from me.

I giggle, loving that we are all completely exhausted. Miguel meets my eyes, grinning.

"I think that was five, *mi amor*."

I burst out laughing, because he's so fucking ridiculous.

"What is he talking about?" Link asks, throwing his arm over his face and stretching lazily.

Greg sits up, pulling me into his lap. I curl up, snuggling onto his chest.

"Counting orgasms?" Greg grunts as he kisses my head.

"Mm-hmm. He wanted to blow my mind. Thank you for helping him," I mumble.

"Bed, baby girl. But first a shower."

Greg picks me up into his arms and Miguel and Link follow us.

I'm halfway asleep by the time we finish showering, drifting off as my guys curl up next to me in bed.

thirty-three

TORI

I wake up to a hand groping my breast. I gasp as it starts to pinch and pull, so I get my revenge by pushing my ass into his groin and rubbing against it.

"Minx," Link growls. "Come shower with me so I can bury my cock in you before I wash you clean." I giggle because that actually sounds like a lot of fun.

"What time is it? Can I have coffee before we talk about fucking first please?" I hear footsteps and Greg walks in quickly with said coffee. "My favorite!" I sit up and make grabby hands.

Greg rolls his eyes and gives it to me. "I'd ask if you meant me or the coffee, but I know better."

I smirk and take a sip. Mmmm coffee. Sighing happily, I scoot my back so it's propped against the pillows.

"Won't choose. You're all my favorites." I take another sip as my eyes close again happily.

Link kisses my shoulder. "Good, because you're our favorite too, pretty girl."

Greg lays at the bottom of the bed as the guys talk quietly. I can't people before another sip or two.

A phone buzzed and I groan. I take another sip quickly. Greg gets up and looks for the phone.

"Hey, baby, it's your phone. Tori, do you know who this is?"

I take it and see it's an unknown number again. Taking a deep breath I suck it up and answer.

"Hello? This is Tori McAllister, how can I help you?"

I glance at the time and see it's six forty-five am. Ugh, so early.

"Hey Tori, it's Griffin. I'm sorry to call you this early, but I wanted to tell you as soon as I could. I submitted a police report on your behalf, and the chief has no other option except to arrest Anthony today for domestic violence and stalking. Unfortunately, we don't have enough to get a restraining order, since we need two acts of stalking or threatening behavior in the state of South Carolina. Technically, Anthony didn't leave you the photos, so we couldn't use that as a second act. I'm hoping we can make his assault stick today though. Can I call you at this number when I have an update?"

I am staring at the phone in shock. I didn't think he'd be able to do anything with my statement, so I'm surprised.

"Ye-yes you can call me back at this number, Griffin. I just can't believe you were able to do anything with my report. I don't have a lot of trust in the police department, but you may manage to change my mind."

Griffin chuckles. *"Tori, I'm really hoping to. I'm so sorry for everything that has happened to you, and I'm still planning on paying my penance for being part of the problem."*

I sigh. "I mean, you weren't really-"

"Yeah, yeah I was. I should have believed that it was exactly as bad as Tesa told me it was. She cried after she found you black and blue Sunday morning. I should have remembered that before opening my stupid insensitive mouth."

Greg looks at me in question and I mouth 'Griffin' and raise a finger to tell him I'll tell him everything in a second. He frowns and nods.

"I really do appreciate it. I just want to live my life in peace, knowing that he can't hurt me. I'm working from home today so I'll have my phone."

"Not home alone, yeah? I don't think that's a good idea."

"No," I shake my head even though he can't see me. "I'm at the guys' house and one of them has been with me since Monday."

"Well good. I want to know that you're safe while this goes down. I'll update you as needed."

We say goodbye, and I stare at my phone in shock.

"Tori?" Greg rubs my shoulder and I shudder from all the emotions running through me.

"That was Griffin, calling in an official capacity. They're going to arrest Anthony today. When I was with him and Tesa yesterday, he took my statement."

"Why didn't you tell us you'd be talking to him about that?" Link asks gently and I lean back onto the pillows.

"Tesa kind of sprung it on me. She wants me to be safe, and she thinks this is one of the only ways to do it. I was also going over to meet Griffin since they're dating, and drop my best friend approval. I also...I'm not used to telling you guys every-thing. Before I had to keep everything to myself, because it made the punishments more mangeable."

"Okay, I get it." Link tugs me into his arms and sighs. "I am glad that Griffin was able to get a warrant for his arrest. I didn't push you to go to the police because they were so unhelpful earlier and I figured you'd tell me if you wanted to go. We just want to keep you safe too."

I snuggle into Link's chest and sigh. "Oh, he was a grade-A dick to me," I giggle as he stiffens.

Greg lays back on the bed, arching his eyebrow. "Griffin is

an acquired taste. If he likes you, then he's ride or die. But, he can often be a jerk."

"He acted like I was being a princess who couldn't take two steps without being the girl who cried wolf. I came in hot because fuck that noise and then he saw my neck. Needless to say, no one who's seen my bruises can say that I did them to myself."

Miguel snorted. "No, they definitely cannot."

My stomach growls and I sigh, then grab my phone and dial Tesa.

"Hi bestie! Who do you need me to bury? It's too early for you to be using the phone."

I snort. This bitch. "I'm starving and I'm going to the kitchen to make breakfast. Come over and eat with us. Bring champagne for the orange juice. It's gonna be one of those days, babe."

"Oh shit. You'll tell me when I get there?"

"Yep. Your boy did a thing. A good thing. I just don't know that it'll stick."

"I'll throw on sweatpants and a hoodie. See you in five."

I toss the phone to the side and stand up. "What is going on?" Miguel asks, sitting up.

"When I'm stressed I cook, and I'm actually hungry, so I'm going to be able to enjoy what I make today. So I'm going to throw down in the kitchen and make another cup of coffee. Go shower." With those instructions, I walk out of the bedroom and to the kitchen.

"I'm so confused, but I heard champagne and Tesa, so I'm also mildly terrified," I overhear Link say and I snort.

When I get into the kitchen, I start the coffee machine, and start pulling out ingredients. I'm craving biscuits from scratch, potato hash with poached eggs, and bacon. Yummy. My stomach rumbles again and I roll my eyes. *Patience.*

I am on my second cup of coffee (I didn't get to finish my first) and I'm working on mixing my ingredients for biscuits when there's a knock at the door. I hear heavy footsteps and go back to what I'm doing, knowing that one of the guys will let Tesa in.

"I'm here!" Tesa walks into the kitchen with a smile and I shake my head, starting to spoon my mixture onto the baking sheet.

"Good morning!" Tesa surveys the kitchen filled with my activity in approval. "Mmm biscuits, what are we celebrating?"

She puts the bottle of champagne on the counter, and then goes to the fridge to get the orange juice out.

"Hopefully Anthony is in jail by the end of the day, Griffin called me this morning."

Tesa squeals, popping the bottle of champagne, and starting on mimosas. A Tesa mimosa is champagne with a dash of orange juice for taste and I'm all about it.

"He asked me for your number last night, and I forgot to tell you. He is really committed to putting Anthony in jail. He's angry that there's so much corruption within the police force of Georgetown. I am surprised that he called so early though. So tell me what happened."

"Do you want the cliff notes or what actually happened?" I ask as I take a sip of my drink and smile happily.

"I need the Tori story. Don't leave anything out."

I giggle and tell her everything as we cook. By the time the boys walk in, the biscuits are ready, the potato hash with peppers, onions, and mushrooms are plated with a poached egg on each, and I'm finishing the bacon.

The guys look around and their jaws drop. They have been cooking while I'm over, and they've never seen me cook like this before.

"Can we keep you?" Link's eyes are huge as he drops to his

knees and wraps his arms around my waist to snuggle my stomach.

I giggle, glancing over at Tesa. She rolls her eyes, mouthing, "told ya so." I remember that she had said not to let the guys know that I cook too, or they'd never go home again. I play with Link's hair with an indulgent smile, simply saying, "Of course, baby."

Link stands up, kissing me hard.

"This is one hell of a good morning, and almost makes up for the fact that I didn't get to fuck you in the shower," he growls in my ear.

I shiver and squeeze my thighs together.

"Stop turning on my bestie and come eat breakfast!" Tesa says as she grabs the filled plates and moves for the table.

Link, Miguel, and Greg follow quickly to help her. We spend breakfast laughing and chatting, and the guys tease her a little about dating Griffin.

Tesa smirks. "Your girl is no pushover. I thought that Griffin was gonna shit a brick when Tori called him out yesterday. He's still groveling, and she's already told him multiple times that it's fine."

Greg snorts. "Yeah, he also knows that he's naturally a jerk, so he's overcompensating. I just hope that it'll result in Anthony going to jail."

Me fucking too.

After breakfast, the guys clean up and I say goodbye to Tesa. She runs back to the house to get dressed for work, and I go upstairs to shower in Link's bathroom. Man, I am going to miss this tiled paradise when I move back to my place.

I giggle as I strip, clean my face, brush my teeth, and then step into the warm water. I wash quickly, because I know that I have some edits waiting for me downstairs.

I dry off when I'm done, and then squeeze the excess water

out of my hair. I quickly work some curling cream into it and leave it to live its best life. Wild hair for the win. I never let my hair do this, so it'll be a nice change.

I am cold today, so I pull out leggings with turtles on them and a green sweater from my bag. It still looks professional if you see me from the waist up, and no one will be seeing me from work today.

I apply more arnica cream onto my neck and put on bright purple socks with crowns on them, then hustle down to the living room and find that the guys are still home.

Miguel reaches out and wraps his arm around my waist as I go to pass him.

"Where's the fire, *mi amor*?"

"Ummm...sitting on my computer. I'm going to work." I laugh as I wiggle in his arms.

"Ugh, why. I can't wait until I can have you screaming my name again. That was fun."

I laugh because last night was fun, and Miguel is a horn-ball. Link steals me from Miguel, rolling his eyes.

"You look gorgeous today," he murmurs, kissing my neck. "Thank you for breakfast. It was amazing. Where did you learn how to cook?"

"Um. It's just something that I've always done. I learned from my parents, and then it became something that I do to work off excess energy or anxiety. I also do it because I love to feed people." I shrug with a smile.

It's been a while since I had anyone to feed, so this is nice. Anthony rarely let me cook, complaining about calories or that I was over seasoning.

"Well, we are keeping you forever now." Link grins.

"I'll be here, love, but I really need to get to work now," I giggle.

Link kisses me and then lets me go. I continue before getting pulled to Greg too.

"I need my morning kisses too," he says, giving me a kiss that has me moaning.

"Gah, and now I'm horny. Y'all suck. Go to work!" I throw my hands up and walk away as they chuckle.

I grab my computer, answer emails, and set up meetings for Monday morning. An hour later, I'm pulled into edits and I shut out the world.

———

I SIGH, sitting back finally. It's seven pm and I've been going non-stop. Miguel dropped off a sandwich to me around noon, and then I hadn't really seen anyone all day.

Oh, Greg popped in and said hello, but I was so engrossed in an edit I had waved at him before going back to the screen.

I put my computer down and stretch. I also stopped for bathroom breaks today and I drank tons of water. I was super thirsty, and again I was blaming the antibiotics.

Shit, did I take that today? I don't think I have. I run upstairs and grab the bottle to count the pills, and find that I haven't taken it yet. I swallow it with water, and then pick up my phone. I left it upstairs all day, and now it is dead. With a sigh, I plug it in, then go find the guys.

I notice that the door to the office is closed. I shrug, not wanting to interrupt Greg while he's working, before walking to the kitchen and starting to pull out ingredients.

Half an hour later, Miguel and Link find me putting a tray of lasagna into the oven.

"I may have died and gone to heaven," Miguel moans, waiting for me to close the oven door before kissing me.

I chat with the boys about their days, and Miguel asks where Greg is.

"I think the office? It was closed, and I just finished for the day myself."

Miguel heads over to the office to see what's going on, and Link and I chat. I make garlic bread as well, add that to the oven, and pull out a bottle of wine.

Greg and Miguel join us thirty minutes after that, just as the timer goes off.

"Ugh, I'm sorry I've been holed up in my office today, baby girl. I saw you were slammed too, and then my whole day imploded. Everyone needed me, so it was crazy."

I smile over my shoulder and shrug as I pull everything out. I know exactly how those days can be and I say as much to him.

We have a great dinner when Miguel gets a text. "Babe, have you been ignoring your phone today? Tesa just asked me if you're okay."

I sigh. "No, tell her I left my phone up in Link's room, and it died. I haven't had it all day and I've been too slammed to realize."

Miguel responds to Tesa and shrugs. "Apparently Griffin is also worried and tried to call you."

"Did something happen with Anthony?"

"She wouldn't tell me. Want to go check your phone for messages?"

I nod and run upstairs. My phone turns on when I push the button and I see that I missed phone calls and texts.

I listen to the voice messages, prioritizing who I need to call now or later. Four of them were for work, so I'll call them tomorrow first thing. The fifth was Griffin asking me to call him.

I hit his number and call him back right away.

"Tori, you good? I thought this was a good number to reach you."

I sigh. "Yeah, it is when I don't leave it in the bedroom. I got sucked into editing and then forgot I didn't have my phone. I am still getting used to this whole work from home situation."

Griffin chuckles. *"Well, hopefully you can go back to work soon. Anthony was taken into custody today, and they're talking to him now. They wouldn't let me sit in the room, but I did hear mention of an alibi."*

"Who would be his alibi though? That person's not telling the truth-"

"I know, Tori. I thought it was odd too. So I'll let you know if I hear anything else that you need to know. He's definitely getting help from someone, so just watch out for yourself, okay? I know I joked about this before, but make sure the guys are with you when you go out."

I nod and thank him before hanging up. I go through my texts and don't see any unknown numbers.

I respond to Tesa and then leave the room with my phone, walking back to the guys. I find them in the living room and wince. I had kind of taken over the area.

Miguel sees me and laughs.

"I'm glad that you're comfortable. What you do is super time consuming from what I understand. Getting sucked into what you're doing is just one reason that you're the best at what you do."

He pulls me into his arms and I snuggle happily. I update them on what Griffin said and shrug. "Hopefully it'll be over soon, but right now I just want to watch a movie and relax."

The guys agree, turning on the opening scenes of the newest *Spider-Man* movie. My eyes get heavy quickly, and I fall asleep as Spider-Man asks for help from Dr. Strange.

thirty-four

GREG

I'm worried about our girl. Tori has been slammed at work, and it's no wonder that she fell asleep early last night. She tends to ignore the world when she gets sucked into her work, and it's part of what makes her the best at her job. I just worry about the stress that she's been under between work, her stalker, and her injuries.

Today she'll have an equally busy day, but I made sure to clear her schedule for a two hour break for lunch and a self-defense class.

That's part of what I was doing yesterday, amongst the shit storm of a day that I had with my employees. I called her bosses to clear a few hours for this. I need her to be clear headed and have energy for her training. Tom and Peter gave Link their business cards when they met with us, and I lifted them from his room yesterday.

I will let Link know later that I took the cards, but right now my brain is moving with the need to protect her. I may not be able to remove her ex from being a problem, but I can teach her to protect herself. For now, this will have to be enough.

Tom and Peter weren't given a lot of details about what had happened to Tori on Saturday, but they had seen Tori's neck in their video call. I explained that I wanted to work self-defense training into her day, but that Tori has been falling into bed exhausted after she was done with work every night. I was concerned that she would be too tired after her work day for the training to be productive. Tom and Peter had agreed to an extended lunch for Tori, since she often works late hours anyways.

It is now eleven am, and I text Miguel to make sure that she is eating lunch.

Miguel: Shit! No, my day is getting away from me. I'm going now...

I roll my eyes. Can she remember to feed herself? Probably, but I have seen how immersed Tori gets when she's editing. She almost passed out on me the other day when I was talking to her, and I was worried about her.

I haven't forgotten about the text messages that I found, but I feel like I'm missing something important about them. They had come from an unknown number, and it wasn't in a tone that I felt she'd invite. She absolutely didn't appreciate rough sex, even though Miguel and I had found that she was open to exploring fun kinks during sex. I should know better than to believe everything that I see, but I find that my perspective is skewed when it comes to her.

There are certain things that I know about Tori, and one of them is that she has so many deadlines to keep up with that she often ignores things like having to pee or eating.

Miguel: Soo... She's in the kitchen and already made herself a salad. She also washed her dishes and is heading back to work.

Fuck, a salad? No, that wouldn't work for the kind of workout I was about to put her through. Maybe I should have remembered to tell her I was planning this. Shit, that's what I get for forgetting.

I decide to text her.

GREG: **Hey baby girl, guess what's today? We are going to work on your self defense training, so I need you to eat a real lunch please.**

Me: **Today? I already ate, but I could make some grilled chicken I guess. There was a lot of protein in my salad already.**

Greg: **Perfect. I didn't mean to spring this on you, but I ran out the door and forgot to tell you.**

Me: **I get it, see you later.** 🌙

THAT WENT WAY SMOOTHER than I expected. Tori is typically pretty chill for the most part, but I don't know what her day has already been like.

Twenty minutes later, I'm walking in the door. Tori is wearing workout clothes with her red hair pulled up in a hair tie. She's on the floor stretching, legs straight out as she pulls herself forward while holding onto her arches.

I squat by her, surprised.

"You're taking this really well for someone who just had her day hijacked." I reach out and put my finger under her chin so she'd look at me. She's really flexible, so she's now bent over while looking up at me. Fuck, she's gorgeous.

Tori grins, shrugging. "I'm used to my day being hijacked. Nothing goes the way you expect it to in publishing. My day is constantly changing, so I've learned to roll with it. Tom also emailed me a few minutes ago to make sure I was taking my extended lunch."

I bite my lip. "Yeah I hope you don't mind that I-"

"I don't mind. I know that I need to learn this, and my week has already been insane. If I don't schedule it, it simply won't happen."

She stands up with a smile and I follow suit. "Let's do this, so I can feel a little safer until I know these charges will stick."

I wish I can tell her that of course they'll stick, but I dug into Anthony St. James' background and I'm not at all sure that they will. He's been making very important connections since he graduated college in this town, and that makes me worried that the charges will be dropped. That makes it even more important that I teach Tori how to defend herself.

Instead, I lead her outside to the backyard and set up mats on the ground for our training area.

The next couple of hours fly by as I explain different holds and how to get out of them. She's tiny at five-foot-two, so with limited time, sparring isn't going to be as helpful as how to get out and then run.

Her eyes widen as I practice attacking her, and she puts what she just learned into action. This is the best way that I know to teach this to her, and other than her initial panic when I run at her, she does well. The initial panic is to be expected. I'm six-foot-two and have solid muscle, so it makes sense for me to practice with her like this. I know that she's been worried about her size difference next to Anthony.

Tori is breathing hard by the time we are done, and she's guzzling water. I watch her carefully, making sure that she doesn't overdo it.

She dramatically throws herself onto the mats on her back to get her breathing under control and I roll my eyes.

I decide to mess with her and climb on top of her.

"Is this an invitation for being such a good teacher," I tease her while kissing up her neck. She sighs and arches into my lips.

"I'm all hot and sweaty, baby." I grin against her neck, smelling the coconut and jasmine scent of her skin.

"You smell delicious. You always smell the best right after a run or dancing for hours. I just want to drink you in and fuck you afterwards."

Wiggling against me, I thrust into her. She mewls as my cock strokes her pussy through our clothes. These pants aren't the best for hiding how hard I am.

I glance around the backyard. It's fenced in, and the walls are high. No one will be able to see anything, but she'll have to be quiet.

I chuckle evilly, and her eyes widen. I don't think she's seen much of my adventurous side yet.

"Can you be a good girl for me and be quiet? I need to be inside of you in the next thirty seconds. Can I make you feel good?"

Tori grins. "Yes fucking please!"

I get onto my knees and pick her up, turning her. All of my training and time in the gym has helped to keep me strong. Tori squeals when she finds herself on her stomach and then I'm pulling her to her knees, with her head and arms still braced on the mat.

I pull her yoga pants down her hips and grin. I leave her pants halfway down her thighs and spread her ass to look at that gorgeous pussy. Her lips are glistening, and I lick her from her pussy to her tight asshole.

I want her ass soon, but that won't be today. I push my tongue into her tight pussy hard, fucking her with it. Tori writhes and whimpers, trying to stay quiet.

"Greg! Ahhhh! God, I'm so so-"

She doesn't get to finish before I suck on her clit and slide two thick fingers into her tight channel. She comes hard, squirting all over my face. I chuckle, knowing that the vibrations will travel through her clit. She shudders as her orgasm makes her twitch.

I push my pants down, fisting my cock, before sliding through her folds. I need to make sure I don't hurt her, so I make sure to coat my cock well in her cream.

"What's it going to be, baby girl? Are you going to be quiet for me? Or are you going to be a brat and scream?"

I slide hard into her pussy and she huffs out the breath that she was going to use to speak. She moans as I slide till I'm balls deep inside of her. Tori does a shit job at being quiet as she gives a little scream when I spank her pretty ass hard, and rub it like the gentleman that I am as I fuck her from behind. Her ass bounces as I thrust into her.

I push her shirt up, trapping her arms in it intentionally. Still looking down as she arches her back towards me, I slide the zipper on her sports bra down so that her tits fall out. I lean forward and grip them firmly, making sure to pull her nipples as I fuck her from a deeper angle now. She is pinned underneath me, so all she can do is take my cock. She's so hot and wet, and I easily slide in out of her tight little hole.

"Fuck, you take my cock so good. I am enjoying watching myself fuck you, but I'm not mad about making you scream. You gonna cream on my cock like a good girl?"

Tori gasps, "Greg, I can't be quiet. Feels too good-"

She's on the edge of being incoherent and I kiss her shoulder.

"Fuck it, everyone is at work, scream for me."

I pull out until only my tip and the bar just below it is inside of her before thrusting so hard her eyes roll as she screams. I reach around her and rub her nub hard as she begs incoherently. She is so responsive, I never want to be with anyone else ever again.

Refusing to look at that thought too hard, I focus on making my girl come. She can't widen her thighs because they are trapped in her pants, so she feels even tighter to me. Neither of us is going to last much longer.

She starts to pebble in goosebumps and I grin. She's getting closer to falling apart for me. I have noticed that sometimes she'll get goosebumps depending on how overloaded her senses are.

"Fuck, you're so perfect, baby girl. Your pussy is so tight and you taste so good. One day that pretty little ass will be mine too, but I think I may make you wear a butt plug to our date. That way you'll think of me and what it'll feel like every time you shift your weight."

Tori shudders and gasps, "Oh my god!"

I grin and decide to check to see if she has any butt plugs in her collection of toys... I remember that Tesa ordered her an array of vibrators, but I haven't checked everything that had been delivered. If not, I will be ordering some because she seems to like the idea.

Her pussy clamps down on me so hard, all I can do is rock into her G spot. I feel a tingle at the base of my spine and I know I'm close.

"Come with me!" I bark in a command and she shudders, screaming as she comes. I bury my head in her shoulder, lightly biting it and groaning as I follow.

Breathing hard, I roll on my side, pulling her with me while still inside of her.

"Don't wanna move," she moans.

"Mmmm, I know. I do need to get you showered so you can go back to work though. I'll carry you up as soon as I get the feeling back in my toes. I don't think I've ever come so hard."

She sighs happily, laying her head on my shoulder as I cuddle her.

My phone buzzes loudly by the back door and I groan. I really don't want to move!

Tori giggles, slowly sitting up and pulling off her yoga pants so she can stand. Her shirt slides down her torso to just barely cover her perky ass. Fuck, now I'm hard again. I stand up, pulling up my pants and tucking my cock away.

"I'll try to meet you in the shower, baby but-"

Tori grins over her shoulder as she walks to the back door.

"Thank you for this break from everything. It was amazing. I get that duty calls, whatever that looks like in your day."

I smile because she's super understanding and then my heart clenches because she has no idea what I do for work. Would that change her mind about being with me?

Tori disappears into the house and I lurch for the phone. Fuck, I missed the call.

I call back while I think. I do run a security firm, but that sometimes means that we extract people from dangerous situations or remove them from the land of the living.

I killed Grace's husband and made it look like an accident when we met five years ago. I felt the weight of her disapproving stare that I hadn't done the same for Tori. Anthony is just too well connected to the police department and the mayor's office, but it doesn't mean that I don't want to.

The person on the other end picks up, and I head back inside to our soundproofed office to talk. I'm surprised that Tori hasn't noticed this yet. She takes a lot of things at face value, and while I love this about her, I also worry how long that can continue.

———

TORI

I SMILE AS I SHOWER. I didn't see this afternoon leading to self defense lessons and screaming orgasms in the backyard. Though I can't say that I'm upset about it in the least.

Greg is always surprising me. I can't figure him out, and sometimes it's fun, like today. I love that he took the time to organize self defense lessons for me, because I honestly really need them. Other times, I can't help but feel like he doesn't trust me.

I still need to tell him about the text messages that he saw that Anthony had sent, but I keep forgetting to. My brain feels pulled into a million different directions, and it's not the only thing that I've forgotten.

Sighing, I realize that I haven't taken my birth control pill either. My phone reset itself somehow, and all of my alarms were deleted. With all of the sex that I'm having, I need to be more careful. I think I'm getting my period soon though, but my cycle has always been hard to track. Tesa has been telling me to track it on my phone, so I'm going to start doing that as soon as my next one begins.

I finish showering, step out, and quickly dry off. I stare at my wet hair with a sigh. Braid it is. I squeeze out the water and then weave my long red hair into a bun. I wash my face and work my way through my skin routine because I don't want to break out after sweating today.

I leave the bathroom, walking over to my duffle bag on Link's bedroom floor. Do I choose comfort or something a little cuter?

I pull out a long sleeved dress, bra and underwear. I may as well look slightly cute if my hair is going to be wet. It's how I balance things. I tug on my clothes, finishing off the style and comfort with a little lip balm. I glance in the mirror and shrug, calling it good enough.

I head downstairs, wondering if I can tempt Greg into snuggling for a little longer before I have to go back to work.

Walking down the hallway, I frown in disappointment when I see that the door is closed again. I put my ear by the door to see if I can hear anything on the other side. I don't want to knock if he's busy, but I can't hear a thing.

I realize again that I don't know much about what Greg does for the security firm. I just know that he is always on the phone, checking on his employees, or going out to meet with clients. Leaning against the wall with a sigh, I make myself a note to ask. I spent way too much time in the dark when I was with Anthony, and now look where I'm at.

I have a stalker and an abusive ex-boyfriend that seems to think he needs to reprogram me so I'll be his 'perfect girl'. The idea that I can be reprogrammed into that quiet, skittish girl that I used to be terrifies me. I don't want to go back to the abuse, and Anthony showed me that he isn't against taking me against my will. I shiver, hoping that Griffin will have good news for me soon. I need to call him and find out if anything has changed.

I know that Greg isn't Anthony, but I can't allow myself to fall back into that pattern. I have to be smarter and more aware, without being a psycho and yelling, "Tell me all your secrets!"

I snort to myself, walking away from the door. Clearly the stress is starting to get to me. Or...maybe it's all this time in the house. Maybe I should think about going back a day early? If Anthony is in custody, what could it hurt? Yes, calling Griffin definitely needs to be a priority, I decide.

The doorbell rings and I glance at the wall clock as I pass it.

It's two in the afternoon, and Greg didn't mention that anyone was coming by.

Deciding that I'm not answering the door to a house that I don't live in, I walk to the living room to finish working on an edit.

Someone starts to bang on the door, yelling about the police and I frown. How does Greg not hear that in the office?

Fuck my life. I walk back out into the foyer and stop, glaring at the door. I really don't want to answer it. Why are they even here? The knocking starts again, and I grumble.

I unlock the front door and open it. There's two police officers standing at the door, and I still can't fathom why they're here. I blink and give a small smile.

"Hi...can I help you?"

"Yes, I'm Officer Potts and this is Officer Keller." They show me their badges and I nod, still confused. "We were asked to come regarding a noise complaint? Someone said there was a woman screaming?"

Screaming? Oh, shit. *How do I manage to get myself into these things?* I blush as I step out and the officer's eyes travel to my neck. I'm sure my blush is making the now yellowing bruises stand out even more.

"Do you need help? Is someone hurting you?" The officer's previous inquiring attitude has now become more hostile, as he puts his hand on his gun. Oh, for fucks sakes.

Knowing my bruises look awful, it reminds me of yet another reason that I shouldn't have answered the door. My hand travels up to my neck, as if I can hide the bruises with it.

"I put in a police report, so I'm hoping that he's in custody. I don't know that he'll be booked though," I shrug to show my level of trust in the system.

The officer frowns at my admission, opening his mouth to say something.

"Can I help you, officers?" I relax as I hear Greg's voice, turning towards him.

He steps out, pulling me into his arms. He's still in workout gear, but I don't care. This conversation is getting seriously uncomfortable.

Officer Potts repeats the concern about noise control and I look up at Greg, biting my lip. Greg's face is unreadable except for the slight twitch of his lips. Gah, asshole.

He leans down to my ear. "I've got this if you want to head back inside. You're blushing so hard, I'm afraid you're gonna hurt yourself."

I roll my eyes. "Thank you for coming to check on us, but I really am fine. Greg was teaching me self defense and it may have gotten a little...heated."

I give them a sunny smile and Greg barks out a laugh. Leaving him to deal with the aftermath, I walk back inside. I swear, it's always something. But I have to admit, that was kind of funny. Fuck, I guess people heard us.

I giggle in embarrassment, walking inside, then back to the living room, and hopping into my nest of pillows and blankets in the living room. There's a wall of windows in here and it's so bright and cheery. I love this room.

I sit and try to remember what I'm supposed to be doing... Fuck, birth control. Thankfully it's in my purse, so I grab it. I take the one I missed, noticing that I skipped yesterday. I really am terrible at taking pills. Maybe I should look at other options.

I grab my computer, and start to do research on what other kinds of birth control methods there are, and make a document with a pro and con list. I allow myself to get lost in the information overload that is the internet for a half hour, before dragging myself out.

Glancing at the time, I realize that it's four o'clock. What was I supposed to do? Looking out into the hallway from where I'm sitting, I notice that Greg isn't outside anymore so he must have sorted the police.

Oh my god...Tori McAllister...what did I want-

Griffin!

Sighing, I grab my phone, happy that it's at least downstairs this time and that it's charged. I glance through my messages and see I missed a few. I decide to call Griffin first before I get distracted.

I dial his number, sitting back on my nest of pillows.

"Hey Tori! Is everything okay? I noticed that the police were called out to your neighborhood today on the scanner. I've been keeping tabs on your area, just in case." My heart hurts a little that this is the first thing he has to ask in my shit show of a life. And then I realize that I need to explain why they were called.

"Uh, yeah. They were called but I'm totally fine-"

"Wait, they were? What happened? Do I need to come check on you?"

I can't help myself and sputter a giggle. "Um, no. Do you really want to know?"

"Oh I feel like this is a good story. I've been having a shit day, and I need to laugh."

I grin, happy that I get along so well now with Griffin. I know that Tesa really likes him and wants us to also be friends.

"Soo, apparently there was screaming in Greg's house and someone reported it..." I start and Griffin cackles.

"I thought you were supposed to be working today, and not getting Greg into trouble, Tori! Oh my god, I need to go bug the officers that went out to the house. Um. Their house is pretty well insulated. How would they hear anything?"

I wonder how he knows that, but maybe he was around when they were constructing it? I don't know, it was just a weird comment.

"I mean...is it? I don't know. We were in the backyard and he was teaching me basic self defense-"

"Is that what we're calling it now, Tori? Did he attack you with his cock? Apparently there was a lot of screaming as I'm reading the dispatch log."

"Nope, none of that. The only person I dish to is Tesa, and we have to change the names when we do so that she doesn't need therapy afterwards."

Griffin snorts. *"I mean, the guys are as close as brothers so I can see that, but I am still laughing that y'all were so loud that the police were called for a noise complaint."*

I cover my face groaning in embarrassment. "Yeah, I almost didn't answer the door, but Greg was in his office and they started yelling through the door. It was so embarrassing."

Griffin laughs hysterically, making jokes about how I need to be defended by the multiple dicks in that house, and I giggle too. So ridiculous. I can see now why Greg and Griffin are friends.

"Anyway," I stress. "I wanted to call for an update. I'm starting to get a little stir crazy in their house. Is Anthony still arrested?"

Griffin sighs. *"Yes, but there are other people that are saying that they saw him throughout the night too. It feels staged, like there's too much interest in where he was so that he could pull out his list of alibis. I just don't like it. I really don't think that they'll be formally charging him. It feels like my bosses are trying to put on a show that they held him for as long as possible before they have to let him go."*

I chew on my lip, because this is what I was worried about. I sigh, but it feels too close to a sob for comfort.

"Hey, Tori. None of that, okay? He's still here, and he hasn't even had a lawyer come in, which is honestly also weird. They've

been asking him about his whereabouts for hours, you'd think he would have asked."

Anthony is very patient. He would have waited so he can say that he was cooperating. I think to myself.

"You there?"

"Mmmhmm, just thinking. I'm fine for now. I wanted to check in before I went back to work."

"Okay. Well, listen. Greg'll tell you that I hate everyone, but you've grown on me. I know Tesa wanted us to be friends too. What if Sunday I go over to your house with movies and food, and the three of us can just hang out? Tesa has been slammed all week, and I refuse to deprive her of bestie time. I'm being slightly selfish, by the way, because this means I get to see her too."

I laugh, and if he notices that my laugh is just a touch hysterical, he wisely doesn't call attention to it.

"I think it must be hard to date someone that has such a close friend at times. I haven't seen her since Tuesday, and I miss her. We got close super fast, but I've gotten used to seeing her everyday for more than a few minutes."

"You'd think, but it's really not. I mean it might've been harder if you were a bitch, but you're not. I like that you call me out when I'm being a jerk. I need a friend like that to remind me because my guy friends just accept that I'm a dick."

My lip twitches as I think about that. "I think they accept it because they have dicks. I have news for you though: You don't have to be a dick just because you have one."

"Hear, hear!" Link comes into the room at that moment and I giggle.

"Who are you imparting dick-wielding advice to, Tori?"

"Ummm...Griffin." I giggle.

"Oh good! I think that the police department may gift you and Tesa with a fruit basket because of your positive influence.

I don't think it'll be enough to make him a former dick, but I appreciate the effort that you're making."

Why are the men in my life so ridiculous?!

I am laughing too hard to continue the conversation, so I tell him to check with Tesa about Sunday but that I'm in.

Link lifts me into his lap and snuggles.

"You're supposed to be working, and instead I come home to Greg telling me about how he made you come in the backyard. Such a naughty, pretty girl."

I shiver and he chuckles. "None of that, now. I need Tori cuddles while I answer emails, and you need to go back to work."

I grin, grabbing my laptop and snuggling into his chest. This part of working from home doesn't suck, and I'm pretty sure I'll miss it. It's only Thursday, but I have a feeling that I won't be coming up for air again until the weekend.

If anything, not being in the office has made my days feel longer.

I returned six calls, answered emails, and read a manuscript by eight o'clock that night that I needed to finish editing by tomorrow. I email the author that I am almost done but that I have a few plot questions, and then call it quits. Link hung out with me for an hour before he went to meet with an inspector for a build.

The only reason that I call it quits is because the guys begged to have dinner and relax. Gah, I love my job, but it sucks to fall behind.

thirty-five

TORI

The next morning I wake up to someone shaking me. I sit up quickly, pushing my hair out of my face. What's happening?!

I moan, looking around, seeing Greg standing in front of me with my phone. He looks scared that he's waking me up, and honestly, he should be.

"Coffee?" I whine and Greg nods when I take the phone, walking quickly towards the kitchen.

I answer the call without looking.

"Hello? It's so early." I am whining but it's- I glance at the alarm clock. Ugh, it's five am. Who hates me?

"Tori, I know you aren't your best in the morning, and I'm so sorry to call you this early." Peter's voice drifts into my ear, but I'm having trouble understanding.

I grab my water, taking a sip. Miguel and Link are snuggled next to me and I'm jealous. I want to be sleeping too. It's not fair.

"Hmm. Hi Peter. Is everything okay?"

"Yes, but I need you to come in today. I know that you weren't

going to return until Monday, but things kind of blew up here
without you. I have two of your authors that are having meltdowns
and need meetings with you, and Tom. I also need you to go through
a list of new manuscripts and decide which authors you're going to
continue working with and which new authors you're going to take
on. We do need you to choose to cut at least five authors that can be
taken over by some of our newer editors that are coming in."

Holy shit that was a lot of information. I blink at the phone
as Greg comes in with coffee and I look up at him.

He rolls his eyes at me. "This is why I'm never waking you
up like this again without caffeine in hand. Is that your boss?"

I nod and take a sip of coffee with a happy sigh.

"Okay, I'm only one-third alive at best right now, Peter. I
was just thinking that I was going a little stir crazy at home
and that I may want to come back to work early."

Greg's jaw dropped and he mouths, *"Really?!"*

I nod at him and take another sip of bliss. Oh my god, I
would worship at the feet of the coffee gods if I could.

"Excellent. I wouldn't ask if I didn't feel like it was important, and I wanted to give you enough time to get ready. I apologize for the early call. I could have probably waited another
hour, but I'm already answering emails for the morning."

My jaw drops. "Already? Have y'all considered hiring
another manager? Cause that's insane!"

Peter chuckles. "Every damn day. I'm waiting for our
finance department to work it into the budget."

Ugh, that sucks. "Boo. Okay, I'll text Tesa that I'm coming
into work since we drive in together. I'll see you there."

I say goodbye and sigh, leaning against the pillows with a
moan, then take another sip of coffee. Miguel and Link are
awake now, and Link moves over to me, wrapping his arms
around my waist and laying his head on my boobs.

We hang out in silence, and I know it's partly because they're counting my sips. It would be funny if it wasn't so true.

I run my fingers through Link's hair and I swear if he was a cat that he'd purr. I take my fourth sip of coffee, pick up my phone and text Tesa that I'm coming to work with her. I also ask her to bring me clothes. I know that the phone will wake her up and she'll come over right away.

Link sits up, sliding his hand through my hair and kisses me hard.

"Good morning, pretty girl. Tell me why you're going to work today?"

"I know it wasn't the plan, but Peter sounded like the world was ending because I haven't been there. I have authors I have meetings with apparently—"

Buzz

I glance back at my phone and see my work email is blowing up. I had synced it to my phone while I was home just in case. I open it and sigh. Peter emailed me that I had two meetings in person today with authors. I briefly touch my neck. Fuck, I need makeup with better coverage.

I finish my mug and walk to the shower, not surprised that the guys followed. I sigh and turn at the doorway, pulling my sleep tank up and over my head.

"Yesss?"

The guys' eyes go straight to my breasts and I smirk. Yep, I still got it. I drop my panties and start to turn.

"Wait!" Miguel says.

Fuck a duck! I should have backed away with my tits on full view.

"I need you to use your words and to stop using your body against us," Miguel grunts, closing his eyes to get a hold of himself.

I giggle, because this wasn't my fault. I take pity on the

guys and explain why I need to go back to work today instead of Monday.

I sigh. "I'm kind of freaking out now because I need to find some makeup to cover up the last of the marks on my neck so that I don't scare people. Tesa is going to come over soon too with clothes for me. I'm also worried because today is now the day of my new promotion, so I'll be phasing out of my last job and into my new one. I just wasn't expecting any of this, so this is my 'oh shit' face."

Greg nods and shrugs, looking determined. "Miguel, you're making more coffee please. I'll call Tesa and go get you makeup, baby girl. Link, distract our girl for a little." Miguel huffs.

"Seriously? Why does he get the fun job?" Miguel is in full on brat mode and it's adorable.

"You broke the spell that is her gorgeous body. You're also Tesa's bitch this morning. She is probably going to want to make breakfast for Tori."

My phone buzzes and Greg walks out to it. He holds it up to me and I shrug.

"Just tell me who's texting me and what they need please, love." He nods and clicks the screen.

"Tesa is coming over now. The message cuts off, but it looks like she is also planning to make breakfast."

I grin because my stomach is starting to grumble. "Does distraction come with orgasms, Link?" I ask before turning and walking to shower with an extra sway in my hips. I'm feeling extra sassy this morning.

Greg barks out a laugh, shaking his head before getting dressed and grabbing his phone to do his errands and letting Tesa into the house.

Miguel grumbles in Spanish. I look over my shoulder as I hear him also talk about spanking my ass.

"Will those come with orgasms too?" And then I slap my hand over my mouth because I should know better than to taunt Miguel like that. Link shakes his head, reaching around me to turn on the water.

He whispers in my ear. "You've definitely bitten off more than you can chew again, pretty girl."

Do I apologize? Fuck, he's gonna make me pay for suggesting that he wouldn't give me orgasms.

Miguel glowers at me and then smirks. "I am going to make you pay for that when you're least expecting it."

Everything tightens and I shiver. Not in a 'I'm scared' shiver, but a 'holy shit why is that so hot?' kind of way.

"That's very big of you," I decide to tease instead, stepping into the now warm water.

Link chuckles, shaking his head. He decides to stroke the fire by picking me up and kissing me.

Miguel curses and walks out of the room, slamming the bedroom door.

"You're so bad, pretty girl. How about I make you scream to start your morning off right?"

He slips his fingers through my folds before entering my tight slick hole. I gasp thrusting into his fingers as he lazily fucks me with them. He drops his head to the side of my neck and kisses down.

"Fuck, I just want to suck on your neck and mark you as my own like a fucking cave man," he growls.

"Anywhere but where you can see!" I gasp because I'm so close. Link grins, kissing me, swallowing my whimpers.

"Really?"

"Yes, ohh. Oh my god, Link!"

"Tell me, pretty girl. Are you close? I can feel you clenching like such a good girl on my fingers."

I mewl, unable to make real words right now and Link chuckles darkly.

"So wet, so ready, so fucking mine," he growls.

He kisses me harder, slipping a third finger inside of me, sliding his thumb over my clit to give it special attention. I mildly remember that Tesa is supposed to come over, and wonder if she'll be able to hear me scream.

Link decides that I'm thinking too hard and sucks on my nipple. He alternates between that and little bites, and it's the bites that send me over the edge.

I scream his name as I come all over his fingers.

He groans as he pulls them away and sucks on them. I watch him with hooded eyes as he enjoys his treat.

"More," he groans.

He props me up against the wall before falling to his knees, grabbing my thighs, he lifts them onto his shoulders. It was one of those incredibly strong things that I always thought would be hot in books. Spoiler alert, it is.

I squeal as he settles between my legs and he grins up at me.

"Come on my face, and then I'll fuck you till you scream. Deal?"

I let out a hard breath, because holy fuck is he hot. His green eyes smolder, and he's smirking at me. I realize that I've lost my train of thought, and all I can do is nod eagerly.

He moans, "Such a good fucking girl," before diving in to eat my pussy like its a peach. He sucks, nips, and slurps. I hold onto the shelf above me and his hair as I ride his face.

I'm on the edge between pain and pleasure because my senses are overwhelmed. He uses his teeth to gently worry the nerve endings in my bud before sucking hard, then resumes fucking my pussy with three fingers, and my core clenches them tight, not wanting to let go.

I'm embarrassingly wet, my arousal covers his face, and all Link can do is smile like he won a medal. I love how much he loves to watch me come, and I love this man more and more everyday. It's almost scary how fast this is happening.

Link smirks as if he knows that my thoughts are drifting and he slips a finger into my ass. I moan, my eyes rolling back and my toes curling as I dig into his back.

He fucks my pussy and my ass with his fingers, sucking my clit hard. I have lost all ability to use words. I moan and thrust my hips as I ride all of the sensations. I shudder and gasp.

"Come on baby, fucking be mine!" The note of possession in his voice throws me over the edge and I scream as I come.

Link uses his fingers to help me ride through my orgasm, sucking hard on the inside of my thigh. Somehow it triggers another orgasm right after and I moan incoherently, shuddering.

He slips his fingers out of me and lets my legs fall down, then picks me up and I am too weak to wrap my legs around his waist. He chuckles darkly.

Rubbing his cock along the folds of my pussy to hit my clit makes me twitch. I'm so overstimulated after those orgasms.

"Hold on to me, okay? We're running out of time."

I wrap my arms around his neck and he thrusts hard into me. Fuck, he's so hard and thick and I can feel the stretch as he pushes inside. The three of them aren't small, but Link's mushroom head is large and in charge.

Resting his head on my shoulder, he kisses my neck, before turning so he's using the wall for support. He bounces me on his cock, lifting and then dropping me so all I can do is moan and hold on tightly to his shoulders.

He watches my tits bounce like it's the best view he's ever had. He looks at me like he's worshiping me, which is exactly how all three of them fuck me. Whether it's hard, playful, or soulful, they all are showing me how much they love me with their bodies.

My body starts to clamp down hard on him, so he rocks into my pussy,

"You're so fucking tight, baby. I need you to cream all over my cock for me. Do you think that you can do that for me?"

He's rocking right against my G spot.

"Right fucking there. Oh my god please don't stop."

I'm not against begging right now if it means that he'll keep going. My eyes are tearing up because it feels so fucking good. Then I'm squirting all over his cock, giving him his own private shower.

Link turns me so my back is against the wall again, bracing against it as he fucks me hard into it. Four thrusts later, he's coming inside of me.

Someone bangs against the door and I scream in surprise.

"Breakfast is almost ready, and Tesa wants to see Tori! Get a move on, or she'll come find you!" Miguel yells through the door and I laugh.

He puts my feet carefully down on the tile floor before bending to kiss me hard.

"Let's go then, gorgeous. You've got a busy day." I smile as I walk into the water.

"I do, so in case I forget to tell you, thank you for the orgasms."

Link laughs in that startled way that he has, as if he's surprised that I said what I did.

We enjoy our time together as we shower and then we are hurtling into the rest of the day to get ready.

―――――

TESA and I run through the lobby. We are so freaking late. Breathlessly we giggle as we hit the button on the elevator. In actuality, we are only five minutes late, but usually we are early so this feels really late.

Greg came through with the foundation to cover my throat, so I felt more self confident today.

I am wearing a blue boat necked top with quarter sleeves, a gray skirt, and blue flats. I have my hair in a pretty low bun that had taken me two seconds to do, and I look reminiscent of a cute ballerina. I wear fairy silver earrings for luck, and I am ready for the day.

I say goodbye to Tesa on her floor and then step out on my floor, walking quickly for my office.

"Not so fast, Tori!" Peter is moving quickly across the office space towards me, and I bit my lip.

"Stop, you're not in trouble, I just need to show you your new office. You're saving my ass by coming back early. I never realized how needy your authors are. You never mentioned it."

My jaw drops as I turn and follow him. "I mean, I don't know that they're needy-"

"Ha!" Peter shakes his head. "Tori, Ms. Peters wanted to know why you haven't returned her call from five minutes ago. Miss Traiton said she couldn't not see your face this week or her book would fail. Oh! And Mrs. Acton needed help plotting her next book and had questions for you. These are so afield of what your job description is, it isn't funny. How do you get it all done?"

I shrug. "I just do?" How else are you supposed to answer a question like that?

Peter shows me my new office. There are more windows here and it's a corner away from the bustle of the rest of the office. I rarely left my office anyway, outside of lunch with coworkers that I was already friendly with, so this works for me.

"Here's a pile of new manuscripts that came in. I need you to decide what authors you're keeping and who will work well with a newer editor. Is there anyone that isn't high maintenance that you can think of that wouldn't mind working with an editor that isn't as busy?"

Off the top of my head, I can name at least three people that were churning out books and needed someone with a lot of availability. I give Peter the names, and he quickly writes himself a note.

"Excellent. Now I need another two before the end of the day so we can start transitioning them. You saw when your meetings are?"

"Yes! I added alarms to my phone to remind me of when I'm meeting with them."

"Perfect. You can work out of your normal office today, but I want you to move into this one by the end of the day. We are moving up the hiring process and are looking at applicants."

I nod, walking back to my soon to be old office. Things are moving in a whirlwind, but I guess that's to be expected.

"Tori! Don't forget these." Peter is walking after me with the pile of manuscripts. Shit, I spaced on that.

I unlock my door and thank him, taking them from him and turning on the light. The next few hours fly as I take meetings, return calls, and work on an edit. Ms. Peters was just being overdramatic, she had been fine with having a video call to go over her questions. Miss Traiton had been upset because I had edited her book, but had not had a chance to go over the developmental edits that I had suggested.

We went over those, and discussed how to change them. She is publishing in less than a month, so I understand her concern. Then Mrs. Acton was a whole other story, and that meeting was traumatizing for me. She spent an hour going over her shifter book, and asking me about what kinds of piercings her lion shifters should have.

I don't have that kind of time, and she spent another twenty minutes yelling at me for not having been immediately available. She went on the list to be moved to another editor. Sorry not sorry.

I sit back from my desk with a sigh. I am already tired. There's a knock on the door and I perk up. Anything to give me a break today, I'll take it.

I yell for them to come in, and Tesa strolls through the door. "Bestie, I do believe that it's time for me to break you from your prison."

I give a slightly hysterical giggle, burying my face in my hands.

"Oh my god, how did you know?!"

"This place has been insane, and you've been gone for almost a week. I knew you'd need me. Lunch?"

I glance at my computer screen for the time. It's already two pm. That's insane.

"Yes, yes please. I'm starving. I grab my purse and go through it. My birth control is staring at me and I sigh. I am tired of staring at it and feeling like a failure that I can't remember to take the damn things, so I chuck it in the garbage.

"So it's that kind of day?" Tesa shakes her head, laughing.

"My hormones are all over the place, and the universe is working against me. I schedule an alarm to take my birth control, and the phone dies. The phone updates in the middle of the night. Fine, great. Somehow it deleted all of my scheduled alarms. I need to find a different form of birth control. The universe is trying to get me pregnant with all of this peen."

Tesa smirks at me. "You're losing it, girl. You're also getting well dicked, judging from the way that I had to send Miguel after you this morning."

I blush and she rolls her eyes. "Mmm-hmm. How many orgasms did my best bitch start her day with?"

"Ummm four or five?"

"That's what I'm talking about!" She high fives me and it's so ridiculously perfect, that I burst out laughing.

I grab my purse and walk out of my office with her, shaking my head. I lock the door and remember that I had talked to Griffin.

"Oh! Did Griffin talk to you about hanging out on Sunday?"

Tesa stares hard at me like she's trying to process what I said and then her eyes widen.

"Oh my god, yes! The three of us are hanging out," she confirms, nodding her head. "He's decided that you're best friends, and that you need to accept it. I told him that as long as I'm first Best Bitch, that I'm fine with it."

I shake my head giggling. "I literally cannot with you two right now."

"Listen," she says as we get into the empty elevator. "I'm not the one who had the police called on her. And yes, young lady, I need to know all of the details. However, for the sake of my poor brain, we shall change Greg's name to Fabio."

I cackle because how the hell can I keep a straight face and then decide that I'm going to go with it.

I tell her about what happened as we walk out of the elevator and into the street. Tesa motions to the left, and I follow her lead. By the time we get to *Blunch*, we are hysterically giggling.

I was slightly worried about coming back here, but then decided that I need to live my life, if only enough to be able to go to lunch with my bestie.

Our flat bread and soup were amazing, and we had sweet tea to get us ready for the rest of the day.

I had to pee before we left, so I gave Tesa my card to split lunch, and headed to the bathroom. I carefully look around, but it's empty. Shrugging off my behavior as silly, I go pee.

As I'm in the bathroom, people come in but they're in heels and dresses. I flush and finish up, going to wash my hands.

"I guess the nice weather really does bring the whores out," says a voice as someone laughs beside her. I look over my shoulder to see that Veronica has walked in with someone else.

I roll my eyes because she can't hurt me. She is all words. I finish washing my hands and go to dry them.

"Do you really think that lying and telling people that Anthony choked you is going to solve anything," she laughs, shaking her head. "I can't even see any marks, do you Sylvia?"

Sylvia shrugs, clearly bored with the conversation, going into a bathroom stall.

"Anthony was with me all night, Saturday, and that's what I told the nice police officers."

I feel like cold water has been thrown over me and I gasp, shaking my head. I was so wrong. Words are equally awful when it means that you're once again going to be hunted.

"There's no freaking way, Veronica, that you said that. What reason could you have to say that to them?"

"Oh honey, we've been fucking like rabbits for months. All of those late nights out of town, and you never thought to check?"

I shudder, suddenly really glad that I had the doctor check for STIs. Motherfucker.

"I don't know what you're playing at, but he's using you. I just want to be free of him, and he wants-" I struggle to breathe, my breaths coming in gasps.

I can't believe that she's letting herself be used right now. Is she really this dumb?

"Anthony wants to own me. He wants to reprogram me and make me someone that I'm not. This isn't something that I'm just making up. There are photos of my neck black and blue. I'm wearing makeup so that I don't get looks today."

Her face slightly crumples, shaking her head. "No, I mean he was going to teach you a lesson so that you learn your place. And that place is on your knees." She draws herself up confidently. "I'll be his queen, and he can keep you as a fuck hole, that man is insatiable and I can't do it all on my own. You are a woman. You don't need independence. What are you really doing with it anyway? Whoring yourself out?"

She's been whispering intently because her friend is in the bathroom stall. When the toilet flushes, she leans away from me, talking louder. I can't catch a full breath and the room spins just enough to be nauseating.

"This is your only warning. Anthony will be out of jail today, if he isn't already. The police threw out all evidence to the contrary, deciding that you're a liar and a waste of resources. Good luck getting anyone to listen later. Your sexcapade that was called into the police station really made the chief of police laugh, I heard, and gave him the excuse to throw out the evidence. You're a tease and a whore."

I stumble away from her, walking out to our table. I need Tesa to call Griffin right now. I can't get my fingers to work because my hands are shaking so hard.

I fall into the chair next to her and her eyes widen.

"What the-"

"Veronica-in bathroom. Call Griffin now please. Anthony is being released."

I take a sip of water, concentrating on my breathing as Tesa fumbles for her phone. She calls him, but it goes to voicemail, twice.

"Come on, I'll try again. Let's walk back to the office to get away from Skanky Veronica, and you can tell me what has you looking whiter than a ghost."

I nod, taking a last sip before standing up.

We walk back to the office as I recount what happened, and the weird reaction that Veronica had as I told her what Anthony said to me, when he held me hostage in the bathroom Saturday night.

Tesa shakes her head, cursing in Spanish as my phone rings. I pull out my cell and see that it's Griffin. I bite my lip, flashing the screen at her. She frowns, motioning at me to pick up.

"Griffin? What-"

"*Tori!*" Griffin sounds like he's been running. There's a bench behind me, and my legs collapse. Tesa sits next to me, telling me to put the phone on speaker.

"*Tori, Anthony is out. I had to go check on a lead with my partner on a case we're working on, but I wouldn't be surprised if it was a bullshit lead. It led nowhere. When I got back, Anthony had been released, and all charges dropped. They're saying that the bruises have to be faked, even though an officer saw them yesterday.*"

"Um, yeah. Two officers saw them when I opened the door!" I give him their names.

"*Unfortunately, neither of them work in our city anymore. One was fired and the other transferred to Myrtle Beach.*"

My jaw drops. What the fuck is happening?

"*I told you he had friends and pull, but I didn't think it was this bad. Where are you right now?*"

I tell him where I am and what happened at lunch.

He sighs. "*Go back to the office, and then have the guard walk you to your car, please. I'll meet you at the guys' house. We need to tell them that he's out. I know that you have a life that you have to live, and you can. I don't think that he'll plan anything soon. Please don't go anywhere by yourself. This includes the bathroom from now on at restaurants and such."*

I nod my head but then realize that he can't see me. I agree, and tell him that I'll let him know when we are done with work.

Today just turned into an absolute shit show. At least it started with orgasms, right?

thirty-six

MIGUEL

I pace my office, filled with anxiety. Tori had texted our group chat to tell us that she was going to be home late and that she needed to tell us something. She wanted to know if we would all be home tonight so that she could talk to us.

I didn't want to pry and insist that she tell us right then, but I have never been very good at waiting. We all told her that we would be home, and then rearranged our schedules to accommodate her.

I need to move and walk out of my office to go find things to do. It's only four in the afternoon and Tori won't be home until closer to seven thirty, she said. Her new promotion has led to some kinks, and I wonder what happened. I walk out onto the floor of the club, checking in to make sure that we are ready to open tonight.

The club is pretty self-sufficient, and it's obvious pretty quickly that I'm just bothering people. I need to do inventory for our alcohol soon because I have to place an order with our vendor. I decide to start on that. I'm not exactly dressed for this in a button down shirt and jeans, but if I don't do something soon it'll be a problem.

I grab my inventory paperwork to keep track of how many bottles we have versus need, and then head into the room. An hour into this, I realize how fucking dusty this room is. I sneeze and bat away a cobweb out of my hair. Gah, why.

I continue in my efforts, and two hours later Bear finds me. He's a big guy, and he chuckles as he spots me on the floor surrounded by bottles.

"Uh, boss? You okay there?"

I sigh, leaning against the wall to take a break. I'm surprised that no one has come to find me before this honestly.

"Yeah, I'm fine. What's up?"

Bear goes into his concerns that we need to hire more security staff now that we are bringing in more people with our themed nights. We are open Tuesday to Saturday night now, and our themed nights have been really popular. We have been playing with the idea of an open mic night on Monday nights, and opening just the first floor for it.

The club has become one of the hottest night spots, and it's exactly what I always wanted. It just means making sure that we have more staff so that they aren't working every night. These were all things that I planned on doing, but time got away from me.

Welp, I have time now. I grab another sheet of paper and pull out my phone.

"You're right. We do need more people. I'll put an ad out, but if you or any current employees know good candidates, get me names and numbers today. I always like to hire from personal recommendations."

Bear knows this and nods. "I have ideas and I think Patrick's brother just got out of the military and is looking for a job too."

I vaguely remember him asking if we would have openings soon. Yeah, that'll work.

I open up my phone, making myself notes. I write **Personal Recommendations** on the paper and hand it up to Bear.

"Listen, if y'all have enough names, then I won't even have to put out an advertisement, which would make me happy. I hate having to deal with that shit. Make sure the guys know that they are putting their stamp of approval on those names, okay? No bullshit."

Bear nods and heads out the door.

I grab another paper and start to make open lists for more bartenders. Also, certain nights we have dancers on the floor dancing hip hop or salsa, and we need more waitstaff.

I get up off the floor, cursing at how dusty it is here. I sneeze three more times and then curse. I send an email to the cleaning service that we use, asking them to clean this room as well when they're in tomorrow. I don't care how bougie that makes me, this is ridiculous.

I walk around the floor to the most senior of each group that I had written out on a piece of paper, asking them to get their list back to me by the end of the day.

I clean up my mess in the inventory closet, and then trudge to my office. I glance at the mirror as I pass it and wrinkle my nose. I am definitely going to have to make time for a shower before I see Tori tonight.

I am coming into the office tomorrow to finish placing the rest of my inventory order. I'm so tired and done, and I sigh in relief when I check the clock. It's finally time to go home. I still have a ton of nervous energy in my body, and it feels like bees are moving under my skin.

I grab my keys and phone, shutting down all of my electronics, then head out to my car, locking up and waving at anyone that I see as I walk. I know that they will let everyone know that the boss has left for the day and step into their roles for the night.

Unlocking the door to my Jeep, I toss my phone into the cup holder and climb in. I shut the door behind me, sighing as I turn on the car.

I don't live far from work, and I'm glad for that now as I drive home. My mind is racing in a million different directions and I realize that we may not have a plan for dinner.

I dial Link with a sigh. "Hey, Griffin and Tesa are coming over with Tori tonight, do we have plans for dinner or do you need me to pick something up?"

Link snorts. *"Do you really think that I would let Tori come home and not have food ready for her. Who do you think I am, you?"*

I roll my eyes. I sucked at taking care of Tori while she was working from home, but I am used to being around fully functioning adults. That's not to say that Tori isn't, but she tends to get hyper focused and then forgets to do things like eat and pee.

"Okay, okay, fucker. I just wanted to make sure. I'm almost home."

"What crawled up your ass, Miguel?"

"Nothing, nothing, I'm just in a foul mood I guess. I'll be there soon." I toss my phone back into the cup holder after hanging up.

I pull into the driveway fifteen minutes later, making sure that I'm not blocking anyone, then I grab my things, get out of the car and walk up the stairs. Link opens the door as I walk in and his eyebrows disappear under all of that hair of his. I know that I look like a mess.

"I had a fight with a dusty room, and the room won during inventory," I grumble. "I'm going to go shower. I'll be down before she gets home."

I start to walk past him and up the stairs. Link closes the door as he watches me go.

"Need any company getting all that dust off?" He smirks at me and looks sexy as fuck.

At that moment I wish that Tori was home because I need to fight or fuck out this energy, and I don't think Link and I are there yet.

I shake my head, continuing. I say over my shoulder, "Not today, *carino*. I'm in a fucked up mood. I don't want you to run afoul of it."

I stride into my room, tearing off my shirt quickly. The dust is starting to itch, and I can't wait to wash this off. I unsnap my jeans, pushing them off my hips, with my boxers following.

"Goddamn, you really are a work of art," I glance over my shoulder and realize that I left the door open.

I smirk, toeing off my shoes as well, and then kick everything off.

"Babe, I really don't want to fight with you, which leaves-"

"So fuck me." Link reaches behind his head for his shirt and pulls it off in a move that is incredibly sexy.

I check for drool as I watch him unveil his abs. His arms flex as his shirt comes off the rest of the way and he throws it to the side. He unsnaps his jeans and pushes them off his hips. He's not wearing underwear. Fuck, he's gorgeous.

He stalks towards me after he kicks off his pants, then grabs my neck and kisses me hard. He pulls me to him hard so that our cocks rub together.

"Link," I groan. "Fuck, if you don't walk away I'm going to turn you around and fuck your tight ass. I don't have it in me to be gentle right now."

He chuckles as he kisses up my neck.

"Baby, when are you ever gentle? You fuck like a stallion. Why would you ever change? I just want to make you feel good. Can I make you feel good?"

He fists my cock, looking down between us to watch as our

cocks are both weeping pre cum. He drags his hand up, dragging his thumb through the salty liquid as it continues to drip out of my tip.

"Fuck, you really are big," he says almost reverently, biting his lip.

"We don't-"

"Yeah, we do. I want to strangle your big fat cock in my ass. Is that direct enough?"

Fuck me, yeah. I attack his mouth, clashing teeth, dueling with his tongue. I kiss him how I'm planning to fuck him, then push him into the bathroom and up against the wall.

I grab the lube from my counter that I've been keeping there just in case we end up one day all in my room. I may never have been a boy scout, but I always come prepared. I then turn, starting the shower so that it'll be ready.

I drop to my knees and lick up his dick, lapping up the moisture that he's leaking. He lets his head fall back onto the wall, running his fingers through my hair, tugging with a moan.

I swirl my tongue around the tip of his cock and he grunts.

"You're such a fucking tease, Miguel."

I chuckle as I wrap my lips around him and suck before swallowing him whole. He gives a strangled cry as I continue to chuckle as I swallow.

Link tugs harder on my hair, fucking my face. I let him as I liberally coat my fingers with lube before rubbing them over his hole. Link clenches and I unsheath my teeth just a little in warning.

He sighs and relaxes, I slip a thick finger into his ass. He pushes out a little, which allows me deeper. He's such a good boy.

I slip a second inside of him fairly quickly, not letting him get used to the first. He breathes hard and I slide up his cock, letting it slip out of my mouth.

"Widen your stance, baby."

Still facing me, he widens his legs. I watch him take my fingers, all the while praising him and reminding him to breathe. I push a third finger into him and he moans, thrusting his hips into the air to help me fuck him.

We are going to run out of time in a hurry soon. I pull my fingers from him, standing up and ease him to the shower. I may not have a shower like Link, but it's a large walk-in. Perfect for fucking him against the wall.

I push him towards the tile, telling him to hold himself against it. I still have the bottle in my hand, so I liberally coat my cock with lube, before hugging Link from behind.

I kiss him hard over his shoulder, thrusting against the crack of his ass. He gasps every time I brush against his hole and shivers. I fist his cock, gliding up and down, thanks to the lube still coating my hand. I pay special attention to the tip.

When I know he's close, I line my cock up against him.

"Are you gonna be a good boy and take every inch of my cock, *mi amor*? I'm going to take you hard and fast and you're gonna come all over my hand so I can lick it off as I fuck you. Can you handle that?"

"Yes! Yes please please fuck me!" Link is overstimulated and greedy for me and I grin. That's exactly what I wanted.

I grip myself to make sure I'm steady, and push his torso forward so that he's braced against the wall. Now I can watch myself fuck him and he can push back into me.

I can't wait any longer and I push hard into him. Link cries out but shoves his ass out to take me deeper. Soon I am balls deep inside of him and I groan. Fuck, he's so hot and tight.

I wrap my arm around his waist and start thrusting. Soon

the only noises are moans, the slapping of my thighs against his ass, and the shower running.

I notice Link goes to wrap his hand around his cock and I slap it away, then grab him around the throat, turning his head to kiss him.

"Mine. You'll come because I made you or not at all."

Link whines and nods. Such a good boy.

I wrap my hand around him, jerking him off. Link looks down, watching me please him as I pound into his tight ass. He can't thrust forward or move because I'm holding him so tightly. He's at my mercy, and it's beautiful to watch him submit to me.

It's a very different experience, fucking Tori versus dominating Link. I have to be more careful with Tori, which I absolutely do not mind. Link just fucking takes it and asks for more. It's a heady feeling knowing that both of them are mine.

Link screams my name, painting the wall and my hand with his cum, and I bury my head in his shoulder as I shudder, and follow soon after.

We breathe hard together, as if we've run several marathons. Lazily, I bring my hand up to my mouth and lick and suck his cum off my fingers. Link laughs breathlessly as he hears me.

"You're un-fucking-believable," he groans, shaking his head.

"I can't let any of this go to waste. It's one of my favorite deserts. The other is the taste of our girl's pussy." I pull out of him gently and grin as my cum follows.

Like the caveman that I am, I shove some back into his hole with my thumb and then smack his ass.

Link yelps, rolling his eyes over his shoulder at me.

"That's mine, and don't forget it." I move to the shower to

wash up, and he follows. "Baby, I'm gonna be feeling your cock for days in my ass. I'm not even sorry."

I grin, completely sated, all my previous anxiety gone. I kiss him hard, biting his lip. I'm really glad that he talked his way into sharing my shower.

———

LINK

I WALK DOWN the stairs with Miguel, with a secret smile. I can feel him still in every step, every shift in my weight. Miguel throws his arms around my shoulders when we move off the last step with an easy grin.

His earlier anger and aggression seems to be gone, so whatever Tori has to tell us, hopefully he'll take it better. We are always so worried about her, but it's been better since her ex was put in jail.

"Tori, are you here yet?" Miguel yells as we walk towards the back of the house.

"In the kitchen!"

We walk into the kitchen and everyone is laughing and talking.

"What am I, chopped liver?" Tesa teases with a giggle, knowing that that isn't true.

"Yeah, yeah." Miguel pulls her into a hug with a chuckle, kissing her temple before going to kiss Tori.

"He's in a good mood," Tesa murmurs to me, eyes questioning.

"Yup," is all I say with a twitch of my lips.

"Oh my...Lalalalala." Tesa spins away and I bark out a laugh.

She's seriously so much fun to mess with. I know that Tori and Tesa change our names when they talk about our 'sexcapades', as she likes to call it. Otherwise Tesa can't enjoy the gossip session.

Shaking my head, I focus on what's happening in the kitchen. Griffin is here and chatting with Greg and Tori. It's so funny to me that he's decided to befriend Tori. He's a jerk ninety percent of the time and Tori is so sweet. I wonder if they're at each other's throats often.

Tesa claps to get everyone's attention. "We need to feed Tori before she turns into a gremlin. It's been hours since that shit show lunch that we had."

Wait...what happened at lunch? The guys and I turn towards Tori with raised eyebrows. Tori glares at Tesa with a growl. Oh shit, maybe she is gonna turn into a gremlin. Her stomach growls and that cinches it.

"Let's all grab food, and Tori can tell us about her day and what she wanted to tell us," I chuckle. I'm not laughing at her, but at Tesa's way of directing the conversation when it comes to Tori.

Tori nods. "I'm starving, and I actually want to eat, so I'm going to take advantage of that."

Griffin frowns as he grabs a plate. "How many tacos do you want Tori, and hard or soft? I'm also aware that you can do this yourself, but I want you to tell me why you aren't eating. You're too tiny as it is for that shit."

I glance at Tesa to see if his attention upsets her and she smiles behind her hand as she gets food. Ohh...sneak attack Tesa. I see you girl.

Tori opens and then closes her mouth, eyes bouncing back and forth between Griffin and Tesa.

"Uh, when I'm super anxious, my stomach cramps and I can't eat. Lately, I haven't even been hungry, and then other times I've been starving. I don't know." She shrugs with a sigh.

"Oh, and all hard please, three tacos." That's my girl. I fist pump where she can't see me, happy that she's eating.

Miguel walks past me on the way to the large kitchen table that we have, squeezing my ass. My butt flexes on reflex and I wince. He chuckles as he sits at the table, winking at me. Such a brat.

Soon, we are all eating, Tori happily dunking chips into queso and doing a wiggle in her seat. I would give almost anything for life to be this simple for her.

We chat about everything but Tori's day so that she can happily eat. We talk about how I got a bid on a new building this week for the construction company, planning to break ground in two weeks. We talk about how Miguel is opening a Monday night open mic night, and Tori's ears prick. I've heard her sing, I idly wonder if she'd consider performing.

We talk about all of the things big or small, until finally we are done eating. Tori takes a big sip of margarita and I wonder why she feels she needs to bolster her courage. Greg made the drinks, and he has a heavy tequila pour. Tori doesn't even flinch.

"Okay," she murmurs, looking up at us. "So, this isn't great. I went to lunch with Tesa, and in the bathroom, I ran into Veronica. She told me that she's been sleeping with Anthony, probably for most of the year that we've been living together. So I feel like I should take a hot shower and I'm super glad I took the STI test because ick." She shudders, then continues, "Anyway, she told me that she was his alibi," her voice hitches and she shakes her head to clear it.

"She told me that they would probably be letting him out within hours at the most. Veronica acted smug, like I was dumb and it was only a matter of time before Anthony had me again. She acted like I would be the side piece, used for his darker fantasties, things that she couldn't fulfill. She was totally blasé about him taking away my freedom and reprogramming me to be his puppet."

I feel the blood rising as I listen, and have a feeling that it's about to get worse.

"Anthony wants to turn me into someone that I will never be for him again. I will never be that weak willed scared person that he wants me to be. Veronica doesn't understand that he probably won't keep her around for long after he's done with her. I was shaken up after I talked with her, and I ran out to Tesa. We called Griffin several times, and that's when we found out that Anthony is walking free. All charges were dropped, and they have no interest in entertaining my statement."

"What the fuck?!" Miguel roars and Tori flinches.

"Dial it down by like a hundred," Tesa says with a sigh.

"Why. Why is this happening?" I bite out. I'm just as pissed about this.

"Corruption." Griffins bites out. "Trust me, I'm angry about this too. I went out on a lead on a case I've been working on that I found out was bullshit. I've been super vocal about Tori's case, and I don't fucking care. But, when I came back, Anthony was gone. They said they couldn't hold him. The chief asked me into his office and sat me down. He said that after the call earlier this week where two officers were called to investigate a noise complaint, it was obvious that you were not someone that needed help from the police. You obviously were a whore that needed to be muzzled."

Our jaws drop.

Griffin raises his hand. "I said that what two consenting adults do behind closed doors, even if it is outside, is up to them. However, you did not consent to being choked, assaulted, or mistreated. He paled at that, but said that the two police officers had not reported any marks. The male officer that came out to the house was fired this week, and the other was transferred to another department three hours away."

Mother-trucking-shitballs.

Tesa shakes her head, reaching out to hold Tori's hand. Her head is down and she's wiping her eyes. "This is so unfair. Her ex is a monster, and everyone is just turning a blind eye to all of this!" Tesa is pissed and I don't blame her. Her best friend is getting the short end of the stick here.

Griffin slams his fist on the table. "Here's what I know from digging a bit at work. Anthony St. James is close to the mayor, the chief, and plays a weekly poker game with over half the officers in Georgetown. He made sure that he was well-connected here. It's not fair that my hands are tied and I can't do anything, especially when there are people who can."

Tori wraps her arms around herself and Griffin narrows his eyes at her. Griffin glares at Greg and he shakes his head at him. You know it's bad when the cop is pissed that the mercenary for hire can't kill his girlfriend's ex boyfriend. His hands are just as tied, and Tori and Tesa don't have any idea about what Greg's job really entails.

Tori's leg starts to bounce and I can't sit still anymore. I stand and pick her up, sitting in her chair, I drap her on my lap.

She sits stiffly instead of cuddling into me, staring off to the side. She's checking out of the conversation and I can feel that she's shaking. Griffin meets my eyes and mouths, "She's spiraling." Fuck, I know.

I rub her arms, and she's covered in goosebumps. "Maybe, maybe I should go. That would be better, right? Staying here is complicated, and it just puts people in danger. I don't want to, but I can't go back to him."

Tesa and the guys look at her in shock and I tighten my

hands around her arms gently and release. Fuck, its so bad that she wants to run. Call me selfish, but I can't lose her. She and Miguel are everything, and... I can't.

Tesa shakes her head. "You're not leaving. You know what, today has been a lot." She stands up, shoving her chair back, which makes Tori look up at her. "I can't believe that Peter threw so much at you and made you come in today. Having all of those meetings and figuring out your new duties. He really should have planned better. How many people cursed you out today?"

Tori chuckles, starting to relax. My jaw drops. I am not worthy, she is masterful.

"No one cursed me out per se. I had three meetings, two emergency video calls, and Peter insisted that I find authors that I can transfer over to newer editors. They're expanding a lot, and I think Peter is overwhelmed. I don't even know what all of my duties will be yet."

"But, wait. If you're transferring people to others, that means less work, right?" Greg is frowning at her, not understanding why she's not more excited.

It's nice to hear her talk about what she does, because we all have no idea, even if it was a distraction tactic to get Tori to talk about something else for now. Somehow, it feels like this promotion will mean more work, not less.

Griffin stands, grabbing the pitcher to refill it. "I feel like this calls for more drinks," he sighs. "At the very least, it may get me laid tonight."

"Dude!" Miguel yells, throwing a napkin at him, and I laugh. I have a feeling that if he had anything heavier that wouldn't break, he'd have thrown that at him.

Griffin ducks his head and runs away as Tesa giggles.

Tori rolls her eyes at their antics. "Yes, I definitely need drinks, but it won't get you laid by me," she giggles. Miguel snorts, and Tori snuggles into me finally, content to take comfort in my arms. Thank god.

"So he gave me a stack of manuscripts and told me to choose ten. He wants me to take on ten new clients. This means scheduling calls, meetings, video chats to make sure we're a good fit, reading and editing their books, and making sure they're ready for publishing before it goes to Tesa in marketing. I already gave him a few names that can be transferred immediately, but now I have to figure out who else to move. Then, I peeked into an email from HR and read something about continuing education credits being mandatory for the job, which is fine. However, they want me to take fifteen credits over the next year. That's just a lot on top of everything that I already do."

"Peter never said any of this," Tesa whispers in horror. "When the hell do I get to see my bestie?! Does it at least pay well?"

"He had me chasing him all over as he talked to me today, and I had to deal with my current position's responsibilities. I know that they want me to sign in on Monday. I guess it does? I started at forty-thousand a year ago and this job would put me at sixty-five-thousand. So yes, it'll pay well, but fuck. I'm so tired and overwhelmed by everything, that I can't tell you the last time I had a vacation." Tori sags in defeat in my arms with a sigh.

We all look at her in aghast. "Hold on, when's the last time you went on a vacation? Don't be dramatic," Griffin demands, as he brings the pitcher to the table.

"I'm really not being dramatic. Soo...this wasn't even really a vacation because it was for school. I did an immersion course the summer of my freshman year of college. It was a two month super intense course where I learned Spanish while I was in Spain. I loved it. I still explored, and did excursions with the university to immerse myself in the culture."

"Wait," Miguel's eyes light up. "So this means I could take you to a Spanish restaurant, and I could have an entire conversation with you in Spanish?"

"Um...you can have an entire conversation with me in Spanish...anywhere, Miguel. But yes," she laughs at him.

"Oh my god, it's a date. How ridiculous is it that we haven't really gone on dates," Miguel sighs.

Tori shrugs like it doesn't bother her. Doesn't every girl want to have dates though? Greg leans forward with a sigh, "Baby girl, about our date tomorrow, I don't think..."

Seriously?! Right this second?

Tori warily looks over at him. "Great. Something else that this man gets to fucking take from me. I'm so sick of-"

"No! Tori, no. I still want to go with you. I was just going to suggest that we not stay in town. Why don't we go to Myrtle Beach? There are festivals happening tomorrow, and it may help you to be outside. You've been really stressed out, and this can be like a mini getaway."

I scowl at Greg. You really should have led with that. Tesa smacks him over the head, cursing at him in Spanish and Miguel sniggers. Griffin smacks his hand on the table and Tori and Tesa jump.

"Ground rules! Or I'm not letting you go. You stay with Greg at all times, and that includes the bathroom. I don't know how he's finding you and that's concerning for me. I don't know if he has people exclusively reporting back to him or if he has some other way to track you."

Oh shit. Tori absently reaches for her necklace for comfort, and I wonder if Anthony may have bugged her phone, or AirTagged something that she keeps with her at all times. I decide to ask Greg if it's possible to check because Griffin makes a good point.

"I know that Greg can protect you, but you've been attacked in enough bathrooms that it's become clichéd. So if you can, make sure that you do the single or family stall and that he waits outside for you. You don't look at anything without the other at your side. If you can't do this, then I'll forbid you from going, understood?"

"Yes, Daddy," Tori and Tesa answer, batting their eyelashes. Oh shit. These two are such brats together, and I often forget it. Griffin looks gobsmacked, as he reaches for a poured glass of margarita and takes a deep sip. He looks up at the ceiling and then shakes his head. He looks back at them and says, "Absolutely not. That shit can never happen again."

Greg, Miguel, and I laugh because we know that he's absolutely not interested in Tori, but I have to admit that if it had been anyone other than Tesa that it would have been hot. I watch Griffin discreetly adjust himself before sitting down and I hide a smile by kissing Tori's shoulder. Griffin has bitten off more than he can chew by deciding to be friends with Tori and dating Tesa.

Tesa and Tori are besides themselves giggling, proud that they got under Griffin's skin, which I have to admit is usually difficult.

We spend the rest of the evening laughing and teasing each other, making sure to keep Tori relaxed and distracted. She's had a crazy day, and she deserves a little peace.

thirty-seven

I head out my door to pick up Tori from her house for our date today. Tori had wanted to sleep in her bed last night, but I heard Tesa tell her to sleep in her bed with her to make sure she didn't have nightmares. Why didn't I know that she has nightmares?

I had met Griffin's eyes over their head as they walked out and he shrugged. He didn't know either. Griffin had gone home that night, saying something about seeing them Sunday for their day, whatever that meant.

I walk across the grass and through the side gate that connects the two properties, and move up the porch steps. Yesterday was a series of ups and downs for our girl. I want to give her a distraction and have fun today.

I still plan to protect her though. My tight jeans pocket is completely cut out, so that I can get to my knife easier. I have a holster strapped to my upper thigh for easy access too. I'm also wearing boots with my jeans, and there's a knife in my boot as well. I'm hoping that I don't have to use any of this, but I have planned for every possibility that I can.

I knock on the front door with a grin, and Tori opens it with a smile.

"Hi, handsome."

She's wearing a pretty blue, cap sleeved flowy dress, with printed white and yellow flowers, and a low neckline. Her dress ends at her calves and she's wearing sandals. Her hair is curled in beachy waves and she has a bracelet on and earrings. I notice that the earrings are in the shape of little unicorns. She's absolutely gorgeous.

She's wearing her parents' necklace again, and I think back to what Link had mentioned to me last night before we headed up to bed. He thought that there may be something on her person that could be bugged with a tracer, and I think he could be right. I'll have to figure out a way to ask her if I could search her for it today. I don't want her to freak out with a possibility that is just a hypothesis right now.

I grin at her, leaning down to kiss her. She relaxes into the kiss, wrapping her arms around my neck.

"Hey, hey! No lewd behavior on the porch!"

Ugh, I thought Griffin went home. I look over my shoulder to see that he is getting out of his car with coffee.

"Hi Griff!" Tori waves happily at him. Ugh, she has a cutesy name for him and everything. They really are officially besties. Weird.

"Hey. You look pretty. Are you going to be safe today?"

Tori nods, raising three fingers in scouts honor and I chuckle. I wonder if she really was a Girl Scout. Griffin rolls his eyes, leaning down to hug her. He cuffs my shoulder with a grin.

"Have fun guys. I am taking Tesa out today too, but I brought you a coffee," Griff says as he hands Tori an iced coffee, ignoring me.

Meh, Tori needs another coffee around this time anyway. I

glance at my watch to make sure we are still on time, and it's exactly ten am. Perfect.

"You have everything, baby girl?"

"Yep! I'm ready!"

I walk her down the stairs to the car, I left outside of the gates, after saying goodbye to Griffin. I open the door for her, helping her in. I packed a cooler with snacks and bottles of water that are now on the floor behind her. I also put a pillow and blanket back there because I know that she's been working non stop. I kiss her, putting her seatbelt on reverently and close the door. I'm in protective mode, and I know Tori can tell. She just smiles at me and lets me proceed.

I am almost bouncing in excitement and I force myself to walk around to my door. This date is a lot of firsts for me, and I want to make sure that I do it right.

"Have fun with our girl, lucky fucker!"

I look behind me as I open my door with a laugh. Miguel and Link are standing on the porch with a grin on their faces, and Miguel has his arm around Link's shoulders. I know exactly how those two will be spending their day, and I shake my head. They're going to lunch and then probably going to fuck their way through the house. Miguel is so much more relaxed lately, and it's about damned time.

"Yeah, yeah! Y'all have fun too." I wink at them, and Link blushes. I can't with how cute they are.

I wave and climb into the cab, then dig into the cooler for snacks, and put a few things next to Tori in the cup holder before turning on the car.

Tori dances in excitement in her seat as she opens up a snack. I chuckle, putting on my seatbelt. I pull up a playlist of songs that I know that she likes and she beams at me, leaning back into her seat happily.

"Need anything, baby girl?"

"No. I'm doing pretty perfect right now, darlin'."

I hit the gas, and we spend the next two hours chatting. Tori decides to play twenty questions, and the time flies by. I learn that her first kiss was when she was nineteen, when she was in Spain, she lost her virginity to Anthony, and her favorite color is royal blue.

She also told me that her favorite guilty pleasure is reading reverse harem, and I remember Tesa's list. I don't think she's actually had time to read for pleasure lately. I know that she's hanging out with Tesa and Griffin tomorrow, and know that Tesa will find a way for her to get her reading time in.

I pull into a parking space, thinking about Griffin and their odd friendship. "Hey," I say, opening her door for her. "How did you and Griffin become friends anyway? Y'all are so different."

"Oh, does it bother you? I know y'all are friends…" She looks at me uncertainly as she turns towards me in the seat.

I shake my head, caging her in my arms. "No, baby. You can be friends with anyone that you want to be friends with." I drag my nose up her neck and her breath hitches. I kiss her pulse on her throat gently, and whisper in her ear, "I really am just curious."

Tori beams at me. "He was an asshole to me and I sassed him. I wasn't gonna take his shit, and he told me we were going to be best friends and that was it."

My jaw drops. "Really?!"

"Yep. I said I would call him out on his shit, and wouldn't let him get away with it. So Tesa, Griffin, and I have kind of become the three musketeers. They have their dates, and Griffin plans our time to hang out."

She shrugs. "I asked Tesa if it bothered her at all, and she said that he said he felt pulled to me like he would a little sister. So he claimed me, and that was that."

Huh. I pull her to me, picking her up to lift her out of the truck. She's so short that she struggled when she got in. I let her slide down my front, kissing her hard.

"I'm glad you have people," I murmur as I stare into her eyes. "You're not alone anymore, so remember that. We're all here for you."

Tori's eyes fill with tears, but I know they aren't sad tears. I kiss her as she blinks them away, then place her on her feet. She has her purse slung across her chest and I close the door, locking it behind her. Tugging her with me, I head towards the food trucks that are at this fall festival. Later in the day, there's a music festival I bought tickets for that I know she'll enjoy too on the beach.

Tori smiles happily when she sees the food trucks. "What are you in the mood for, baby girl?"

"Hmm. I really want street corn and tacos!"

Of course she does. I grin because that sounds absolutely amazing right now. She's hyped up on caffeine and excitement and I let her lead me to the food truck. We grab tacos and eat as we walk, checking out the different art stalls, jewelry, and knick knacks that are being sold. We take fun photos at the different photo backdrops that they have up, and soon we're walking up the road to the beach.

We left the truck because it's a gorgeous day, and parking was sure to be a nightmare at the music festival.

She looks up at me with a smile, and I can't believe that I'm out with her today. It's been easy, fun, and she hasn't shown any real signs of anxiety. I wish that she could have more easy days like this, and I have felt guilty for weeks.

I remove people who are problems for a living. Even Griffin, who's a police officer, thinks that her ex needs to die. I've dug into his history, and there's too many people who would miss him. He also doesn't keep any real schedule. He's rarely home, and when I hacked into his email and phone messages, I didn't see anything that would show that he's a bad person.

The only thing that I can think of, is that he has a burner phone. I believe that this man needs to die. I've seen the marks, I have experienced Tori's anxiety attacks and how twitchy she is. Link told me that he found her talking to herself in the shower, asking who would miss her, and my heart clenched. I can't imagine life without this gorgeous girl in it. I just need more time to find a way.

I pull out my tickets, handing them over as we go in. The concerts are on the beach, and I can hear the sound checks starting. Tori bounces on her toes and bites her lip. I lift my eyebrow at her in askance.

"I have to pee." She rolls her eyes and I throw my head back and laugh.

She has the world's tiniest bladder when she's moving, so we have hit the bathrooms together a lot. It's adorable.

"Let's go before the music starts, baby girl. Wait till I tell the guys that you actually have the world's tiniest bladder when you're not working. They won't believe it."

I go with her to the restrooms, waiting outside for her to come out.

"Hey, aren't you waiting outside of the wrong restrooms?" I glance up from my phone to see a bottled blonde with huge breasts beside me flirting. Eh, super not interested. Maybe in a club before Tori, but that's not the case anymore.

I give her an uninterested look. "Nope. Waiting for my girl."

The woman huffs. "You don't trust her to go to the bath-room by herself? Are you that controlling?"

I chuckle darkly, shaking my head. "No. I trust her just fine. I don't trust the rest of the fuckers in the world. Have a good night."

I dismiss her with an eye roll as Tori walks out. I tried to be nice, and she decided to unsheath the claws. Bad habits die hard, so she got the asshole. I wrap my arm around Tori's shoulders and kiss her head. Tori wraps her arms around my waist and squeezes.

The bottle blonde walks up to Tori and says, "Hey! I just wanted to let you know that your boyfriend hit on me. Girls have to stick together, you know."

I look at her in horror as the bitch tosses her hair over her shoulder and looks at me with a smirk.

"My boyfriends have better taste than that." Tori shrugs with a smile. "Have the night you deserve, babe."

I snort and move around the girl with Tori, whispering, "Burn," in her ear.

Tori giggles. "I feel like I deserve a drink after that."

"You get whatever your pixie heart desires, sweet girl. That was bad ass. I thought you were gonna kill me," I confess to her.

"I mean, why? It's true, you have way better taste than that." She smirks. "Even when you were a fuck boy."

"Ha! You're feisty today! I'm here for it."

I grab us both a bottle of beer, and then find a spot on the beach with her. Everything is open space, no seats, and there's this excitement in the air.

It's a rock concert, and Tori jumps up and down in front of me as the first band goes up. She dances with me, sings, and we have the best time. We don't have any issues the rest of the night, and around nine we are walking out to the car.

Tori danced off her buzz, and she's happily humming as she walks with me. It's a max exodus of people that had done what we had and parked a few blocks away.

It's dark, so I have her walk slightly in front of me so my hands are free, scanning the area as we move. I don't think it's paranoia when we've had so much shit happen recently. I want the night to end as drama free as it has been all day.

We get to the car and I help Tori in. However when I turn as I close the door, I'm met with a fist. There are three guys around me, so I shake it off and yell at Tori to lock the doors.

I hear the snick of the doors locking and I unleash the part that I keep hidden from her.

I grab the guy who tried to punch me again, turning him and yanking his arm up. He screams and I grin. Yes, I enjoy my moments of violence too in my line of work. This is just for fun, since they tried to fuck up my first date.

"Anyone want to explain what the fuck this is about?" I ask. As I twist his arm up higher, I know that it will break soon. I keep my eye on the other two men as I kick the guy's legs out from under him.

"You, you hit on my girl!" The burly blond to the right of me roars and I indulge in a small eye roll.

"Bro, you see the bombshell I have in my car? I absolutely wouldn't hit on your girl. You're either lying or you're getting played. So which is it? 'Cause if it was the bottle blonde with the fake tits, then I vote that you were played."

"They're not fake!" The girl comes out from behind the car to say this and I sigh. Called it.

"Are we really gonna continue this?"

I get my answer when the disgruntled boyfriend comes running at me, so I break the fucker's arm that I'm holding and the punk screams, then passes out. Pathetic.

I make short work of the other two, putting one in a sleeper hold, and slamming the other into his own car. I keep the girl in my sights the entire time, until I have to turn slightly to get momentum to knock out the last guy. I hear a gun cock and I sigh. *Fuck this bitch.* I slip my hand into my pocket where my knife is with a relaxed grin. There are few lights in this parking area and everything is covered in shadows. I doubt that she's proficient enough with a gun to hit me.

But I don't want to be shot today so I make myself a smaller target by shifting my body so that I'm turned sideways.

"Are you really that shallow that you had to pull this shit? I don't even know your name." I snort.

"I don't like to be turned down," she growls.

I sigh. "Then make better life choices!"

I fake to the right and then make a run for her, knocking her arm upwards as the gun goes off. Shot goes wide and I yank the gun out of her hand, then push her on the ground and she gasps in shock. Idiot.

I call the emergency line, and ask for a patrol to come pick up the trash. Due to higher traffic here, there are more police patrols out. Two police cars pull into where I am and I make sure to kick the gun away from me before they can see me and raise my hands. I explain the situation to the police officer who comes up to me and he shakes his head as he looks around the parking lot.

"For fucks sakes," he mutters.

"Yup. Sorry I broke one of their arms, but he came at me, ya know?"

"Yeah. No, don't worry. I apologize for the disturbance on your night out with your girl. She good?"

We look over at the truck and I motion for her to come over. She unlocks the door and jumps from the cab, running for me. She slams into my body hard and I rock back but stand my ground.

"I'm okay, baby. I'm totally fine." She's breathing hard and crying.

The police officer chuckles. "It's probably a good thing you stayed in the truck, miss. It looks like your partner had it under control. You're free to head home, we'll be taking things from here."

I kiss Tori hard and she relaxes into my arms. I was impressed by her jump from the truck, and glad that she didn't hurt herself. I walk her back to the open door and pick her up into the cab. She wraps her arms around her and I close the door, then run around the front, get in and look at her, turning on the light.

"What the fuck, Greg? I had no idea you could fight like that, and then...when she pulled out the gun and you ran *towards* her...I couldn't believe it!"

"Baby. I knew it would be fine. She obviously didn't have much training with the stupid gun. I was fine the whole time. I am sometimes in dangerous situations at work. I learned how to make sure that I always come home."

This gets her attention and she relaxes. I know that my time is running out and I'll have to tell her soon, but she's already upset. I can't tell her yet. I distract her by changing the subject, then shut off the overhead light, and turn on the car.

"We almost made it out scot-free," I tease her.

She giggles. "It wasn't my fault!" She throws her hands up and does an adorable wiggle.

I want to tell her that it's never her fault, but I don't bring it up. We head home, and she falls asleep on the drive back. I sigh and call Griffin. I tell him about what happened and he snorts.

"When are you gonna tell her that you're basically a ninja?"

I roll my eyes. I am fucking not a ninja. Ass-hat.

"Soon, and you know I'm none of that. I'm just really good at what I do," I mutter the last part.

"Mmhmm. Look, you do good work. You're fair, you're not just for hire. You're one of the few that have a code. I will always look the other way on that. It just pisses me off that you haven't told her. She's important to me, and I can't help but feel like this is all going

to blow up in your face. I don't want to have to pick up the pieces because you stuck your head in the sand."

He's right and I hate it. I hit the steering wheel and sigh. "I'll tell her this week, okay? I just need to figure out how."

"Yeah, okay man, whatever. I won't say anything. Tomorrow is bestie day."

I snort. "Bestie day?"

"Yep. My time with Tesa and Tori, uninterrupted by you fuckers."

"They have you wrapped around their fingers, you know that right?"

Griffin laughs. *"Yep. I don't have any problems with this. I really like Tesa and Tori... Tori as a friend. Tesa said that she claimed her and that was just it, and that's exactly what it's like to be around her. You want to see her smile, protect her, and be one of her people. I've never in my life been friends with a girl. She reminds me of my sister, and I'm going to invite her to come visit me soon to meet them I think."*

I knew he wasn't sexually interested in Tori because when she teased and called him daddy he had been less than amused. She's like his bratty best friend that can call you on your shit. I think it's good that she has friends outside of just us. She deserves to be able to let loose and enjoy herself with friends. Her choice of friend in Griffin will always make me laugh though. I finish my call with Griffin and soon we are home. Tori wakes up sleepily. She's fucking adorable.

"We're here?"

"Yeah, baby girl, we are. You sleeping with us or your house?"

"Mmmm. Mine please. I know Tesa has a whole day planned together, starting with breakfast." I walk her to the door and kiss her hard.

"I had fun today," she says smiling, not mentioning the less than fun things.

"Good. That was the first date that I've ever been on, and I'm glad that it was with you. Sweet dreams, baby girl."

Tori sighs happily, hugging me goodbye, before unlocking the door and going in.

I know that I'm going to have a lot to answer for soon, but today was a pretty perfect day.

————

TORI

I SIT up abruptly from a nightmare gasping for air. *Just a dream, not real.* I turn on the light, watching as the shadows are dispelled, then grab my phone and curse. Five am? On a Sunday?! Come on.

Knowing that I won't be able to sleep, I get up and pee. I wash my face, dry it, and then stalk back and forth in my room. I need to run. Fuck. Maybe I can see if the guys will come with me? They'll ask questions though... argh.

I dress in running clothes, put on my shoes, then grab my arm band, and my phone. What the hell am I going to do now? Double crap, I don't know what to do.

I open my door and start walking, trying to figure out how I'm going to expel all of this energy. My anxiety is getting higher as I walk and I shake out my hands.

"Tori?" Griffin steps out of Tesa's room in low slung shorts and no shirt. "Why are you up?"

"I-it's dumb."

Griffin crosses his arms over his chest and frowns. "Nope.

Start over." I huff out a breath, bouncing up and down on my toes.

"Okay, fine. I woke up and now I have all of this energy and I have to go running. But I can't because I'm not supposed to go by myself and I'm kind of losing it."

"Tell me why you woke up and I'll go with you." Griffin's eyes are stormy as he says this and his stance tells me that he'll bug the shit out of me until I tell him.

God freaking dammit. "I dreamed it was dark and raining and I was panicking. I was running away from something but I couldn't see what. Then something tackled me, everything went black, and I woke up."

Griffin nods. "K, I'll meet you downstairs in five."

I blink, bouncing coming to a standstill. "That's it?"

"Yep. Time's a-wastin' babes. Leave a note on the coffee maker for Tesa."

I giggle that he knows that I leave my notes there for her and start walking. I move downstairs, head to the kitchen to fill up my water bottle, and then write a quick note for Tesa. I'm usually back by the time that she wakes up, but I still do it just in case.

I head to the front door as Griffin is walking down the stairs. "Ready?"

I nod, my ability to use words before coffee exceeded. Griffin snorts, knowing all about the four sip rule. Listen, rules are there for the safety of others. I turn off the alarm, walk out with Griffin and lock up. I click a button to reset everything with a sigh. He stares impassively as I finish.

"Warm up, and then we'll go."

His voice is a little cold, but I ignore it. I did kind of drag him out of his girlfriend's bed. I slip on my AirPods, set my music to *About Damn Time* by Lizzo, and start stretching. Once

I'm done, I glance at him and he nods towards the road. Cool, he can be my bodyguard while I run.

I ignore him from then on out once I hit the pavement. I let my feet take me where they want, my playlist encouraging me to run faster, harder. I feel like I'm running away from my nightmare, from Anthony, from my shit show of a life, but I refuse to examine the metaphor. I know my trauma, I understand that the nightmares aren't normal, or the room starting to darken from anxiety, and losing my breath from a panic attack.

I know that all, and still. Still I can't do anything about it because the threat to my existence, to the Tori that I am now is still out there. He'll never stop.

Never.

All of a sudden I'm yanked back, and I stop. I glance behind me and see it's Griffin. I focus on my breathing. I'm out of breath, but that's what I was going for. He pulls my AirPods out of my ears, glaring at me.

"Is that how you always run?! How are you not sick and puking right now?"

I can't talk because I don't have the breath to. I lean over with my hands on my knees and force out, "Never eat before a run."

Griffin glares at me.

"You're two steps from collapsing, Tori-girl. You can't run from your demons forever." Griffin's Irish and I can hear his brogue come out more when he's angry, like now. I have a hard time understanding why he's mad. The guys have watched me run. I typically run just like this. My legs do feel a little rubbery, which isn't completely normal and I sigh. We were passing a park, so I walk over and collapse onto the grass.

I open my water and carefully drink this time, knowing that I very well may puke and then that'll set Griff off all over again. Hey, if he can have nicknames for me then so can I. He sits next me, still holding my AirPods and glaring at me.

"I always run like this," I tell him with a shrug, taking another sip of water.

"Bull-fucking-shit. The guys would have said something if you run like the hounds of hell are after you."

"They're all taller than me, used to running hard. So they really don't notice. They paced me after I got hurt, but that was fine because I really did hurt. I've been conditioned," I shudder as I admit this, "to run this hard. Usually I don't think about it, but I told you I had a nightmare. So, I had to run it out and today was worse than usual."

He sighs. "Fuck me," he mutters.

"Not my job." I sing-song and he snorts.

"Such a brat, I can't."

I shrug because I am what I am and I can not lie. Fuck, I'm officially loopy. Okay, maybe I did overdo it, but I won't admit it.

"Listen, have you thought about talking to someone about this? You're not, um, coping well."

I laugh slightly hysterically. "Cope with what? That I'll never have a normal life as long as I'm in this godforsaken town with him? When am I supposed to start coping? I can't even go on a date without something crazy happening."

Griffin winces. "Yeah, I heard. Wanna talk about it?"

"Nope. I need coffee and my bestie. You suck monkey balls."

"Tori!" He sounds equally amused and horrified and I smirk. Win for me. I hold my hand out for my AirPods and he shakes his head.

"You need to cool down. You need to walk home and talk to me."

I huff and feel tears start to well. It's too early for this shit. "I don't wanna."

Griffin groans. "Why!" He throws his hands up in the air. "Why do I suck? For telling you the truth? I'm worried about you." I sigh and stand up, starting to walk. Fuck the music. "Tori!" he shouts after me. He's gonna wake up the neighborhood, but that's not my problem. I keep walking. He catches up to me and I sigh.

"I wasn't myself for a lot of years. I was what he wanted me to be. I dressed the way that he wanted me to. I spoke when I was told, and I ran every day at five am because I was fat."

Griffin bites his fist and I know he's trying not to say anything. "I have a shit relationship with food because of Anthony. I have a little voice in my head and when it gets too loud, I can't eat. I may as well not even try. On Sunday, exactly a week ago, I asked myself why I was still here? Why am I living this shitty life, where Anthony can find me wherever I am, and take up where he left off? He doesn't want to be my boyfriend again, he wants me to be his fuck toy. His perfect Stepford girl that does whatever he wants. I can't be that person anymore, so I thought if I died, then he can't have me. I'll still belong to me."

Griffin grabs my arm and turns me to him, horrified. "*No!*" he yells. "Absolutely fucking not."

I sigh, shrugging. I mean it wasn't the ideal or best thought that I've ever had and I can own up to it. "My thoughts are kind of dark. Not as much as they were on Sunday, but yeah. I can't go back to being his perfect little toy. I am finally finding myself again, and I'm super broken but I belong to me. I have nightmares often, and Tesa can usually tell if I'm going to have one so she'll drag me to her bed to sleep with her. I didn't really have a trigger last night, so I don't know why I did."

He looks pensive and I flap my hand at him, "What?"

"You and Tesa are close and my dating her is kind of fucking with your bestie mind meld. I-"

"Nope. It really isn't, so stop. She and I would be super pissed if you decided to stop dating her over something so dumb. Like I said," I slide a hand around myself, "super broken. Ignore me."

I pull away from him, swiping my hand along my cheeks to catch the tears from falling. I start to walk faster because I'm already tired of the conversation that surrounds the little broken girl.

"Tori," he starts again, following me. "You really aren't broken. That's not what I meant. I just don't know how to help. My way didn't do shit, and now he's out and I don't know how to fix this. I'm pissed at the system and that I can't help you."

I smile tightly. "Sometimes," my voice is full of tears and he flinches. "There's nothing you can do because the system is broken and the bad guys win."

"You can't seriously think that. Between all of us, we can keep you safe. You have to know that we are here and we want to help."

I get that. I'm grateful for that. I'm just not in a good headspace.

"I know," is all I can say as I wipe my tears and head inside to smile my way through whatever it is that they have planned to distract me from my life.

thirty-eight

MIGUEL

I'm sitting outside with the guys, doing a shit job of pretending that we aren't checking on Tori. Tesa, Tori and Griffin have been outside drinking and talking. Tori giggles and it sounds slightly hysterical and I glance at Greg. He frowns and takes a long pull from his beer.

"What happened between your date day and today?" Link asks with a growl.

"I don't know but she doesn't sound like herself," Greg sighs, glancing over at the cottage next door.

Tesa and Griffin start teasing her and her voice becomes more normal. Pretty soon I hear them grilling and chatting.

My phone buzzes, and I check it.

Griffin: **Tori is having a rough day. She had a nightmare and I went for a run with her but I made it worse. I don't know her as well yet, and I mentioned seeing a therapist.**

I growl. Link and Greg crowd around me and read over my shoulder.

"How is a therapist going to help her with a psycho ex that's stalking her, outside of telling her to go to the nice police officers that can't fucking help her?" Link spits out.

I glance over at the fence, but we're far enough away that she can't hear us. I want to ask them to come hang out with us, take a swim, but we promised to leave them to their bestie time. I just have to hope that they can help her turn her mood around.

MIGUEL: **A therapist is unable to help her with her very real fears of being kidnapped and reprogrammed by her ex.** *Griffin*: **What?!**

I DON'T HEAR anything else and I shrug. It's not my fault if he doesn't understand her very real fears. Greg gets an alert on his phone and reaches over for it. He activates the camera for the front door and sees that Griffin is banging on the door.

"Uhh...did he not get the whole line in the sand bestie versus boyfriend day?" I ask.

Link snorts, shaking his head. "Baby, that's not a thing." I shrug. *It's a thing!* We walk inside and Greg opens the door.

"How are you explaining that you're here?" I ask him.

"I'm out of ice cream and raiding your fridge," Griffin smoothly says as he storms inside.

He turns to face us as the door shuts behind him. "I didn't realize that she was this rattled. She's depressed, possibly suicidal, and having nightmares. I feel like shit because she sleeps with Tesa to keep away the nightmares and I was with Tesa last night. Like how the fuck do you do this?! I'm not used to worrying about anyone like this. And I'm all tied up in fucking knots over her. We've had breakfast, watched movies, I've given her shit that she's living her best reverse harem life, and now I'm grilling because the girls decided they needed steak in their lives today."

I snort, rolling my eyes. "Don't you have a sister?"

"Yeah, but she's seventeen, and she doesn't talk to me about how hormonal her feelings are. I'm not used to this. Tesa just rolls with it, deflects, and does it like a pro. I've had more side eyes today because I'm fucking up more than I ever have in my life. Do I have to go back?!" He's whining and I chuckle.

"You wanted to be her person. So be there," I tell him with a shrug. "You can't fix her problems. At least not right now. So help her have fun. Get her out of her head. Tesa deflects because she can tell when Tori has had her fill of reality. She's masterful at it but she's known her for longer. Give yourself a break and just follow her lead. That's what we do. We have a list of dos and don'ts for Tori because we're guys and we tend to fuck shit up."

I can own that we aren't perfect. Griffin nods with a sigh. "I hate to see her the way I did this morning. And I was a dick. I didn't mean to be but she scared me. She ran so hard her legs practically collapsed out from under her."

Greg shakes his head. "That's why you have to run next to her and then she'll run at your pace. You can't coddle her or it'll frustrate her, but you can't let her just go either. She can run for miles once she gets going and gets into her head."

"I didn't realize. I should have run next to her but she was super upset, so I let her run ahead. I fucked up. I'll do better." Griffin grimly walks to our freezer and starts grabbing ice cream. You'd think he was headed to the executioner.

"Are you sure you can do this?" Link looks at him skeptically.

"Yeah, I'm just pissed that I fucked up on our run. Tesa says that before coffee you have a small window to make sure that Tori has a good day. Well I pissed on that window, and now I have morose, slightly manic Tori. It's terrifying."

Ha. So he can learn. "Go fix it with ice cream and then

either a nap or more coffee," I suggest. Those things usually help.

Griffin nods, walking out of the house with his ice cream resolutely.

"Poor fucker," Greg says, shaking his head.

"It sucks that there are only so many things that we can do for her. She's holding on by a thread, and really it's more than anyone can expect." Link blows out a breath in frustration and we know more than anyone how fast things can spiral with depression.

We did, after all, almost lose Link.

We spend the next few hours watching movies, and trying to keep our minds off of Tori when I hear a squeal outside. I wouldn't usually hear anything, but Greg had opened the door to grab something from the car.

Greg laughs, and I walk out onto the porch with Link.

Tori and Tesa are pelting water balloons at Griffin while he shoots them with a water cannon. Welp, that's one way to get her out of her head.

Tori is in a pair of, I swear, the tiniest shorts that I've ever seen and a bikini top. Her tits bounce in her top as she runs and I'm just waiting for a nip slip. I'll have to kill Griffin, but I'll make it up to Tesa, I promise. I don't think she's super attached to him yet.

Her legs are strong as she divides and conquers the front yard with Tesa with her balloons clutched in her arm as she throws them at her opponent. Tori and Tesa also have a mean throw.

"Get him, pretty girl!" Link cheers, leaning over the porch and laughing.

"What the fuck guys?! Whose team are you on?" Griffin yells as he gets pelted with balloons.

They have buckets set up with ammunition all over the

yard and I laugh. My sister has always had a mind for tactical takedowns when it came to water fights, snowball fights, or laser tag. Griffin had no idea what he just got himself into, which is par for the course with these girls.

Tesa's motto is, *"Tesa always wins."*

I stopped laughing about this motto around twelve years old when I realized how much she meant it. It's one of the reasons that I'm always worried about being poisoned by her. She wouldn't kill me, but she would enjoy making me shit my brains out.

I watch the girls run around the corner towards the back of the house as they chase him with balloons and realize that he's out of ammunition. "Help!" He yells as he runs.

"Keep running! Tesa always wins!" I crow and the boys shake their heads in amusement.

Poor bastard. He just wasn't ready. I roll my eyes at their antics and laugh. Tesa definitely got him back for fucking up Tori's morning.

————

TORI

I SMILE to myself after the water fight. Griffin definitely wasn't ready, and he cried uncle about an hour into the fight. I'm currently laying out in the sun to dry in my bikini and bottoms. I had taken off my shorts which are now soaked.

I've been in a shit mood all day and Tesa definitely noticed. She made breakfast and made me coffee, and I forced a big smile thanking her. She looked between Griffin and I and then glared at Griffin. I could tell that she wanted to yell at him and demand answers but I wanted quiet and food. I took a big bite and she stilled. She watched me chew and swallow and then relaxed.

I wasn't okay, but I was hungry and eating. I knew that she would let it go for now.

After breakfast we watched eighties movies and Tesa and I schooled Griffin on our favorite parts. He was amused by it all, teasing us about the actors that we crushed on. I know that these movies were made before I was even born, but that didn't change how much fun they were. They embody teenage angst and romance.

It was after the movies that my day unraveled a little. The three of us had talked and laughed, hanging out outside while Griffin grilled. The weather was gorgeous after the cold this morning, and we had wanted to enjoy the sunshine.

Griffin was digging. He asked seemingly innocuous questions about past boyfriends but I've only ever had one boyfriend: Anthony. I lost my virginity to him, and had every first except my first kiss with him.

My first kiss happened in Spain on a night out with friends. We went bar hopping, danced, and I kissed a stranger that I had ended up spending half the night dancing with. He was from Madrid and taught me how to flirt in Spanish. The kiss had been smoking hot and then he had to leave a little while later. It was kind of the perfect first kiss.

I would have to use my flirty Spanish speaking skills with Miguel, but we'd probably end up having sex in an alley. I laughed then, and I have to admit that the laugh wasn't my normal. Tesa looked questioningly at me and I shook my head. I couldn't tell her what I was thinking about. He was her brother, and there's only so many code words we could give my boyfriends.

Around that time, Griffin had grumbled about being out of ice cream and stalked out of the house.

"I know I'm not my best today, but that was a little excessive," I rolled my eyes at his antics.

"He's worried about you. Somewhere today he fucked up with you and he won't tell me how."

I sighed. "I'm...okay. I'm not fine but I'm better?"

"If you're questioning that, then that's the same as a lie. Don't lie to me. It's okay to not be okay." Tesa arched her eyebrow at me.

Fuck. I felt my eyes filling with tears and I blinked rapidly.

"Don't be nice to me!" I exclaim. I'll be a mess if she continues and I know it. Griffin is holding on to a thread as it is, and he may run if I cry.

"Okay, you're a twat who stole my boyfriend out of bed this morning. Is that better?"

I sputtered out a laugh. "You heffer! Yes that was much better thank you. Margs?"

"Yep!"

After lunch, Tesa had recommended that I take a nap, so I did. I had too much peopling today and I was tired of keeping it together.

I took an hour nap, and then when I got up Tesa had been scheming. No one will understand how diabolical this woman's brain is. If she didn't love books and marketing as much as she does, she'd probably be an evil dictator somewhere. I freaking love her crazy.

This is how we had ended up in our water balloon fight that had made Griffin re-examine his life choices.

I giggle and smother it because I'm alone in the backyard and only crazy people giggle to themselves, right?

Tesa and Griffin had left to hang out for a bit, and I think that this really meant stroking his, ah ego and pumping him for information. I giggle again and take another sip of my drink. I'm officially tipsy and I'm not mad about it.

My phone buzzes and I pick it up. It's the boys and my group chat.

Miguel: Did you make Griffin flee already, *mi amor*?

I snort. "As if," I mutter to myself.

I decide to respond to him for real, instead of talking to myself.

Me: Nope. He got his panties in a twist because he lost so epically.

I hear laughing over the fence and I roll my eyes. "Y'all! Are you for real right now?!" I yell over the fence.

"We miss you... and bestie day is over now they're gone. Come over with whatever you're drinking and help me with a situation I have, baby girl." Greg has a situation? Huh?

I slide my legs over the lounger and stand up, then grab my drink and walk around the house, letting myself out of the side gate and to their gate. I walk around the house and see the guys sprawled in chairs around their pool. I wonder if they spent part of their day spying on me.

The guys grin, sitting up as they see me. They all are drinking beers and eye my margarita.

"Do you need water after that or another drink?" Link asks.

"Umm, I've only had one since my water escapades," I pout, not really understanding why he's asking. Link gets up and kisses me.

"Then I'll make up a pitcher while you hang with us, pretty girl. I don't know how long your bathing suit will last with us though. You look fucking gorgeous."

His eyes smolder as he looks at me and it clicks. Ohh. Well the rest of my day will be fun. Link heads inside and Greg makes grabby hands for me. I laugh and climb onto his lap, taking a sip of my drink and putting it to the side.

"Did y'all miss me?" I tease.

Greg pulls me hard into his lap and I can feel how much he missed me. He hits my clit perfectly and I moan.

"Wait, we cannot have the cops called again due to public indecency, Greg," I say with a giggle, shaking my head.

He holds my waist with his arms with a huff of frustration. "Ughh. Your skin is all warm, you smell like coconut sunscreen, and you're so soft...everywhere."

He rocks me back over him and my eyes roll with a sigh. He tugs my bikini down and stares greedily.

"*Mi amor*, I kept envisioning your tits falling out of your suit when you were running earlier today and I plotted Griffin's death vividly."

Miguel is languid and completely serene in his thoughts like this is completely normal behavior. My men are cavemen! But...fuck, if I didn't kind of miss them, too.

"Ooh! Ooh! Her tits are out! Are we making up for lost time?" Link is very excited as he walks out with my pitcher and refills my cup. I giggle, shaking my head again.

"Y'all are impossible."

"Mmm but you missed us, didn't you, pretty girl?" Link kisses up my neck, his fingers plucking at my nipples and I writhe, moving up and down Greg's cock for friction. I whimper and shake my head, removing his hands and standing up. My breasts are still bouncing now that they've pulled them out of my bathing suit top, but I'd rather move then end up fucking them in the backyard.

"Ummm none of that. I came over to hang out with y'all, not have screaming orgasms in the backyard and have the police called again. The neighborhood is already ready to deliver a Scarlet letter. Poor Mrs. Henderson gave me the stink eye today after our water balloon fight."

Miguel chuckles, leaning back in his chair kicking his feet out wide. God, why is that so hot. He's not wearing a shirt and his abs make me lick my lips. *Bad Tori!* Miguel is completely oblivious to my struggles.

"*Mi gringa linda*, Mrs. Henderson is in her nineties and mourning her youth when she looks at you. Did you know that your tits are still out? Come here at least so I can warm them up with my mouth. Your nipples are all flushed and hard."

He sucks on his bottom lip and I feel warm. I'm sure that my chest is pink now and my nipples are darker too.

"Fuck, baby you're killing me," I groan.

I shove my breasts back into my top and jump into the pool. I was two seconds from climbing that man's pole. The water is freezing and exactly what I needed to cool down.

I push up from the bottom and breathe deeply when my head breaks out of the water. Miguel is standing, eyes wide.

"Really?! You're running from me?"

"Yep!" I gasp, slightly out of breath with a laugh. "Come cool off, *papi*. You look a little over heated." I know that I'm playing with fire and his eyes get hooded.

"Wait...what did she say?" Greg looks confused. I roll my lips inwards to contain my smirk.

Miguel jumps into the water and I squeal, swimming away. We play keep away for a bit until the guys jump in too, corralling me and kissing me hard.

"I figured out where I went wrong when I fucked you outside," Greg murmurs.

"What? How?"

I'm a little out of it as Miguel's hand curls around my neck possessively without squeezing, before turning me to kiss slowly.

Greg chuckles darkly. "I needed one of the guys to gag you with their cock."

Lord have mercy. I moan, shivering with need. I've had

anxious energy all day, and I never once thought to let the boys fuck it out of me. Clearly my priorities were skewed.

"Now, these perfect tits need attention I think," Greg growls.

He takes my top completely off and throws it. I twist in protest, and Miguel wraps his other arm around my waist.

He twists my nipples hard and I wrap my legs around his waist. Fuck it, you only live once, right?

"So fucking gorgeous." He drags his tongue around my nipple, refusing to give me more and I mewl into Miguel's mouth.

"Shh, your boy will give you what you want. He's just gonna torture you a little for running away. You should know better than that."

"Don't we owe her multiple forced orgasms for something? I don't remember why, but it sounds good to me, she's such a fucking brat."

"I'm not a brat-"

Greg takes that moment to suck on my nipple and I moan. Miguel takes care of the sound by cutting off my breath. His hand tightened just enough that all I can do is writhe between them in silence.

Greg and Miguel have me sandwiched between them and I grind hard against Greg's cock as Miguel grinds against my ass.

Greg releases my nipple and Miguel loosens his hand so that I can pull in a breath.

"Is that okay?" Miguel growls into my ear, kissing up my neck.

"Yes! I didn't think I'd like that but I do with you."

"You're so fucking good for us," Miguel sighs happily.

I didn't think that I would be okay with not being able to breathe during sex, especially after the bathroom incident with

Anthony. With Miguel, I just feel safe and loved. It's kind of a mind fuck that I feel like that, but everything about these men feels different.

Greg tips my head back to look at him. "If you don't like something, and you can't say something, hit my arm twice, K?"

I nod eagerly and he goes back to sucking hard on my other nipple while plucking on the one that he just left.

Miguel kisses me hard again, plunging his tongue into my mouth, clashing our teeth. It's so hot. He's fighting me for dominance and it's yet another thing that I'm finding that I like.

I never experimented a lot with Anthony, because it never felt safe. He always took and very seldom gave unless there was a price attached.

I forget everything else when the strings on my bottoms are pulled away and a very hard cock is pushing against my entrance. I'm more than ready.

I can't see who it is because Miguel is still dominating my mouth.

I feel the first piercing as he pushes inside of me and I moan. Greg feels amazing.

Miguel turns me to look at Greg and slowly tightens his hand around my neck. I feel no anxiety at all as my eyes roll in pleasure.

"That's our good girl," Greg growls.

He wraps his arm around my waist and I really am caged between these two powerful men. Men that would never hurt me, and say they love me.

My nerve endings fire as my core tightens. Greg lowers his mouth, kissing and sucking on my breasts again.

Miguel finds a rhythm, choking me for longer and longer periods of time, checking for signs of distress and growling in pleasure every time he finds that I'm fine.

Greg tilts my hips just a bit as he thrusts and he hits that perfect spot. He does this just as Miguel releases my neck and I gasp a breath to scream before he cuts it off again.

I explode, squeezing Greg tightly and he grunts.

"Yeah, fuck. Baby, coat me in all of you. Keep coming on my cock. So fucking good. God!"

"You come so prettily for us. Your face is all flushed, your nipples are dark and purple from Greg playing with them. We need to push you more often. God, I can think of so many things we can do."

Miguel pushes down his swim shorts and grinds on my ass. "Only you could tame us, *mi amor*. You are everything we need. All ours." Miguel releases my throat again to kiss me.

"Scream into Miguel, baby girl. Give it to him."

"Fuck," Link groans.

"Enjoying the view, man?" Greg chuckles before he goes back to torturing my nipples. He's started pulling them between his teeth.

"Yeah, it's always my favorite view to watch my girl get fucked how she deserves. Mmm. Fuck I'm close," Link moans.

Greg twists his hips as he fucks me and one of his piercings at the base of his cock grinds into my clit.

I try to thrust up because it feels good and he chuckles. "More?"

Miguel lets me face him and I nod.

"It feels so good. I'm so close. I need more, baby."

I'm panting as I talk, knowing that my ability to speak is limited. I love that I never know when Miguel will steal my breath with his hand that wraps completely around my throat. Huge hands and a huge cock. Give it all to me.

Greg grins, pulling slowly out as my eyes roll and I moan. "Your wish is my command, princess."

Greg thrusts hard into me and I scream. There's no sound though, because Miguel is taking his job very seriously.

My toes start to curl around Greg's back and he grins knowingly.

"Our girl is gonna explode. We've got curled toes, Miguel."

Miguel turns my head to look at Link. He's sitting on the side of the pool watching us, fisting and twisting around his cock.

"Mmm. Link's gonna blow too. Paint those delicious abs with your cum, baby boy. I wanna see it all."

Miguel has such a filthy mouth. The last thing I see is Link's head tilted back as he comes hard. My eyesight whites out as I come and my ears ring. I slowly come back to myself with Greg watching me closely.

"We lost you for a little bit, beautiful. You good?"

I nod. He's holding me tightly to his body, and he smiles, kissing me.

"Yo! Are you fucking my bestie?" Tesa yells as I hear her open the guy's side gate.

"Fuck!" I whisper panicked.

The guys scramble to grab my bathing suit. Miguel ties the strings to my bottom and Greg quickly helps me with my top.

Link jumps into the pool with a laugh, splashing water on himself to clean himself up and pulls his shorts up.

"Man that's such a waste," Miguel laments and Link throws him a sexy smile.

"Next time you can clean me up with your tongue, baby."

I quickly dunk myself underwater to cool off. I still feel warm after everything. I check my top as I come back up just as Griffin and Tesa walk into the backyard. Griffin looks at us suspiciously and I shrug with a grin that I mean for the first time all day.

"Mmmm. So I see you fucked the funk out of her," Tesa says

with a grin. "Good men. I'm gonna get a glass. You want a beer, Griffin?"

Griffin looks gobsmacked and I giggle. "Yeah, baby, sure thanks."

Tesa walks inside and I walk to the side of the pool to look up at him with a smile.

"If I knew that was what you needed, I would have sent you over earlier," Griffin laughs, shaking his head.

"Honestly, most days lately I don't even know what I need. I can just take it an hour at a time. I know I wasn't the best to be around today. I'm sorry."

Griffin frowns and shakes his head, sitting next to the pool in his swim trunks.

"No. Don't apologize. I'm a fixer and it's a bitter pill to swallow to realize that I can't fix everything. I can just be here for you. I didn't do a great job of that this morning. I also insinuated that there was something wrong with you. There's not. Even strong people need a break. You're so strong, Tori-girl. I'm sorry too."

"Are my people having a heart to heart?" Tesa comes back out with a grin.

Griffin tips his head over his shoulder to look at Tesa. "Just admitting when I'm wrong."

"Mmmm. It's so sexy when a man can do that." Tesa pops the top off his beer and hands it to him.

Griffin rolls his eyes and I grin. My world is back to what it needs to be again.

thirty-nine

TORI

My alarm woke me up this morning with a screech. Ugh, the next few days will be insane. I slept alone last night but I didn't have a single bad dream. I was probably too tired to. I sit up as there's a knock on the door.

"You decent?" Griffin yells through the door and I laugh. I can't believe he almost saw me in all my glory yesterday. I glance down and I'm in a band shirt and sleep shorts. No nip slips here!

"All good!"

Griffin walks in with coffee and I sigh happily.

"I hear it's your first full day in your new position. Drink this, then come down. I'm making waffles and Tesa is making breakfast potatoes and eggs."

I make grabby hands for the coffee and take a sip. "Y'all are my favorites." I mumble happily.

"Glad to hear it. Get a move on, Tori-girl."

I'm starting to really love that nickname.

I drink my coffee as I head into the bathroom. Yes, I absolutely took a shower with my coffee. He told me that I needed to hurry, and I can't do that without coffee. After my shower I stare at myself in the mirror, scrunching my face. I dry off, trying to decide what to do with my hair. I blast it with heat before putting it in a pretty, smooth bun at the base of my head. I put on makeup and then open my door.

Thank god that I'm still in my towel because Tesa is in my bed with food and the door to my room is wide open.

"Ummm, really?"

"Breakfast is happening in your bed today, so get dressed before he comes back up babes," Tesa snickers.

"Fuck I hate y'all," I grouse.

Green scoop necked shirt, flowy patterned skirt and green pointed flats is what I decide on. I step out of my closet to see Griffin is eating breakfast on my bed with Tesa, all cuddled up. Today is weird.

I grab green and silver vine earrings that crawl up my ear and put them on before crawling onto the bed for food. The three of us sit with our backs to the headboard as we eat. I drink my second cup of coffee, and I enjoy the sensation that I have people that care about me. Hmm. Okay, this is a good weird thing I've decided.

"How busy will you be today, babes?" I think before I answer Tesa.

"I have to see HR in the morning, then I have to go through those ten manuscripts first to decide who I'm taking on that's new. Once I decide, I have to email those that I've chosen for phone calls, and I'm going to be lazy and blind copy Peter and Tom on those so I don't have to write separate emails to them. Work smart, right?"

"Okay, how much of your old position are you still doing in the meantime?"

We strategize my day and decide that I will force myself to stop at two to go to lunch. We're going to *The Java Spot* because we are more likely to have a peaceful lunch there. Griffin looks between us with a smirk?

"What?" We say in unison.

"Do you really have to plan lunch like this? And why did you only plan Tori's day?"

"Oh, my days are fine. I have nowhere near as chaotic of a schedule as Tori. Her days are hijacked by something nearly seventy percent of the time. My days are long, but I can go to lunch whenever. If I don't remind Tori to eat, she'll be sucked in and then hangry by four pm."

"I don't understand what is so stressful about editing," Griffin retorts.

"It's not the actual editing, it's the magnitude of my editing. I edit four manuscripts a week while also conducting video calls about the edits. I do developmental editing too, so I check for plot holes, or if a character's eye color changes suddenly, or a character pops up somewhere that he or she shouldn't be. Say they're in a restaurant and the other people are walking to them and all of a sudden they're talking in the scene. Obviously that person can't be in two places at once, so I mark it to ask the author about it. This way everything runs smoothly."

"Huh. And you work nine to five?"

Tesa snorts. "You know we don't, baby. Don't be silly. Usually it's closer to nine to six or seven."

Griffin shakes his head. "And your boss wants to do continuing education classes too? Ugh, we'll never see you!"

I throw my head back and laugh because this is why Tesa was whining earlier when we talked about it. Now he gets it.

"We'll work it out. But this is why I have to strategize. My boss has also made it a rule that if I'm outside of the door and the door is locked, I'm not allowed to go back inside to answer a call. They'll call at all hours for things so they don't forget to ask or tell me something."

"Isn't that what email is for?" Griffin says dryly.

"Yep, but not all of my authors like email. So I come back into work with ten voicemails to go through when I walk in. It's just my job, which I love, I just have to make sure that I take care of myself too during the day."

Griffin nods approvingly. "What time do you have to go in?" I check my phone and see a message.

"Umm...soon. Who is this?" Griffin looks over my shoulder as I open the text.

Unknown: Did you really think you could get rid of me so easily, little whore?

I gnaw on my lip uneasily. "That's him, isn't it?" Griffin growls.

"Yeah..."

Unknown: I hope you enjoyed your freedom, because you'll be mine again soon. I'll always find you.

I shiver. "Fuck this. Tesa, how safe is work?"

"Pretty safe. Peter and Tom are just as worried about her stalker situation, so the guard makes sure to walk us out to our car. On the way into work there's a ton of people, so we are pretty safe too. Anthony tried to get into the building once and he was escorted out. They aren't playing around with her safety."

Griffin sighs. "That's the best we have for right now. Don't go anywhere alone, please. If you need to, call for an escort. I don't care how ridiculous you feel doing it."

I nod, scooting off the bed to brush my teeth again and fix my lipstick. Griffin picks up all the plates and walks out to wash them.

I raise my eyebrow and Tesa grins. "He comes housebroken, isn't it fabulous?"

I snort, shaking my head. "See you in five, boo."

Tesa nods, rushing out to finish as well.

Before we know it, we are running out the door to the car. Griffin kisses Tesa goodbye first as I lock the door and arm the house. Griffin walks towards his car too, waving goodbye.

Tesa grins goofily as she settles in the car. "That good, huh?" I tease.

"Yeah. I really like him."

I nod, smiling. "We're keeping him."

Tesa throws her head back, laughing. "Definitely keeping him!"

She drives us to work and I run into the HR office before heading up to my office. This is the beginning of a crazy week.

————

I SIT BACK from my chair with a sigh. It's now Thursday, and it's been a flurry of work. My new authors write contemporary, fantasy, wolf shifters, angels, omegaverse and more. I love how different they all are, and their creative processes are all so different. Three are pantsers, meaning that they don't plot but are linear writers. Everything goes forward as they write, so it all makes sense. The others plot excessively and are super organized.

During the last few days I've figured out my work life and now have twenty authors that I work with in total. It sounds like a lot, but they all publish at different times. I also talked to Peter about the continuing education courses, and he said that he wanted me to start in January.

I'm okay with this because I'll have more time to get the hang of everything. So far I'm happy with my new job responsibilities, but I have still been getting out around six every night. I haven't really had a chance to see the guys outside of waving to them on the way into the house. Yesterday, they surprised Tesa and I with Chinese food, and we hung out for a little bit. I didn't realize how much I had missed them.

Miguel: **I miss you!!**

I giggle. It's like he knew I was thinking about him.

Me: **I miss you too, I am actually going to be done at a normal time today. (Knock on wood lol.)**

Miguel: **Don't jinx it, *mi cielo*. Come over today around seven? We want to feed you and give you screaming orgasms.**

Mmmm god yes please.

Me: **I'll be there. My schedule is starting to ease up a little so I'll be able to be home more.**

Miguel: **I'll tell the guys. See you soon *gringa linda*. I love you.**

Me: **I love you too, *mi amor*.**

Miguel sends me a photo of him blowing a kiss and I melt. This man is amazing. I send him one back.

Miguel: **Is it wrong that I can't stop thinking about your lips wrapped around my cock now?**

Me: **Can it be seven now?**

I put my phone away with a smirk and get through the last couple of hours of my day.

———

MY PHONE DINGS and I see it's five thirty.

Tesa: **Let's go girl!**

Me: **Locking the door now!**

Okay, slight exaggeration, I think to myself as I grab my things and race for the door. I lock it and my office phone rings.

"Marked safe from answering another phone!" Tom booms as he walks past me and I burst out laughing. He's not wrong. I fall into step with him.

"Tell me about what's new. Any hiccups so far?" I think back but I can't pinpoint a single thing.

"Ohh! So I had a couple of authors that were upset that they were being transferred..."

We discussed which ones and he said he'd personally call them tomorrow morning to smooth things over. He walks me to the elevator and hits the down button.

"How are things personally?" He pitches his voice lower, though the offices are mostly empty now. "Is that man in jail still?"

I shake my head sadly. "Nope. He's out and he's sent me some texts. The police don't seem to care though. All I can really do is make sure that I'm never alone."

Tom scoffs, angry for me. "For how long though?"

"I don't know," I whisper. He gives me a hug, surprising me.

"Security still walks you out?"

"Yes."

"I'm walking you down then," he says resolutely, escorting me into the elevator.

I wish I could say it wasn't necessary, but it very well may be. I still don't know how he keeps finding me. I idly touch my necklace with my St. Benedict medal and send a prayer up to my parents. I ask them to forgive me for being so trusting and ask them to protect me. I swipe away a tear when we get to the lobby. Tom glances at me and I nod quickly. I don't know what I'm agreeing to but I'm as okay as I can be right now.

He walks me into the lobby and there's Tesa. "Excellent. You're still riding together." Tom smiles happily, and I know he's glad that I'm no longer alone.

"We are!" Tesa rushes up to us with a smile. "Thank you so much for walking her down. I was just starting to go up to find her, worried that she had been pulled back into work."

Tom snorts because that happens often. "Be safe ladies. Tori, I'll see you tomorrow."

He turns and hits the button to go back up to his office. My heart warms that he only came down for me. Tesa and I start walking towards the guard's table together.

"I see you told Tom a little about what's happened?" She's fishing and I roll my eyes at her.

"He asked me if Anthony was still in jail and I said no. Honestly, there's nothing I can do except not be alone right now. I feel a little like a ticking time bomb, especially with his last messages to me."

Tesa scowls. "You won't be alone at all today. Miguel told me that the guys are making you dinner and miss you. I let Griffin know and he'll probably come over later tonight too. This week's been crazy!"

We wave at the guard at the table and he smiles, nodding. He calls for someone to come take over his post, and then walks us out. "Be careful getting home. This storm is going to be bad. The radar is showing that it'll be raining most of the night."

I glance up with a frown. It had been gorgeous all day, but the weather could change so quickly. The sky is now dark and the clouds look heavy with rain. "We promise to be careful, Derek. Thank you so much for walking us out," I say with a smile.

Tesa and I get into the car quickly. "Girl, I can't wait for the weekend. We should plan a big group date out for Saturday. Think the guys would go for it?"

I grin. "Yeah! Ooh that sounds like fun. I think they would, depending on what it is. We had fun when we went to Myrtle Beach."

Tesa nods. "There's a fall festival happening just outside of town actually!"

"Totally sold. I love all things fall. I cannot wait for Halloween!"

Tesa and I brainstorm about costumes and whether to do couples or even try for a group costume. It's honestly just so nice to feel normal for once.

When we get home I decide that I need to change quickly before I go over to the guys place.

Tesa and I head into the house, continually glancing at the sky. It's totally going to rain by the time I walk out. Dammit. I run upstairs as Tesa yells at me to hurry.

"Yeah, yeah. Fuck why does it have to rain today!" I walk down the hall quickly, throwing open my closet door.

"Comfortable but cute...where are you?"

I strip down to my bralette and cheeky undies, glaring at my wardrobe. I know damn well it's not my clothes fault, I just miss the guys and want to see them.

I grab a pair of cute ripped jeans, pulling them on. Next I decide on a slouchy off the shoulder sweatshirt because it's cold now that the wind is kicking up.

"Tori! Ya gotta move babes!"

I grab my boots and socks and call it. I plop my butt on the floor to pull them one, then I push myself up off the floor and look at the mirror. Okay, I'm cute!

I fluff my hair, playing with the cute waves. My makeup is still holding well from this morning too. Sweet!

I grab my phone and glance at the screen. It's seven ten but I don't have any missed calls or messages. Maybe the guys saw that Tesa and I were home and were just waiting for me to come over.

Hmm.

"I'll watch you walk over from the porch, babes. I'll call Griffin after and see what he's picking up for us."

I'm vibrating with excitement as I walk out the door with a smile. The rain starts up and I make a run for it. Tesa laughs.

"You're cute even when you're a drowned rat, babes! Have fun!"

I walk up the guys' porch steps because I don't want to fall and ring the doorbell. I expect it may take a second because I've noticed that they rarely hear the bell.

I guess they're expecting me because Greg opens the door.

"Hey! I missed-"

"I think you should stop there, Tori." Greg cuts me off coldly, stepping out onto the porch.

Miguel and Link follow him. They take up so much space that I step back to give them room. They're all scowling at me and Miguel is holding something in his hand. Are they papers?

They walk forward and slowly I'm crowded down the stairs.

"Why are you looking at me like that? Did something happen?"

I'm standing in the rain now and I shiver, but not from the cold. Something is very wrong. Link hasn't looked at me like that since we first met and Miguel is looking at me with anger.

What? Did I do something?!

"You've got to be kidding me. Did you need something from us or expect something? Did you plan to get money from us?" Greg spits out.

"I don't understand! I have my own money. I don't need anything from you. What are you talking about?"

"No, you no longer have a home. I don't want a whore like you living with my sister, freeloading. You don't even pay her rent, do you?"

"She won't let me!" I yell at him, frustrated. Why are they harping on rent? She can tell them this herself.

I turn towards the house and Miguel yells.

"No! My sister can't help you now. It was fun, but it's over. Thanks for being a warm cunt and a great fuck toy."

A what? Holy shit.

"What planet am I living on right now that you think you can talk to me like this?" I scream. "Who the fuck are you right now?!"

"There she is. The victim. Poor little Tori. I really thought that you were like me. I wanted to protect you. You're not a victim though. You're a whore. Show her, Miguel." Link looks over at Miguel and he sneers at me.

I throw open my arms. "Yes, please show me why you're treating me like this. There has to be a reason. You couldn't possibly be this cruel just for shits and giggles."

Miguel throws the papers that he has in his hand at me and I struggle to grab a few as they fly everywhere and the wind whips it up.

I blink as I hold one up and the photo is of Anthony and myself. I'm arched back as he fingers me and I look at the photo and then them. This was the night that we were in the bathroom and he withheld my orgasms. This was the night that I started to question things with him. Why do they care about an old photo?

How did they get these?!

I look at the next one and see that I'm on the bed at my old apartment and he's fucking me from behind. The photo has been enlarged and you can see...everything. They're all black and white. And then it hits me and I feel sick. The cameras in the apartment. He had them on when we were having sex. He also replaced the camera in the bathroom. That motherfucker.

That still doesn't explain why they're mad at me. My eyes start to well from tears, but I'm unsure if it's from sadness or anger.

I throw the photos down on the floor. "You knew I had a

sexual relationship with Anthony. We were dating. I don't understand-"

Greg rolls his eyes. "Let the adults talk now. You were a warm, tight pussy, but it's obvious that you're still fucking him. Message has been received."

He tosses a note at me and I catch it.

I TOLD *YOU SHE'D ALWAYS BE MINE. PHOTOS DON'T LIE. I'VE BEEN FUCKING THE LITTLE LIAR THE WHOLE TIME. BETTER LUCK NEXT TIME.*

WHAT THE FUCK IS HAPPENING?!

Shocked, I take a step back, my stomach starting to rebel. "I didn't do any of this. Don't you see that this is all him? I don't understand how you can believe this?!"

Miguel shrugs. "I mean, who would really go to all of this trouble for some pussy? He can have you. You were a fun ride, your pussy was a great fuck, but now it's time to run along like the little whore that you've shown yourself to be."

The guys turn away as if they decided to and the rain starts to come down harder. I scream as I watch them leave, breathing hard. I have no one now. Tesa will hate me, everyone will and he'll take me again.

I am gulping at the air as I walk away. I need to run. I need to go. I run through the side door that connects the yards before turning and puking. My body is just over today. Shuddering, I run up the porch steps.

The front door was still unlocked. I run up to what was my room, grab a duffle and throw in my clothes, wallet, and keys before running back downstairs.

"Tori?"

I can't look. I can't turn or I'll lose it. And if I see the hatred or hear the words that those boys said out of her mouth...I fucking can't.

"I'm sorry. I never meant for this to happen. Your brother hates me. They all do. And you will too." I rip open the door and run into the rain.

"Tori, what the fuck!" Tesa screams into the storm as I run for my car.

We've been driving Tesa's car to work, just another example of how codependent I am. I unlock my door, throw in my bag and get in. I shove in the key and turn it, hoping the engine will turn. When it does, I whisper a little prayer.

I have my necklace, some clothes, and my wallet. I'll start over. I'll have to. There's nothing here for me and Anthony is coming. My skin itches and I shudder, shaking my head.

"Keep it together, just a little longer Tori." I start talking to myself, but really who else do I have?

Everyone leaves. Or Anthony takes them from me.

I slam the car into reverse, leaving Tesa screaming for me to come back, to talk to her. I see her running for the guys' house and I know that soon she'll hate me too. Pulling onto the road, I'm quickly reminded of how much I hate this drive when it rains.

The road twists and turns and I have someone on my ass. I find myself speeding up because I feel like I'm going to slow. Shouldn't I be going slower when I can't see?

I squint at the road as it turns sharply. I want to slow down but I can't. The car is too close and it doesn't look like he'll let me slow down.

"Oh my god, why are you riding me right now? Just back up please!"

I'm screaming as I drive, terrified because my windshield

wipers are on full blast and I can't see shit. My wheel hydroplanes.

"Motherfucker! Why?"

I've completely lost it. My anxiety is riding high, my heart is broken, and-

Lights on my right startle me from my musings and then I'm being hit on my right side and behind. All of a sudden the car is spinning. I can't do anything, all I can do is hold on and scream. The car flips twice before I'm upside down. My head hurts and I see lights coming towards me. I'm on the side of the road, upside down. Something drips from my forehead and I touch it. Looking at it makes my vision swim when I see its blood.

I hear a swish and look up. I see a big truck with a grill pull up behind me. A Good Samaritan maybe?

My heart sinks though when I see the shoes that step down from the cab. They're pointy and unusually shiny, and I remember Anthony polishing them often in another life. This person takes another step and I recognize him.

"No. No, god please no," I whisper, starting to struggle.

I can't get out and my seatbelt is stuck. Fuck. I move too fast and I gag against nausea. I idly wonder if this is a concussion. My breathing is coming too fast as I freak out, and my vision starts to go black.

No, he can't have me...please.

epilogue

ANTHONY

I grin as I watch my pet struggle. I step towards her, listening as the glass crunches under my feet. She crashed according to plan, and there's no way she'll be able to get out of the car without assistance.

I can see perfectly into the windshield, the terror in her eyes as she recognizes me, the blood that's dripping into them from when she hit the steering wheel. All of her injuries will make it easier for me to steal her away, but not enough to kill her.

I can see it all happened exactly how I imagined it would. There's no way that she can run from me now. I had my friend deliver the older photos of us fucking from the apartment, and he streamed the fight that occurred after to my phone. I laughed my ass off and was rock hard as I watched.

It made me happy to implode her life. She really thought those guys loved her. She thought they'd be able to protect her, but she was so wrong. No one can protect her from me. She's always been mine. She just forgot about that for a while. It's okay though, I'll remind her.

No one will want her now, and it's time to retrain her to be my perfect pet again. I've always known where she was. She was never free, thanks to the tracker in her necklace. Stupid girl. She thought the chain was a benevolent gift from me. I'm far from kind though.

I grin as I watch her. I own a lot of people in this town. One of them is coming in an ambulance to pick her up and take her to my cabin. No one will know where she is, and everyone will wonder how she disappeared. They won't find her though and soon everyone will forget. Then, I'll get to take my time with her, punish her for all of the willful things that she's done to deserve my wrath.

I watch as my pet's head lolls to the side and realize that she's passed out. Even better. Now she won't fight when I pretend I'm saving her. I grin in anticipation as I take another step towards her.

My head turns as I hear a siren beep and a police officer come alongside her car. Fuck...do I know this person? Can he be paid to look the other way?

I turn to see in the window and see that I don't. Shit. This won't work. I pull out my phone and send a text that says: abort.

The ambulance was coming up behind me and turns his lights and sirens on as he continues past.

All these careful plans to be fucked up by one of the only not dirty cops in this town. Shit. I step back quickly and get into my car. I don't need to hang around and get pulled into his investigation. I was lucky to have so many favors that the chief of police threw out my assault charges.

The do-gooder cop gets out and puts out his hand to stop me, and I purposely misunderstand him. I raise my hand to say goodbye, pull into a hole in traffic and race away.

Soon my pet will be mine, but not today. This is just a small hiccup. There's no one else to stand in my way, now.

"I'll be seeing you soon, little whore."

Living Words

afterword

So that was something, wasn't it? I left lots of Easter eggs, but they don't come together till the last moment. Is your phone ok? Your kindle? I'm not gonna lie, I kind of blew up Tori's life. I promise that everything will work out in the end...mostly.

When I started writing Living Words, all I could see was the beginning...and the end. The rest was as much of a surprise to me as it was to you. Buckle up y'all, the ride will continue in Taking Chances.

If you want to yell in our spoilers post, be sure to join my author group here, and it would mean the world to me if you'd yell a little in a review, too. And if you're interested in the music that inspired this doozy, you can check out the playlist for Living Words on Spotify here!

also by jenn bullard

Living Words

Unwritten Truths Duet Book One

Taking Chances

Unwritten Truths Duet Book Two

Coming November 15th, 2022

The Darkest Chord

The Darkest Night Duet Book One

Coming February 2023

acknowledgments

Oh my goodness y'all. They say that new adventures take a village and this is so true. Thank you A.K. Graves for telling a tiny pixie that her words would be fun to read! I literally started writing a few weeks later.

Thank you Amber Nicole for telling me that I could do this, being my sounding board when I felt like I was stuck, and telling me to keep going. Thank you Nicole for helping me through the maze of the indie author world and make sense of it!

Thank you Sarah Klinger PA for kidnapping me, and then kicking me out of the baby author nest. You are such an amazing cheerleader.

Thank you to my stabby alpha/betas: Nicole, Kate,Cindy, Danielle, Allie Santos, Asheley, Jessi, Kerrie-Louise, Heather, and Oriane. I love how so many of you voice and messaged to yell at me about the cliffhanger in this book. Thank you for loving my characters, helping me through find ways to make the book better, and bring part of my team!

And a huge thank you to Veronica Lancet for bringing my books to life with her covers and being my sounding board too.

Thank you to my readers who took a chance on a debut author. Thank you for jumping on this journey with me and loving on my characters enough to be angry and stabby about them.

I am sure I'm missing someone, and that's the problem with writing under pressure. Thank you for all the new friendships in the indie author community and welcoming a tiny pixie with alphas in her head that won't be quiet!

JENN BULLARD

about the author

Jenn Bullard is a tiny pixie debuting author that loves to read. She has three daughters and is married to her cinnamon roll. Most of the time, Jenn is ruled by her characters: they drive, she just tells their story. If Jenn could tell her readers anything: it's to follow your dreams. She wouldn't be writing if she hadn't.

jennbullardwrites@gmail.com